HEART ATTACK™

CREATED BY SHAWN KITTELSEN & ERIC ZAWADZKI

SKYBOUND ENTERTAINMENT

Robert Kirkman Chairman • **David Alpert** CEO • **Sean Mackiewicz** SVP, Editor-in-Chief • **Shawn Kirkham** SVP, Business Development • **Brian Huntington** VP, Online Content •
Shauna Wynne Publicity Director • **Andres Juarez** Art Director • **Alex Antone** Senior Editor • **Jon Moisan** Editor • **Arielle Basich** Associate Editor • **Carina Taylor** Graphic Designer
• **Paul Shin** Business Development Manager • **Johnny O'Dell** Social Media Manager • **Dan Petersen** Sr. Director of Operations & Events
Foreign Rights Inquiries: ag@sequentialrights.com **Other Licensing Inquiries:** contact@skybound.com **SKYBOUND.COM**

IMAGE COMICS, INC.

Robert Kirkman Chief Operating Officer • **Erik Larsen** Chief Financial Officer • **Todd McFarlane** President • **Marc Silvestri** Chief Executive Officer • **Jim Valentino** Vice
President • **Eric Stephenson** Publisher / Chief Creative Officer • **Jeff Boisan** Director of Sales & Publishing Planning • **Jeff Stang** Director of Direct Market Sales • **Kat Salazar**
Director of PR & Marketing • **Drew Gill** Cover Editor • **Heather Doornink** Production Director • **Nicole Lapalme** Controller
IMAGECOMICS.COM

SHAWN KITTELSEN
WRITER, CREATOR

ERIC ZAWADZKI
ARTIST, CREATOR

MICHAEL GARLAND
COLORIST (CH 1-3)

MIKE SPICER
COLORIST (CH 4-6)

PAT BROSSEAU
LETTERER

JON MOISAN
EDITOR

ANDRES JUAREZ
LOGO DESIGN

CARINA TAYLOR
PRODUCTION DESIGN

HEART ATTACK VOLUME 1. JULY 2020. ISBN: 978-1-5343-1594-5 Published by Image Comics, inc. Office of publication: 2701 NW Vaughn St., Ste. 780, Portland, or 97210.

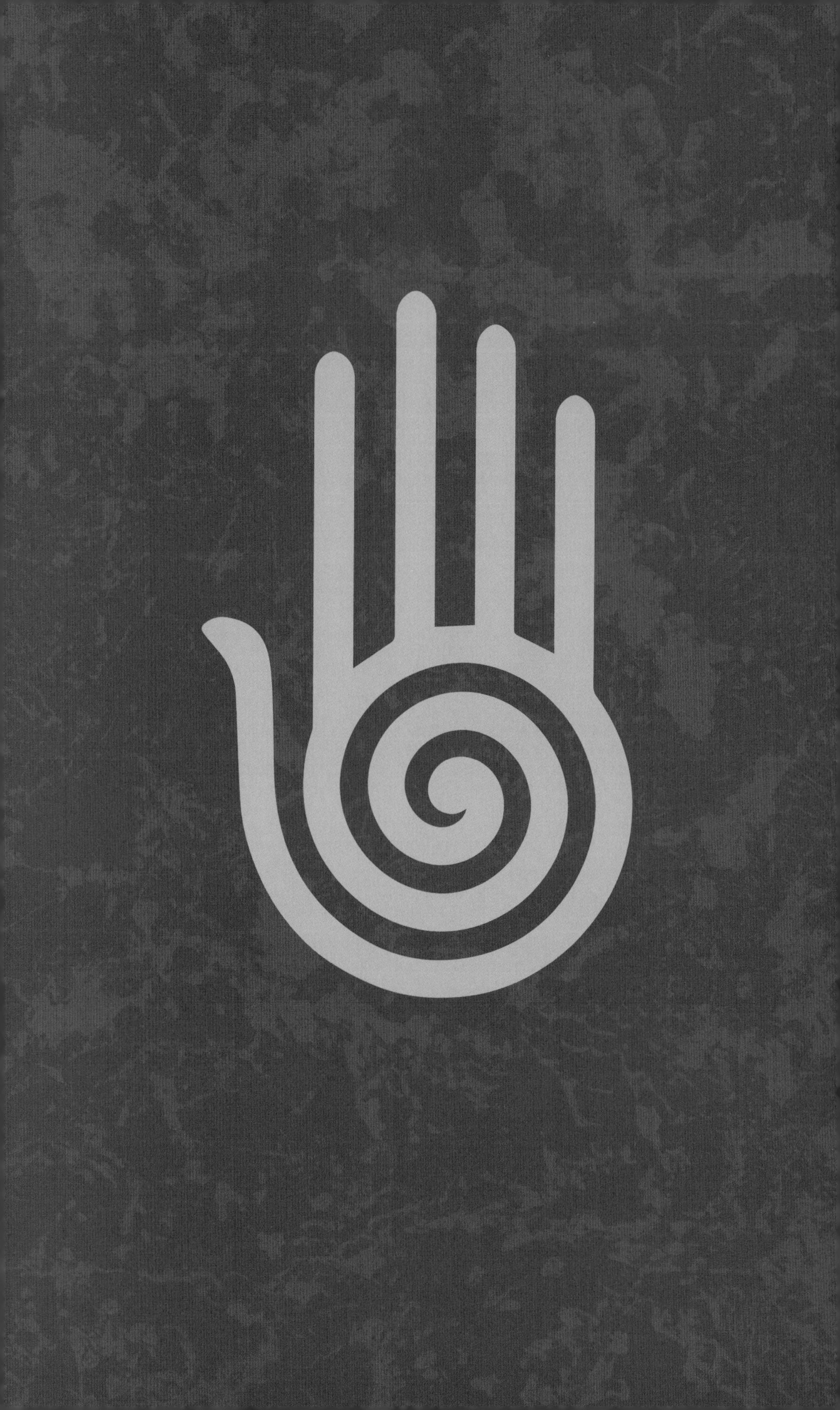

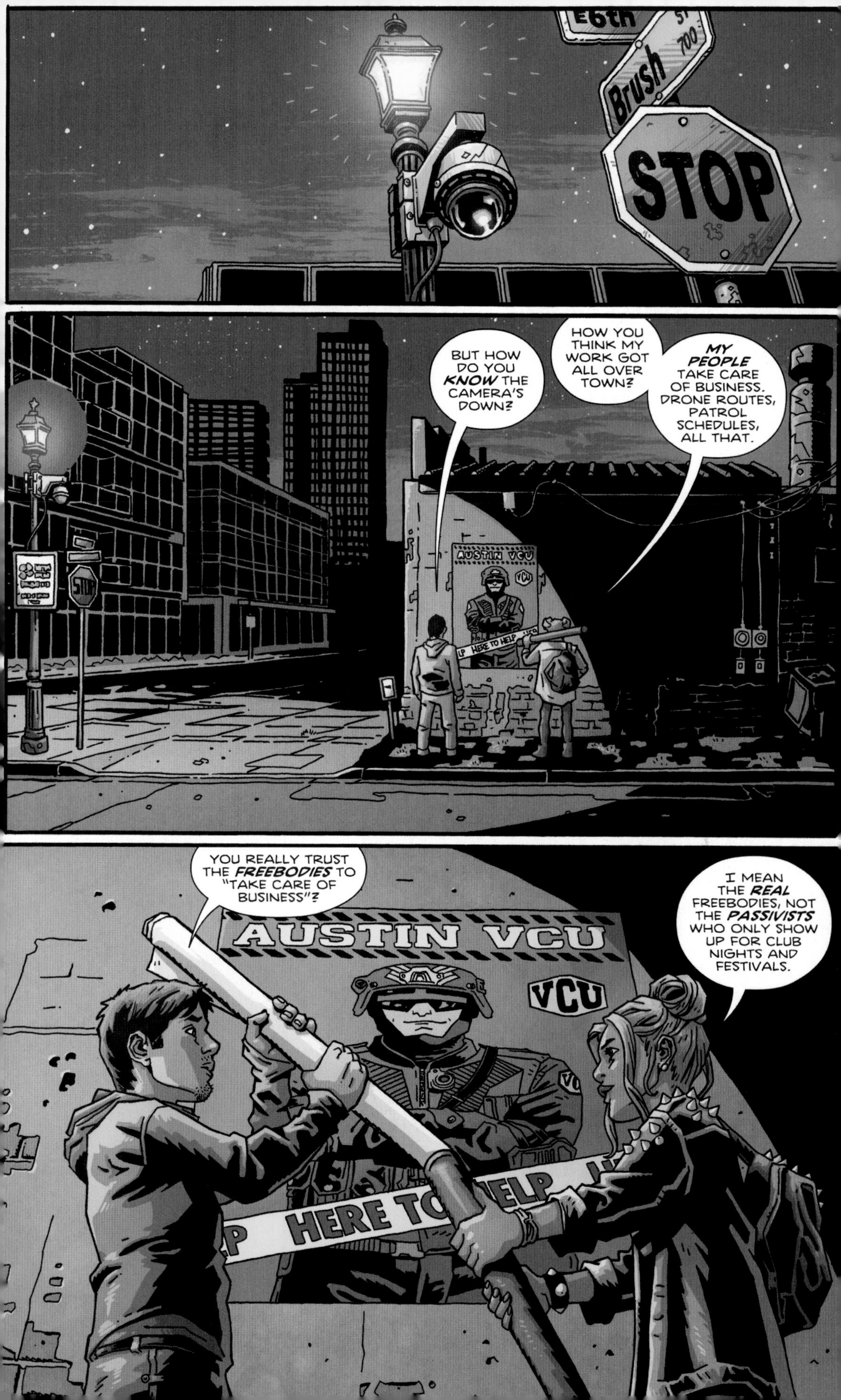
E6th
Brush ST 700
STOP
BUT HOW DO YOU *KNOW* THE CAMERA'S DOWN?
HOW YOU THINK MY WORK GOT ALL OVER TOWN?
MY PEOPLE TAKE CARE OF BUSINESS. DRONE ROUTES, PATROL SCHEDULES, ALL THAT.
AUSTIN VCU
VCU
HERE TO HELP
YOU REALLY TRUST THE *FREEBODIES* TO "TAKE CARE OF BUSINESS"?
I MEAN THE *REAL* FREEBODIES, NOT THE *PASSIVISTS* WHO ONLY SHOW UP FOR CLUB NIGHTS AND FESTIVALS.

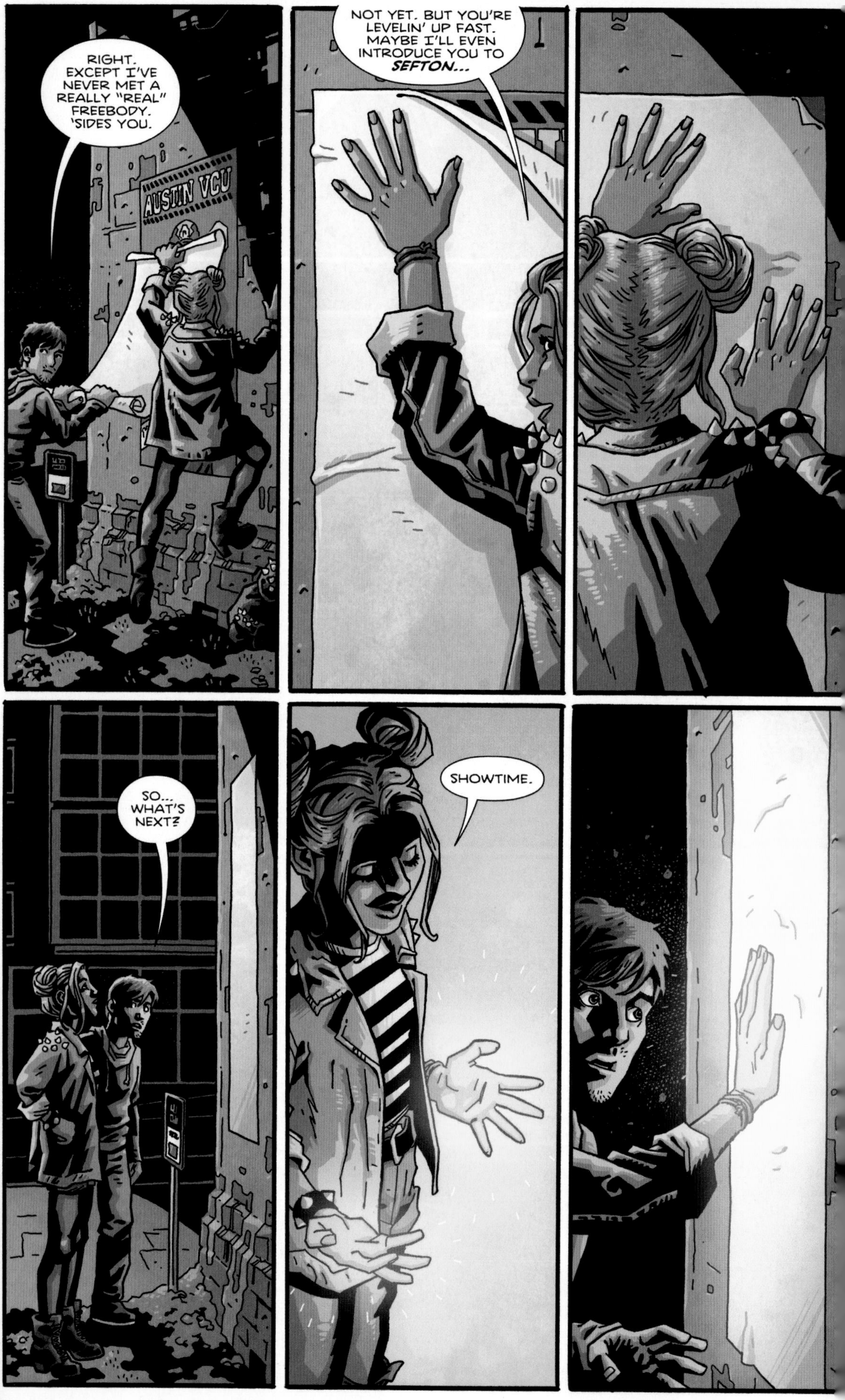
RIGHT. EXCEPT I'VE NEVER MET A REALLY "REAL" FREEBODY. 'SIDES YOU.
AUSTIN VCU
NOT YET. BUT YOU'RE LEVELIN' UP FAST. MAYBE I'LL EVEN INTRODUCE YOU TO SEFTON...
SO... WHAT'S NEXT?
SHOWTIME.

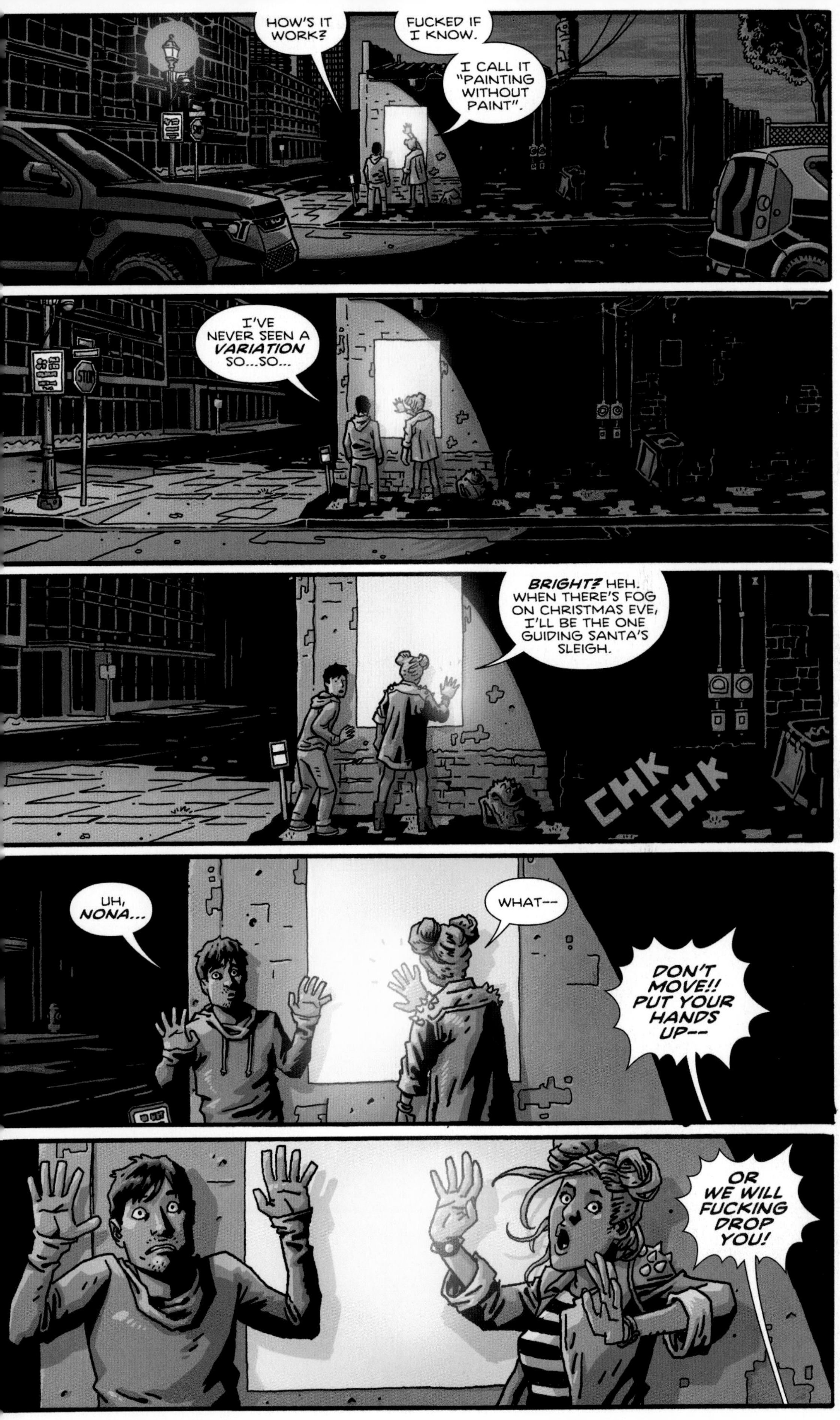
HOW'S IT WORK?
FUCKED IF I KNOW.
I CALL IT "PAINTING WITHOUT PAINT".
I'VE NEVER SEEN A VARIATION SO...SO...
BRIGHT? HEH. WHEN THERE'S FOG ON CHRISTMAS EVE, I'LL BE THE ONE GUIDING SANTA'S SLEIGH.
CHK CHK
UH, NONA...
WHAT--
DON'T MOVE!! PUT YOUR HANDS UP--
OR WE WILL FUCKING DROP YOU!

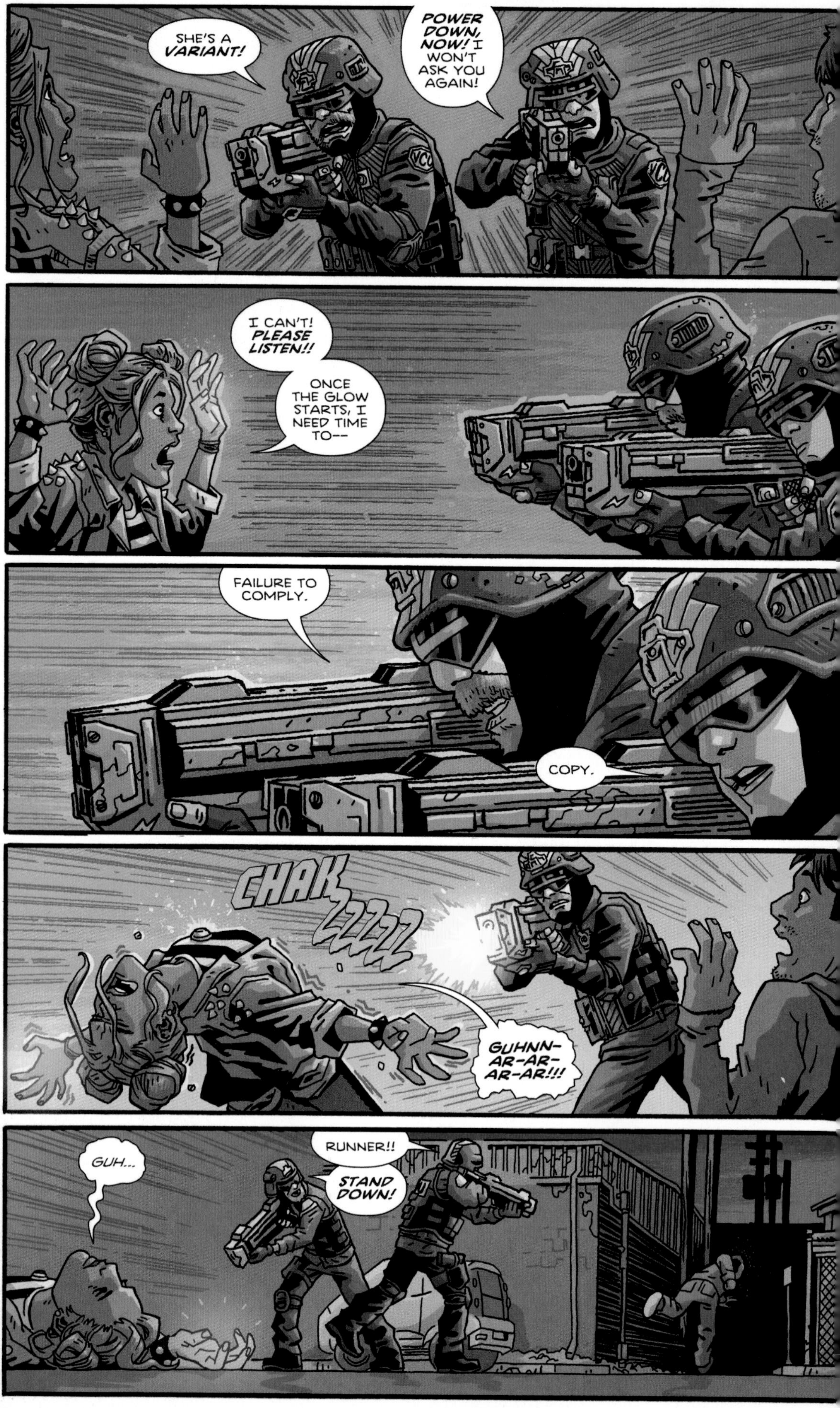
SHE'S A VARIANT!
POWER DOWN, NOW! I WON'T ASK YOU AGAIN!
I CAN'T! PLEASE LISTEN!!
ONCE THE GLOW STARTS, I NEED TIME TO--
FAILURE TO COMPLY.
COPY.
CHAK ZZZZZ
GUHNN-AR-AR-AR-AR!!!
GUH...
RUNNER!!
STAND DOWN!

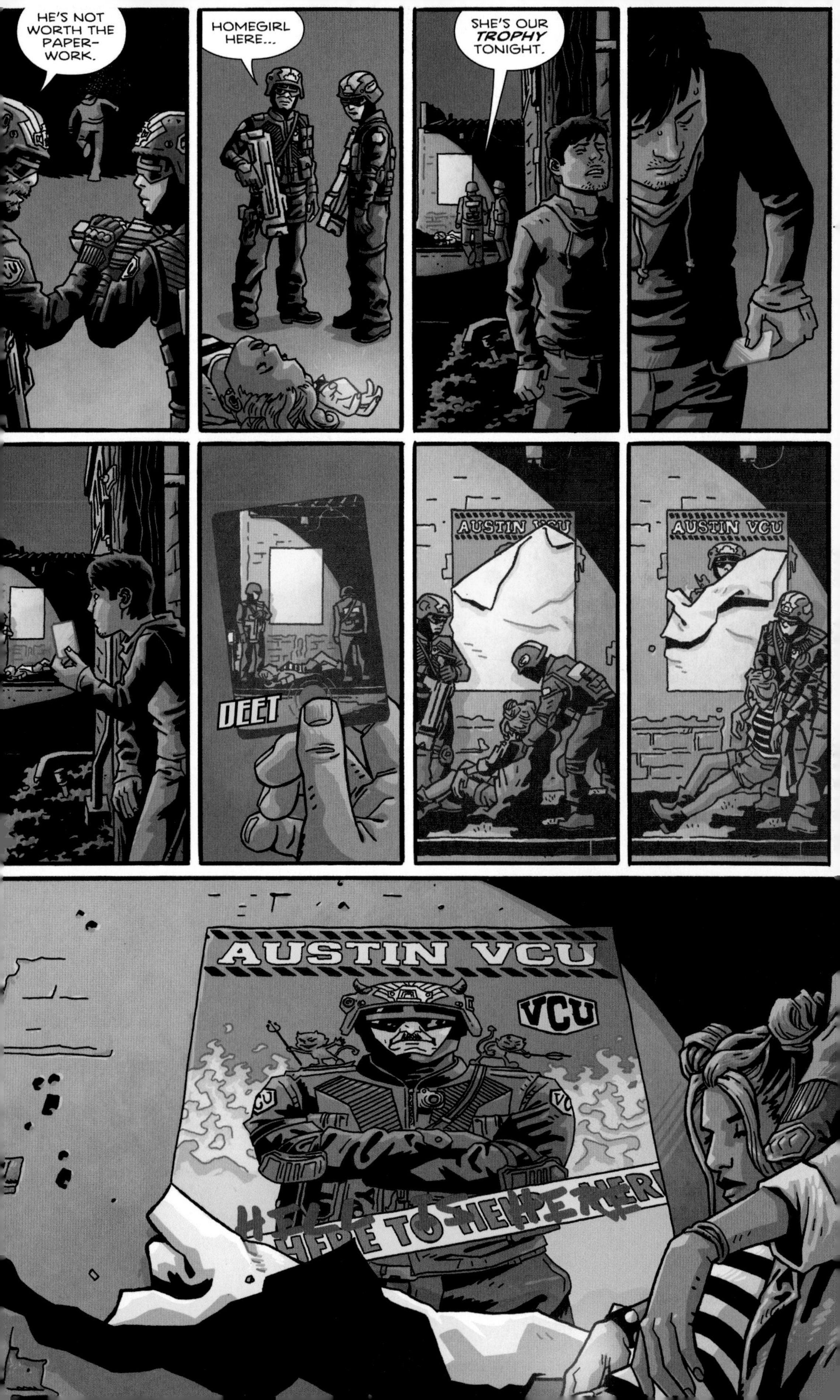
HE'S NOT WORTH THE PAPER-WORK.
HOMEGIRL HERE...
SHE'S OUR *TROPHY* TONIGHT.
DEET
AUSTIN VCU
AUSTIN VCU
AUSTIN VCU
VCU
HELL IS HERE
HERE TO

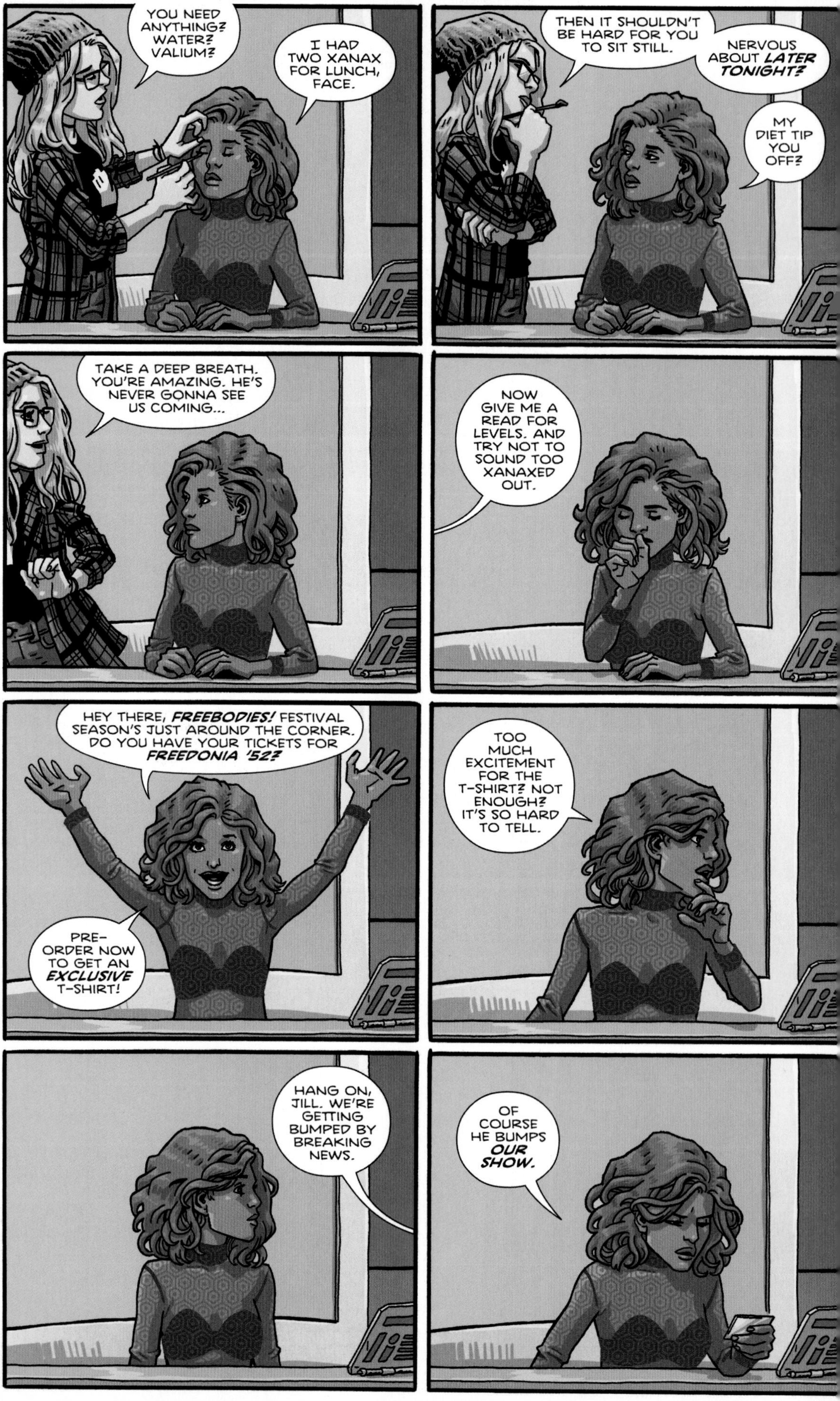
YOU NEED ANYTHING? WATER? VALIUM?
I HAD TWO XANAX FOR LUNCH, FACE.
THEN IT SHOULDN'T BE HARD FOR YOU TO SIT STILL.
NERVOUS ABOUT *LATER TONIGHT?*
MY DIET TIP YOU OFF?
TAKE A DEEP BREATH. YOU'RE AMAZING. HE'S NEVER GONNA SEE US COMING...
NOW GIVE ME A READ FOR LEVELS. AND TRY NOT TO SOUND TOO XANAXED OUT.
HEY THERE, *FREEBODIES!* FESTIVAL SEASON'S JUST AROUND THE CORNER. DO YOU HAVE YOUR TICKETS FOR *FREEDONIA '52?*
PRE-ORDER NOW TO GET AN *EXCLUSIVE* T-SHIRT!
TOO MUCH EXCITEMENT FOR THE T-SHIRT? NOT ENOUGH? IT'S SO HARD TO TELL.
HANG ON, JILL. WE'RE GETTING BUMPED BY BREAKING NEWS.
OF COURSE HE BUMPS *OUR SHOW.*

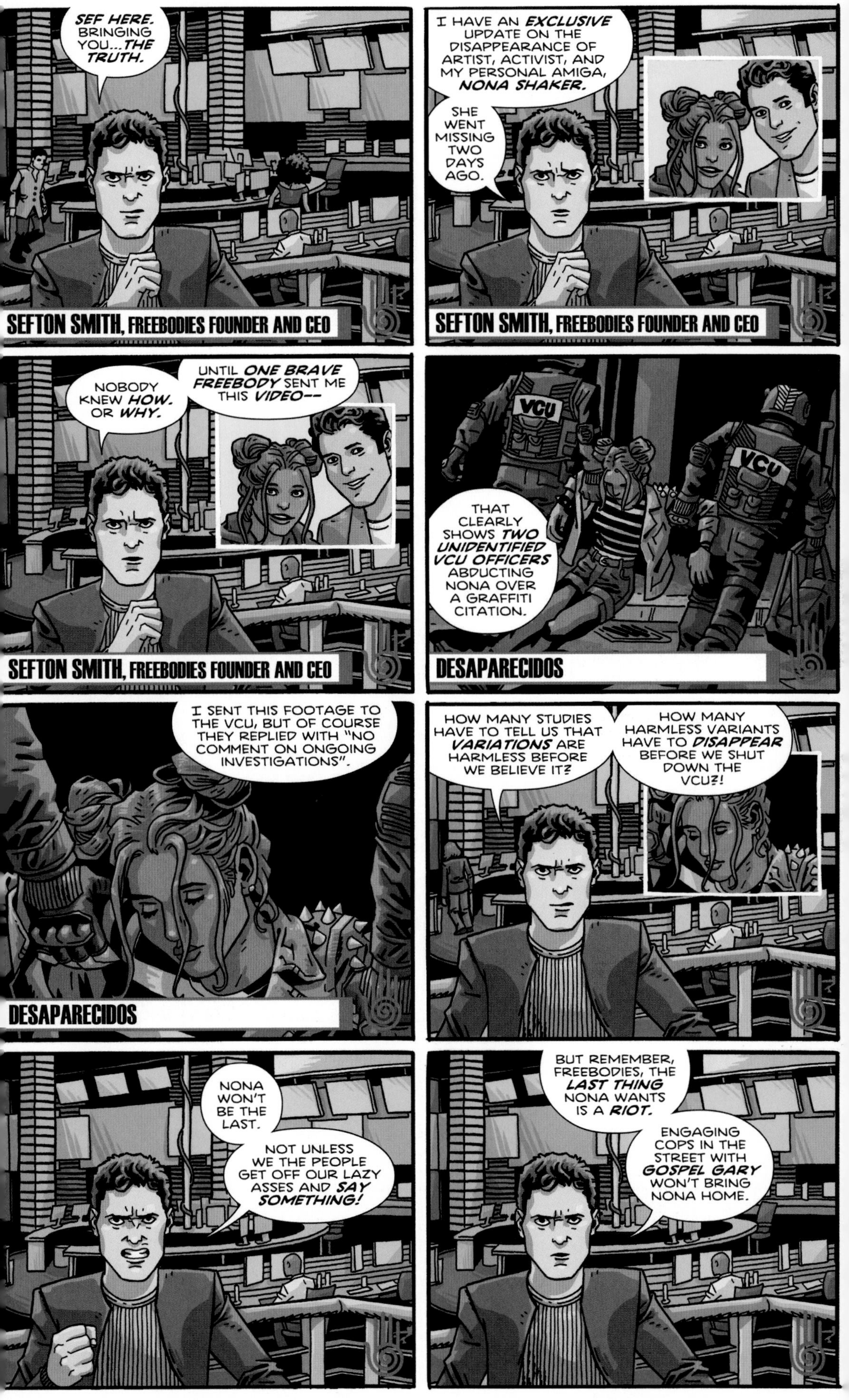
SEF HERE. BRINGING YOU...THE TRUTH.
SEFTON SMITH, FREEBODIES FOUNDER AND CEO
I HAVE AN EXCLUSIVE UPDATE ON THE DISAPPEARANCE OF ARTIST, ACTIVIST, AND MY PERSONAL AMIGA, NONA SHAKER.
SHE WENT MISSING TWO DAYS AGO.
SEFTON SMITH, FREEBODIES FOUNDER AND CEO
NOBODY KNEW HOW. OR WHY.
UNTIL ONE BRAVE FREEBODY SENT ME THIS VIDEO--
SEFTON SMITH, FREEBODIES FOUNDER AND CEO
VCU
VCU
THAT CLEARLY SHOWS TWO UNIDENTIFIED VCU OFFICERS ABDUCTING NONA OVER A GRAFFITI CITATION.
DESAPARECIDOS
I SENT THIS FOOTAGE TO THE VCU, BUT OF COURSE THEY REPLIED WITH "NO COMMENT ON ONGOING INVESTIGATIONS".
DESAPARECIDOS
HOW MANY STUDIES HAVE TO TELL US THAT VARIATIONS ARE HARMLESS BEFORE WE BELIEVE IT?
HOW MANY HARMLESS VARIANTS HAVE TO DISAPPEAR BEFORE WE SHUT DOWN THE VCU?!
NONA WON'T BE THE LAST.
NOT UNLESS WE THE PEOPLE GET OFF OUR LAZY ASSES AND SAY SOMETHING!
BUT REMEMBER, FREEBODIES, THE LAST THING NONA WANTS IS A RIOT.
ENGAGING COPS IN THE STREET WITH GOSPEL GARY WON'T BRING NONA HOME.

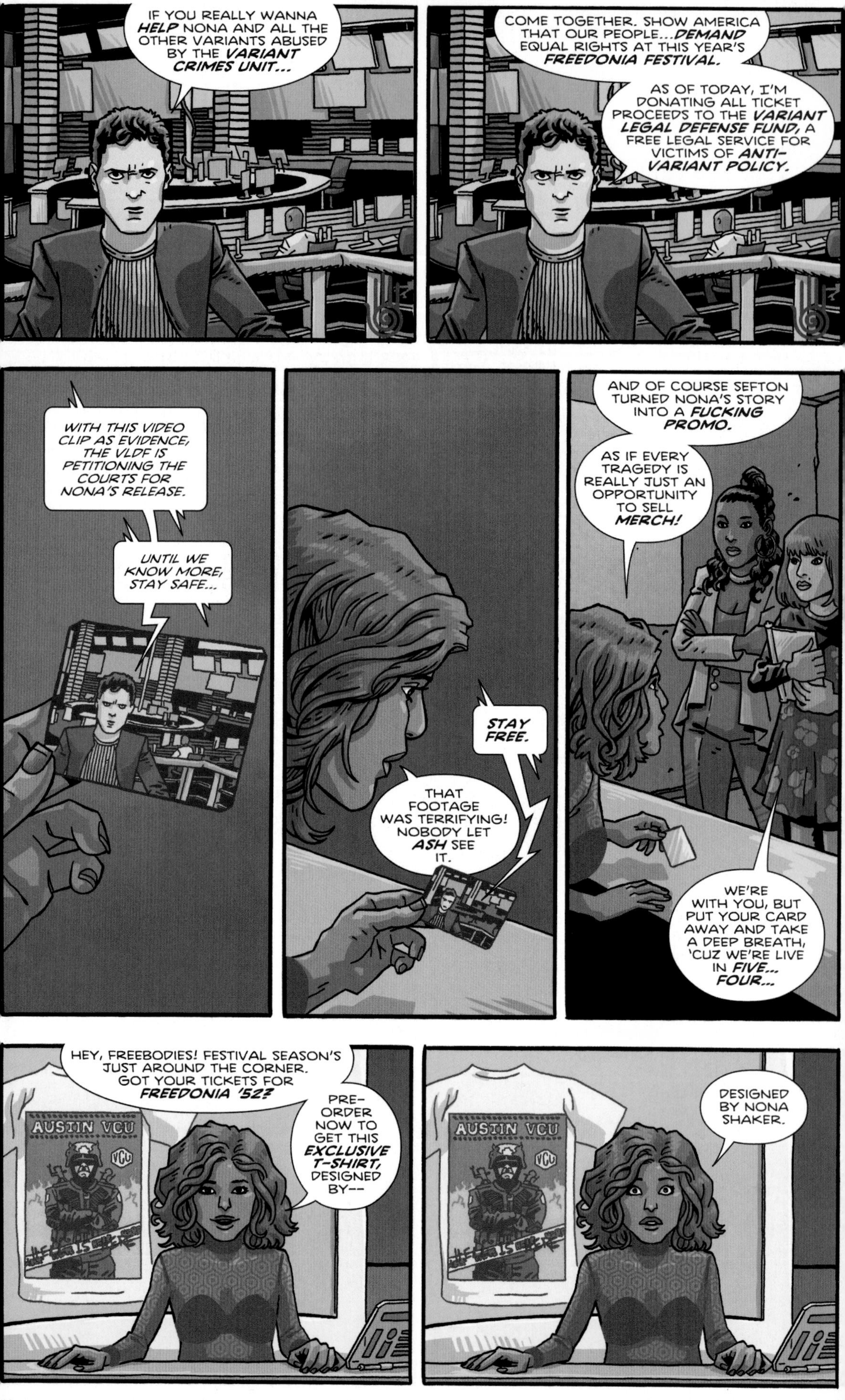

IF YOU REALLY WANNA HELP NONA AND ALL THE OTHER VARIANTS ABUSED BY THE VARIANT CRIMES UNIT...
COME TOGETHER. SHOW AMERICA THAT OUR PEOPLE...DEMAND EQUAL RIGHTS AT THIS YEAR'S FREEDONIA FESTIVAL.
AS OF TODAY, I'M DONATING ALL TICKET PROCEEDS TO THE VARIANT LEGAL DEFENSE FUND, A FREE LEGAL SERVICE FOR VICTIMS OF ANTI-VARIANT POLICY.
WITH THIS VIDEO CLIP AS EVIDENCE, THE VLDF IS PETITIONING THE COURTS FOR NONA'S RELEASE.
UNTIL WE KNOW MORE, STAY SAFE...
STAY FREE.
THAT FOOTAGE WAS TERRIFYING! NOBODY LET ASH SEE IT.
AND OF COURSE SEFTON TURNED NONA'S STORY INTO A FUCKING PROMO.
AS IF EVERY TRAGEDY IS REALLY JUST AN OPPORTUNITY TO SELL MERCH!
WE'RE WITH YOU, BUT PUT YOUR CARD AWAY AND TAKE A DEEP BREATH, 'CUZ WE'RE LIVE IN FIVE... FOUR...
HEY, FREEBODIES! FESTIVAL SEASON'S JUST AROUND THE CORNER. GOT YOUR TICKETS FOR FREEDONIA '52?
AUSTIN VCU
VCU
PRE-ORDER NOW TO GET THIS EXCLUSIVE T-SHIRT, DESIGNED BY--
AUSTIN VCU
VCU
DESIGNED BY NONA SHAKER.

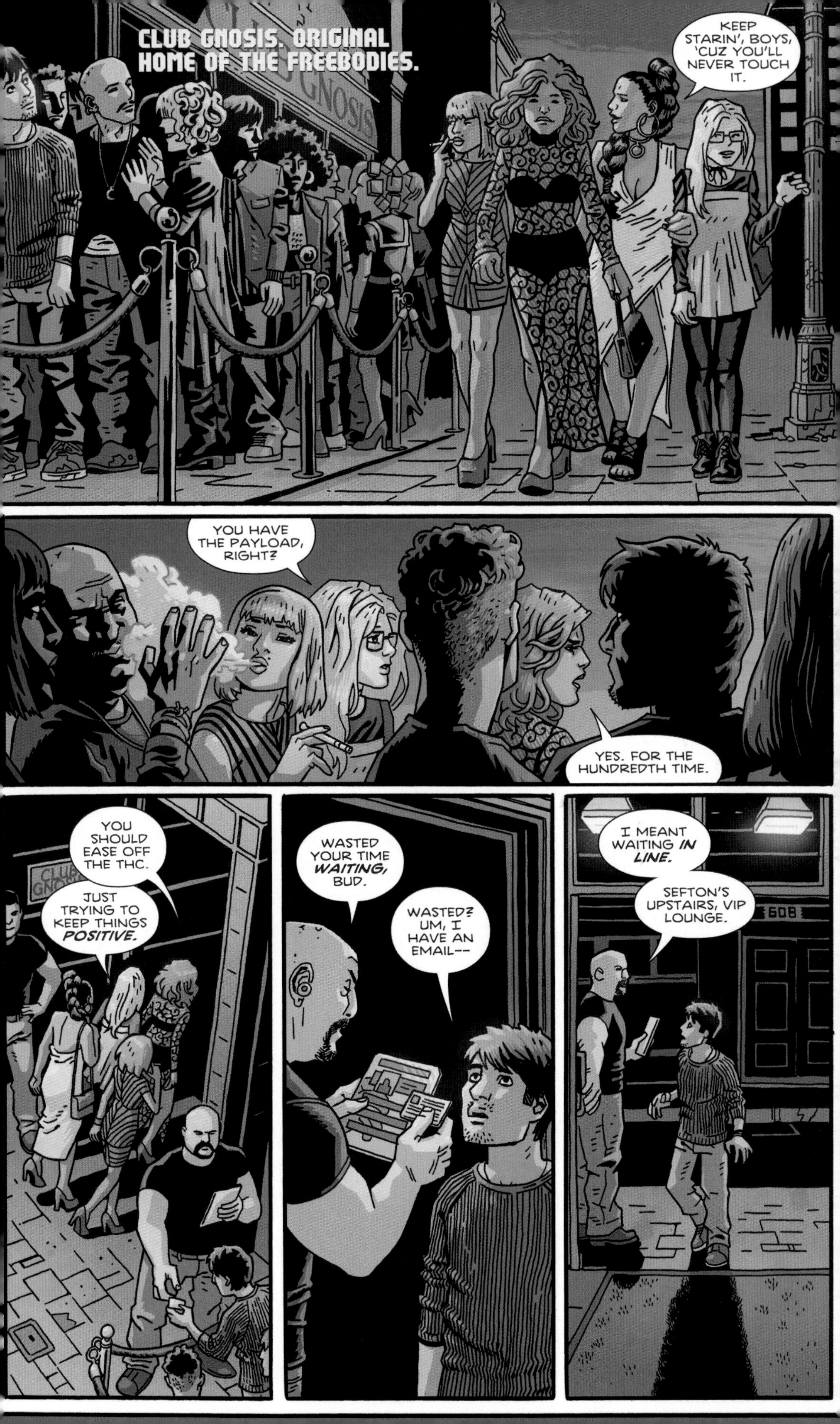
CLUB GNOSIS. ORIGINAL HOME OF THE FREEBODIES.
KEEP STARIN', BOYS, 'CUZ YOU'LL NEVER TOUCH IT.
YOU HAVE THE PAYLOAD, RIGHT?
YES. FOR THE HUNDREDTH TIME.
YOU SHOULD EASE OFF THE THC.
JUST TRYING TO KEEP THINGS POSITIVE.
WASTED YOUR TIME WAITING, BUD.
WASTED? UM, I HAVE AN EMAIL--
I MEANT WAITING IN LINE.
SEFTON'S UPSTAIRS, VIP LOUNGE.

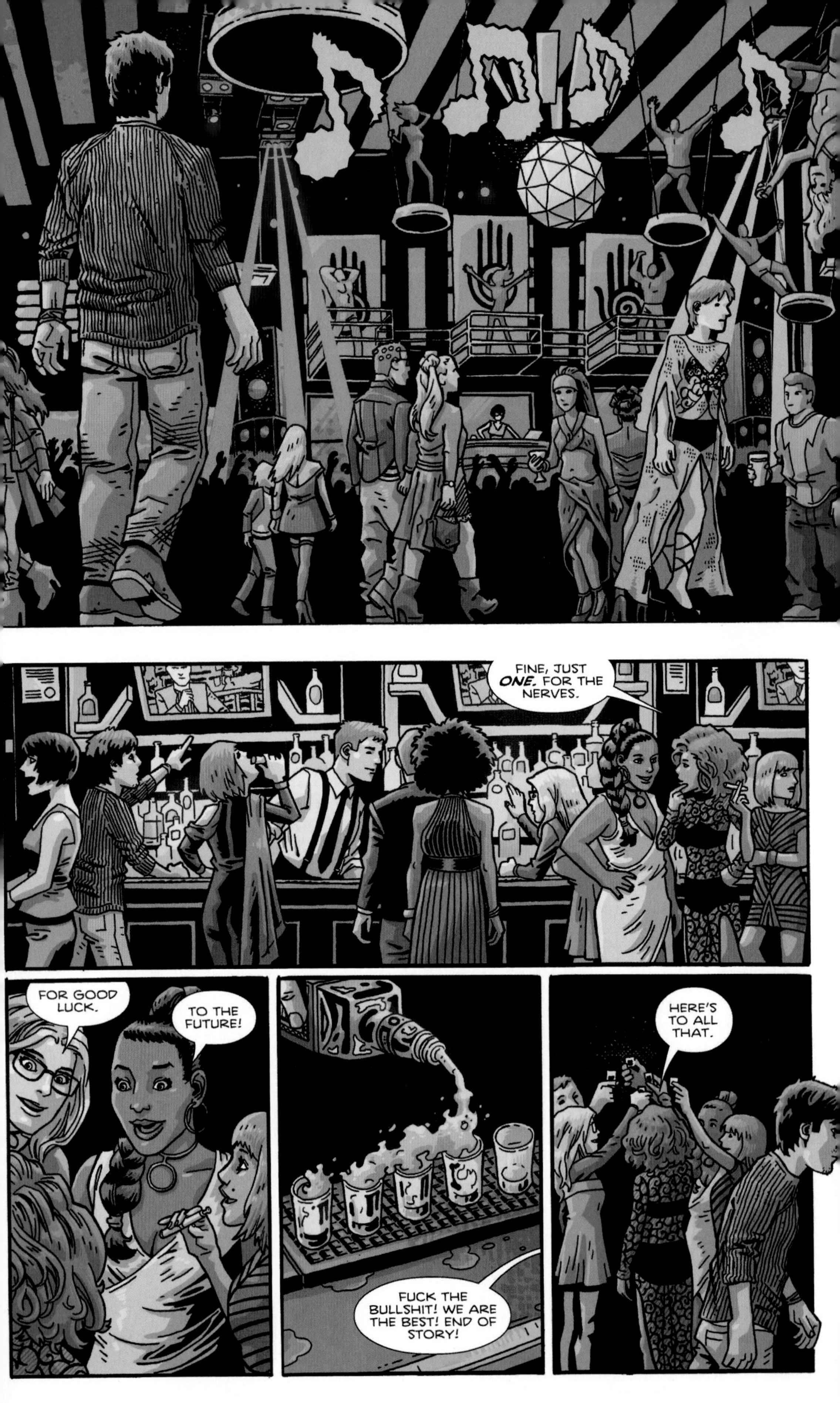
FINE, JUST ONE. FOR THE NERVES.
FOR GOOD LUCK.
TO THE FUTURE!
FUCK THE BULLSHIT! WE ARE THE BEST! END OF STORY!
HERE'S TO ALL THAT.

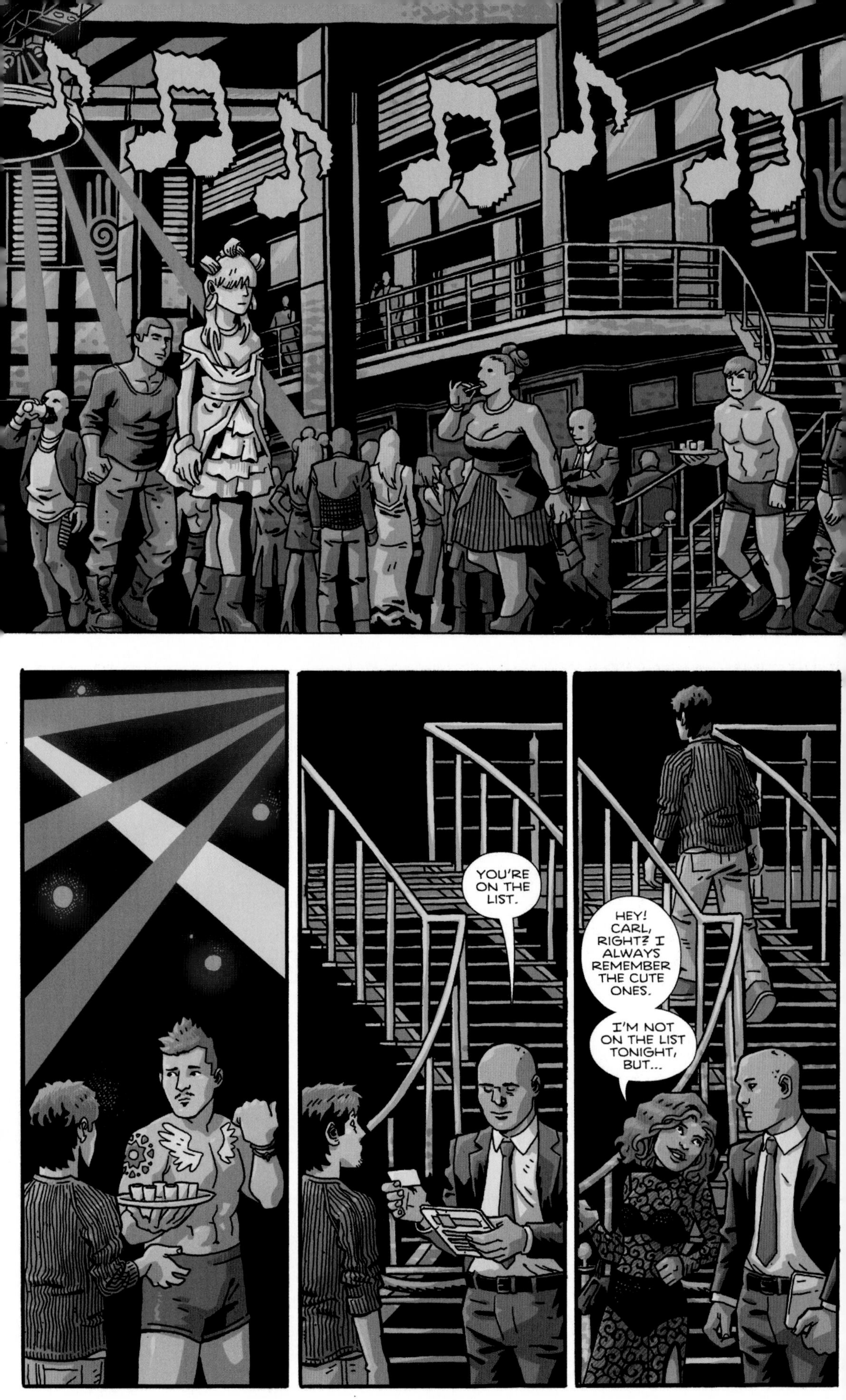
YOU'RE ON THE LIST.
HEY! CARL, RIGHT? I ALWAYS REMEMBER THE CUTE ONES.
I'M NOT ON THE LIST TONIGHT, BUT...

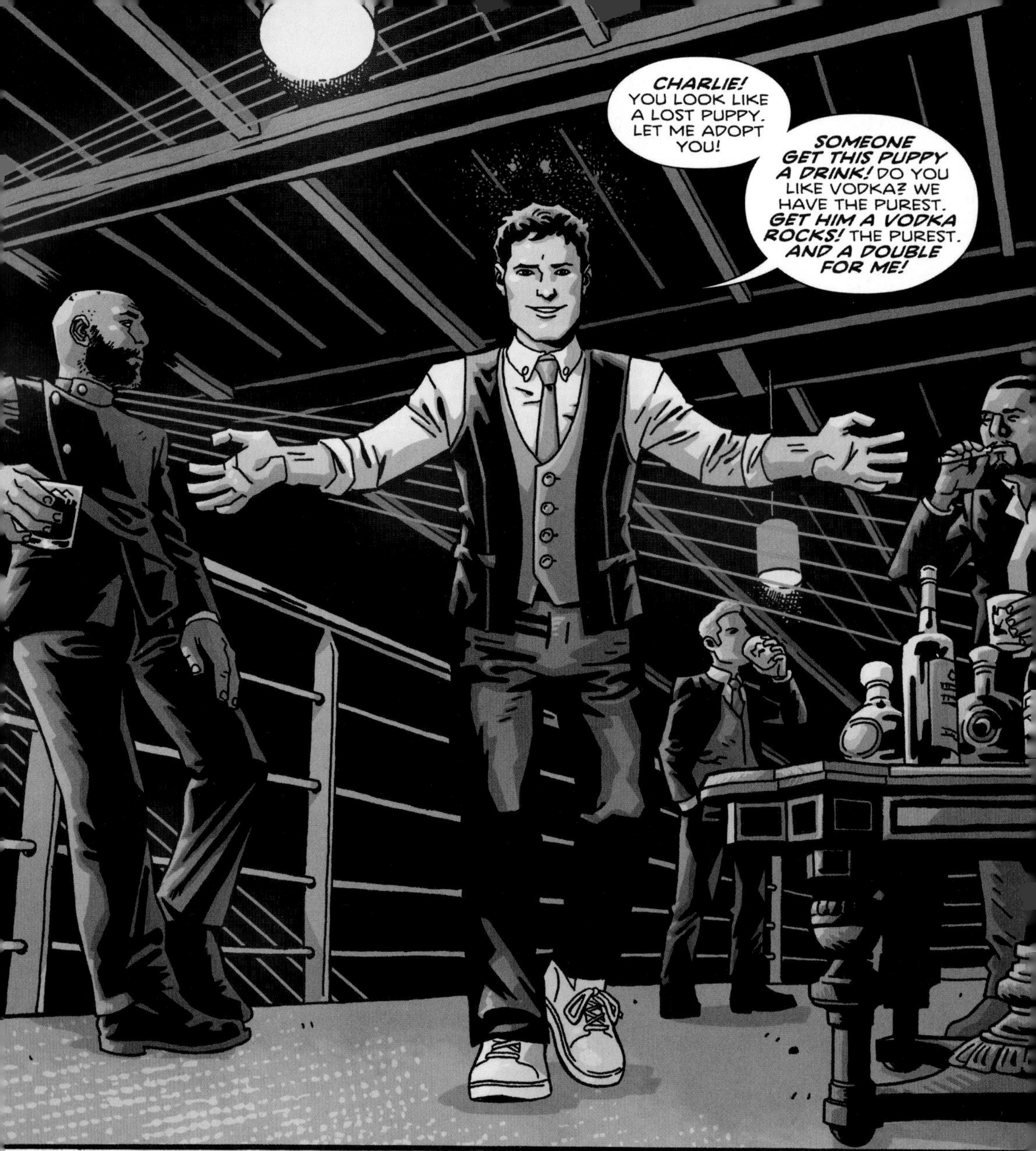
CHARLIE! YOU LOOK LIKE A LOST PUPPY. LET ME ADOPT YOU!
SOMEONE GET THIS PUPPY A DRINK! DO YOU LIKE VODKA? WE HAVE THE PUREST. GET HIM A VODKA ROCKS! THE PUREST. AND A DOUBLE FOR ME!

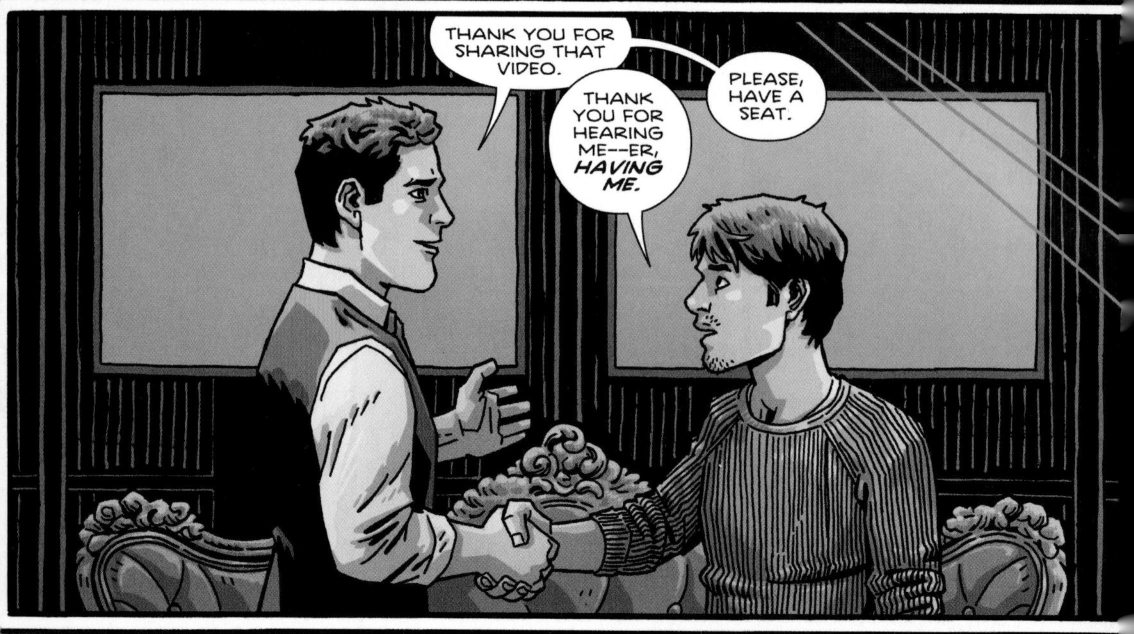
THANK YOU FOR SHARING THAT VIDEO.
PLEASE, HAVE A SEAT.
THANK YOU FOR HEARING ME--ER, HAVING ME.

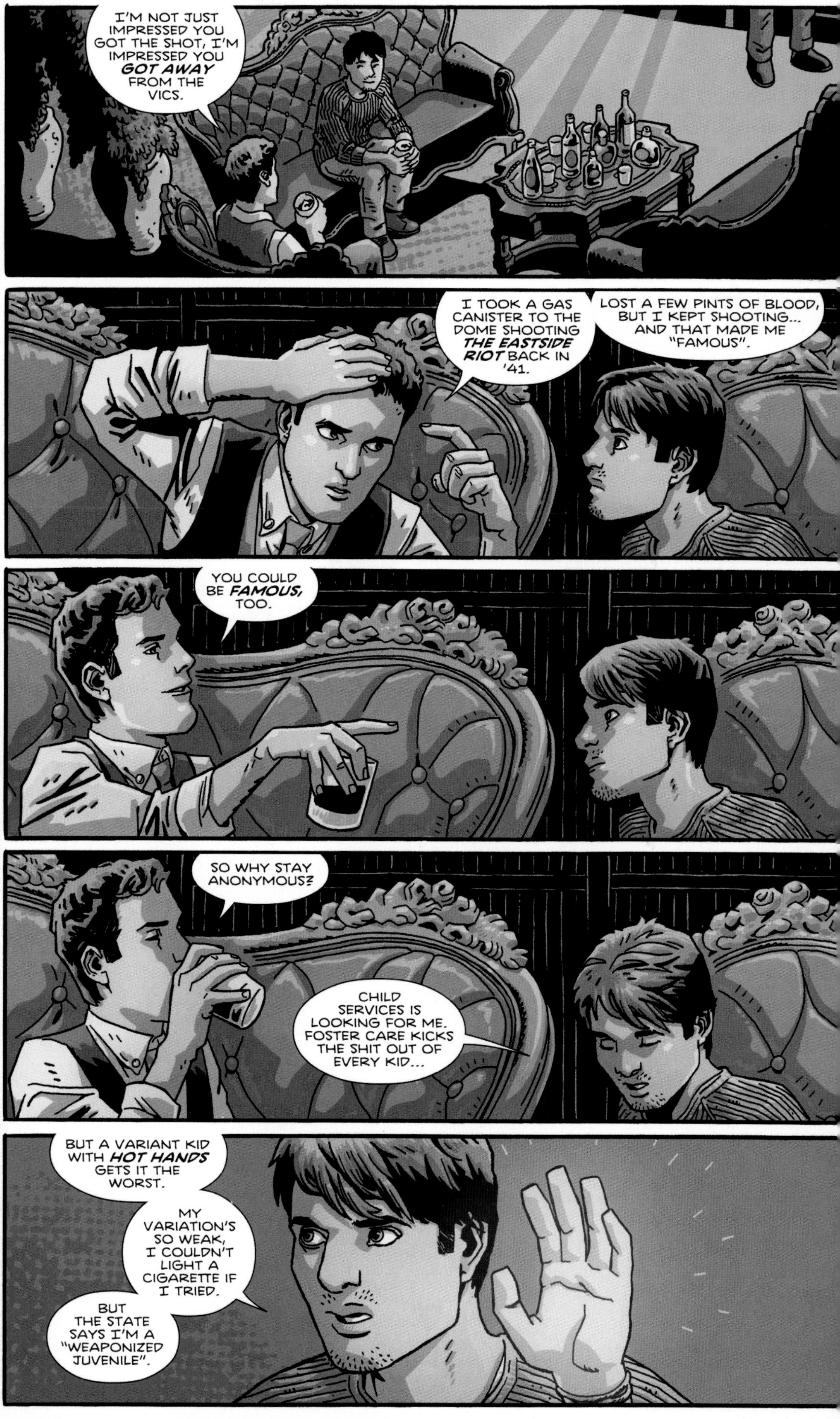
I'M NOT JUST IMPRESSED YOU GOT THE SHOT, I'M IMPRESSED YOU GOT AWAY FROM THE VICS.
I TOOK A GAS CANISTER TO THE DOME SHOOTING THE EASTSIDE RIOT BACK IN '41.
LOST A FEW PINTS OF BLOOD, BUT I KEPT SHOOTING... AND THAT MADE ME "FAMOUS".
YOU COULD BE FAMOUS, TOO.
SO WHY STAY ANONYMOUS?
CHILD SERVICES IS LOOKING FOR ME. FOSTER CARE KICKS THE SHIT OUT OF EVERY KID...
BUT A VARIANT KID WITH HOT HANDS GETS IT THE WORST.
MY VARIATION'S SO WEAK, I COULDN'T LIGHT A CIGARETTE IF I TRIED.
BUT THE STATE SAYS I'M A "WEAPONIZED JUVENILE".

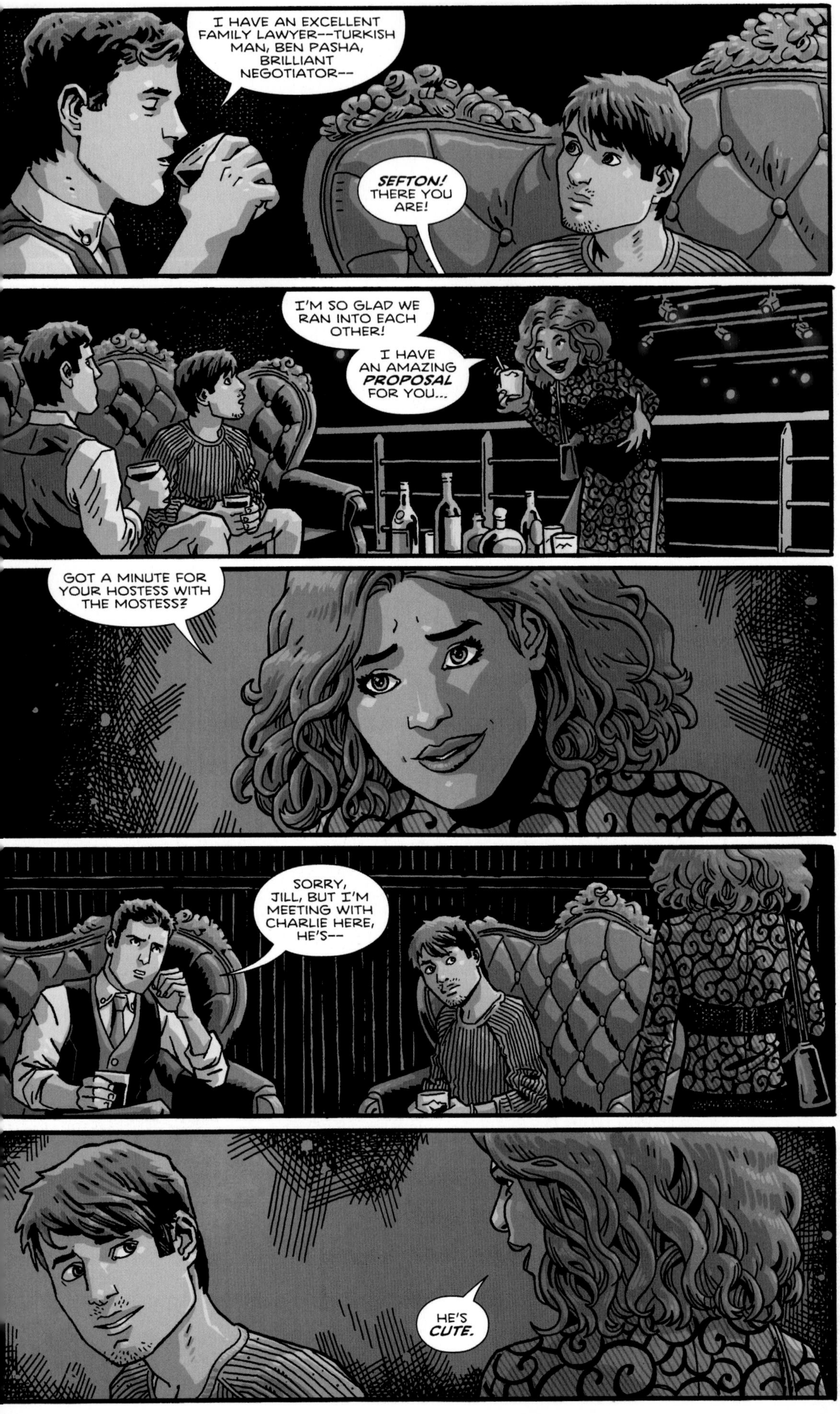
I HAVE AN EXCELLENT FAMILY LAWYER--TURKISH MAN, BEN PASHA, BRILLIANT NEGOTIATOR--
SEFTON! THERE YOU ARE!
I'M SO GLAD WE RAN INTO EACH OTHER!
I HAVE AN AMAZING PROPOSAL FOR YOU...
GOT A MINUTE FOR YOUR HOSTESS WITH THE MOSTESS?
SORRY, JILL, BUT I'M MEETING WITH CHARLIE HERE, HE'S--
HE'S CUTE.

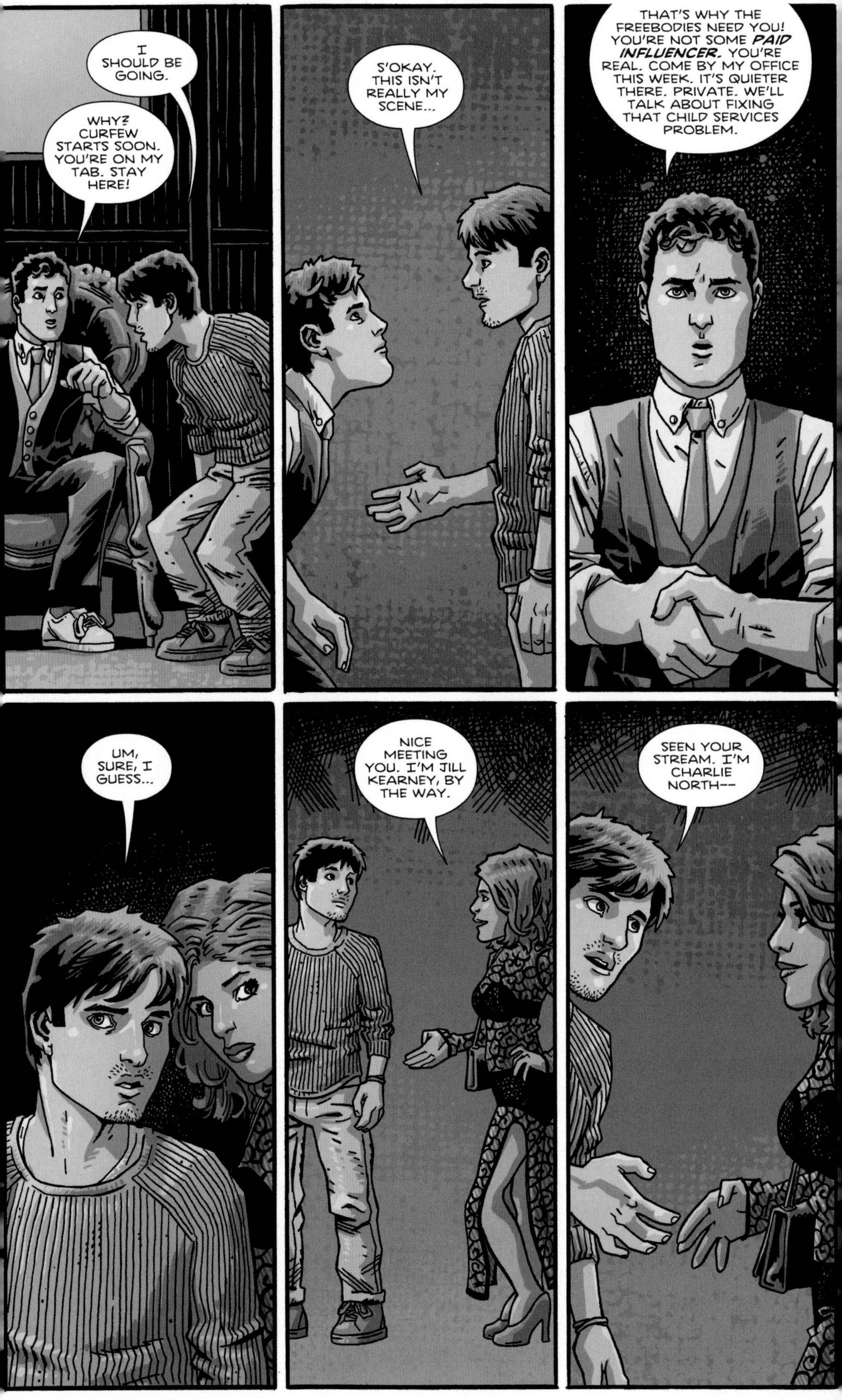
I SHOULD BE GOING.
WHY? CURFEW STARTS SOON. YOU'RE ON MY TAB. STAY HERE!
S'OKAY. THIS ISN'T REALLY MY SCENE...
THAT'S WHY THE FREEBODIES NEED YOU! YOU'RE NOT SOME *PAID INFLUENCER.* YOU'RE REAL. COME BY MY OFFICE THIS WEEK. IT'S QUIETER THERE. PRIVATE. WE'LL TALK ABOUT FIXING THAT CHILD SERVICES PROBLEM.
UM, SURE, I GUESS...
NICE MEETING YOU. I'M JILL KEARNEY, BY THE WAY.
SEEN YOUR STREAM. I'M CHARLIE NORTH--

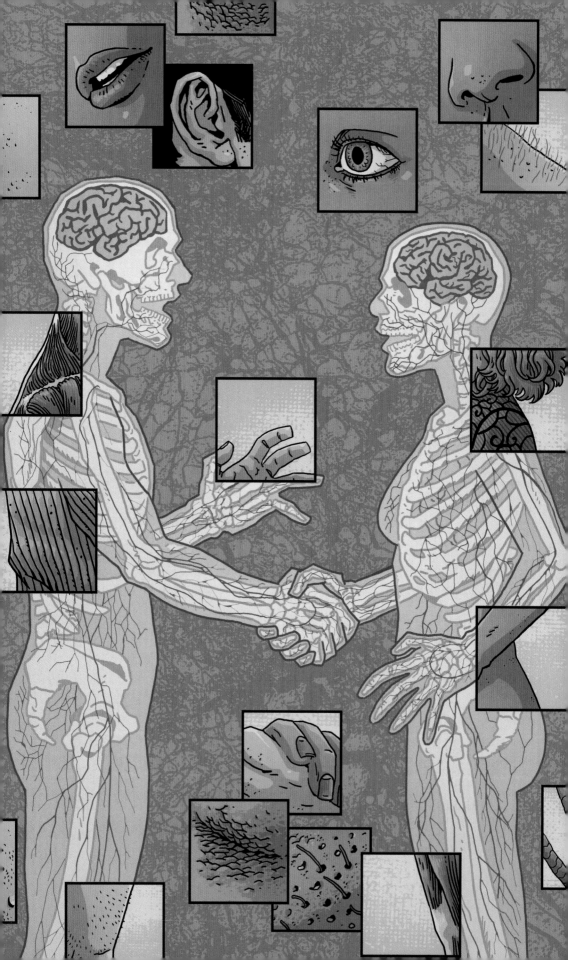

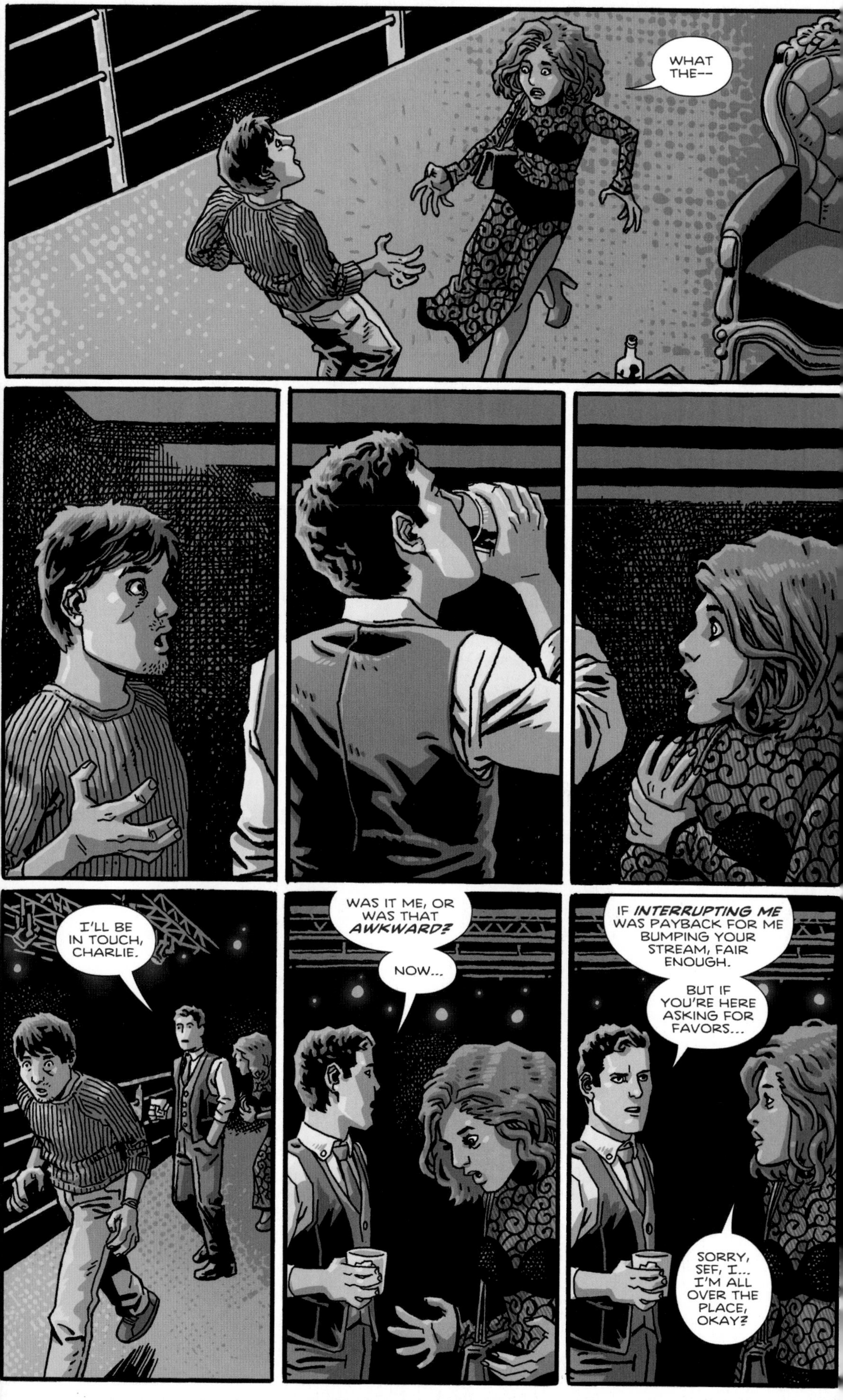

WHAT THE--
I'LL BE IN TOUCH, CHARLIE.
WAS IT ME, OR WAS THAT *AWKWARD?*
NOW...
IF *INTERRUPTING ME* WAS PAYBACK FOR ME BUMPING YOUR STREAM, FAIR ENOUGH.
BUT IF YOU'RE HERE ASKING FOR FAVORS...
SORRY, SEF, I... I'M ALL OVER THE PLACE, OKAY?

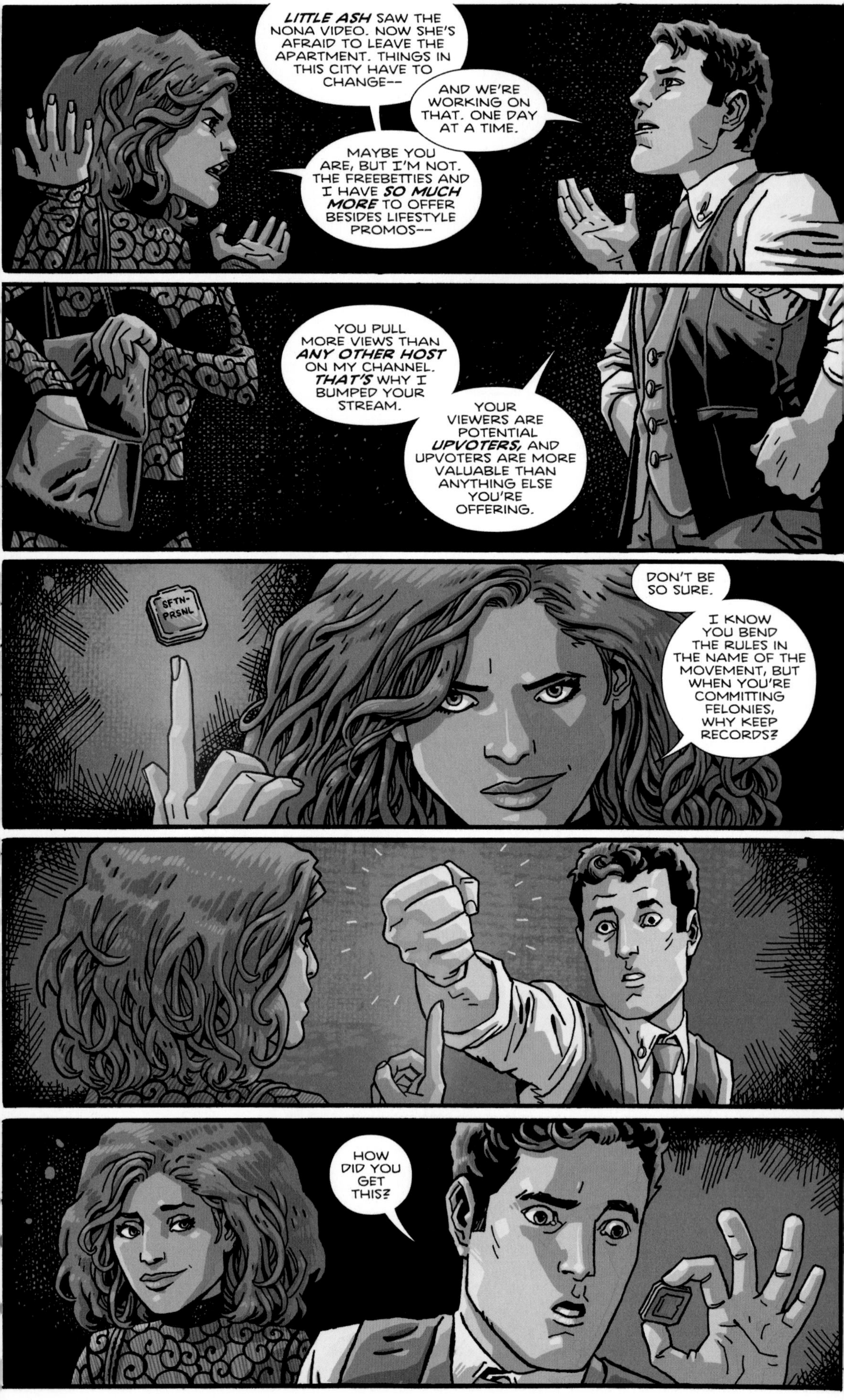

LITTLE ASH SAW THE NONA VIDEO. NOW SHE'S AFRAID TO LEAVE THE APARTMENT. THINGS IN THIS CITY HAVE TO CHANGE--
AND WE'RE WORKING ON THAT. ONE DAY AT A TIME.
MAYBE YOU ARE, BUT I'M NOT. THE FREEBETTIES AND I HAVE SO MUCH MORE TO OFFER BESIDES LIFESTYLE PROMOS--
YOU PULL MORE VIEWS THAN ANY OTHER HOST ON MY CHANNEL. THAT'S WHY I BUMPED YOUR STREAM.
YOUR VIEWERS ARE POTENTIAL UPVOTERS, AND UPVOTERS ARE MORE VALUABLE THAN ANYTHING ELSE YOU'RE OFFERING.
SFTN-PRSNL
DON'T BE SO SURE.
I KNOW YOU BEND THE RULES IN THE NAME OF THE MOVEMENT, BUT WHEN YOU'RE COMMITTING FELONIES, WHY KEEP RECORDS?
HOW DID YOU GET THIS?

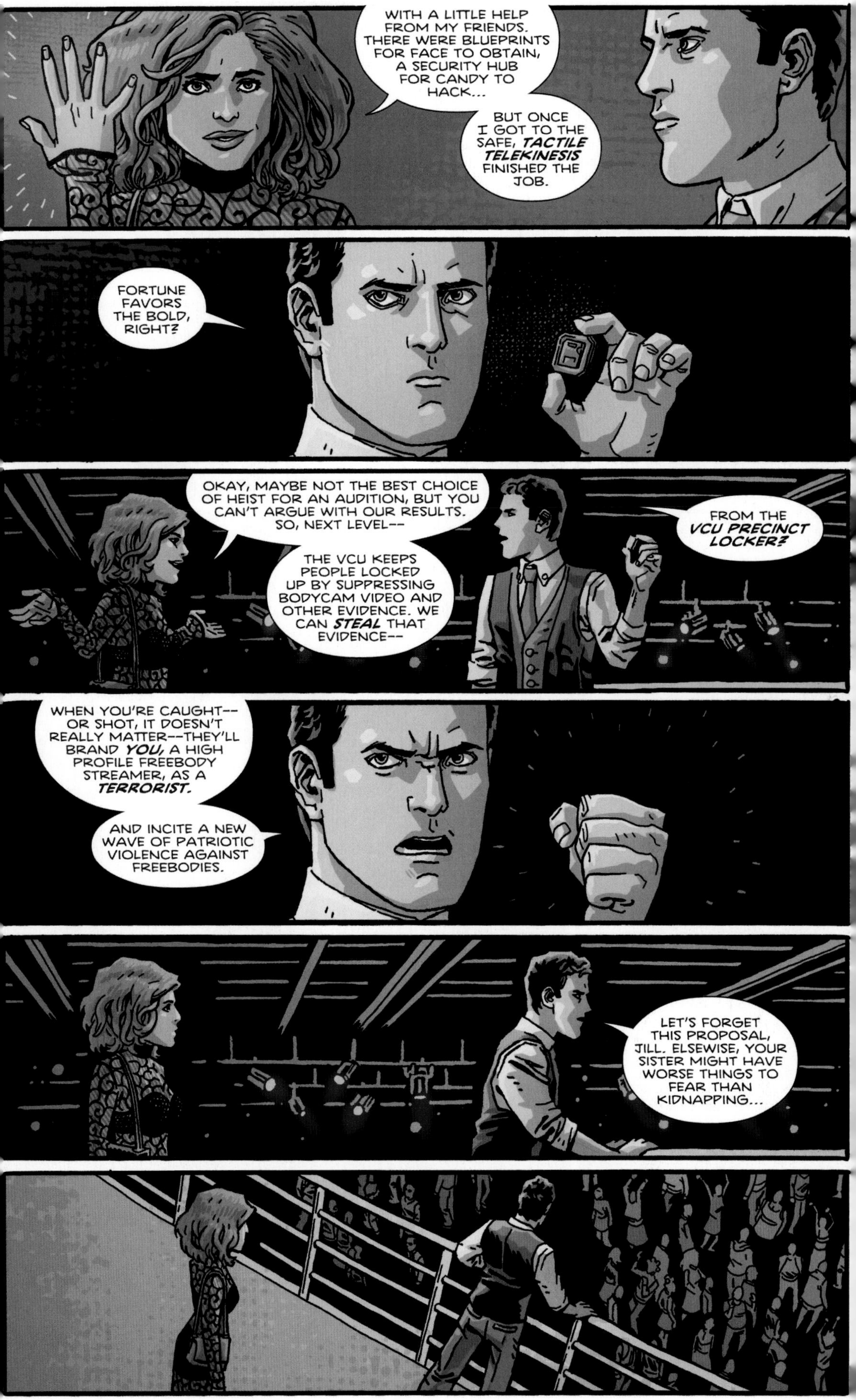
WITH A LITTLE HELP FROM MY FRIENDS. THERE WERE BLUEPRINTS FOR FACE TO OBTAIN, A SECURITY HUB FOR CANDY TO HACK...
BUT ONCE I GOT TO THE SAFE, *TACTILE TELEKINESIS* FINISHED THE JOB.
FORTUNE FAVORS THE BOLD, RIGHT?
OKAY, MAYBE NOT THE BEST CHOICE OF HEIST FOR AN AUDITION, BUT YOU CAN'T ARGUE WITH OUR RESULTS. SO, NEXT LEVEL--
FROM THE *VCU PRECINCT LOCKER?*
THE VCU KEEPS PEOPLE LOCKED UP BY SUPPRESSING BODYCAM VIDEO AND OTHER EVIDENCE. WE CAN *STEAL* THAT EVIDENCE--
WHEN YOU'RE CAUGHT-- OR SHOT, IT DOESN'T REALLY MATTER--THEY'LL BRAND *YOU,* A HIGH PROFILE FREEBODY STREAMER, AS A *TERRORIST.*
AND INCITE A NEW WAVE OF PATRIOTIC VIOLENCE AGAINST FREEBODIES.
LET'S FORGET THIS PROPOSAL, JILL. ELSEWISE, YOUR SISTER MIGHT HAVE WORSE THINGS TO FEAR THAN KIDNAPPING...

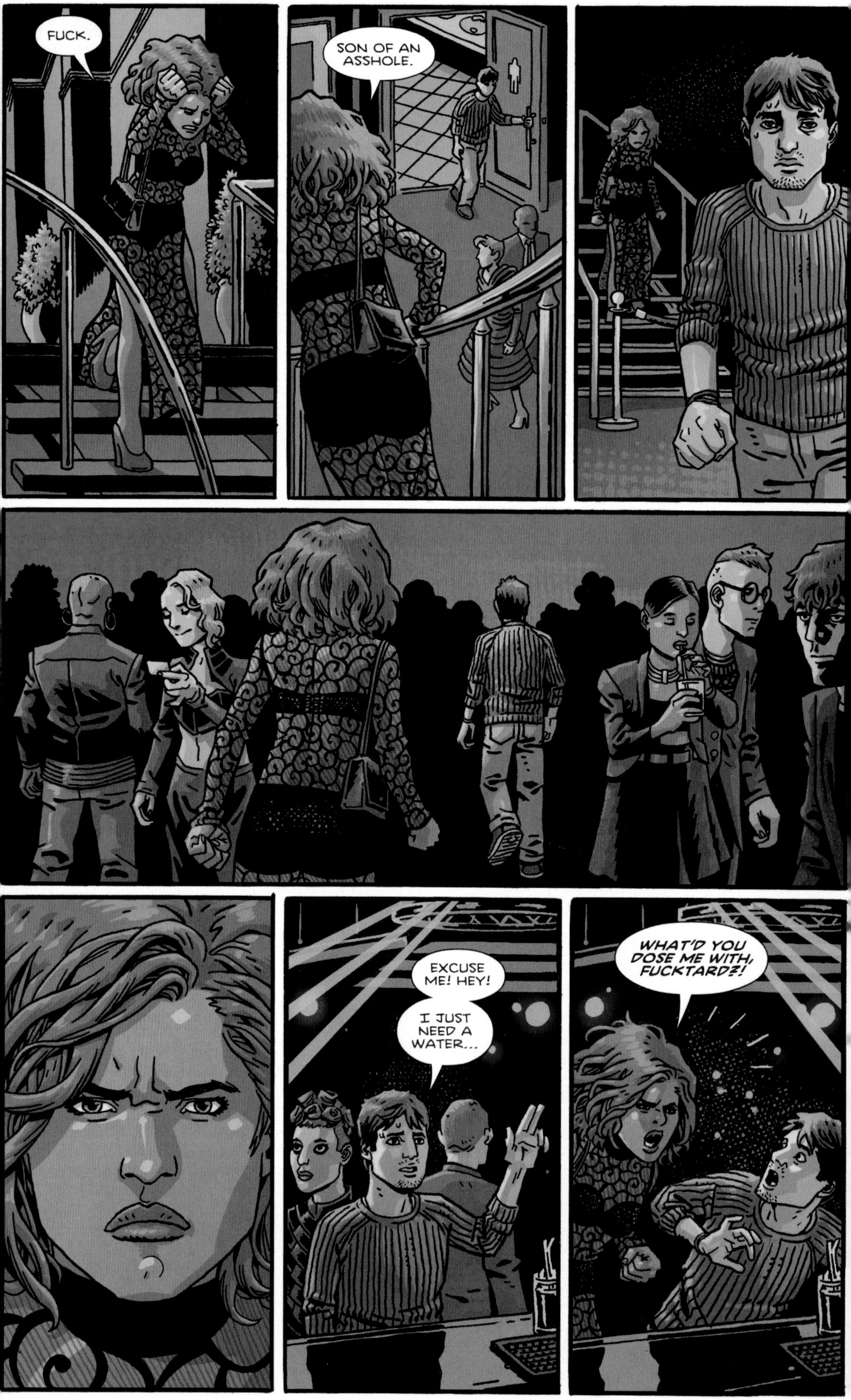
FUCK.
SON OF AN ASSHOLE.
EXCUSE ME! HEY!
I JUST NEED A WATER...
WHAT'D YOU DOSE ME WITH, FUCKTARD?!

WHAT WAS IT, TRANSDERMAL DMT? SERAPH DUST? SCOPOLAMINE?

UH...JILL, RIGHT? LOOK, I HAD SOME KIND OF SEIZURE OR SOMETHING UP THERE--

NO, YOU HIT ME WITH *SOMETHING* UP THERE. THEN YOU LEFT...

AND I SHOT MY CAREER IN THE FACE.

I'M NOT FOLLOWING...

WHAT'D YOU DOSE ME WITH, YOU--

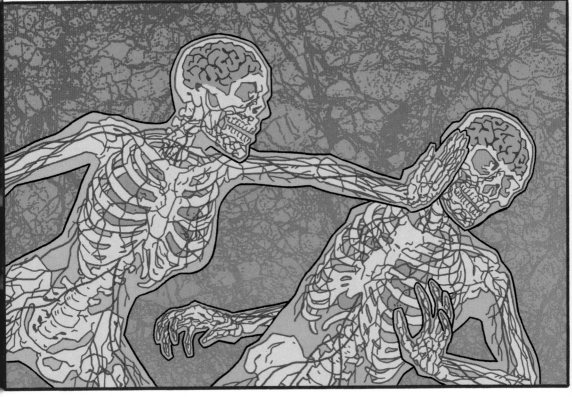

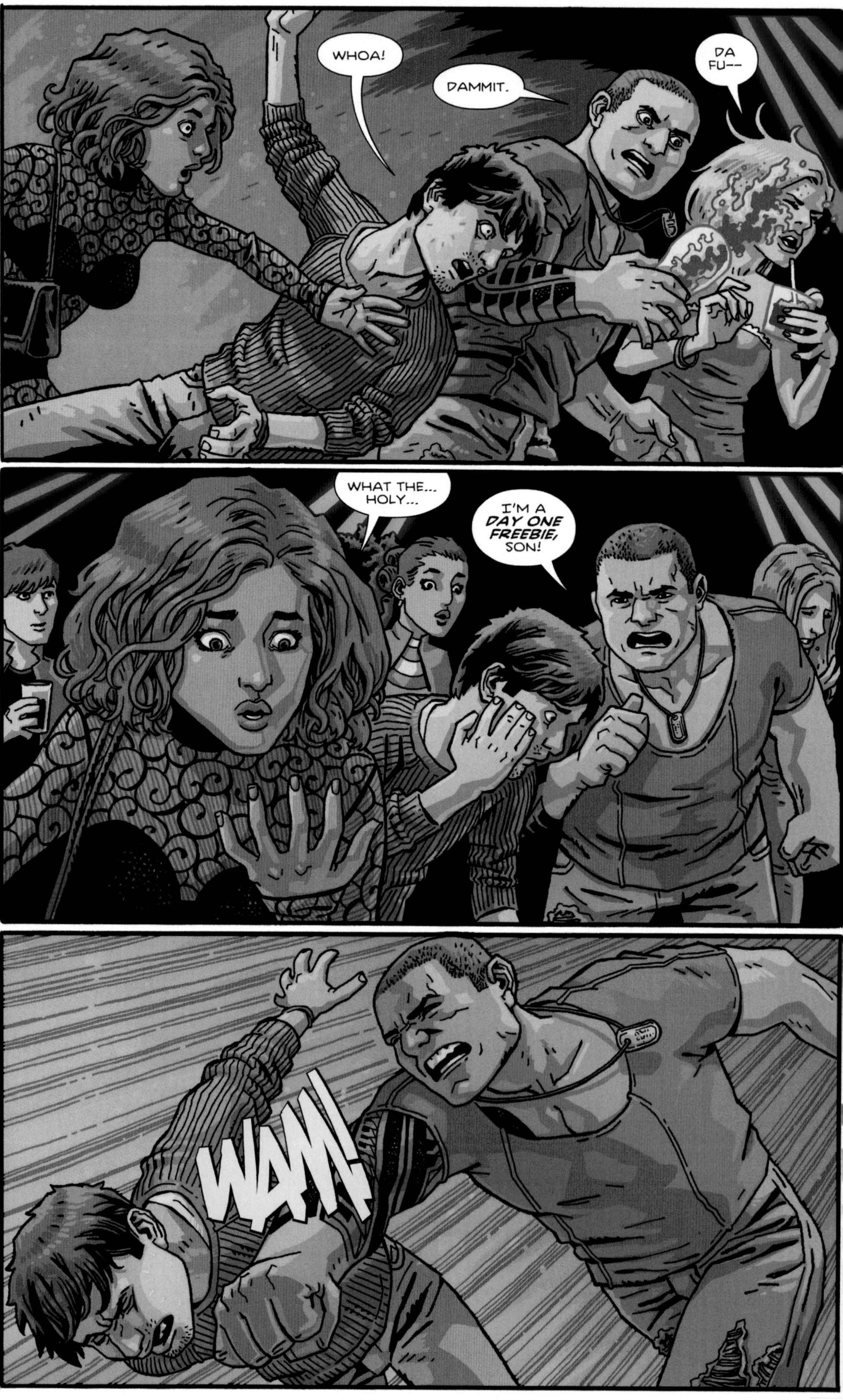

WHOA!
DAMMIT.
DA FU--
WHAT THE... HOLY...
I'M A *DAY ONE FREEBIE,* SON!
WAM!

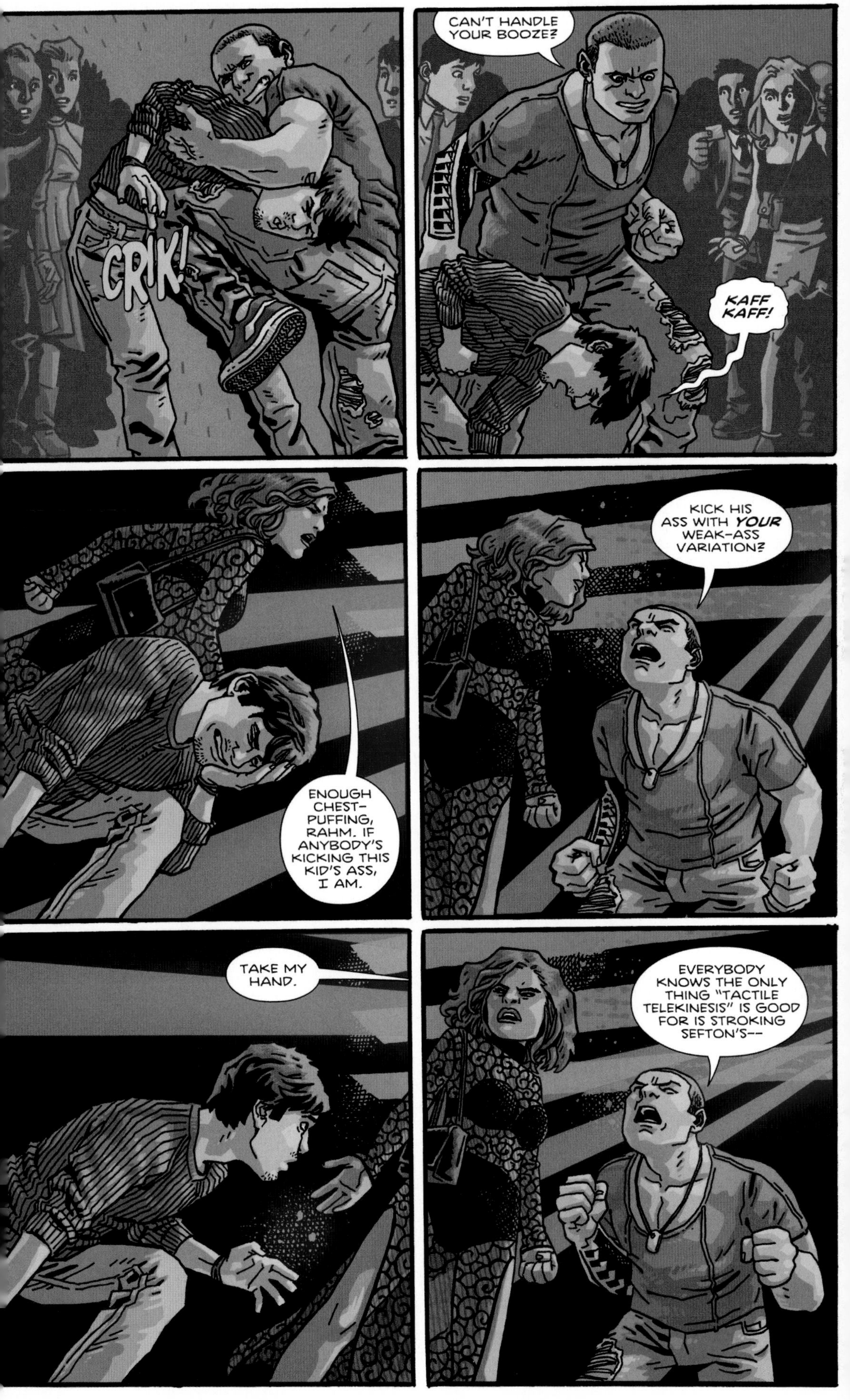
CRIK!
CAN'T HANDLE YOUR BOOZE?
KAFF KAFF!
ENOUGH CHEST-PUFFING, RAHM. IF ANYBODY'S KICKING THIS KID'S ASS, I AM.
KICK HIS ASS WITH *YOUR* WEAK-ASS VARIATION?
TAKE MY HAND.
EVERYBODY KNOWS THE ONLY THING "TACTILE TELEKINESIS" IS GOOD FOR IS STROKING SEFTON'S--

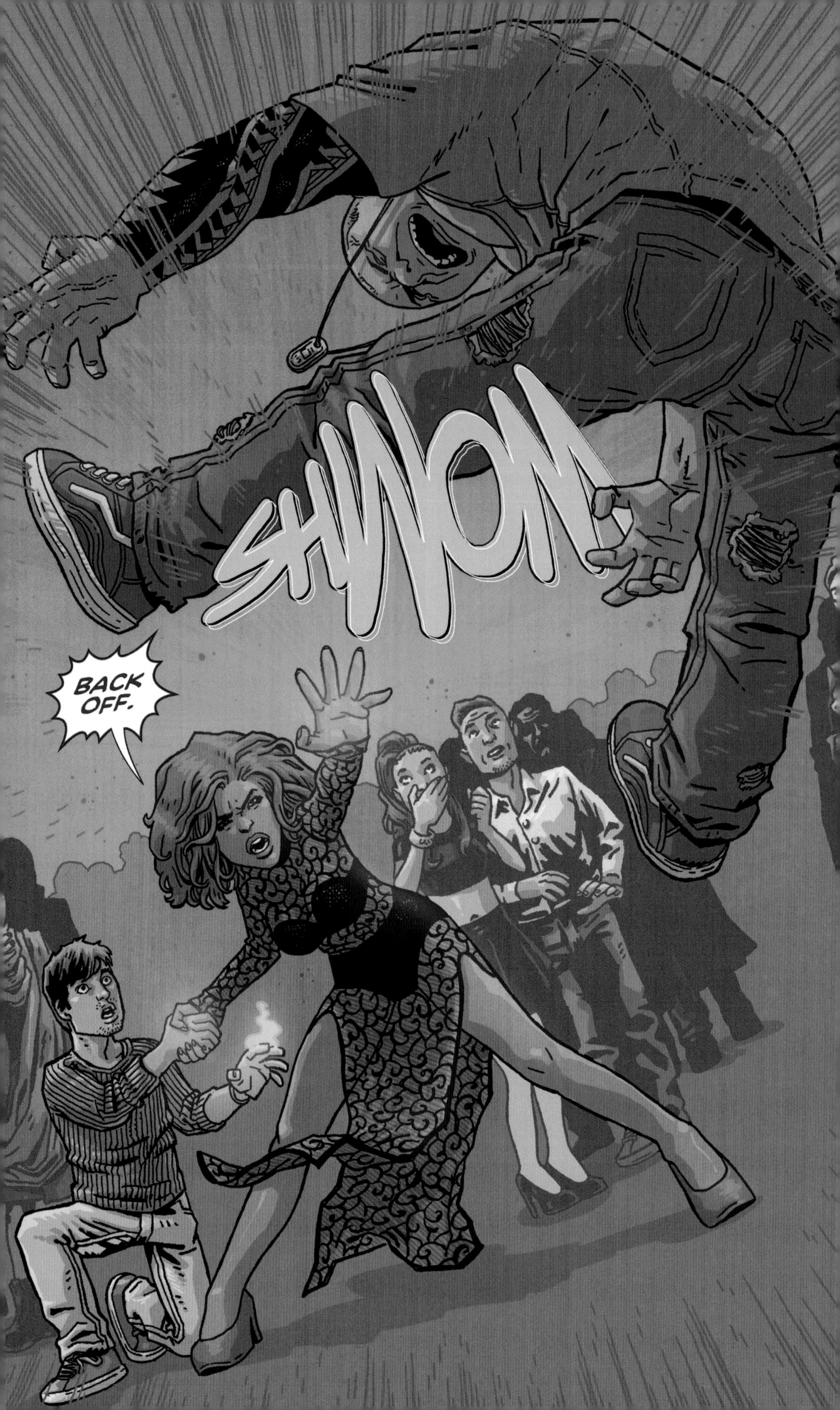
SHWOM!
BACK OFF.

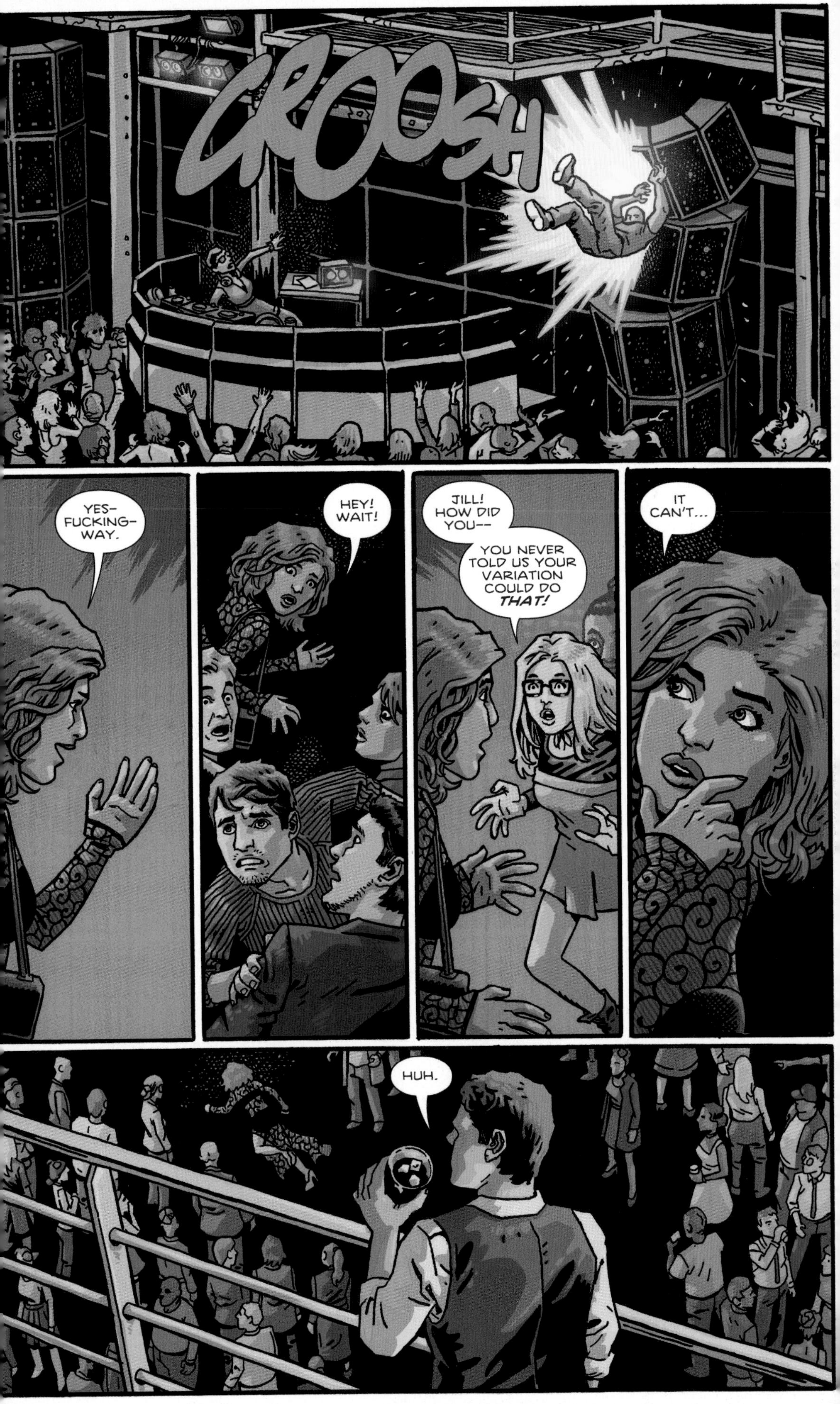
CROOSH
YES-FUCKING-WAY.
HEY! WAIT!
JILL! HOW DID YOU--
YOU NEVER TOLD US YOUR VARIATION COULD DO *THAT!*
IT CAN'T...
HUH.

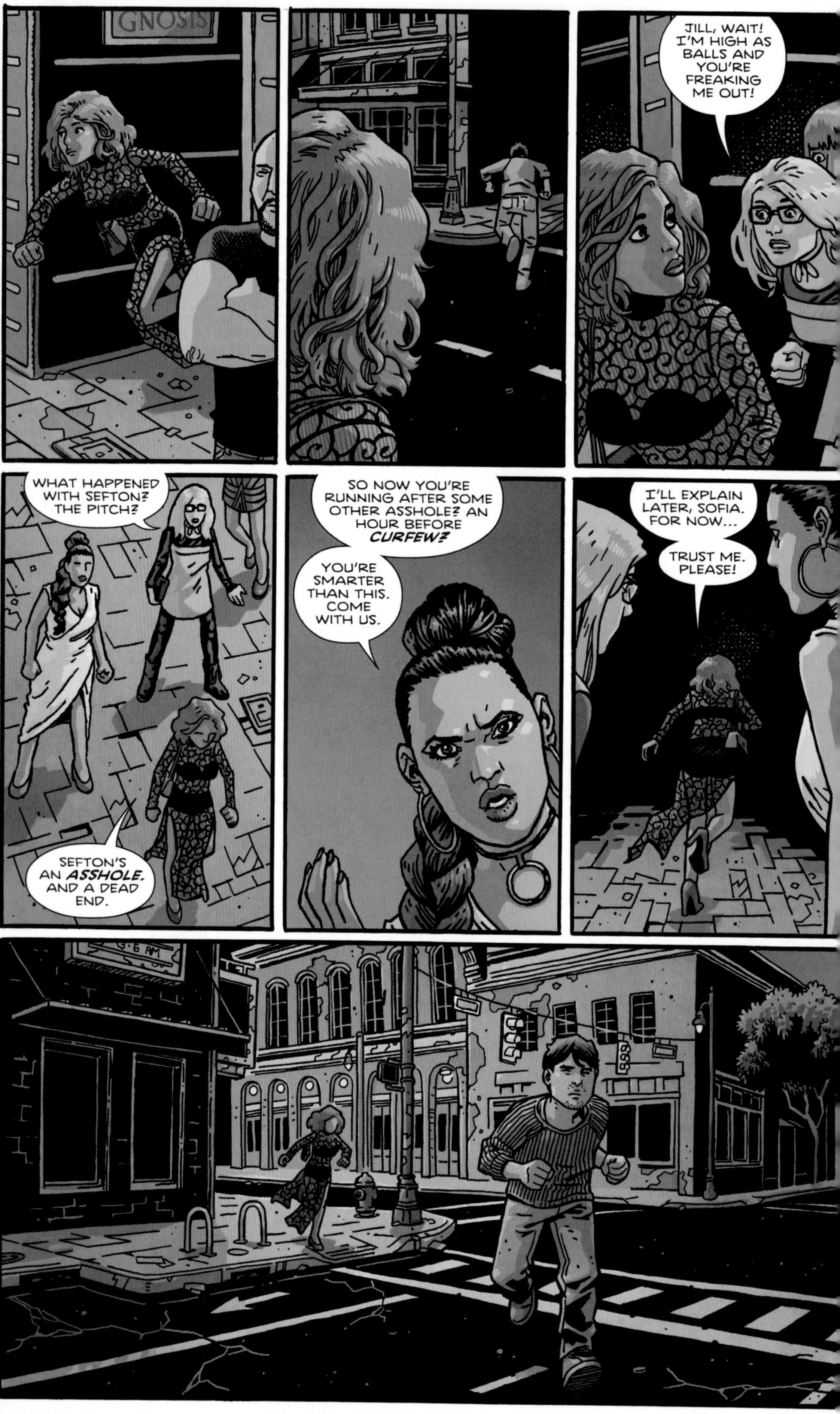
GNOSIS
JILL, WAIT! I'M HIGH AS BALLS AND YOU'RE FREAKING ME OUT!
WHAT HAPPENED WITH SEFTON? THE PITCH?
SEFTON'S AN ASSHOLE. AND A DEAD END.
SO NOW YOU'RE RUNNING AFTER SOME OTHER ASSHOLE? AN HOUR BEFORE CURFEW?
YOU'RE SMARTER THAN THIS. COME WITH US.
I'LL EXPLAIN LATER, SOFIA. FOR NOW...
TRUST ME. PLEASE!

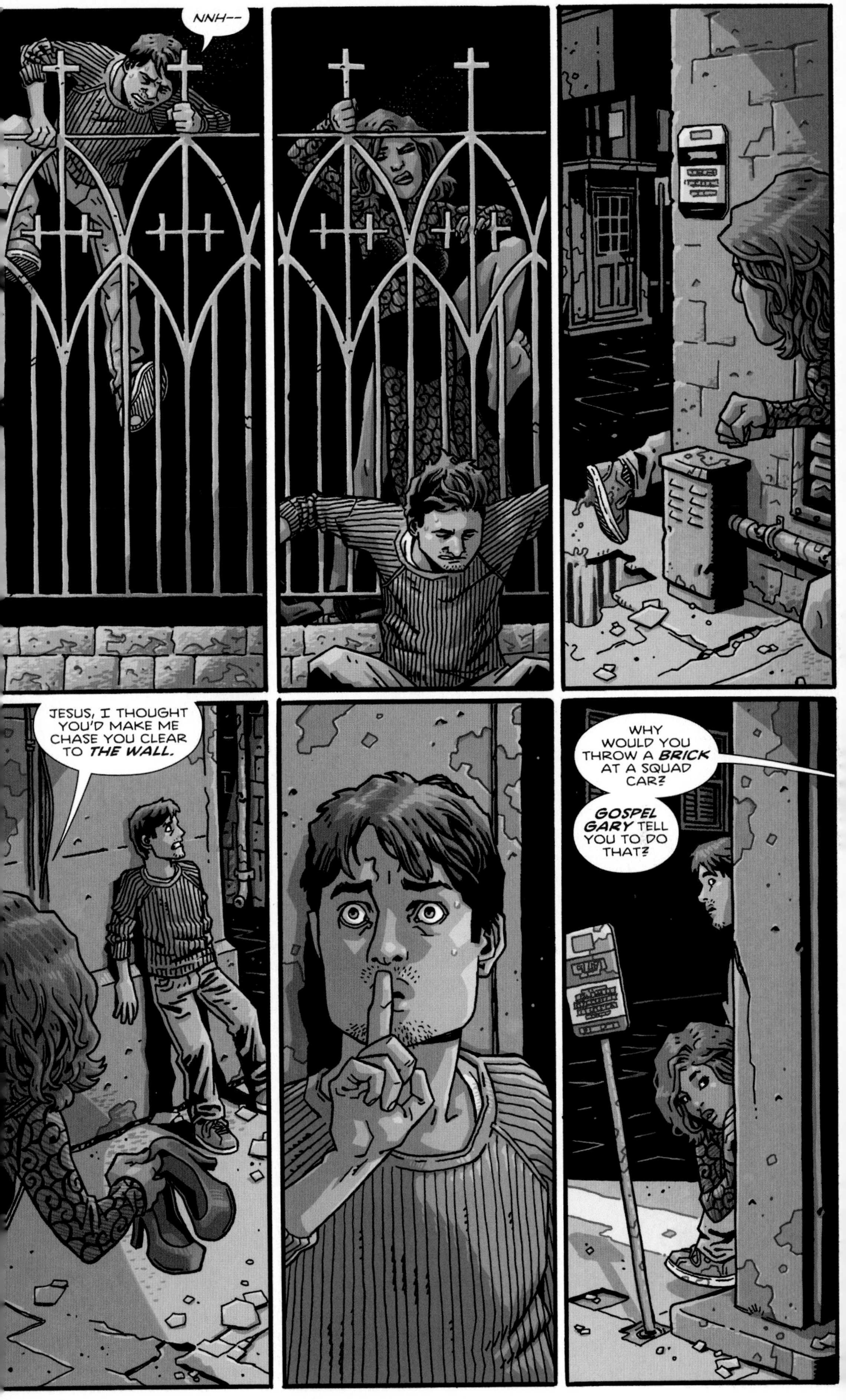
NNH--
JESUS, I THOUGHT YOU'D MAKE ME CHASE YOU CLEAR TO THE WALL.
WHY WOULD YOU THROW A BRICK AT A SQUAD CAR?
GOSPEL GARY TELL YOU TO DO THAT?

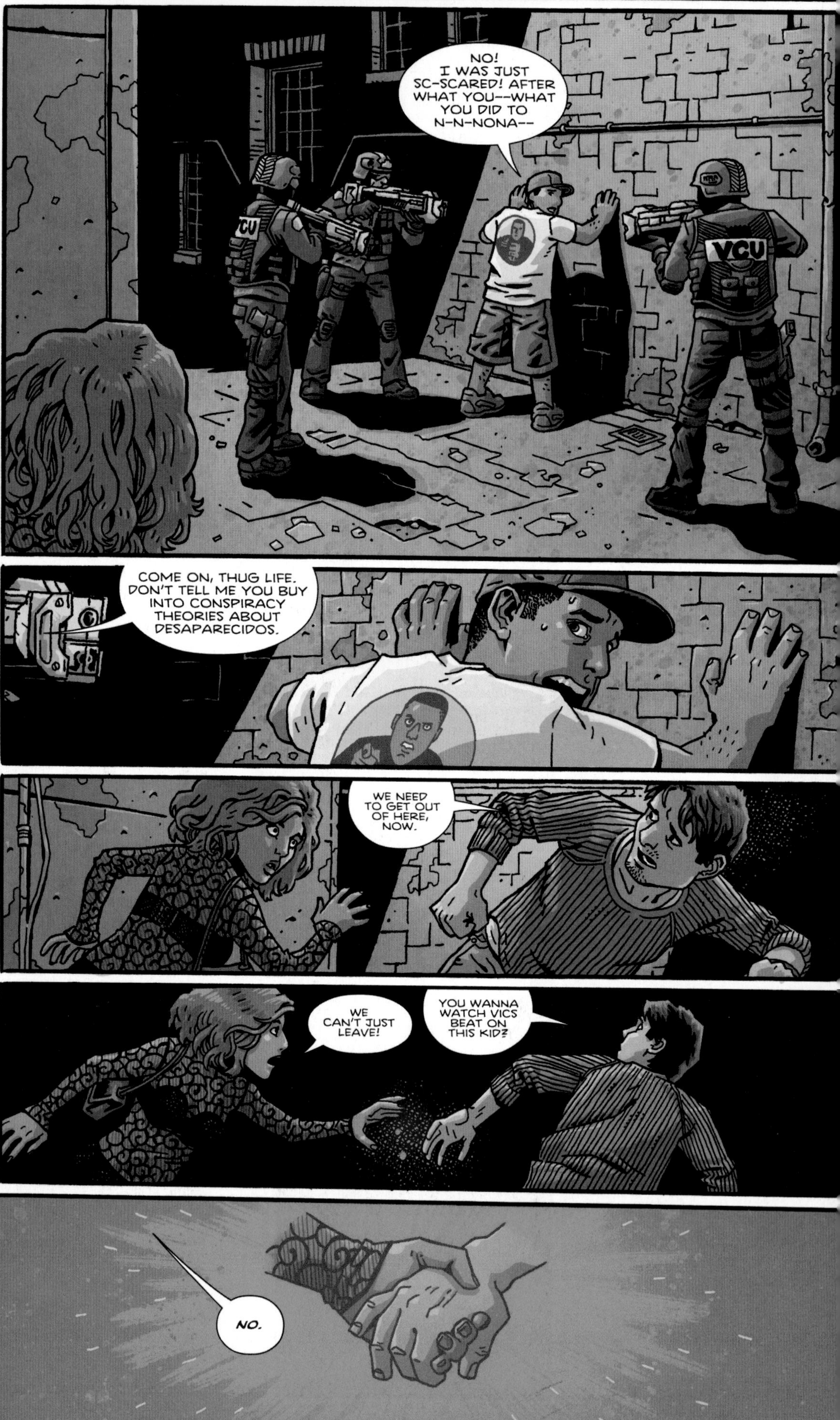
NO! I WAS JUST SC-SCARED! AFTER WHAT YOU--WHAT YOU DID TO N-N-NONA--
COME ON, THUG LIFE. DON'T TELL ME YOU BUY INTO CONSPIRACY THEORIES ABOUT DESAPARECIDOS.
WE NEED TO GET OUT OF HERE, NOW.
WE CAN'T JUST LEAVE!
YOU WANNA WATCH VICS BEAT ON THIS KID?
NO.

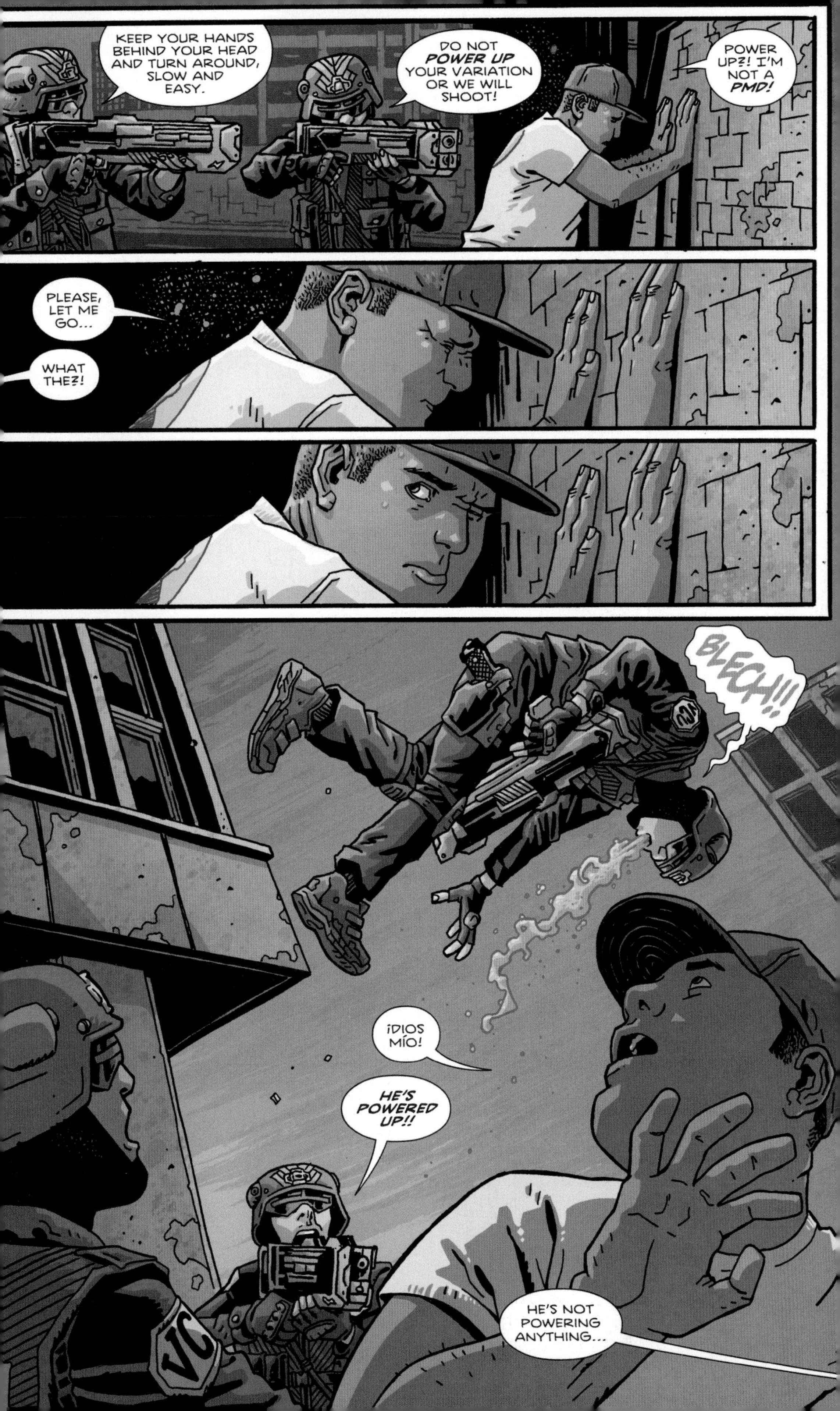

KEEP YOUR HANDS BEHIND YOUR HEAD AND TURN AROUND, SLOW AND EASY.
DO NOT *POWER UP* YOUR VARIATION OR WE WILL SHOOT!
POWER UP?! I'M NOT A *PMD!*
PLEASE, LET ME GO...
WHAT THE?!
BLECH!!
¡DIOS MÍO!
HE'S POWERED UP!!
HE'S NOT POWERING ANYTHING...

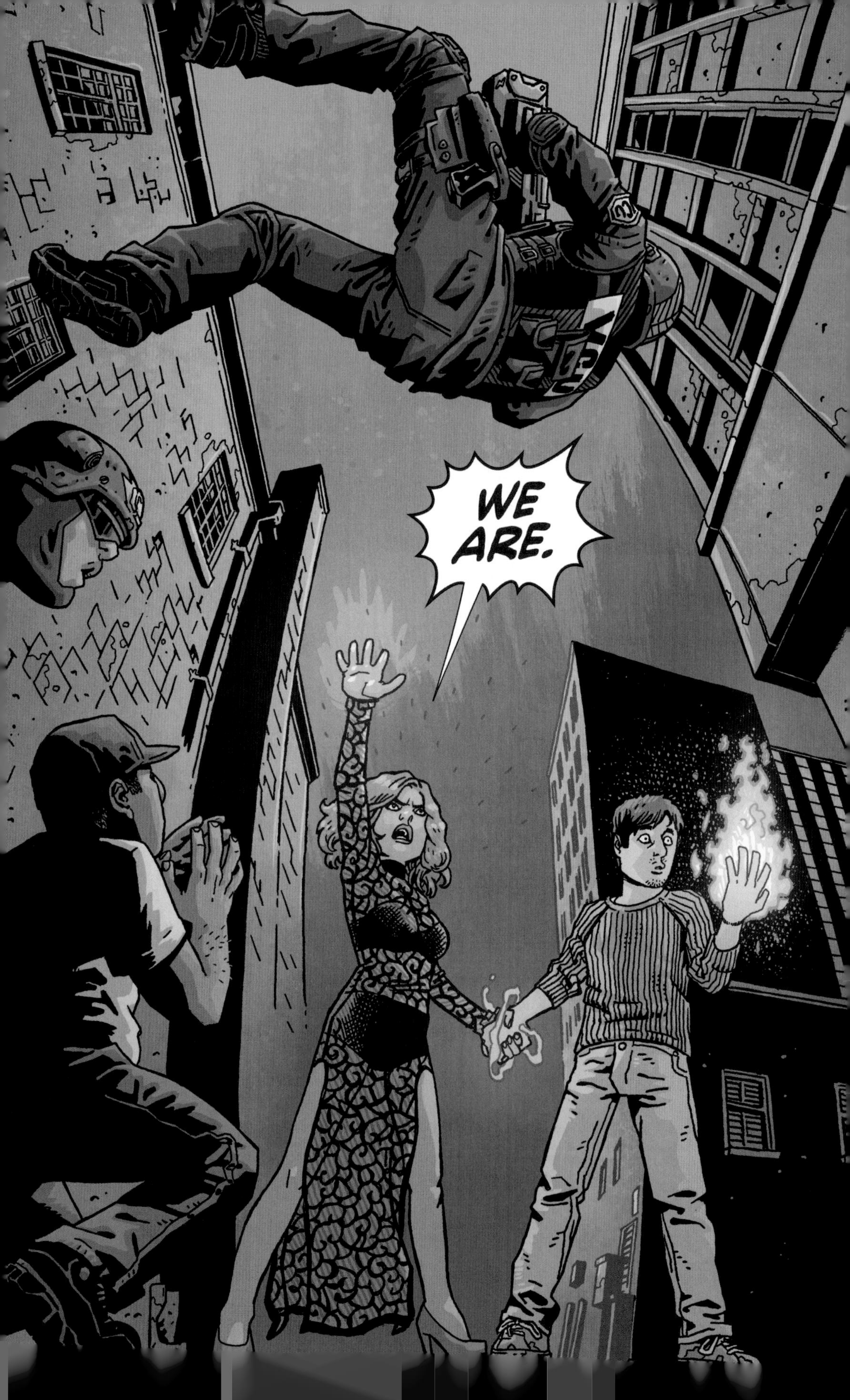
WE ARE.

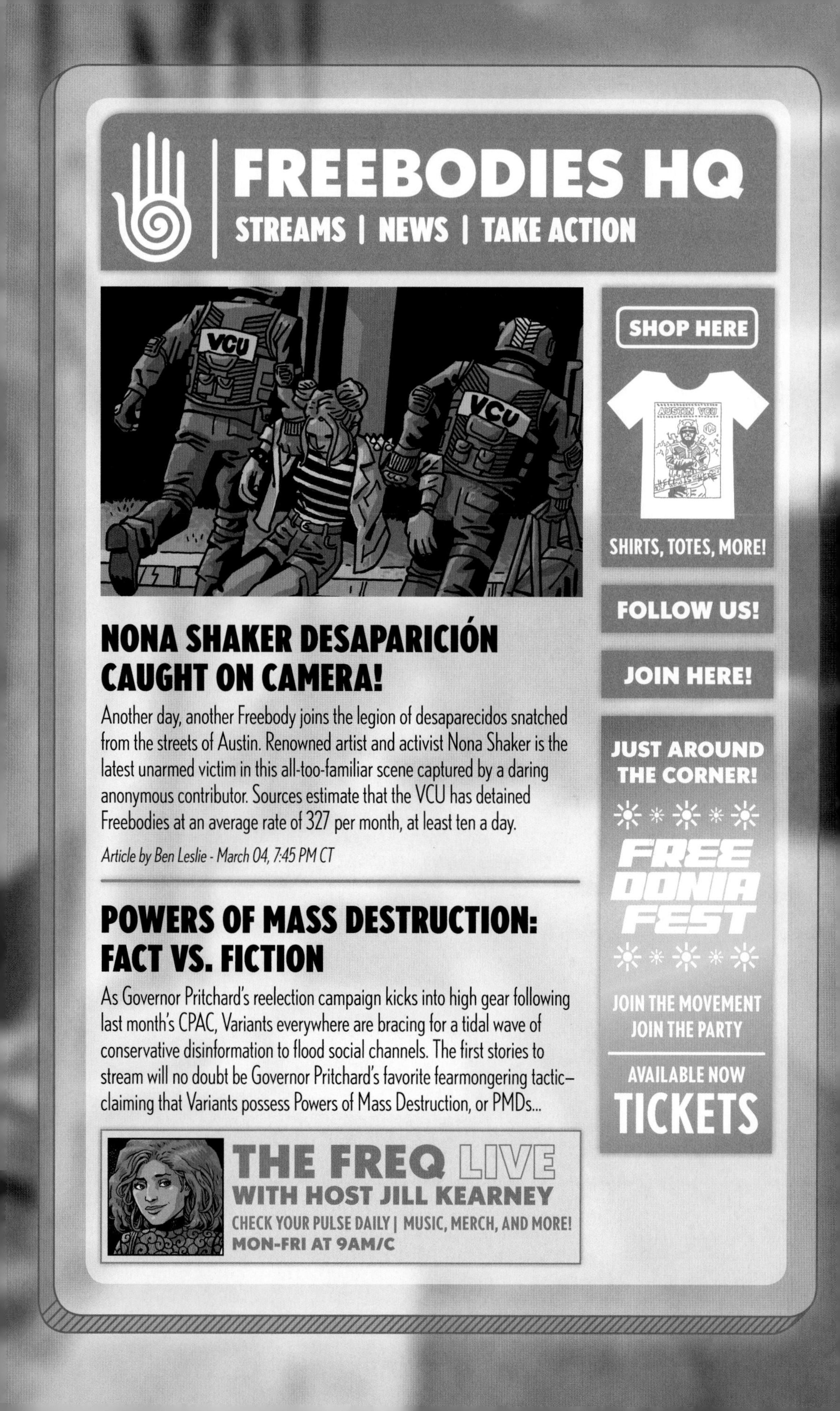
FREEBODIES HQ
STREAMS | NEWS | TAKE ACTION
VCU
VCU
SHOP HERE
AUSTIN VCU
SHIRTS, TOTES, MORE!
FOLLOW US!
JOIN HERE!
NONA SHAKER DESAPARICIÓN CAUGHT ON CAMERA!
Another day, another Freebody joins the legion of desaparecidos snatched from the streets of Austin. Renowned artist and activist Nona Shaker is the latest unarmed victim in this all-too-familiar scene captured by a daring anonymous contributor. Sources estimate that the VCU has detained Freebodies at an average rate of 327 per month, at least ten a day.
Article by Ben Leslie - March 04, 7:45 PM CT
POWERS OF MASS DESTRUCTION: FACT VS. FICTION
As Governor Pritchard's reelection campaign kicks into high gear following last month's CPAC, Variants everywhere are bracing for a tidal wave of conservative disinformation to flood social channels. The first stories to stream will no doubt be Governor Pritchard's favorite fearmongering tactic–claiming that Variants possess Powers of Mass Destruction, or PMDs...
JUST AROUND THE CORNER!
FREE DONIA FEST
JOIN THE MOVEMENT
JOIN THE PARTY
AVAILABLE NOW
TICKETS
THE FREQ LIVE
WITH HOST JILL KEARNEY
CHECK YOUR PULSE DAILY | MUSIC, MERCH, AND MORE!
MON-FRI AT 9AM/C

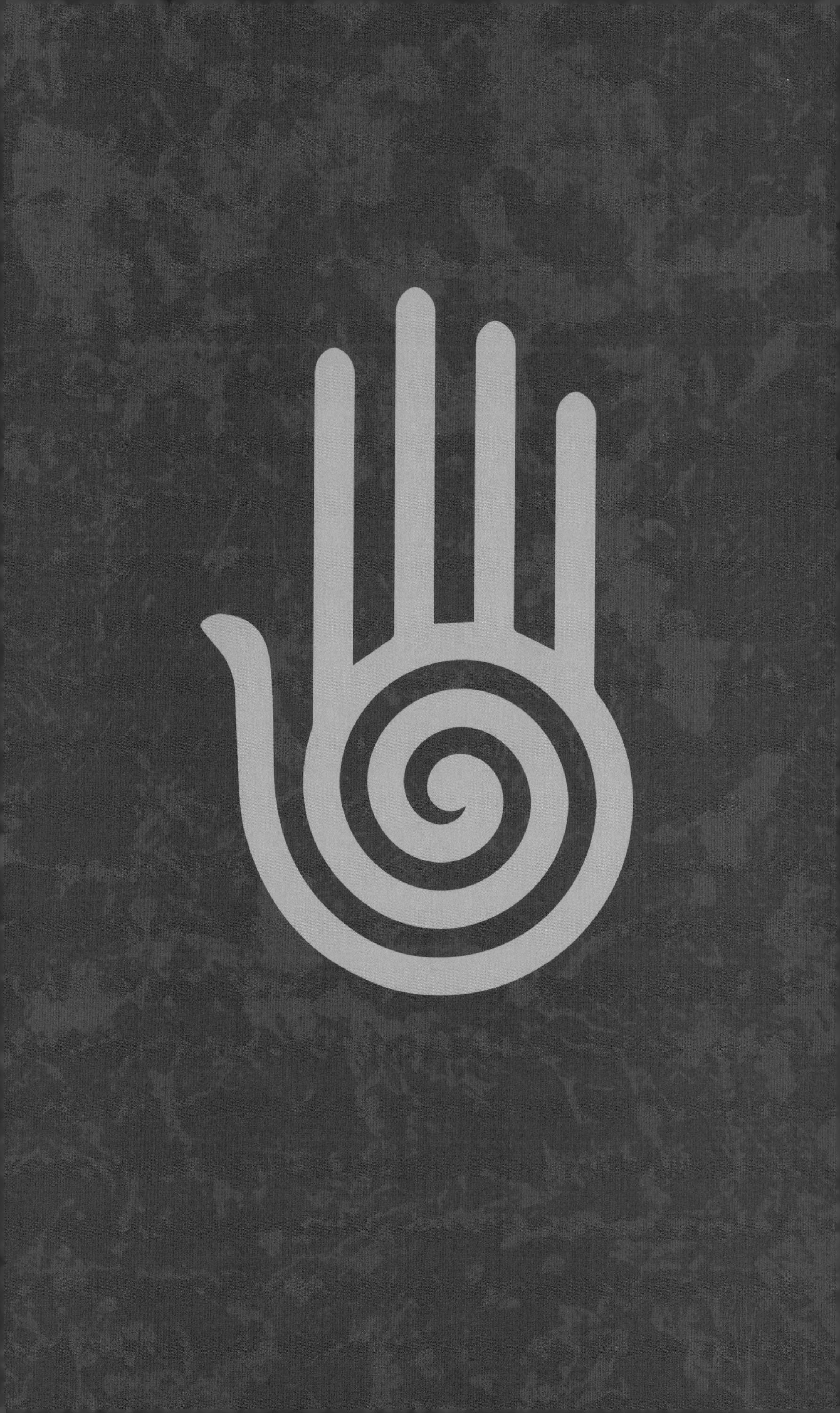

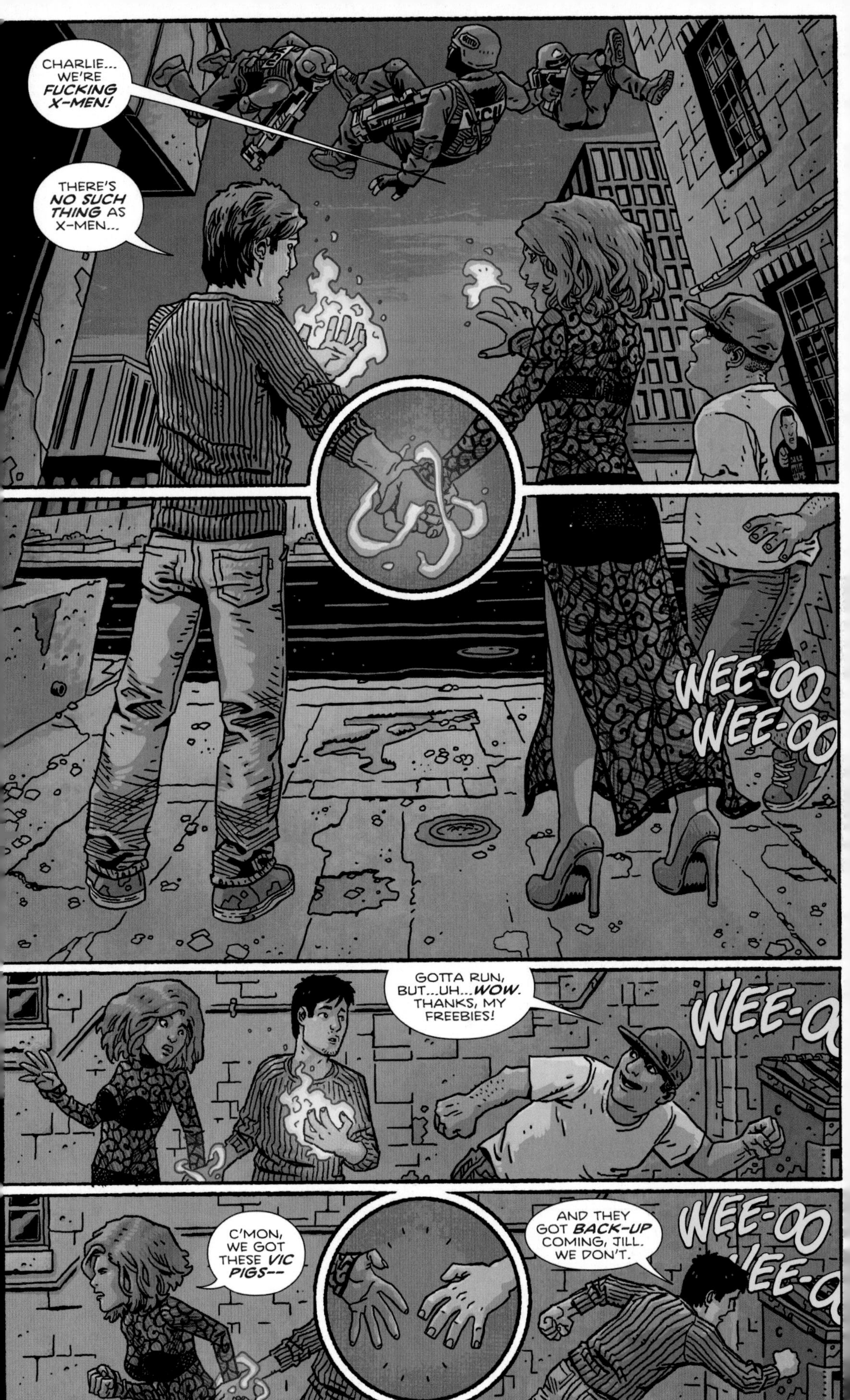
CHARLIE... WE'RE *FUCKING X-MEN!*
THERE'S *NO SUCH THING* AS X-MEN...
WEE-OO WEE-OO
GOTTA RUN, BUT...UH...*WOW*. THANKS, MY FREEBIES!
WEE-OO
C'MON, WE GOT THESE *VIC PIGS--*
AND THEY GOT *BACK-UP* COMING, JILL. WE DON'T.
WEE-OO WEE-OO

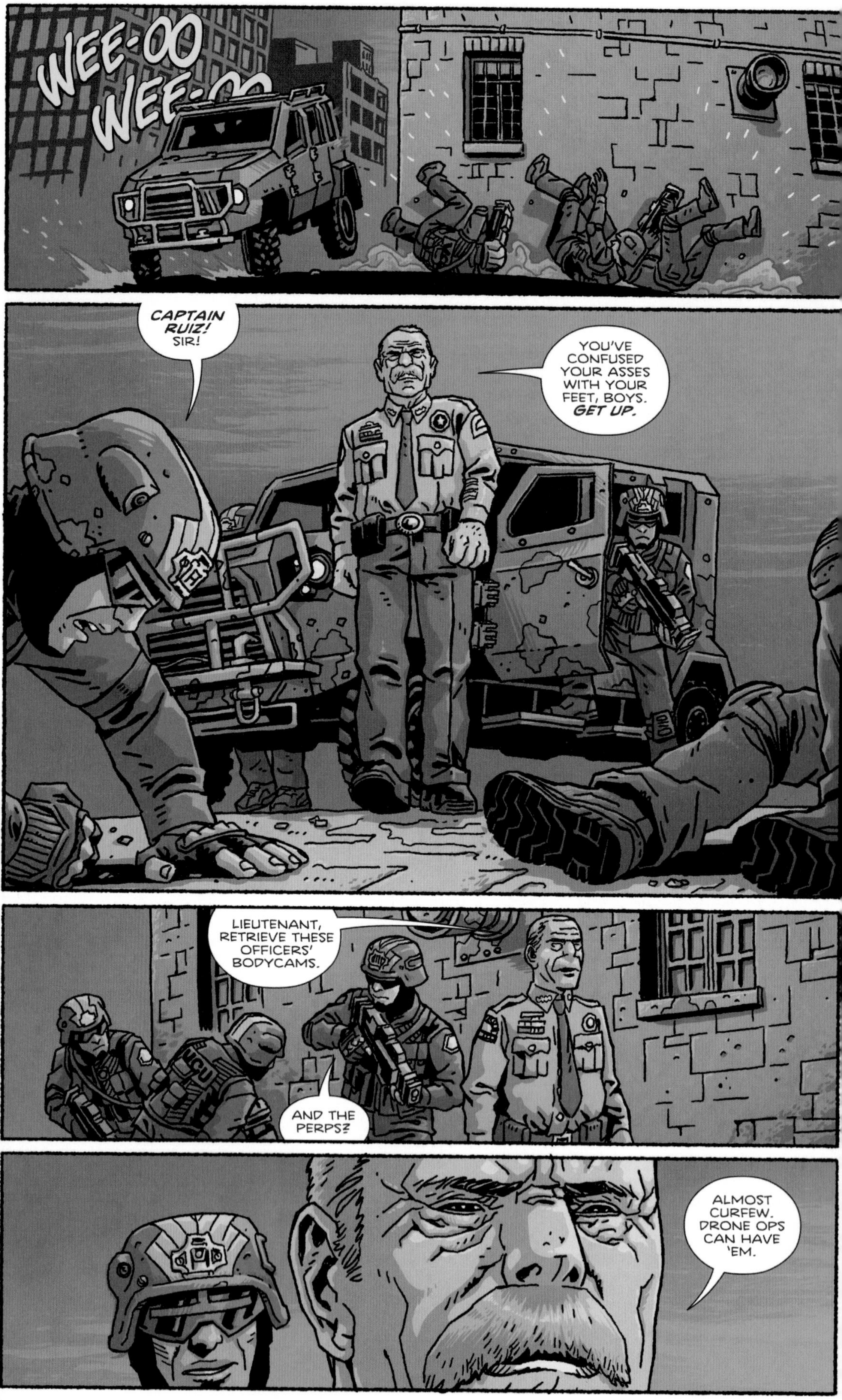
WEE-OO WEE-OO
CAPTAIN RUIZ! SIR!
YOU'VE CONFUSED YOUR ASSES WITH YOUR FEET, BOYS. GET UP.
LIEUTENANT, RETRIEVE THESE OFFICERS' BODYCAMS.
AND THE PERPS?
ALMOST CURFEW. DRONE OPS CAN HAVE 'EM.

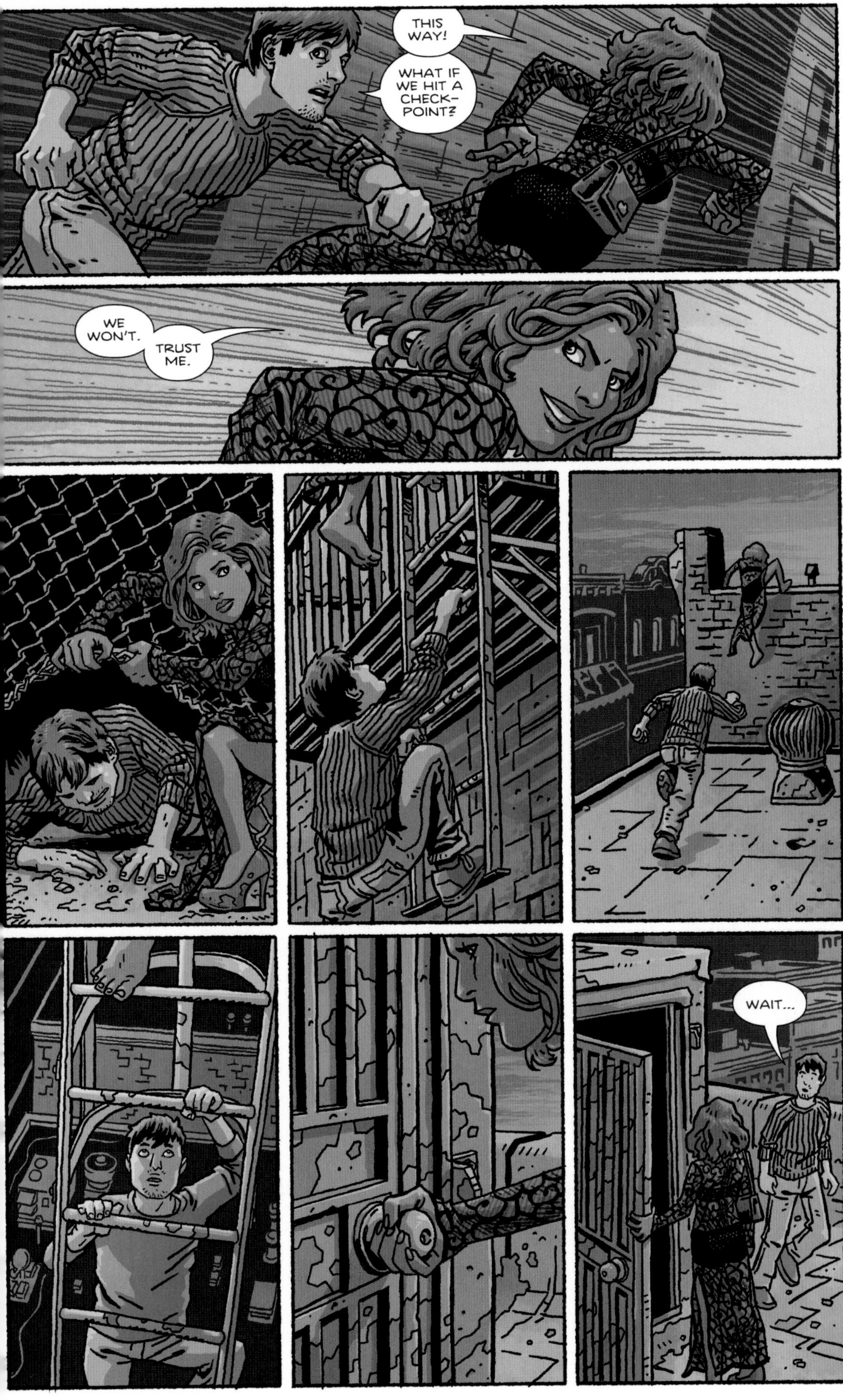
THIS WAY!
WHAT IF WE HIT A CHECK-POINT?
WE WON'T.
TRUST ME.
WAIT...

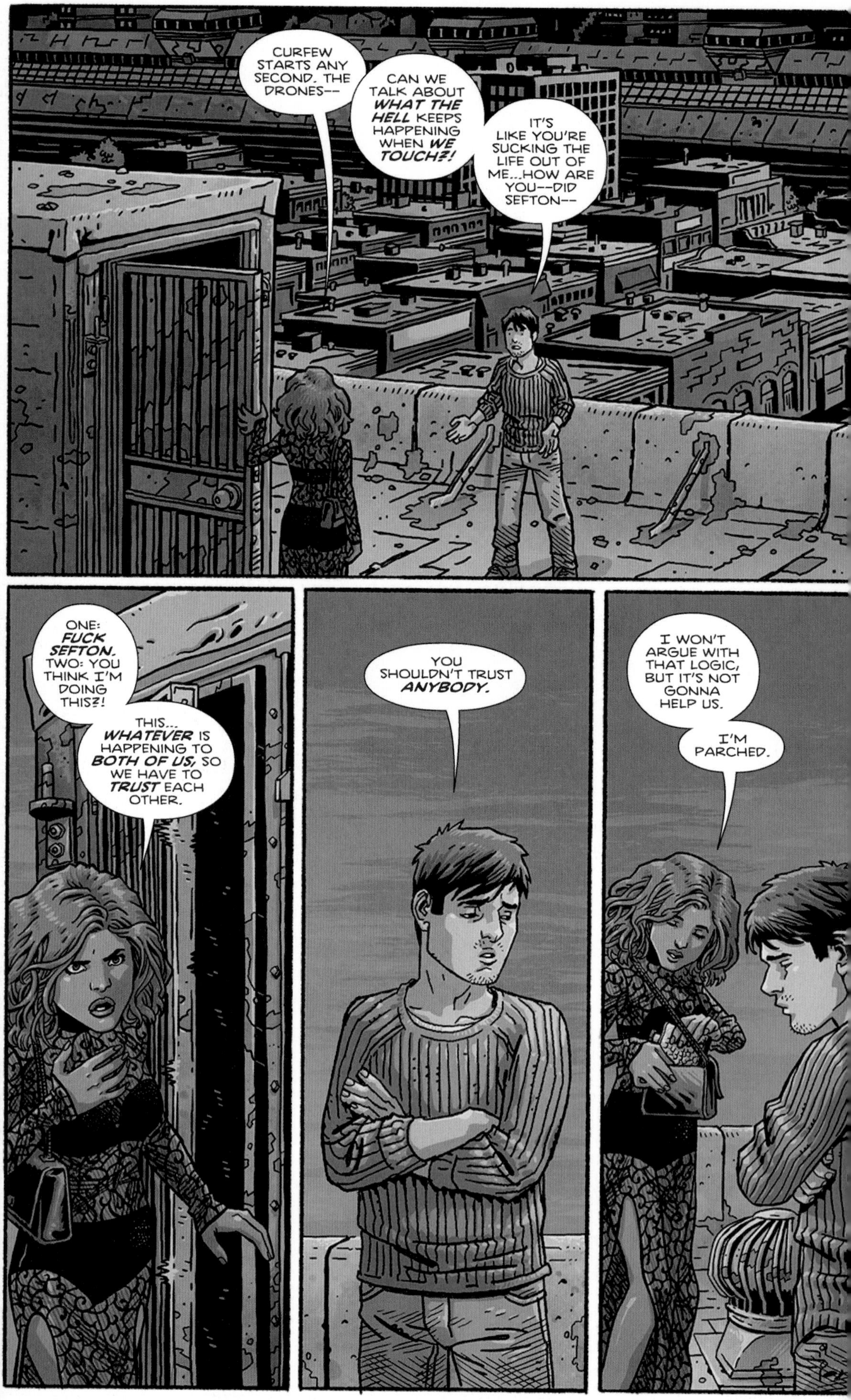
CURFEW STARTS ANY SECOND. THE DRONES--
CAN WE TALK ABOUT WHAT THE HELL KEEPS HAPPENING WHEN WE TOUCH?!
IT'S LIKE YOU'RE SUCKING THE LIFE OUT OF ME...HOW ARE YOU--DID SEFTON--
ONE: FUCK SEFTON. TWO: YOU THINK I'M DOING THIS?!
THIS... WHATEVER IS HAPPENING TO BOTH OF US, SO WE HAVE TO TRUST EACH OTHER.
YOU SHOULDN'T TRUST ANYBODY.
I WON'T ARGUE WITH THAT LOGIC, BUT IT'S NOT GONNA HELP US.
I'M PARCHED.

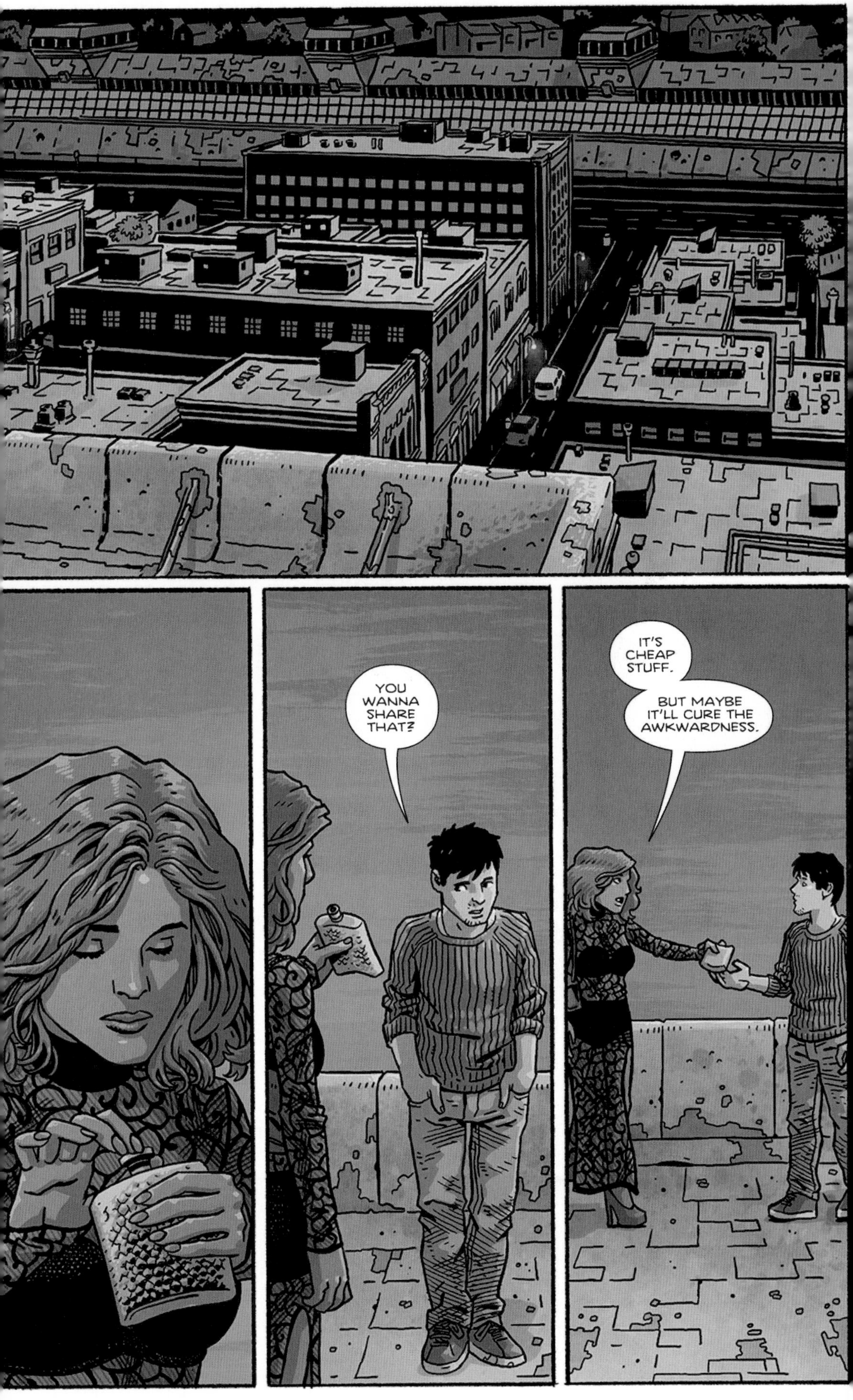
YOU WANNA SHARE THAT?
IT'S CHEAP STUFF.
BUT MAYBE IT'LL CURE THE AWKWARDNESS.

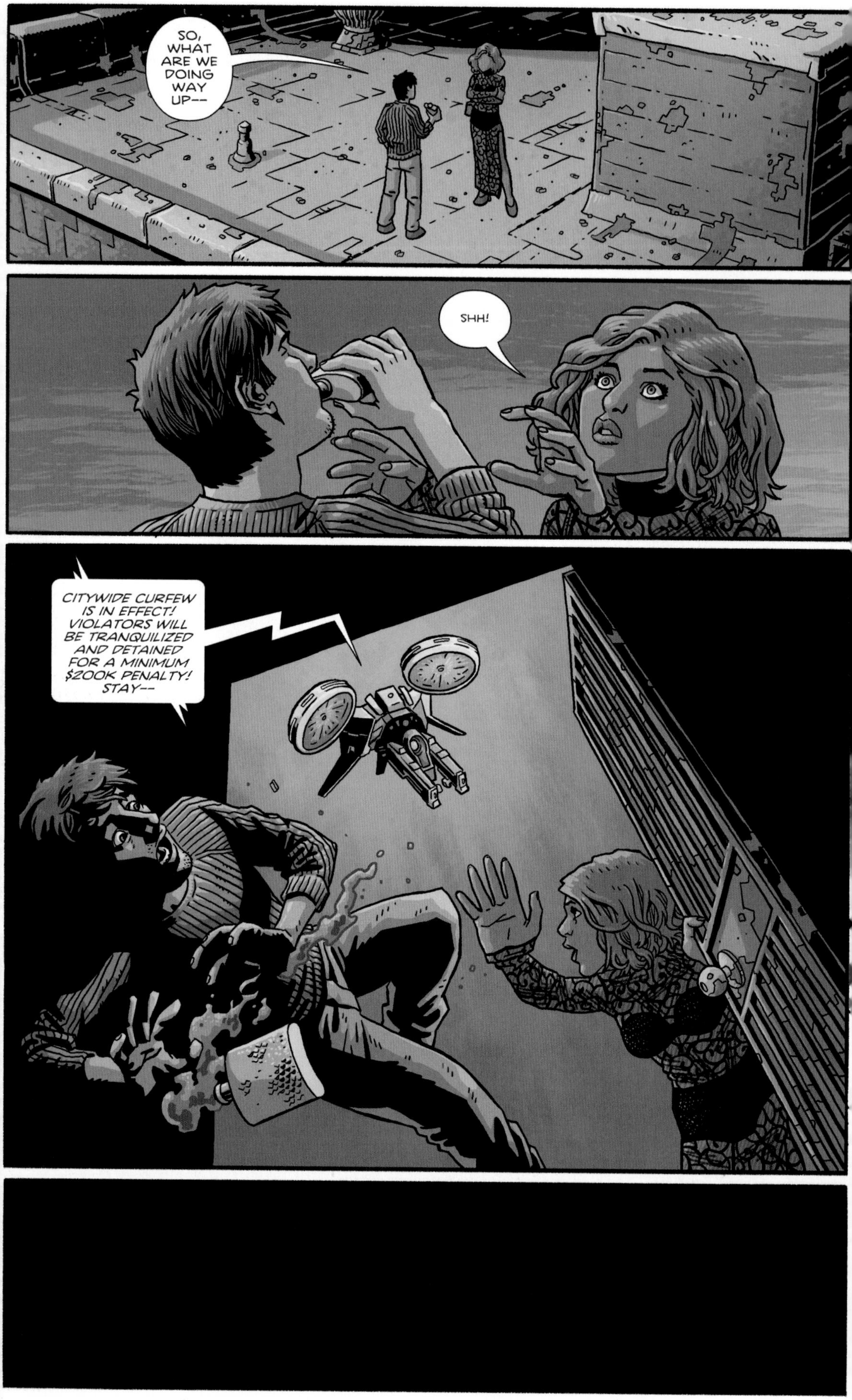
SO, WHAT ARE WE DOING WAY UP--
SHH!
CITYWIDE CURFEW IS IN EFFECT! VIOLATORS WILL BE TRANQUILIZED AND DETAINED FOR A MINIMUM $200K PENALTY! STAY--

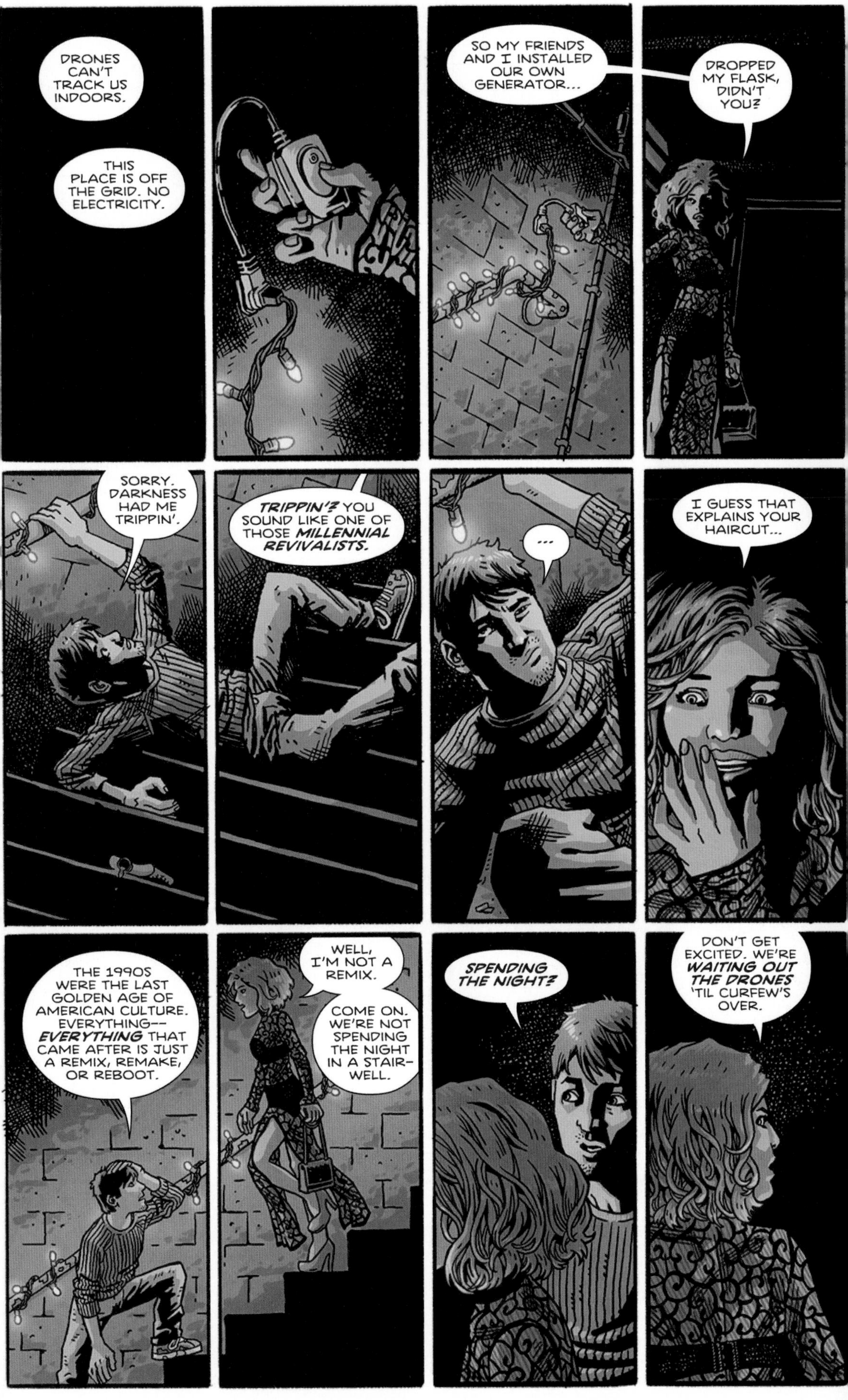
DRONES CAN'T TRACK US INDOORS.
THIS PLACE IS OFF THE GRID. NO ELECTRICITY.
SO MY FRIENDS AND I INSTALLED OUR OWN GENERATOR...
DROPPED MY FLASK, DIDN'T YOU?
SORRY. DARKNESS HAD ME TRIPPIN'.
TRIPPIN'? YOU SOUND LIKE ONE OF THOSE *MILLENNIAL REVIVALISTS.*
...
I GUESS THAT EXPLAINS YOUR HAIRCUT...
THE 1990S WERE THE LAST GOLDEN AGE OF AMERICAN CULTURE. EVERYTHING-- *EVERYTHING* THAT CAME AFTER IS JUST A REMIX, REMAKE, OR REBOOT.
WELL, I'M NOT A REMIX.
COME ON. WE'RE NOT SPENDING THE NIGHT IN A STAIR-WELL.
SPENDING THE NIGHT?
DON'T GET EXCITED. WE'RE *WAITING OUT THE DRONES* 'TIL CURFEW'S OVER.

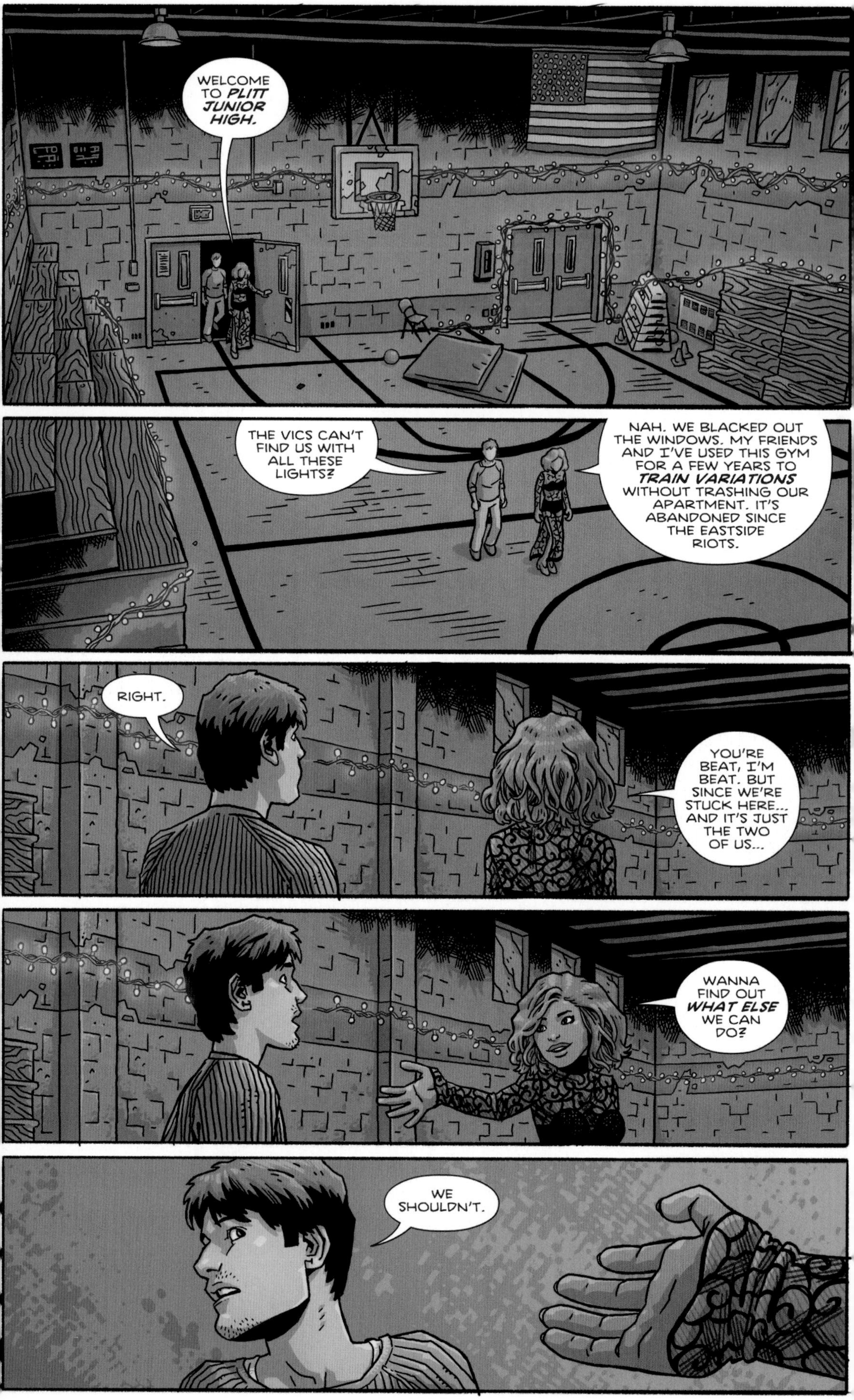
WELCOME TO PLITT JUNIOR HIGH.
THE VICS CAN'T FIND US WITH ALL THESE LIGHTS?
NAH. WE BLACKED OUT THE WINDOWS. MY FRIENDS AND I'VE USED THIS GYM FOR A FEW YEARS TO TRAIN VARIATIONS WITHOUT TRASHING OUR APARTMENT. IT'S ABANDONED SINCE THE EASTSIDE RIOTS.
RIGHT.
YOU'RE BEAT, I'M BEAT. BUT SINCE WE'RE STUCK HERE... AND IT'S JUST THE TWO OF US...
WANNA FIND OUT WHAT ELSE WE CAN DO?
WE SHOULDN'T.

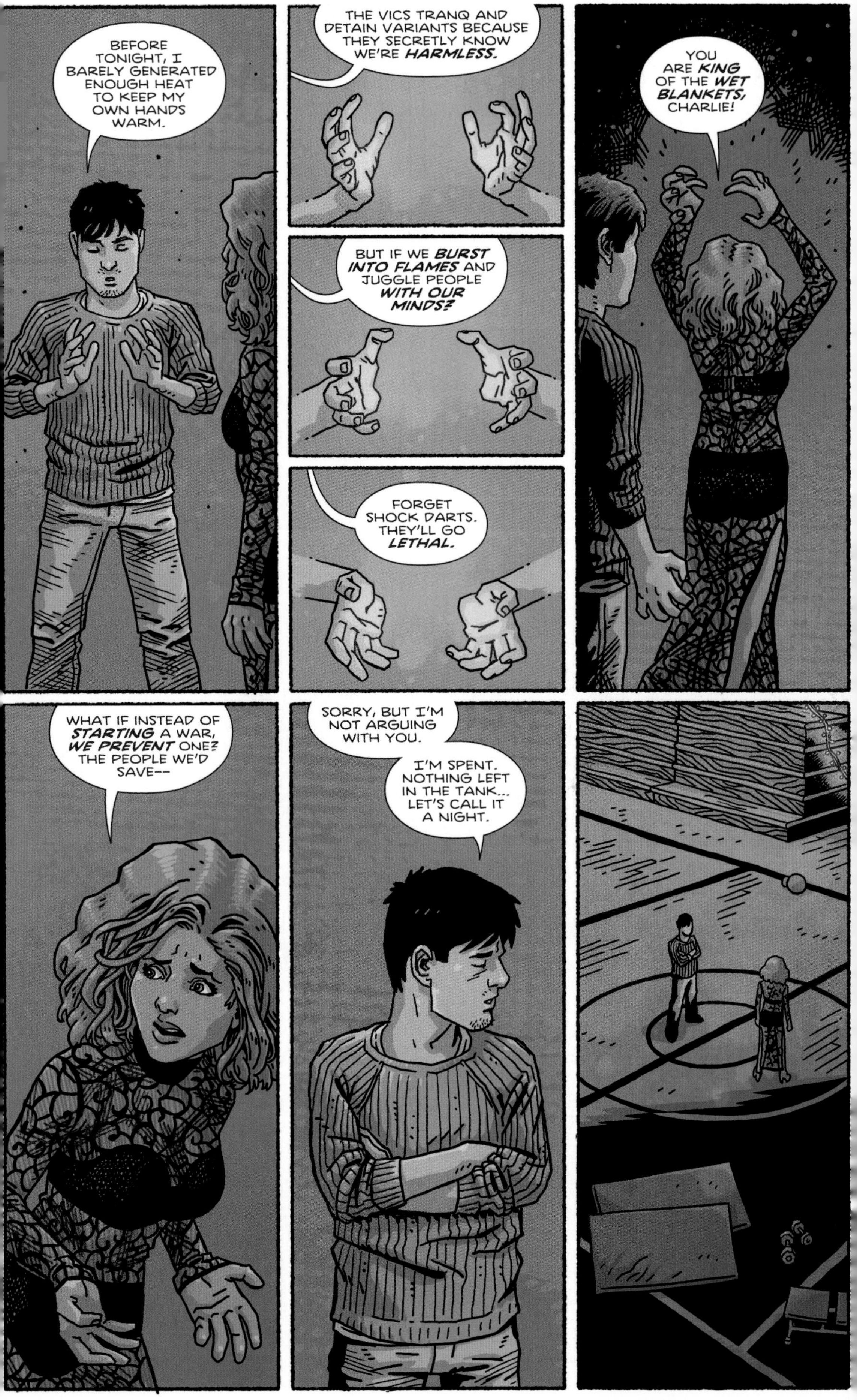
BEFORE TONIGHT, I BARELY GENERATED ENOUGH HEAT TO KEEP MY OWN HANDS WARM.
THE VICS TRANQ AND DETAIN VARIANTS BECAUSE THEY SECRETLY KNOW WE'RE *HARMLESS.*
BUT IF WE *BURST INTO FLAMES* AND JUGGLE PEOPLE *WITH OUR MINDS?*
FORGET SHOCK DARTS. THEY'LL GO *LETHAL.*
YOU ARE *KING* OF THE *WET BLANKETS,* CHARLIE!
WHAT IF INSTEAD OF *STARTING* A WAR, *WE PREVENT* ONE? THE PEOPLE WE'D SAVE--
SORRY, BUT I'M NOT ARGUING WITH YOU.
I'M SPENT. NOTHING LEFT IN THE TANK... LET'S CALL IT A NIGHT.

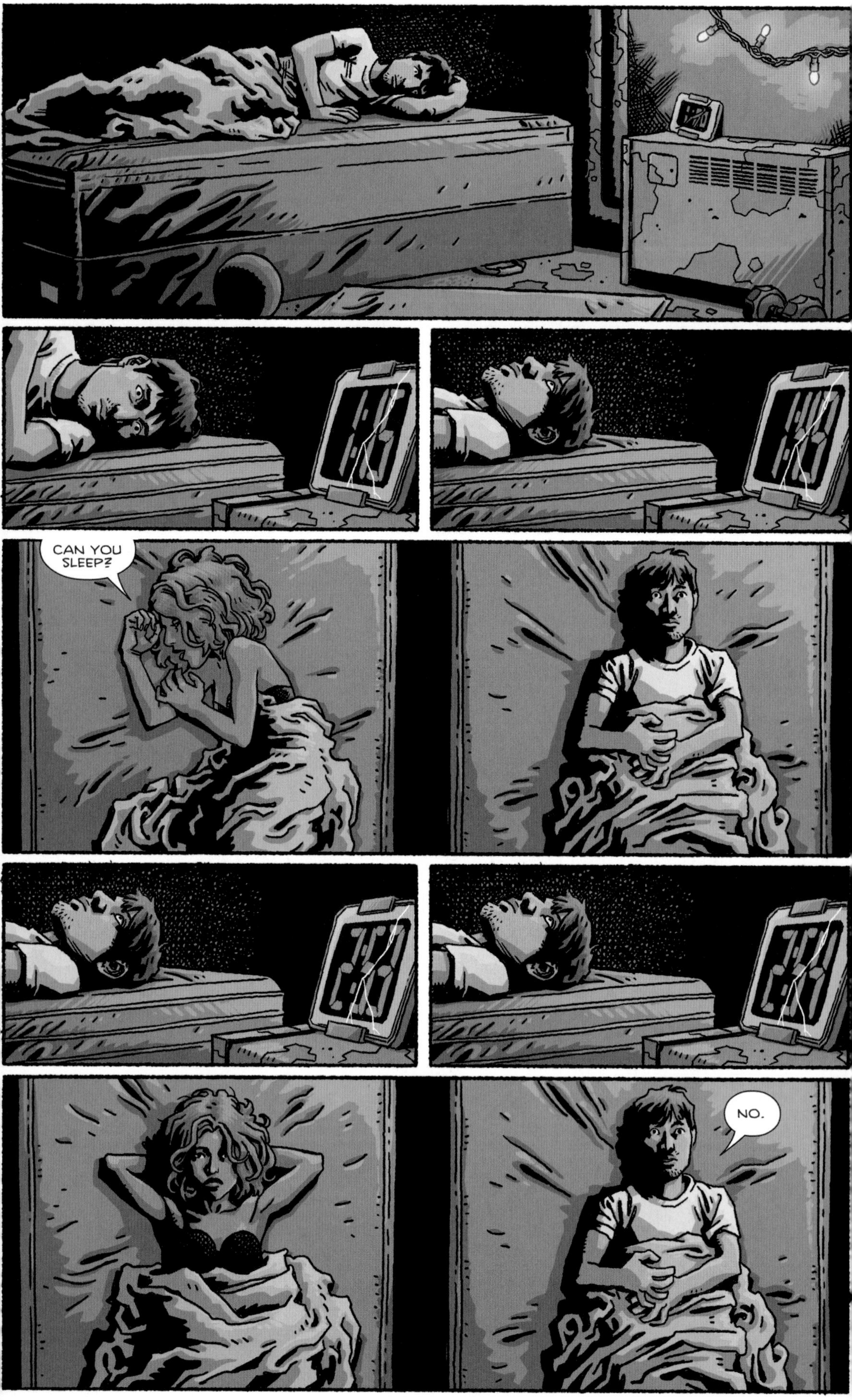
CAN YOU SLEEP?
NO.

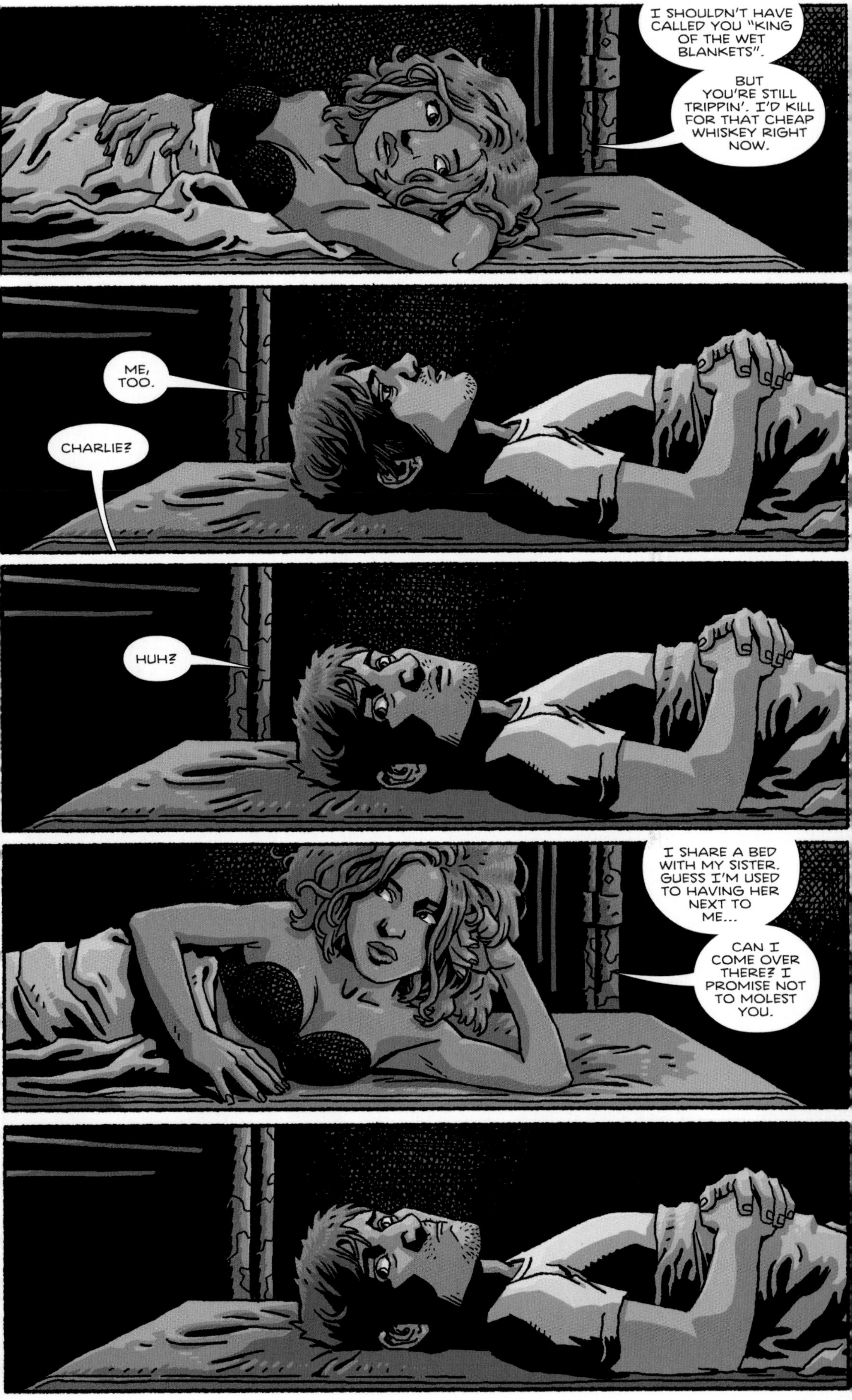
I SHOULDN'T HAVE CALLED YOU "KING OF THE WET BLANKETS".
BUT YOU'RE STILL TRIPPIN'. I'D KILL FOR THAT CHEAP WHISKEY RIGHT NOW.
ME, TOO.
CHARLIE?
HUH?
I SHARE A BED WITH MY SISTER. GUESS I'M USED TO HAVING HER NEXT TO ME...
CAN I COME OVER THERE? I PROMISE NOT TO MOLEST YOU.

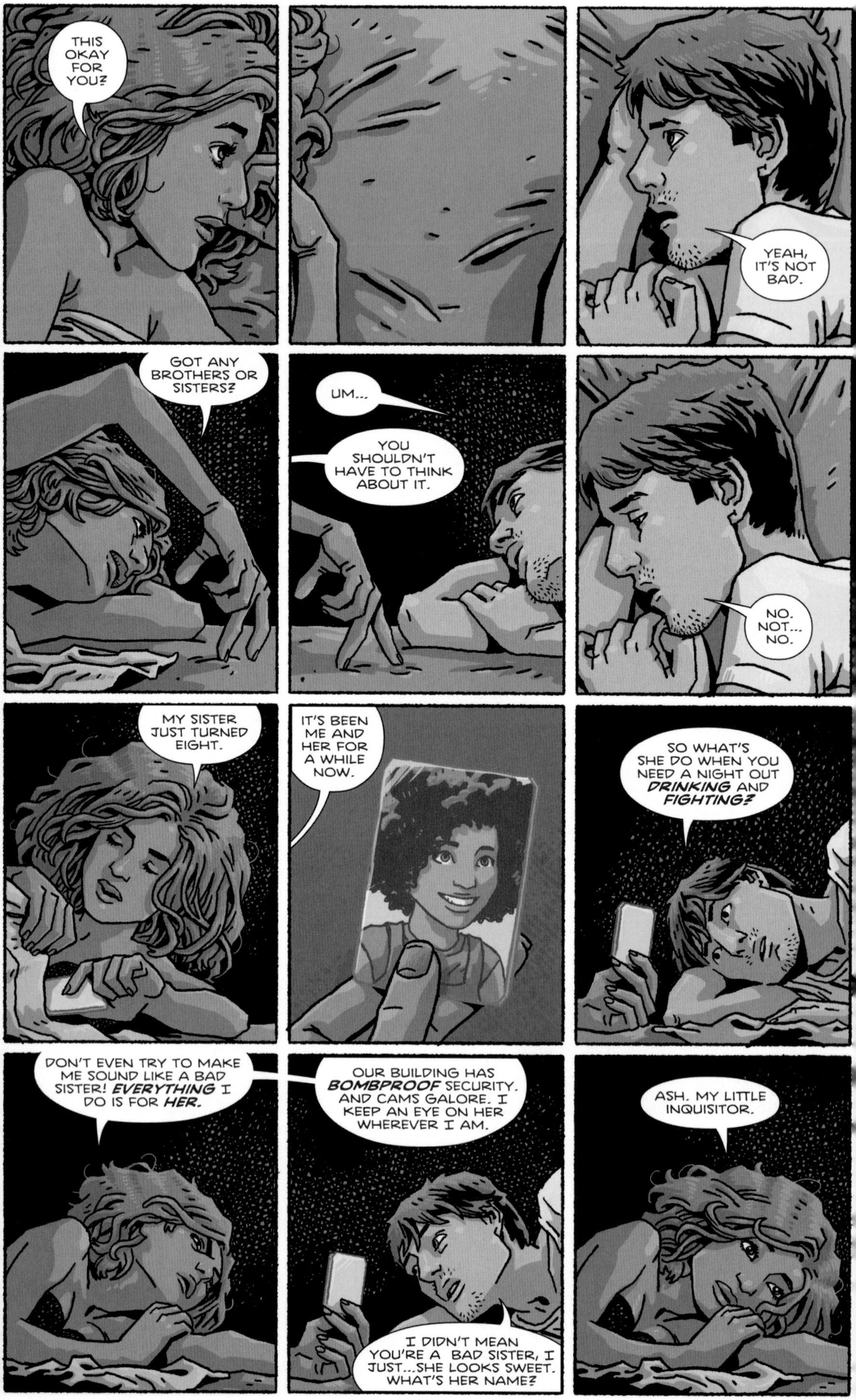
THIS OKAY FOR YOU?
YEAH, IT'S NOT BAD.
GOT ANY BROTHERS OR SISTERS?
UM...
YOU SHOULDN'T HAVE TO THINK ABOUT IT.
NO. NOT... NO.
MY SISTER JUST TURNED EIGHT.
IT'S BEEN ME AND HER FOR A WHILE NOW.
SO WHAT'S SHE DO WHEN YOU NEED A NIGHT OUT DRINKING AND FIGHTING?
DON'T EVEN TRY TO MAKE ME SOUND LIKE A BAD SISTER! EVERYTHING I DO IS FOR HER.
OUR BUILDING HAS BOMBPROOF SECURITY. AND CAMS GALORE. I KEEP AN EYE ON HER WHEREVER I AM.
I DIDN'T MEAN YOU'RE A BAD SISTER, I JUST...SHE LOOKS SWEET. WHAT'S HER NAME?
ASH. MY LITTLE INQUISITOR.

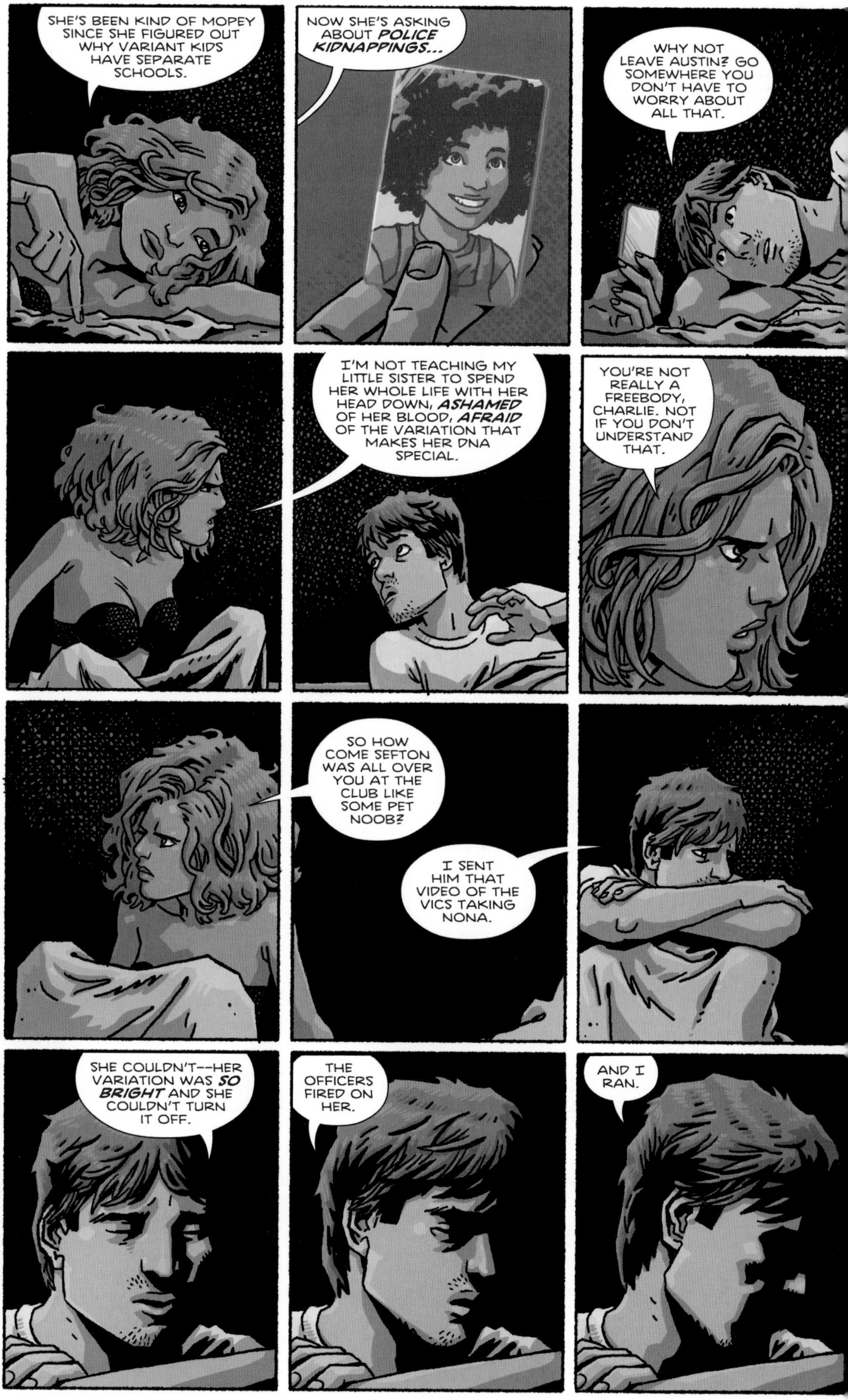
SHE'S BEEN KIND OF MOPEY SINCE SHE FIGURED OUT WHY VARIANT KIDS HAVE SEPARATE SCHOOLS.
NOW SHE'S ASKING ABOUT *POLICE KIDNAPPINGS...*
WHY NOT LEAVE AUSTIN? GO SOMEWHERE YOU DON'T HAVE TO WORRY ABOUT ALL THAT.
I'M NOT TEACHING MY LITTLE SISTER TO SPEND HER WHOLE LIFE WITH HER HEAD DOWN, *ASHAMED* OF HER BLOOD, *AFRAID* OF THE VARIATION THAT MAKES HER DNA SPECIAL.
YOU'RE NOT REALLY A FREEBODY, CHARLIE. NOT IF YOU DON'T UNDERSTAND THAT.
SO HOW COME SEFTON WAS ALL OVER YOU AT THE CLUB LIKE SOME PET NOOB?
I SENT HIM THAT VIDEO OF THE VICS TAKING NONA.
SHE COULDN'T--HER VARIATION WAS *SO BRIGHT* AND SHE COULDN'T TURN IT OFF.
THE OFFICERS FIRED ON HER.
AND I RAN.

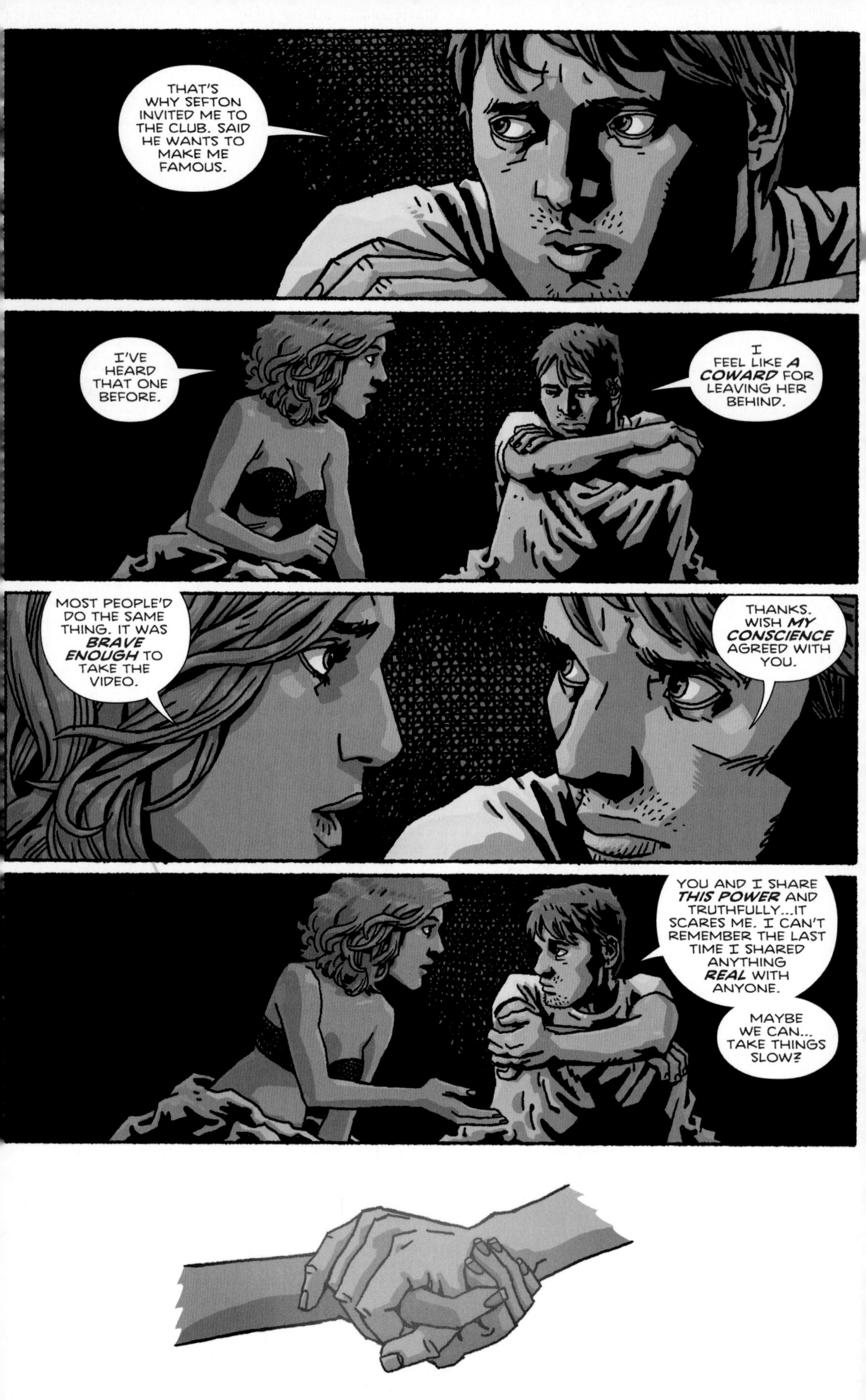
THAT'S WHY SEFTON INVITED ME TO THE CLUB. SAID HE WANTS TO MAKE ME FAMOUS.
I'VE HEARD THAT ONE BEFORE.
I FEEL LIKE A COWARD FOR LEAVING HER BEHIND.
MOST PEOPLE'D DO THE SAME THING. IT WAS BRAVE ENOUGH TO TAKE THE VIDEO.
THANKS. WISH MY CONSCIENCE AGREED WITH YOU.
YOU AND I SHARE THIS POWER AND TRUTHFULLY...IT SCARES ME. I CAN'T REMEMBER THE LAST TIME I SHARED ANYTHING REAL WITH ANYONE.
MAYBE WE CAN... TAKE THINGS SLOW?

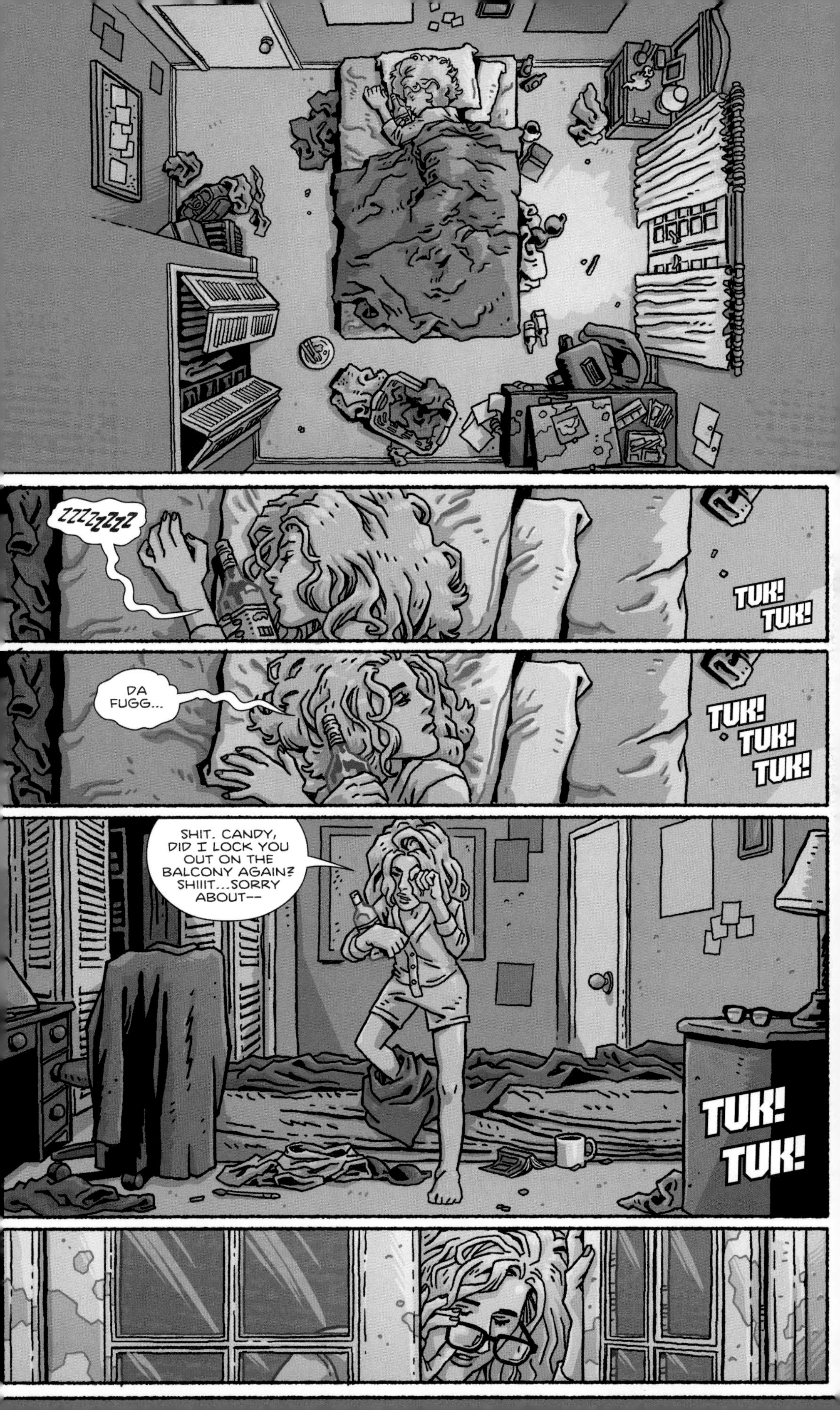
ZZZZZZZZ
TUK! TUK!
DA FUGG...
TUK! TUK! TUK!
SHIT. CANDY, DID I LOCK YOU OUT ON THE BALCONY AGAIN? SHIIIT...SORRY ABOUT--
TUK! TUK!

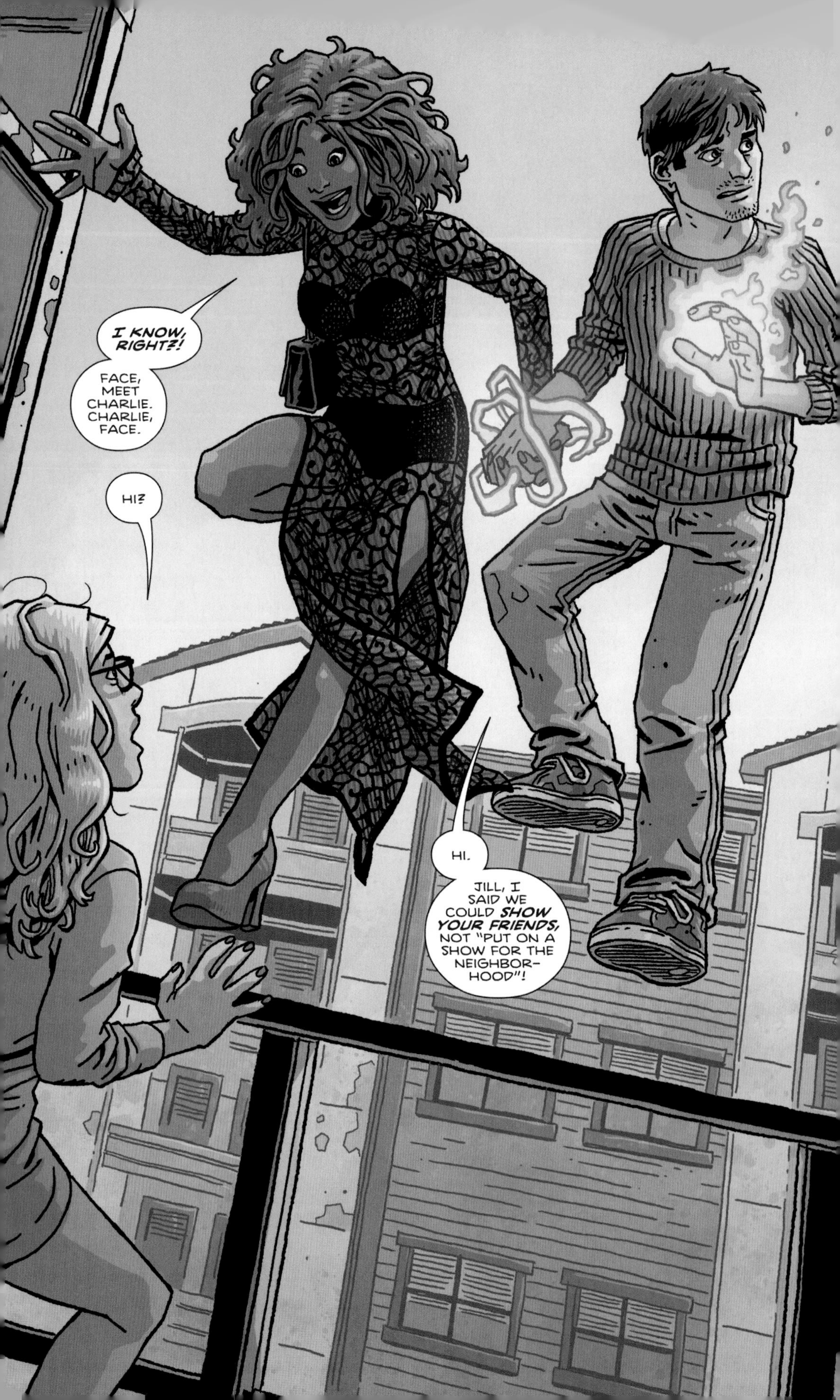

I KNOW, RIGHT?!
FACE, MEET CHARLIE. CHARLIE, FACE.
HI?
HI.
JILL, I SAID WE COULD SHOW YOUR FRIENDS, NOT "PUT ON A SHOW FOR THE NEIGHBOR-HOOD"!

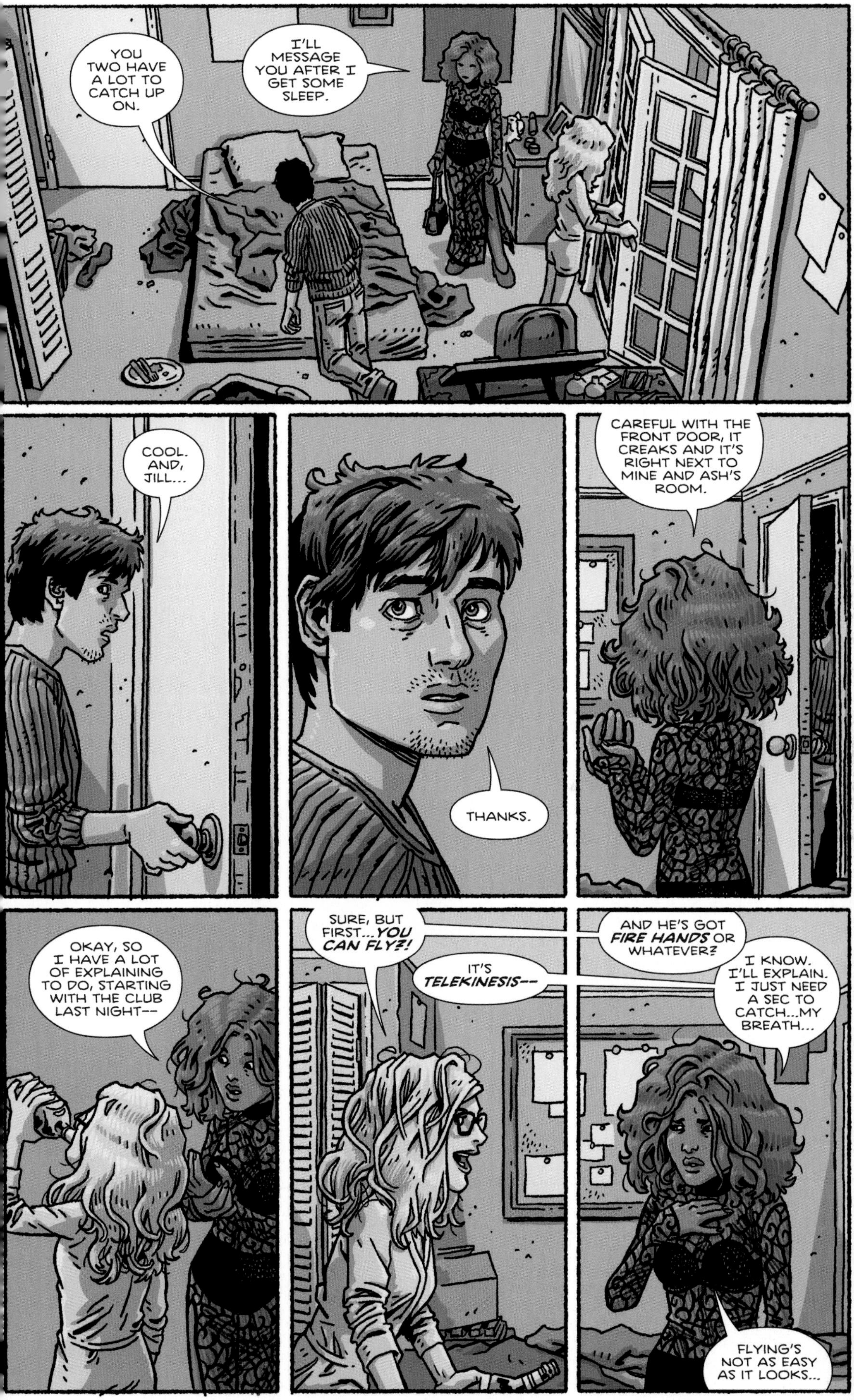
YOU TWO HAVE A LOT TO CATCH UP ON.
I'LL MESSAGE YOU AFTER I GET SOME SLEEP.
COOL. AND, JILL...
THANKS.
CAREFUL WITH THE FRONT DOOR, IT CREAKS AND IT'S RIGHT NEXT TO MINE AND ASH'S ROOM.
OKAY, SO I HAVE A LOT OF EXPLAINING TO DO, STARTING WITH THE CLUB LAST NIGHT--
SURE, BUT FIRST... *YOU CAN FLY?!*
AND HE'S GOT *FIRE HANDS* OR WHATEVER?
IT'S *TELEKINESIS--*
I KNOW. I'LL EXPLAIN. I JUST NEED A SEC TO CATCH...MY BREATH...
FLYING'S NOT AS EASY AS IT LOOKS...

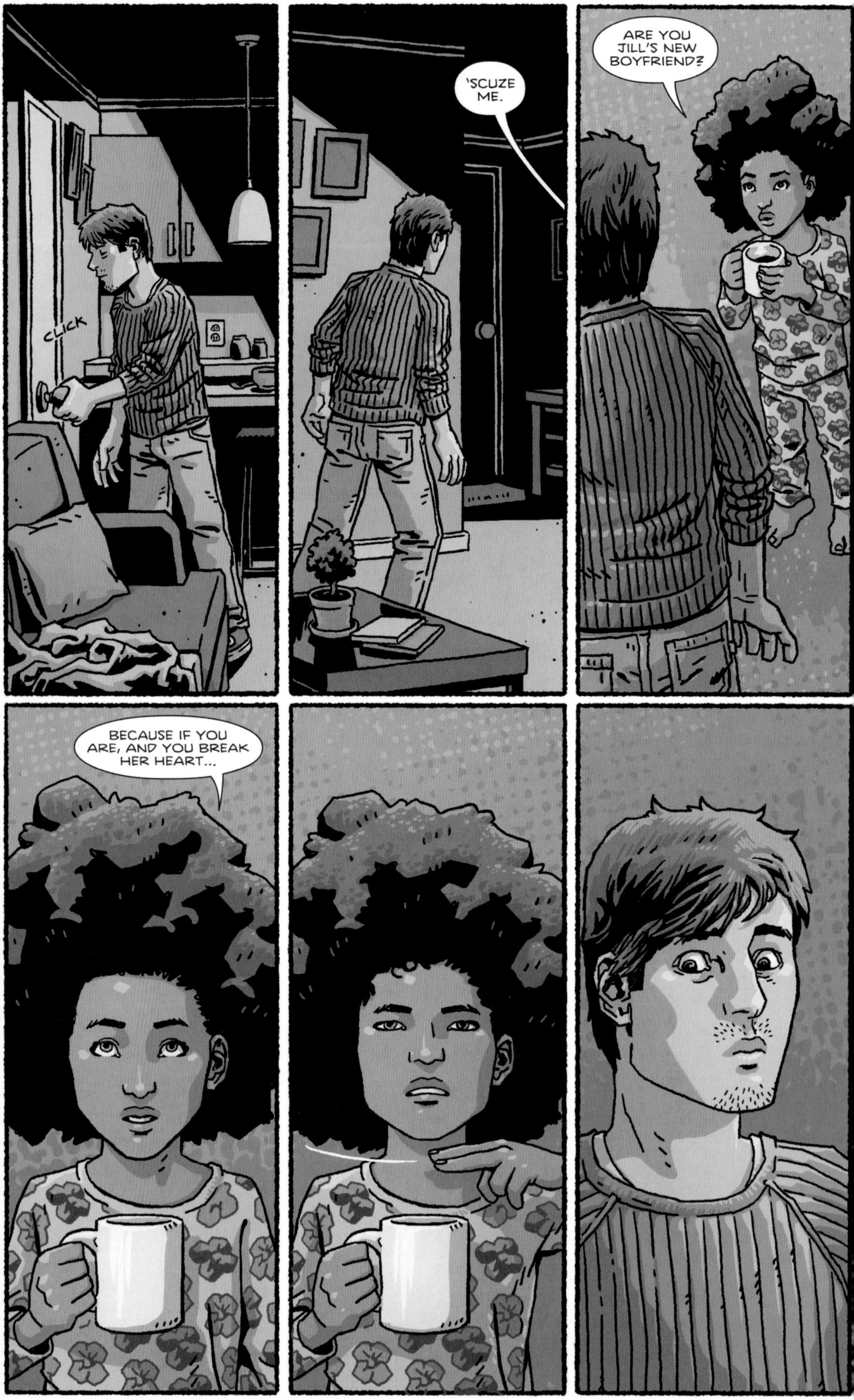
CLICK
'SCUZE ME.
ARE YOU JILL'S NEW BOYFRIEND?
BECAUSE IF YOU ARE, AND YOU BREAK HER HEART...

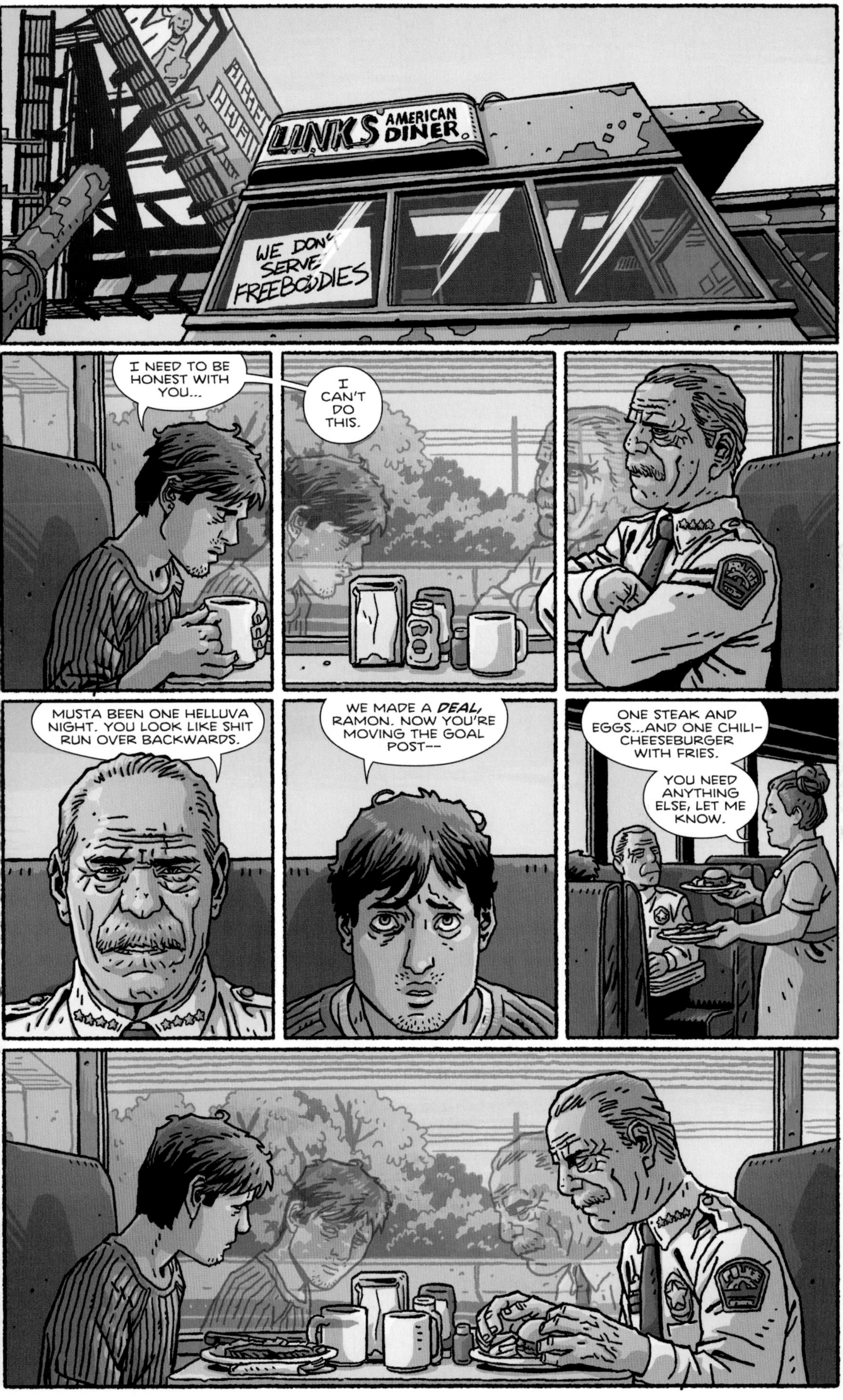
LINKS AMERICAN DINER
WE DON'T SERVE FREEBODDIES
I NEED TO BE HONEST WITH YOU...
I CAN'T DO THIS.
MUSTA BEEN ONE HELLUVA NIGHT. YOU LOOK LIKE SHIT RUN OVER BACKWARDS.
WE MADE A *DEAL,* RAMON. NOW YOU'RE MOVING THE GOAL POST--
ONE STEAK AND EGGS...AND ONE CHILI-CHEESEBURGER WITH FRIES.
YOU NEED ANYTHING ELSE, LET ME KNOW.

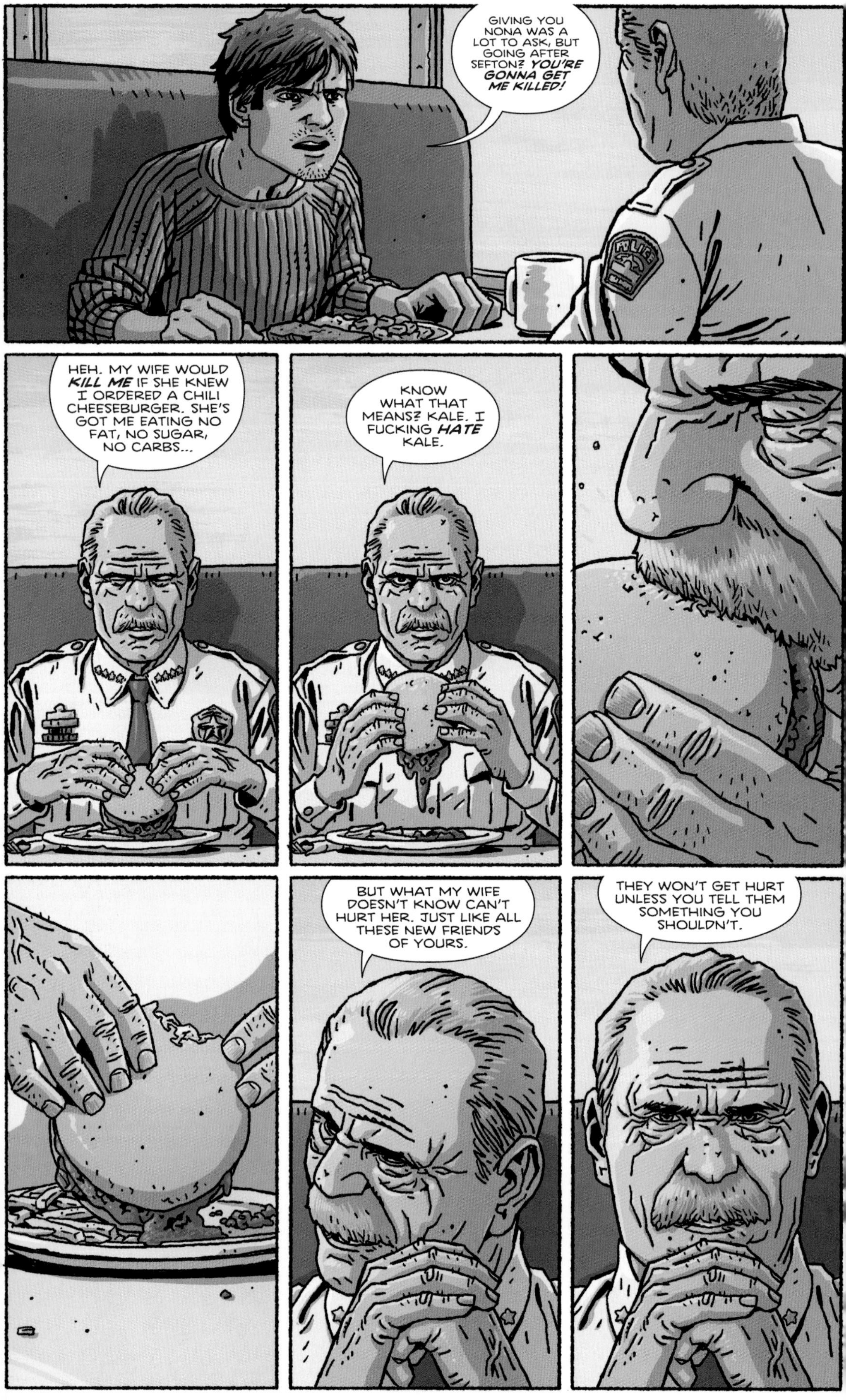
GIVING YOU NONA WAS A LOT TO ASK, BUT GOING AFTER SEFTON? YOU'RE GONNA GET ME KILLED!
HEH. MY WIFE WOULD KILL ME IF SHE KNEW I ORDERED A CHILI CHEESEBURGER. SHE'S GOT ME EATING NO FAT, NO SUGAR, NO CARBS...
KNOW WHAT THAT MEANS? KALE. I FUCKING HATE KALE.
BUT WHAT MY WIFE DOESN'T KNOW CAN'T HURT HER. JUST LIKE ALL THESE NEW FRIENDS OF YOURS.
THEY WON'T GET HURT UNLESS YOU TELL THEM SOMETHING YOU SHOULDN'T.

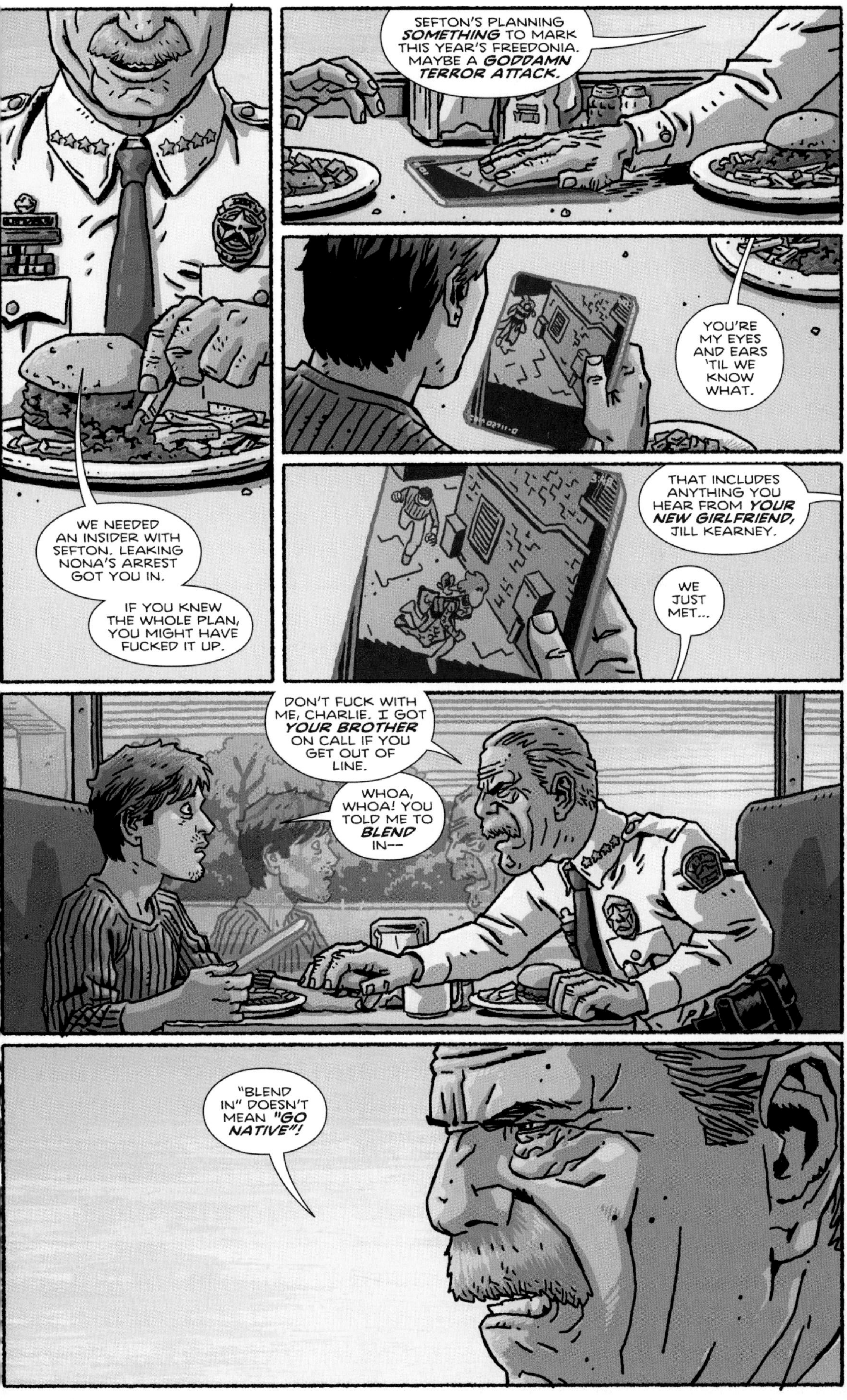
SEFTON'S PLANNING SOMETHING TO MARK THIS YEAR'S FREEDONIA. MAYBE A GODDAMN TERROR ATTACK.
WE NEEDED AN INSIDER WITH SEFTON. LEAKING NONA'S ARREST GOT YOU IN.
IF YOU KNEW THE WHOLE PLAN, YOU MIGHT HAVE FUCKED IT UP.
YOU'RE MY EYES AND EARS 'TIL WE KNOW WHAT.
THAT INCLUDES ANYTHING YOU HEAR FROM YOUR NEW GIRLFRIEND, JILL KEARNEY.
WE JUST MET...
DON'T FUCK WITH ME, CHARLIE. I GOT YOUR BROTHER ON CALL IF YOU GET OUT OF LINE.
WHOA, WHOA! YOU TOLD ME TO BLEND IN--
"BLEND IN" DOESN'T MEAN "GO NATIVE"!

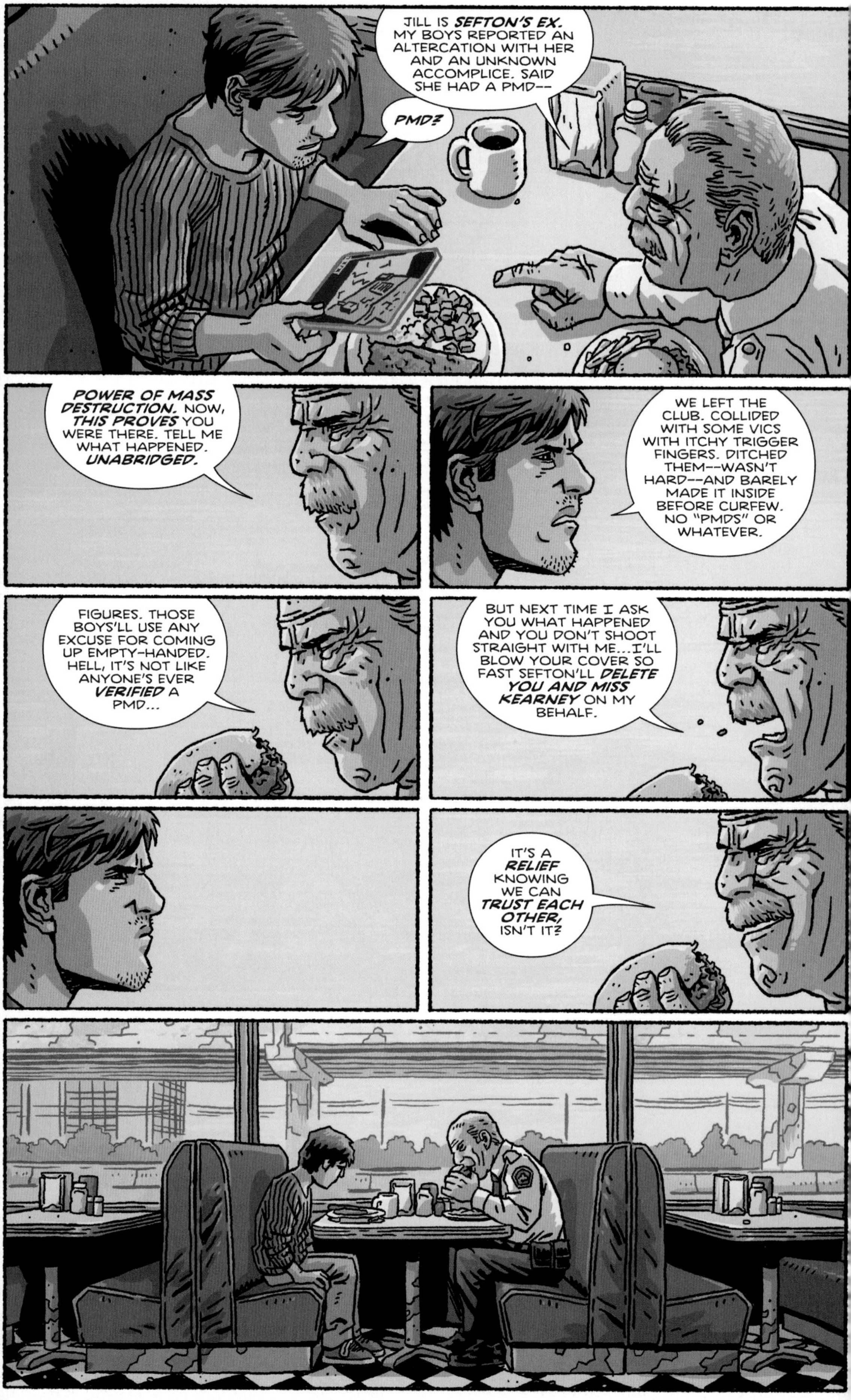
JILL IS SEFTON'S EX. MY BOYS REPORTED AN ALTERCATION WITH HER AND AN UNKNOWN ACCOMPLICE. SAID SHE HAD A PMD--
PMD?
POWER OF MASS DESTRUCTION. NOW, THIS PROVES YOU WERE THERE. TELL ME WHAT HAPPENED. UNABRIDGED.
WE LEFT THE CLUB. COLLIDED WITH SOME VICS WITH ITCHY TRIGGER FINGERS. DITCHED THEM--WASN'T HARD--AND BARELY MADE IT INSIDE BEFORE CURFEW. NO "PMDS" OR WHATEVER.
FIGURES. THOSE BOYS'LL USE ANY EXCUSE FOR COMING UP EMPTY-HANDED. HELL, IT'S NOT LIKE ANYONE'S EVER VERIFIED A PMD...
BUT NEXT TIME I ASK YOU WHAT HAPPENED AND YOU DON'T SHOOT STRAIGHT WITH ME...I'LL BLOW YOUR COVER SO FAST SEFTON'LL DELETE YOU AND MISS KEARNEY ON MY BEHALF.
IT'S A RELIEF KNOWING WE CAN TRUST EACH OTHER, ISN'T IT?

CARNAGE REPORT
9:34 AM

U.S.A. Local Freedom Watch Pods Vids Options

AUSTIN NEEDS MORE WALLS

AND PATRIOTIC WARRIORS TO PATROL THEM | OP/ED

By Michael Maverick

I used to be able to enjoy Friday nights out on Rainey Street. The food, the drink, the atmosphere of a summer night at Banger's Sausage House & Beer Garden, with a buzz on my brain and air thick with romance. Some drunken stranger might spontaneously burst into song – and everyone else in the crowd would join the fun.

Nobody bursts into song on Rainey Street anymore. How could they? The Freebodies are ruining it.

Last Friday, every two steps on Rainey Street, one of these "Variant rights activists" or, as I call them, "Unemployed Genetic Aberrations," confronts me and demands to know how I personally plan to end Governor Pritchard's "paramilitary occupation of the Wall." Then they point at the gigantic, obvious Wall just a couple blocks away as if I could have somehow missed it. "Do you see that? That was a quarantine center. Now it's Governor Pritchard's weapon against Variants – her Death Star!"

To suggest that a citizen as honorable, stylish, and beloved as Governor Pritchard is anything less than the hero of the story makes it clear that these Freebodies and their cult leader, Sefton Smith, are trafficking in alternative facts.

Most Freebodies are Variants. Behavioralists have documented higher rates of depression and aggressive behaviors among Variants. Arguing with this thug on Rainey Street could be dangerous.

So, what do I say to these Freebodies who are ruining Rainey Street and spouting lies in my face?

I point at that gigantic, obvious Wall just a couple blocks away as if he/she/whatever could have somehow missed it, and I say, "I'm glad that Wall is there. If it were up to me, we'd have more walls, and that wall would be taller." At this point the Variant's eyes pop out.

I go on: "I'm glad there's a paramilitary team there. That makes me feel safer. I like knowing Austin is safe from riots, gang violence, and the unpredictable nature of Variantism."

I walk a few steps from that stupefied activist, but I turn back for just a moment, to say, "This place used to be fun. The Wall didn't ruin it. Pritchard didn't ruin it. Variants are ruining it."

And then I leave, knowing that I'm right. And you know what that activist does? Not a goddamned thing, because they are an unemployed genetic aberration, and that's all they'll ever be.

_____ Published 8:23 AM ET, Wed Nov 11

HAVE YOU SEEN ILLEGAL ALIENS? REPORT & DEPORT!

CALL ICE

LIVE NEAR THE BORDER? PARTICIPATE IN YOUR CIVIC DUTY

VALOR FREEDOM TENACITY LOYALTY CITIZENSHIP

CALL TODAY | OPERATORS AVAILABLE 24/7 | CALL 1-1-1

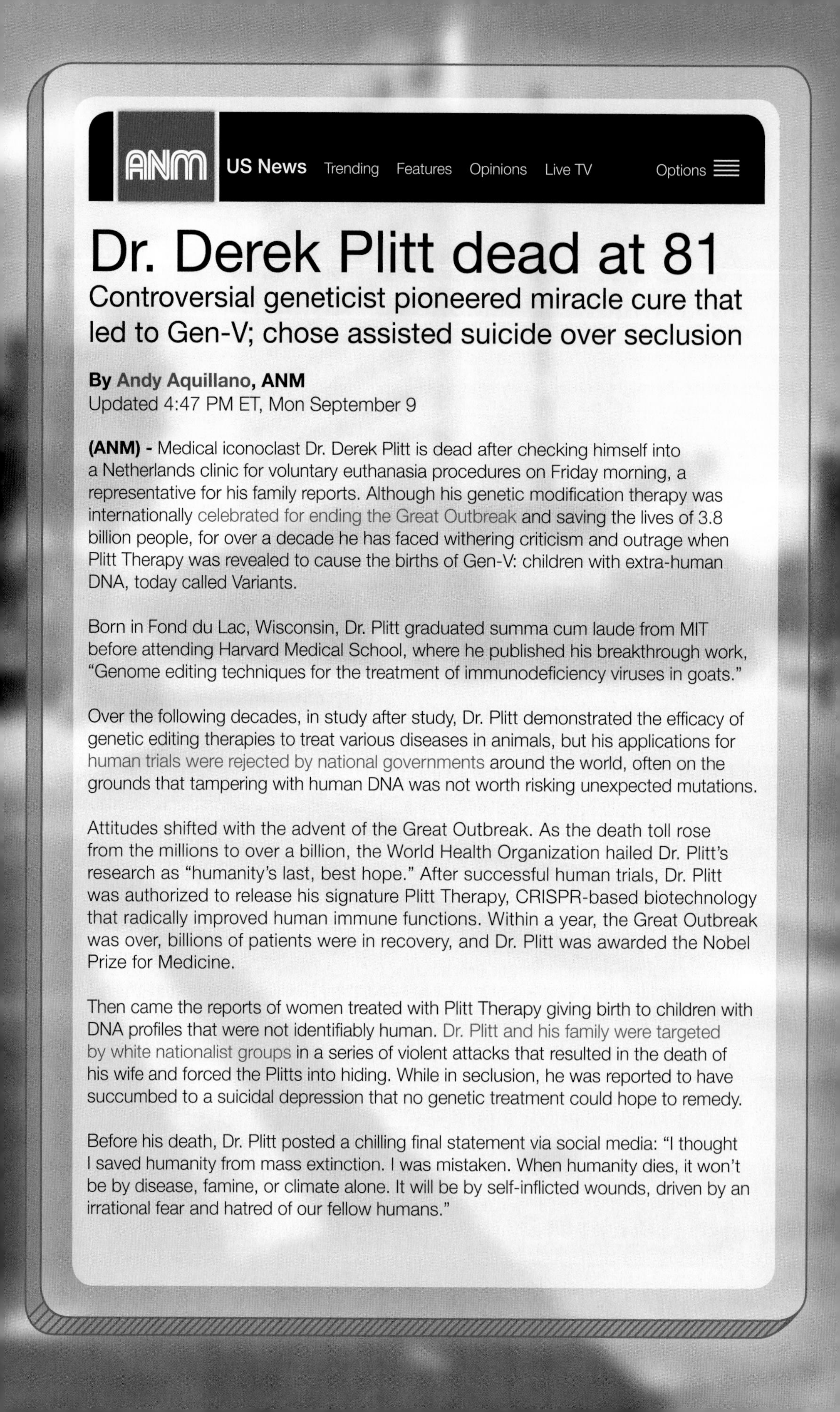

ANM | US News | Trending | Features | Opinions | Live TV | Options

Dr. Derek Plitt dead at 81

Controversial geneticist pioneered miracle cure that led to Gen-V; chose assisted suicide over seclusion

By Andy Aquillano, ANM
Updated 4:47 PM ET, Mon September 9

(ANM) - Medical iconoclast Dr. Derek Plitt is dead after checking himself into a Netherlands clinic for voluntary euthanasia procedures on Friday morning, a representative for his family reports. Although his genetic modification therapy was internationally celebrated for ending the Great Outbreak and saving the lives of 3.8 billion people, for over a decade he has faced withering criticism and outrage when Plitt Therapy was revealed to cause the births of Gen-V: children with extra-human DNA, today called Variants.

Born in Fond du Lac, Wisconsin, Dr. Plitt graduated summa cum laude from MIT before attending Harvard Medical School, where he published his breakthrough work, "Genome editing techniques for the treatment of immunodeficiency viruses in goats."

Over the following decades, in study after study, Dr. Plitt demonstrated the efficacy of genetic editing therapies to treat various diseases in animals, but his applications for human trials were rejected by national governments around the world, often on the grounds that tampering with human DNA was not worth risking unexpected mutations.

Attitudes shifted with the advent of the Great Outbreak. As the death toll rose from the millions to over a billion, the World Health Organization hailed Dr. Plitt's research as "humanity's last, best hope." After successful human trials, Dr. Plitt was authorized to release his signature Plitt Therapy, CRISPR-based biotechnology that radically improved human immune functions. Within a year, the Great Outbreak was over, billions of patients were in recovery, and Dr. Plitt was awarded the Nobel Prize for Medicine.

Then came the reports of women treated with Plitt Therapy giving birth to children with DNA profiles that were not identifiably human. Dr. Plitt and his family were targeted by white nationalist groups in a series of violent attacks that resulted in the death of his wife and forced the Plitts into hiding. While in seclusion, he was reported to have succumbed to a suicidal depression that no genetic treatment could hope to remedy.

Before his death, Dr. Plitt posted a chilling final statement via social media: "I thought I saved humanity from mass extinction. I was mistaken. When humanity dies, it won't be by disease, famine, or climate alone. It will be by self-inflicted wounds, driven by an irrational fear and hatred of our fellow humans."

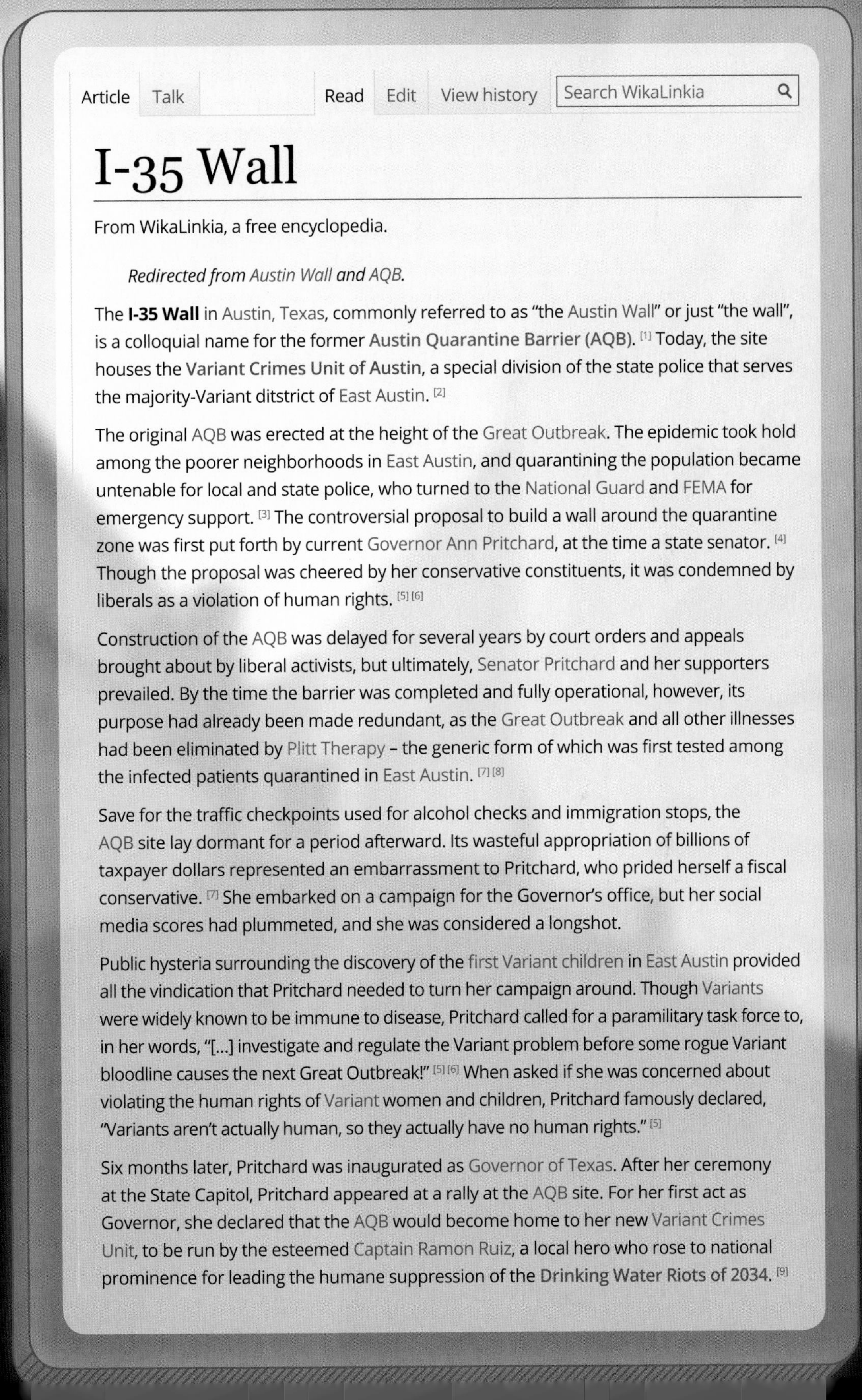
Article
Talk
Read
Edit
View history
Search WikaLinkia
I-35 Wall
From WikaLinkia, a free encyclopedia.
Redirected from Austin Wall and AQB.
The I-35 Wall in Austin, Texas, commonly referred to as "the Austin Wall" or just "the wall", is a colloquial name for the former Austin Quarantine Barrier (AQB). [1] Today, the site houses the Variant Crimes Unit of Austin, a special division of the state police that serves the majority-Variant ditstrict of East Austin. [2]
The original AQB was erected at the height of the Great Outbreak. The epidemic took hold among the poorer neighborhoods in East Austin, and quarantining the population became untenable for local and state police, who turned to the National Guard and FEMA for emergency support. [3] The controversial proposal to build a wall around the quarantine zone was first put forth by current Governor Ann Pritchard, at the time a state senator. [4] Though the proposal was cheered by her conservative constituents, it was condemned by liberals as a violation of human rights. [5] [6]
Construction of the AQB was delayed for several years by court orders and appeals brought about by liberal activists, but ultimately, Senator Pritchard and her supporters prevailed. By the time the barrier was completed and fully operational, however, its purpose had already been made redundant, as the Great Outbreak and all other illnesses had been eliminated by Plitt Therapy – the generic form of which was first tested among the infected patients quarantined in East Austin. [7] [8]
Save for the traffic checkpoints used for alcohol checks and immigration stops, the AQB site lay dormant for a period afterward. Its wasteful appropriation of billions of taxpayer dollars represented an embarrassment to Pritchard, who prided herself a fiscal conservative. [7] She embarked on a campaign for the Governor's office, but her social media scores had plummeted, and she was considered a longshot.
Public hysteria surrounding the discovery of the first Variant children in East Austin provided all the vindication that Pritchard needed to turn her campaign around. Though Variants were widely known to be immune to disease, Pritchard called for a paramilitary task force to, in her words, "[...] investigate and regulate the Variant problem before some rogue Variant bloodline causes the next Great Outbreak!" [5] [6] When asked if she was concerned about violating the human rights of Variant women and children, Pritchard famously declared, "Variants aren't actually human, so they actually have no human rights." [5]
Six months later, Pritchard was inaugurated as Governor of Texas. After her ceremony at the State Capitol, Pritchard appeared at a rally at the AQB site. For her first act as Governor, she declared that the AQB would become home to her new Variant Crimes Unit, to be run by the esteemed Captain Ramon Ruiz, a local hero who rose to national prominence for leading the humane suppression of the Drinking Water Riots of 2034. [9]

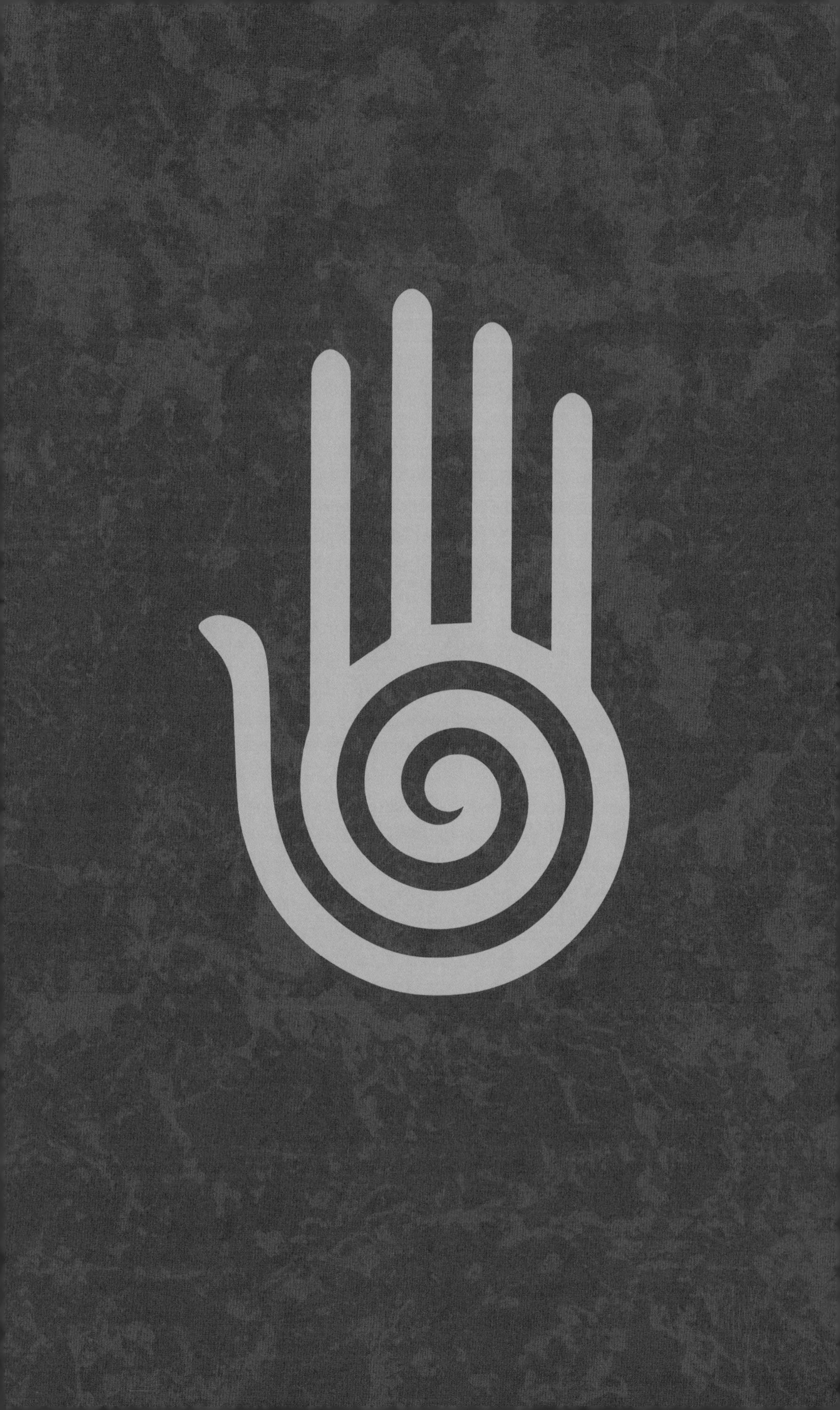

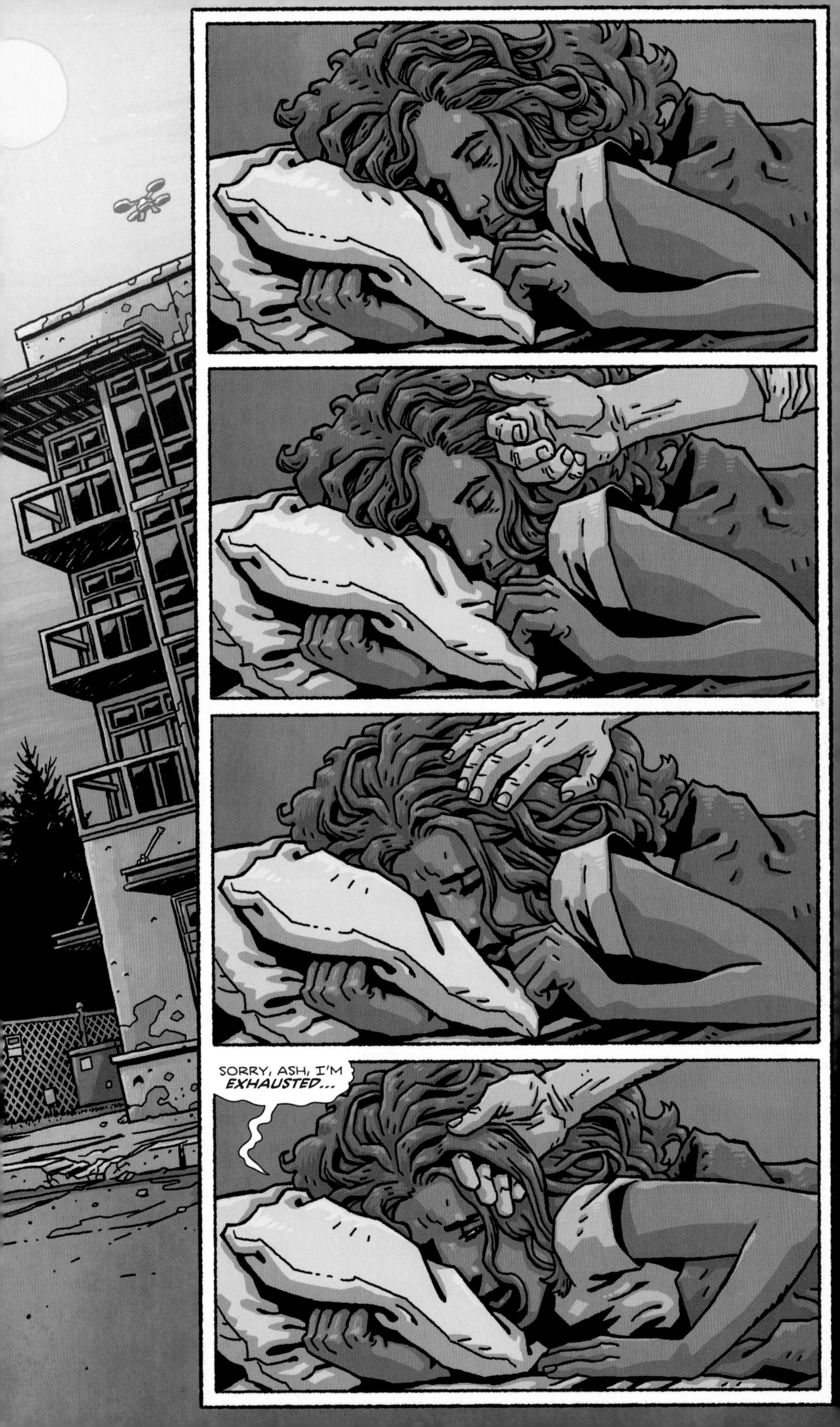
SORRY, ASH, I'M *EXHAUSTED...*

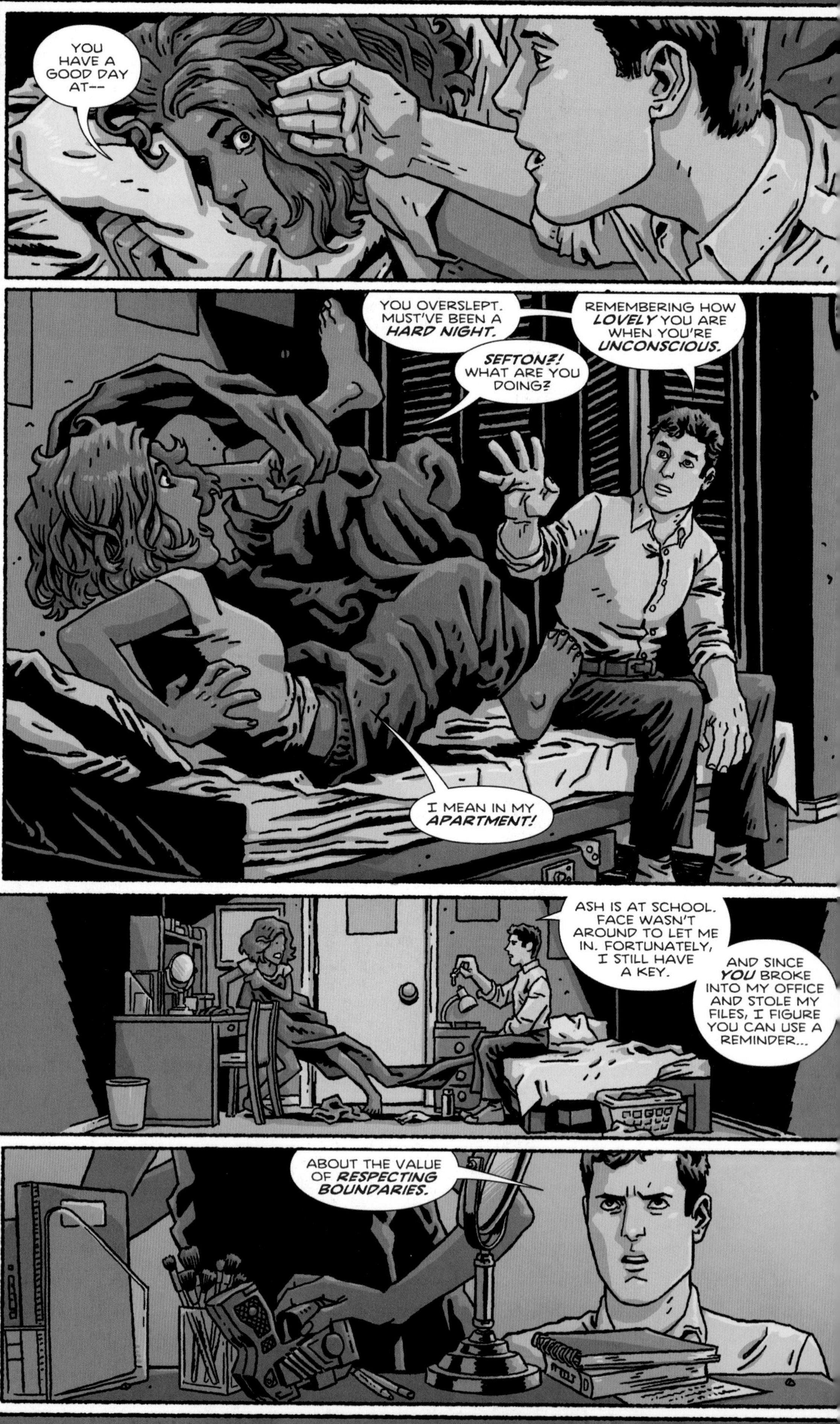
YOU HAVE A GOOD DAY AT--
YOU OVERSLEPT. MUST'VE BEEN A HARD NIGHT.
REMEMBERING HOW LOVELY YOU ARE WHEN YOU'RE UNCONSCIOUS.
SEFTON?! WHAT ARE YOU DOING?
I MEAN IN MY APARTMENT!
ASH IS AT SCHOOL. FACE WASN'T AROUND TO LET ME IN. FORTUNATELY, I STILL HAVE A KEY.
AND SINCE YOU BROKE INTO MY OFFICE AND STOLE MY FILES, I FIGURE YOU CAN USE A REMINDER...
ABOUT THE VALUE OF RESPECTING BOUNDARIES.

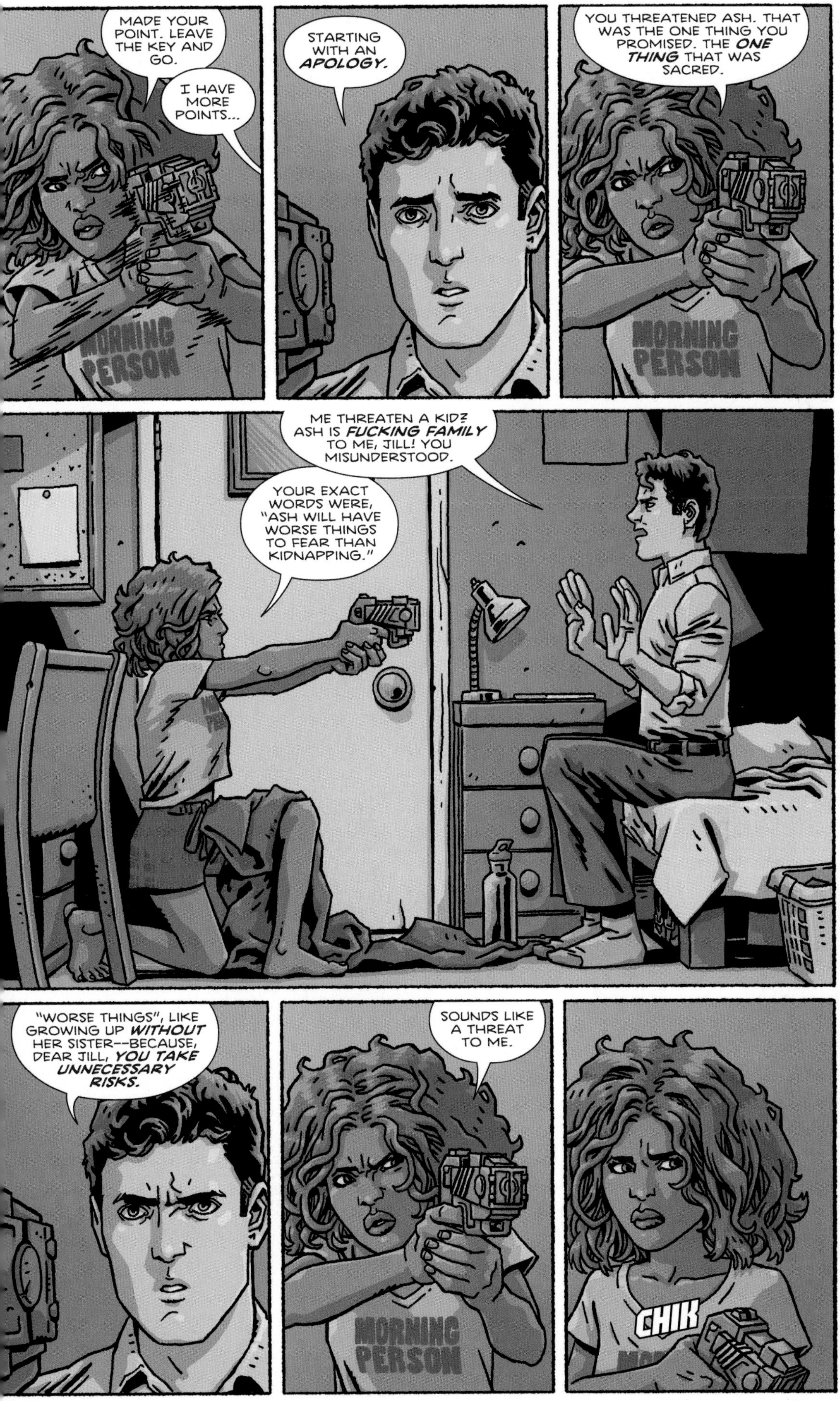

MADE YOUR POINT. LEAVE THE KEY AND GO.
I HAVE MORE POINTS...
STARTING WITH AN *APOLOGY.*
YOU THREATENED ASH. THAT WAS THE ONE THING YOU PROMISED. THE *ONE THING* THAT WAS SACRED.
ME THREATEN A KID? ASH IS *FUCKING FAMILY* TO ME, JILL! YOU MISUNDERSTOOD.
YOUR EXACT WORDS WERE, "ASH WILL HAVE WORSE THINGS TO FEAR THAN KIDNAPPING."
"WORSE THINGS", LIKE GROWING UP *WITHOUT* HER SISTER--BECAUSE, DEAR JILL, *YOU TAKE UNNECESSARY RISKS.*
SOUNDS LIKE A THREAT TO ME.
CHIK

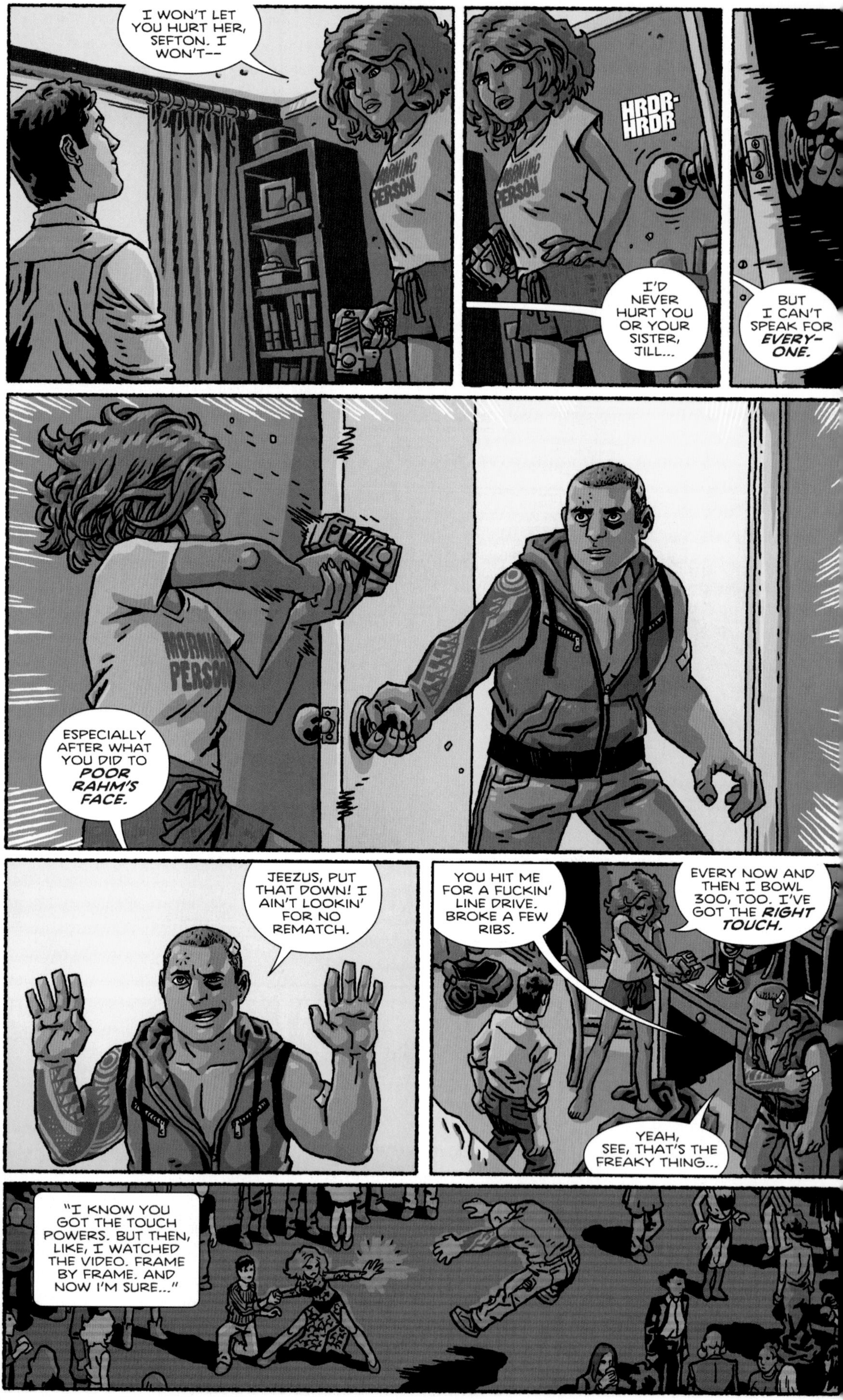
I WON'T LET YOU HURT HER, SEFTON. I WON'T--
HRDR-HRDR
I'D NEVER HURT YOU OR YOUR SISTER, JILL...
BUT I CAN'T SPEAK FOR EVERY-ONE.
ESPECIALLY AFTER WHAT YOU DID TO POOR RAHM'S FACE.
JEEZUS, PUT THAT DOWN! I AIN'T LOOKIN' FOR NO REMATCH.
YOU HIT ME FOR A FUCKIN' LINE DRIVE. BROKE A FEW RIBS.
EVERY NOW AND THEN I BOWL 300, TOO. I'VE GOT THE RIGHT TOUCH.
YEAH, SEE, THAT'S THE FREAKY THING...
"I KNOW YOU GOT THE TOUCH POWERS. BUT THEN, LIKE, I WATCHED THE VIDEO. FRAME BY FRAME. AND NOW I'M SURE..."

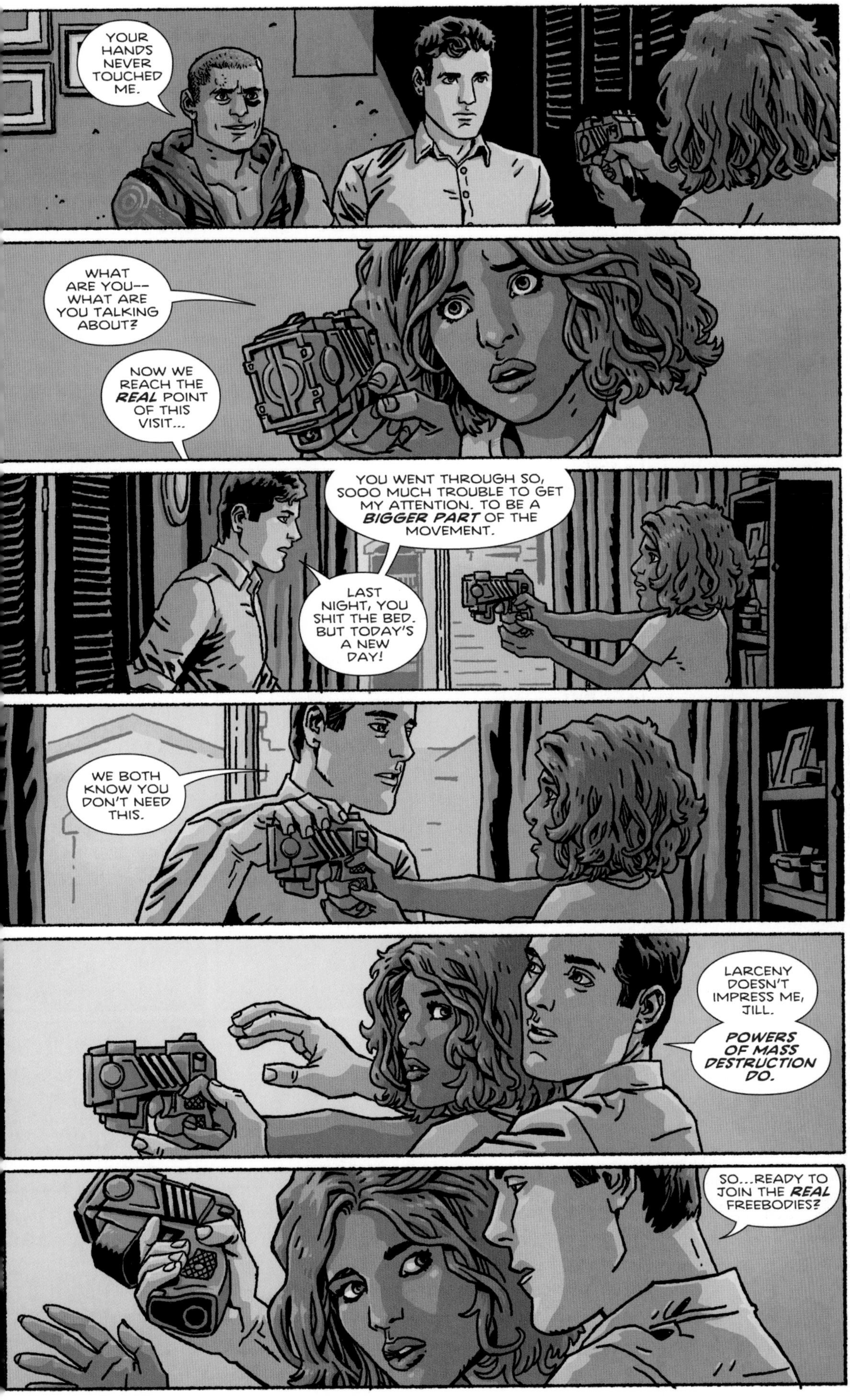

YOUR HANDS NEVER TOUCHED ME.
WHAT ARE YOU-- WHAT ARE YOU TALKING ABOUT?
NOW WE REACH THE *REAL* POINT OF THIS VISIT...
YOU WENT THROUGH SO, SOOO MUCH TROUBLE TO GET MY ATTENTION. TO BE A *BIGGER PART* OF THE MOVEMENT.
LAST NIGHT, YOU SHIT THE BED. BUT TODAY'S A NEW DAY!
WE BOTH KNOW YOU DON'T NEED THIS.
LARCENY DOESN'T IMPRESS ME, JILL.
POWERS OF MASS DESTRUCTION DO.
SO...READY TO JOIN THE *REAL* FREEBODIES?

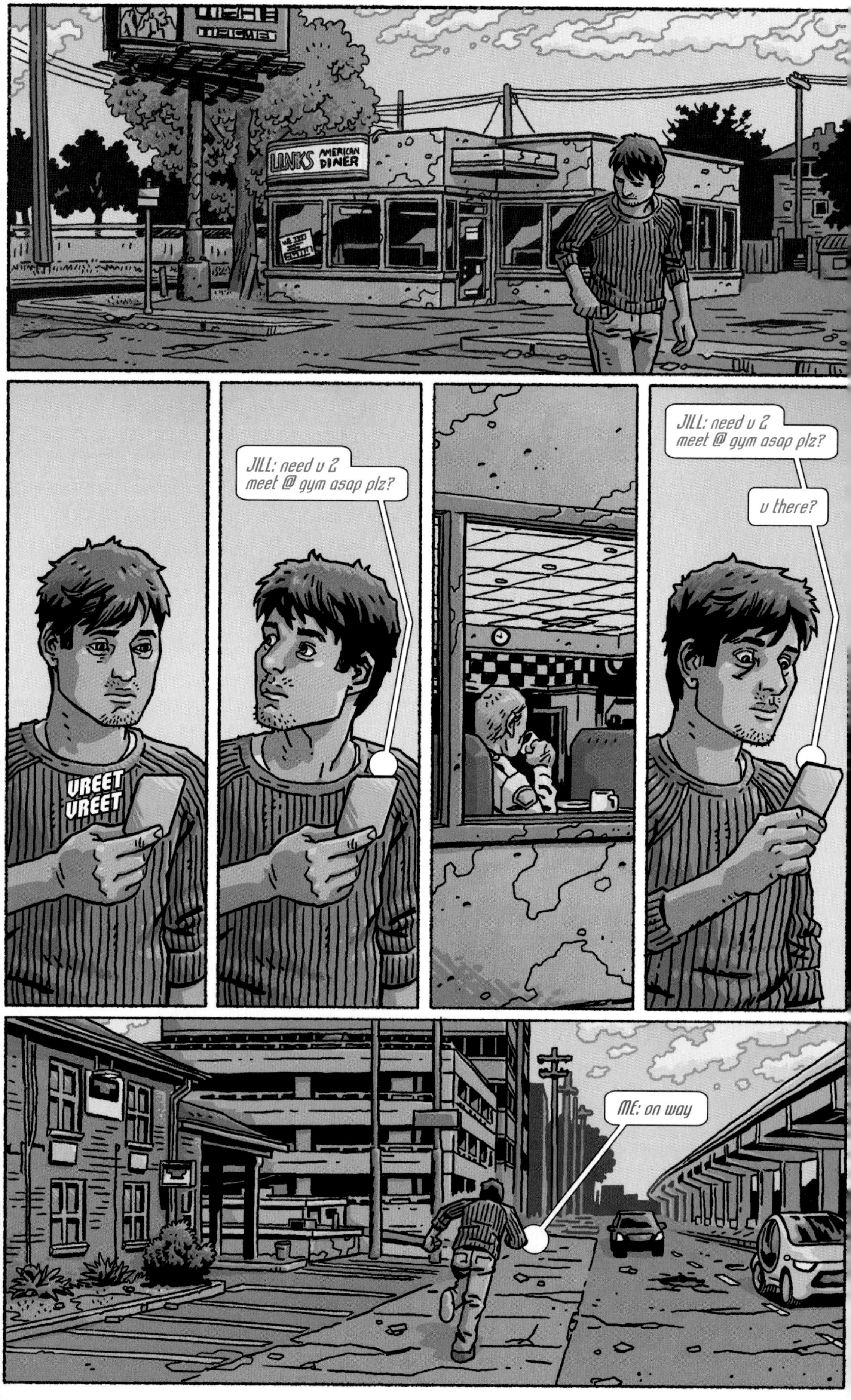
LINKS AMERICAN DINER
VREET VREET
JILL: need u 2 meet @ gym asap plz?
JILL: need u 2 meet @ gym asap plz?
u there?
ME: on way

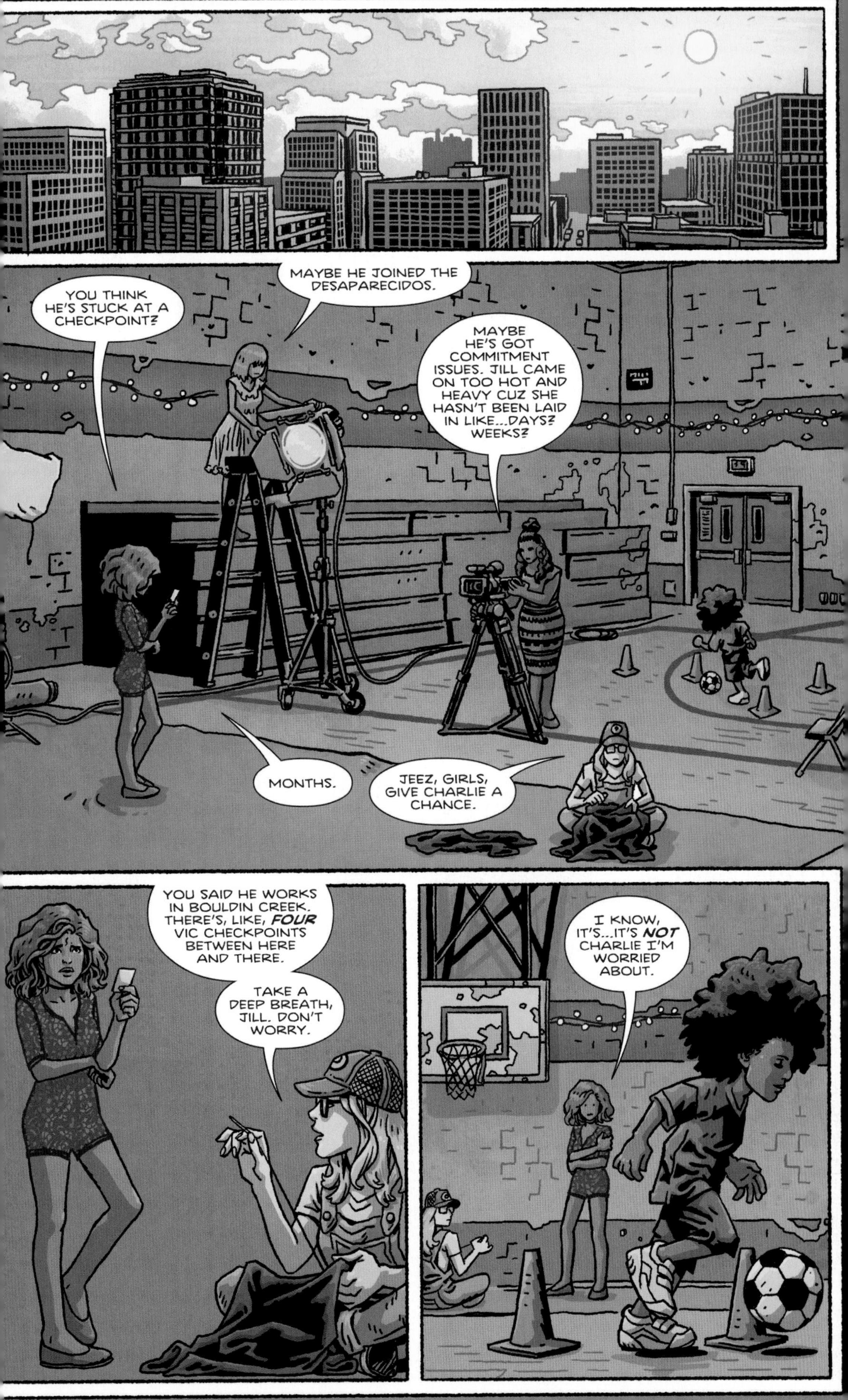
YOU THINK HE'S STUCK AT A CHECKPOINT?
MAYBE HE JOINED THE DESAPARECIDOS.
MAYBE HE'S GOT COMMITMENT ISSUES. JILL CAME ON TOO HOT AND HEAVY CUZ SHE HASN'T BEEN LAID IN LIKE...DAYS? WEEKS?
MONTHS.
JEEZ, GIRLS, GIVE CHARLIE A CHANCE.
YOU SAID HE WORKS IN BOULDIN CREEK. THERE'S, LIKE, FOUR VIC CHECKPOINTS BETWEEN HERE AND THERE.
TAKE A DEEP BREATH, JILL. DON'T WORRY.
I KNOW, IT'S...IT'S NOT CHARLIE I'M WORRIED ABOUT.

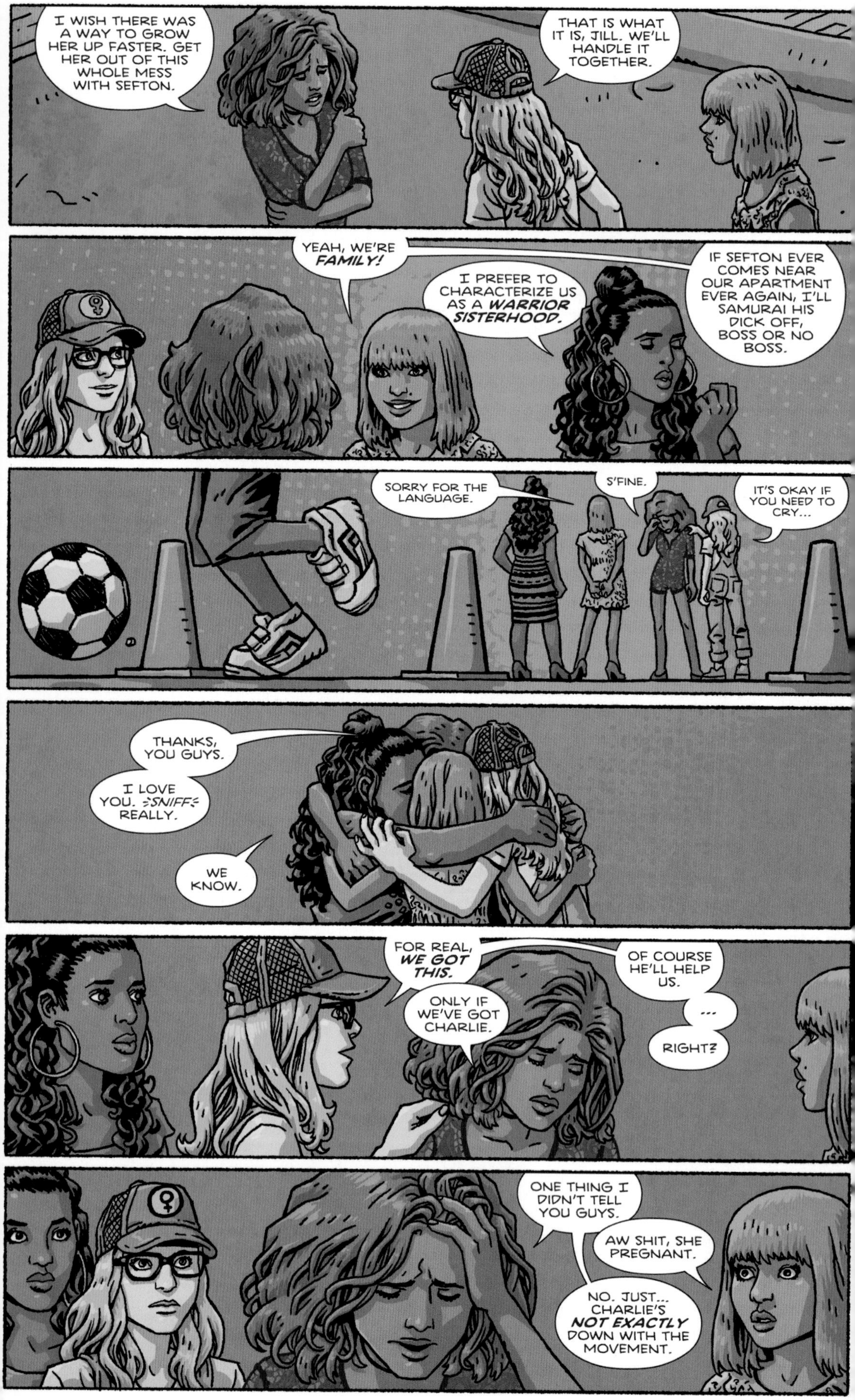
I WISH THERE WAS A WAY TO GROW HER UP FASTER. GET HER OUT OF THIS WHOLE MESS WITH SEFTON.
THAT IS WHAT IT IS, JILL. WE'LL HANDLE IT TOGETHER.
YEAH, WE'RE *FAMILY!*
I PREFER TO CHARACTERIZE US AS A *WARRIOR SISTERHOOD.*
IF SEFTON EVER COMES NEAR OUR APARTMENT EVER AGAIN, I'LL SAMURAI HIS DICK OFF, BOSS OR NO BOSS.
SORRY FOR THE LANGUAGE.
S'FINE.
IT'S OKAY IF YOU NEED TO CRY...
THANKS, YOU GUYS.
I LOVE YOU. *SNIFF* REALLY.
WE KNOW.
FOR REAL, *WE GOT THIS.*
ONLY IF WE'VE GOT CHARLIE.
OF COURSE HE'LL HELP US.
...
RIGHT?
ONE THING I DIDN'T TELL YOU GUYS.
AW SHIT, SHE PREGNANT.
NO. JUST... CHARLIE'S *NOT EXACTLY* DOWN WITH THE MOVEMENT.

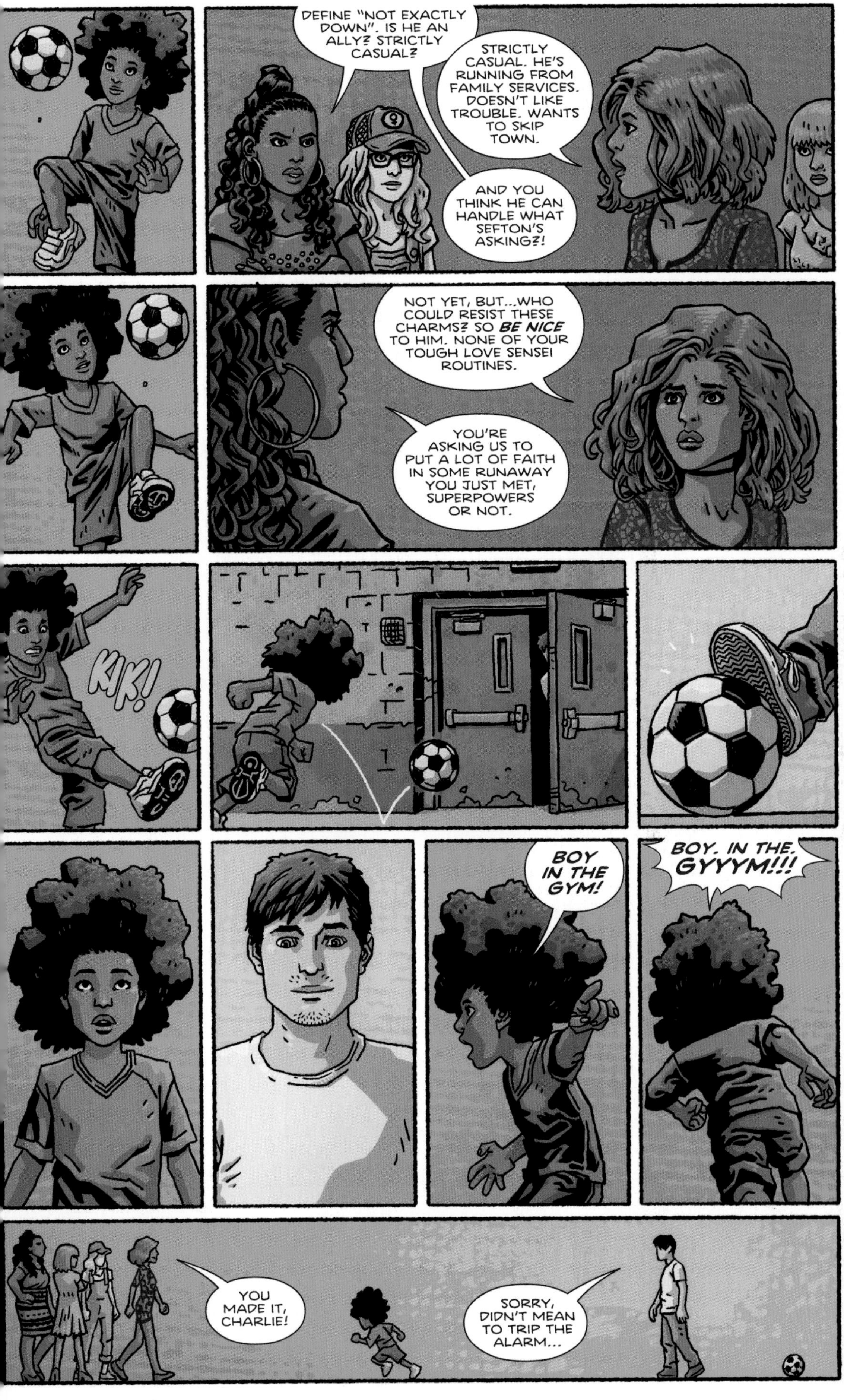
DEFINE "NOT EXACTLY DOWN". IS HE AN ALLY? STRICTLY CASUAL?
STRICTLY CASUAL. HE'S RUNNING FROM FAMILY SERVICES. DOESN'T LIKE TROUBLE. WANTS TO SKIP TOWN.
AND YOU THINK HE CAN HANDLE WHAT SEFTON'S ASKING?!
NOT YET, BUT...WHO COULD RESIST THESE CHARMS? SO *BE NICE* TO HIM. NONE OF YOUR TOUGH LOVE SENSEI ROUTINES.
YOU'RE ASKING US TO PUT A LOT OF FAITH IN SOME RUNAWAY YOU JUST MET, SUPERPOWERS OR NOT.
KIK!
BOY IN THE GYM!
BOY. IN THE. GYYYM!!!
YOU MADE IT, CHARLIE!
SORRY, DIDN'T MEAN TO TRIP THE ALARM...

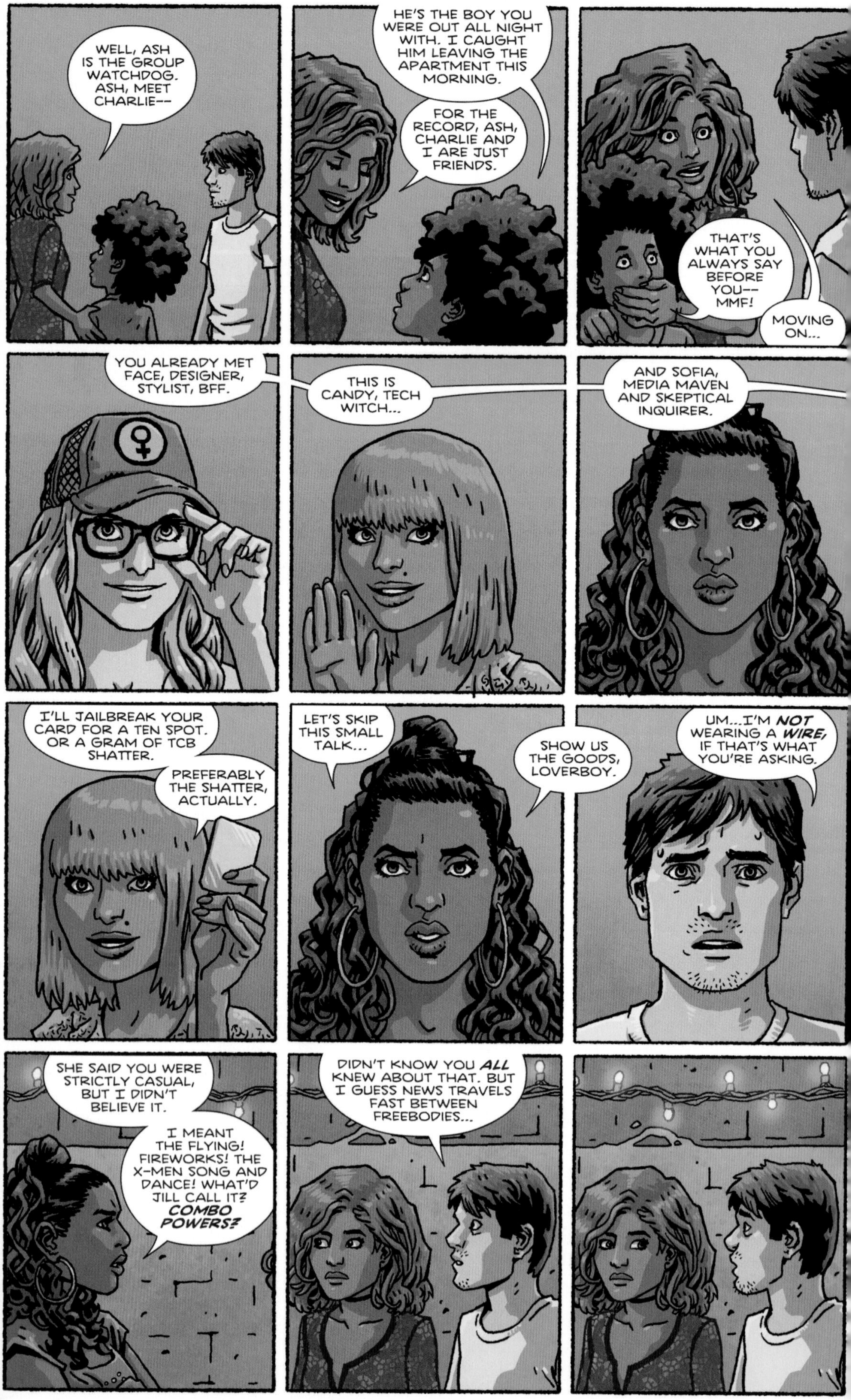
WELL, ASH IS THE GROUP WATCHDOG. ASH, MEET CHARLIE--
HE'S THE BOY YOU WERE OUT ALL NIGHT WITH. I CAUGHT HIM LEAVING THE APARTMENT THIS MORNING.
FOR THE RECORD, ASH, CHARLIE AND I ARE JUST FRIENDS.
THAT'S WHAT YOU ALWAYS SAY BEFORE YOU-- MMF!
MOVING ON...
YOU ALREADY MET FACE, DESIGNER, STYLIST, BFF.
THIS IS CANDY, TECH WITCH...
AND SOFIA, MEDIA MAVEN AND SKEPTICAL INQUIRER.
I'LL JAILBREAK YOUR CARD FOR A TEN SPOT. OR A GRAM OF TCB SHATTER.
PREFERABLY THE SHATTER, ACTUALLY.
LET'S SKIP THIS SMALL TALK...
SHOW US THE GOODS, LOVERBOY.
UM...I'M NOT WEARING A WIRE, IF THAT'S WHAT YOU'RE ASKING.
SHE SAID YOU WERE STRICTLY CASUAL, BUT I DIDN'T BELIEVE IT.
I MEANT THE FLYING! FIREWORKS! THE X-MEN SONG AND DANCE! WHAT'D JILL CALL IT? COMBO POWERS?
DIDN'T KNOW YOU ALL KNEW ABOUT THAT. BUT I GUESS NEWS TRAVELS FAST BETWEEN FREEBODIES...

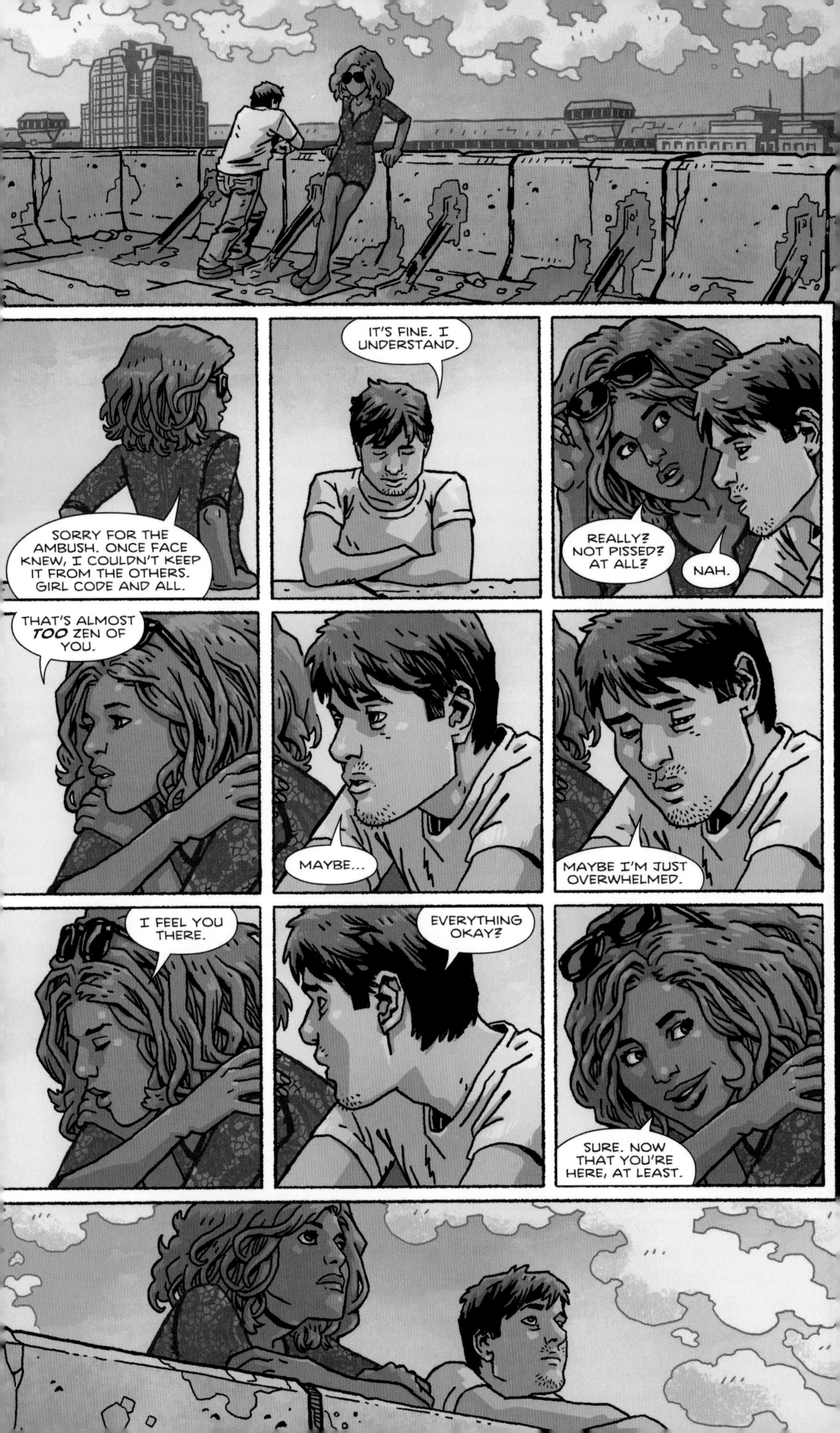
SORRY FOR THE AMBUSH. ONCE FACE KNEW, I COULDN'T KEEP IT FROM THE OTHERS. GIRL CODE AND ALL.
IT'S FINE. I UNDERSTAND.
REALLY? NOT PISSED? AT ALL?
NAH.
THAT'S ALMOST *TOO* ZEN OF YOU.
MAYBE...
MAYBE I'M JUST OVERWHELMED.
I FEEL YOU THERE.
EVERYTHING OKAY?
SURE. NOW THAT YOU'RE HERE, AT LEAST.

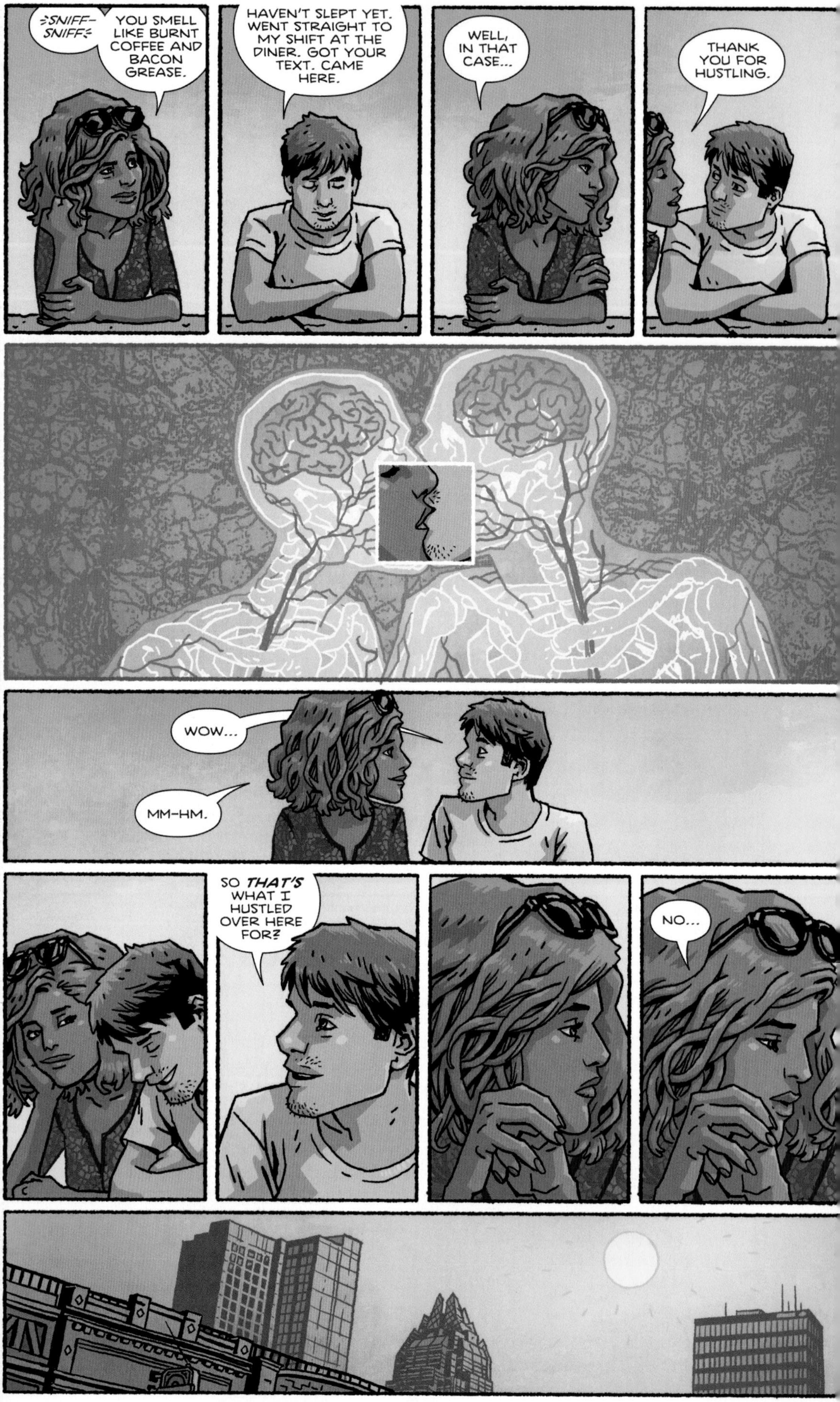
SNIFF-SNIFF
YOU SMELL LIKE BURNT COFFEE AND BACON GREASE.
HAVEN'T SLEPT YET. WENT STRAIGHT TO MY SHIFT AT THE DINER. GOT YOUR TEXT. CAME HERE.
WELL, IN THAT CASE...
THANK YOU FOR HUSTLING.
WOW...
MM-HM.
SO *THAT'S* WHAT I HUSTLED OVER HERE FOR?
NO...

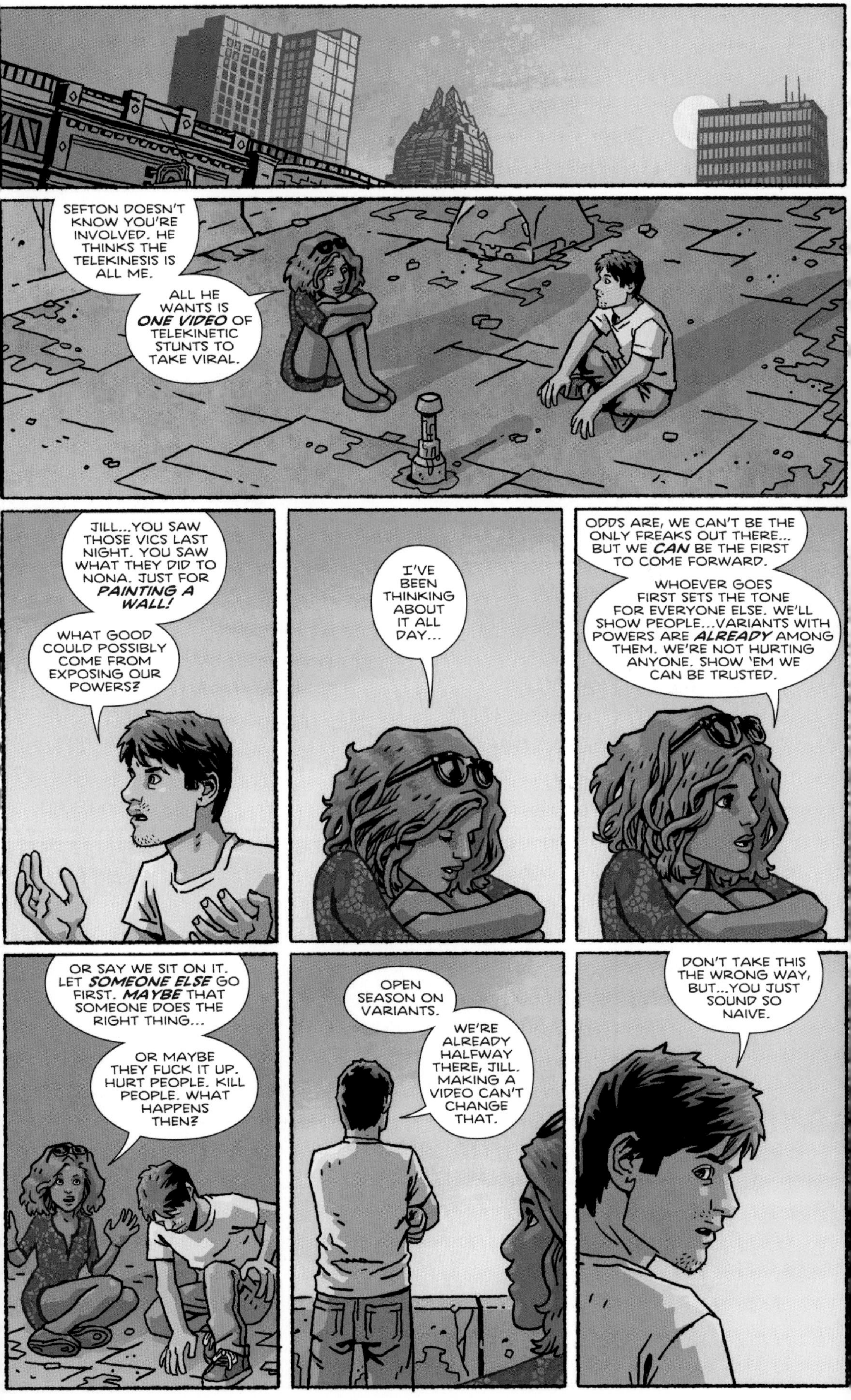
SEFTON DOESN'T KNOW YOU'RE INVOLVED. HE THINKS THE TELEKINESIS IS ALL ME.
ALL HE WANTS IS ONE VIDEO OF TELEKINETIC STUNTS TO TAKE VIRAL.
JILL...YOU SAW THOSE VICS LAST NIGHT. YOU SAW WHAT THEY DID TO NONA. JUST FOR PAINTING A WALL!
WHAT GOOD COULD POSSIBLY COME FROM EXPOSING OUR POWERS?
I'VE BEEN THINKING ABOUT IT ALL DAY...
ODDS ARE, WE CAN'T BE THE ONLY FREAKS OUT THERE... BUT WE CAN BE THE FIRST TO COME FORWARD.
WHOEVER GOES FIRST SETS THE TONE FOR EVERYONE ELSE. WE'LL SHOW PEOPLE...VARIANTS WITH POWERS ARE ALREADY AMONG THEM. WE'RE NOT HURTING ANYONE. SHOW 'EM WE CAN BE TRUSTED.
OR SAY WE SIT ON IT. LET SOMEONE ELSE GO FIRST. MAYBE THAT SOMEONE DOES THE RIGHT THING...
OR MAYBE THEY FUCK IT UP. HURT PEOPLE. KILL PEOPLE. WHAT HAPPENS THEN?
OPEN SEASON ON VARIANTS.
WE'RE ALREADY HALFWAY THERE, JILL. MAKING A VIDEO CAN'T CHANGE THAT.
DON'T TAKE THIS THE WRONG WAY, BUT...YOU JUST SOUND SO NAIVE.

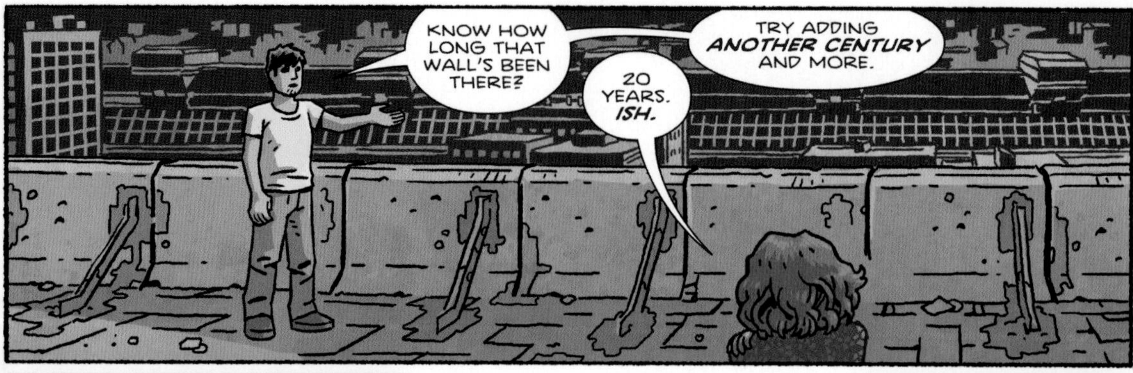
KNOW HOW LONG THAT WALL'S BEEN THERE?
20 YEARS. *ISH.*
TRY ADDING *ANOTHER CENTURY* AND MORE.

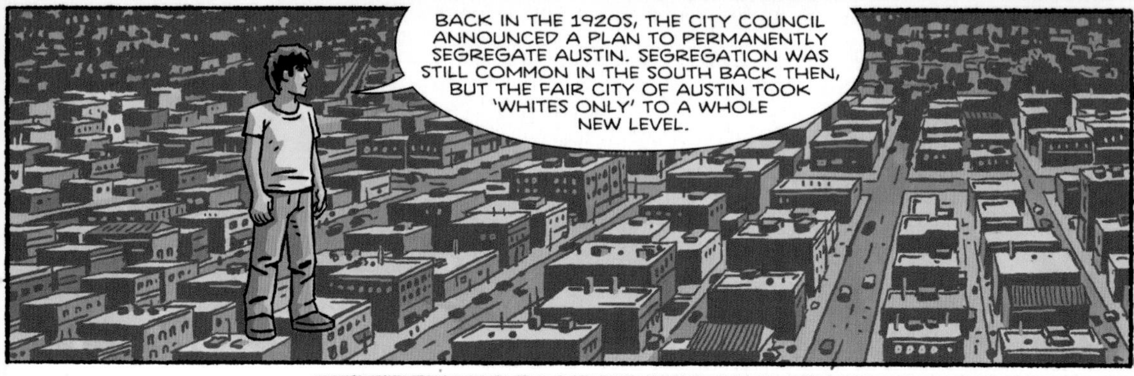
BACK IN THE 1920S, THE CITY COUNCIL ANNOUNCED A PLAN TO PERMANENTLY SEGREGATE AUSTIN. SEGREGATION WAS STILL COMMON IN THE SOUTH BACK THEN, BUT THE FAIR CITY OF AUSTIN TOOK 'WHITES ONLY' TO A WHOLE NEW LEVEL.

"THEY DECLARED THE POOREST NEIGHBORHOODS IN TOWN-- AN INDUSTRIAL AREA EAST OF EAST AVENUE-- 'THE NEGRO DISTRICT'.

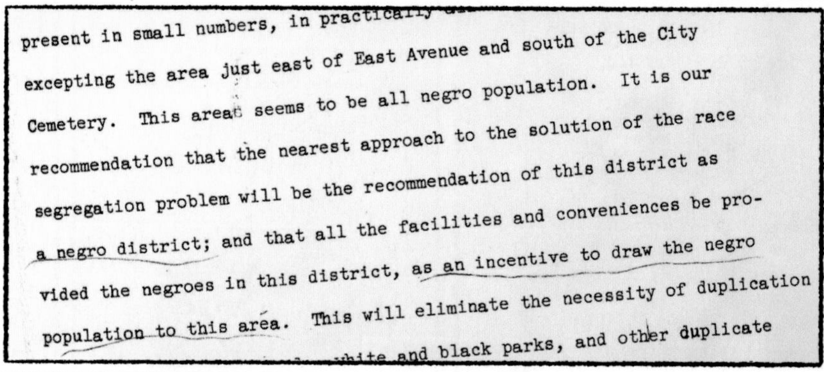
present in small numbers, in practically ...
excepting the area just east of East Avenue and south of the City
Cemetery. This area seems to be all negro population. It is our
recommendation that the nearest approach to the solution of the race
segregation problem will be the recommendation of this district as
a negro district; and that all the facilities and conveniences be provided the negroes in this district, as an incentive to draw the negro
population to this area. This will eliminate the necessity of duplication
... white and black parks, and other duplicate

"TO PERSUADE THE BLACK POPULATION TO MOVE EAST, THE CITY SHUT DOWN EVERY BLACK FACILITY IN WEST AUSTIN... INCLUDING BLACK SCHOOLS.

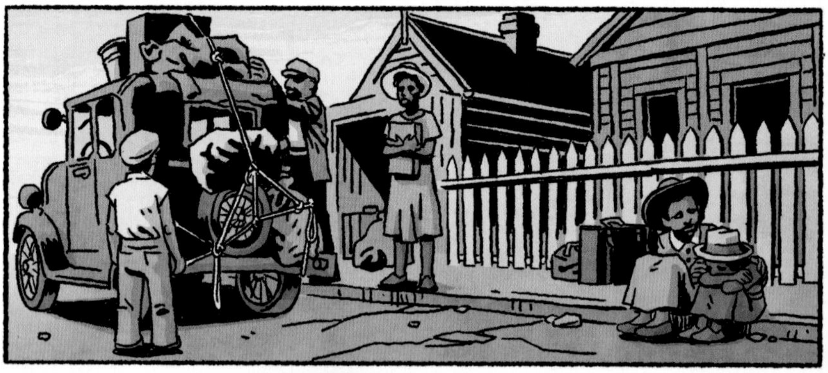

"THE PLAN WORKED.

"WITHIN A FEW YEARS, THE CITY HAD ITS NEGRO DISTRICT.

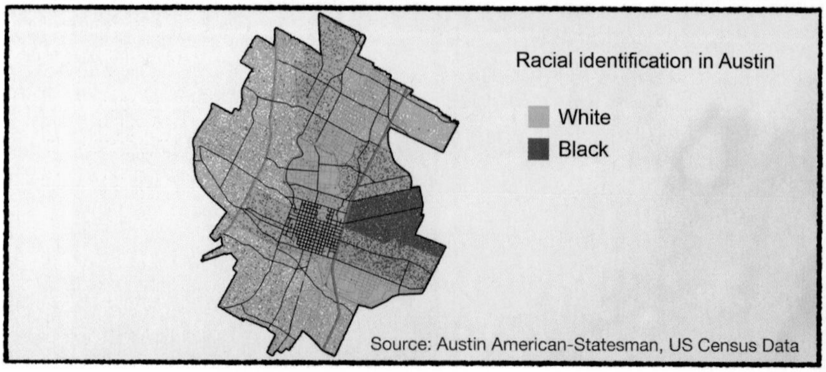
Racial identification in Austin
White
Black
Source: Austin American-Statesman, US Census Data

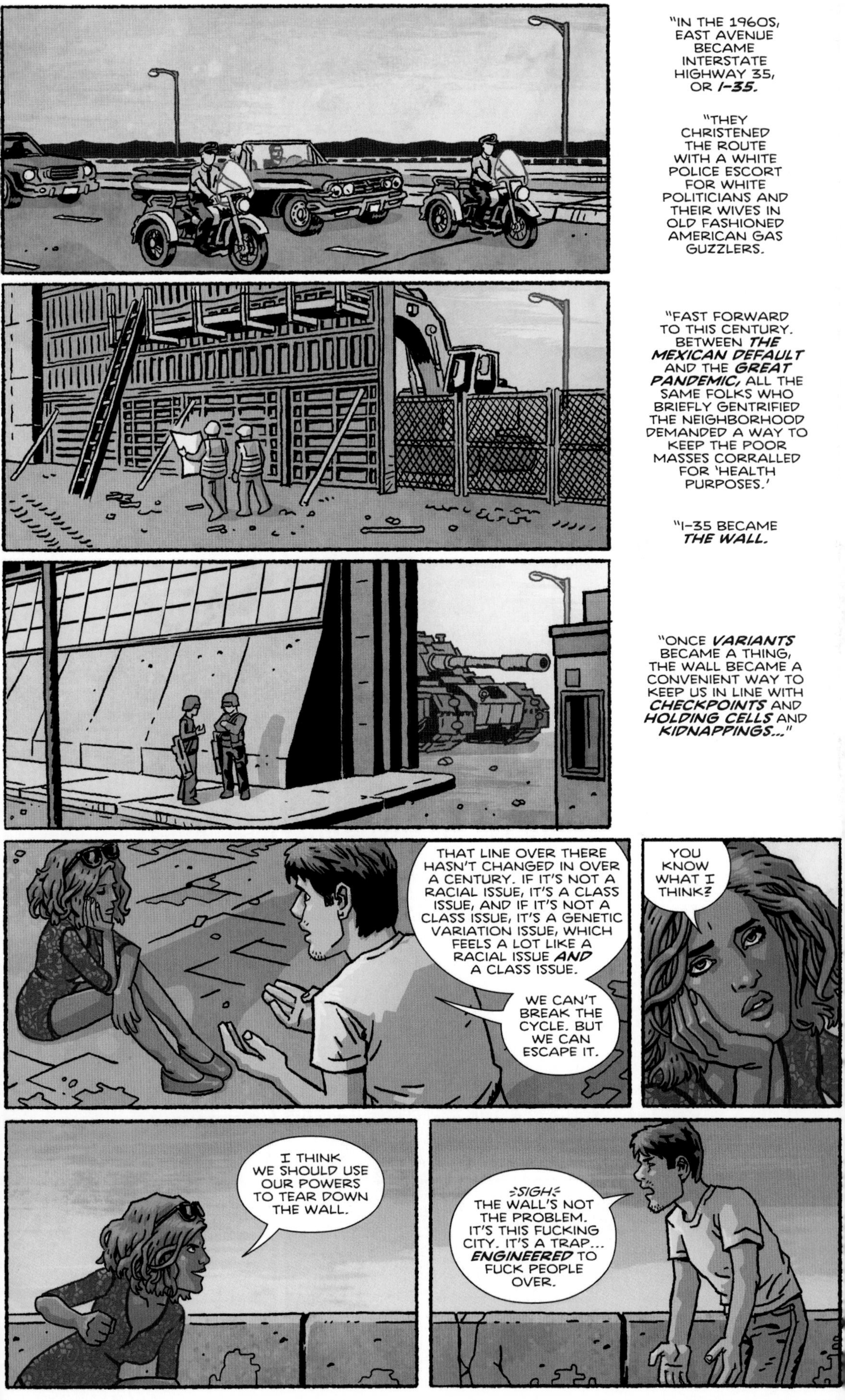
"IN THE 1960S, EAST AVENUE BECAME INTERSTATE HIGHWAY 35, OR *I-35.*
"THEY CHRISTENED THE ROUTE WITH A WHITE POLICE ESCORT FOR WHITE POLITICIANS AND THEIR WIVES IN OLD FASHIONED AMERICAN GAS GUZZLERS.
"FAST FORWARD TO THIS CENTURY. BETWEEN *THE MEXICAN DEFAULT* AND THE *GREAT PANDEMIC,* ALL THE SAME FOLKS WHO BRIEFLY GENTRIFIED THE NEIGHBORHOOD DEMANDED A WAY TO KEEP THE POOR MASSES CORRALLED FOR 'HEALTH PURPOSES.'
"I-35 BECAME *THE WALL.*
"ONCE *VARIANTS* BECAME A THING, THE WALL BECAME A CONVENIENT WAY TO KEEP US IN LINE WITH *CHECKPOINTS* AND *HOLDING CELLS* AND *KIDNAPPINGS...*"
THAT LINE OVER THERE HASN'T CHANGED IN OVER A CENTURY. IF IT'S NOT A RACIAL ISSUE, IT'S A CLASS ISSUE, AND IF IT'S NOT A CLASS ISSUE, IT'S A GENETIC VARIATION ISSUE, WHICH FEELS A LOT LIKE A RACIAL ISSUE *AND* A CLASS ISSUE.
WE CAN'T BREAK THE CYCLE. BUT WE CAN ESCAPE IT.
YOU KNOW WHAT I THINK?
I THINK WE SHOULD USE OUR POWERS TO TEAR DOWN THE WALL.
SIGH
THE WALL'S NOT THE PROBLEM. IT'S THIS FUCKING CITY. IT'S A TRAP... *ENGINEERED* TO FUCK PEOPLE OVER.

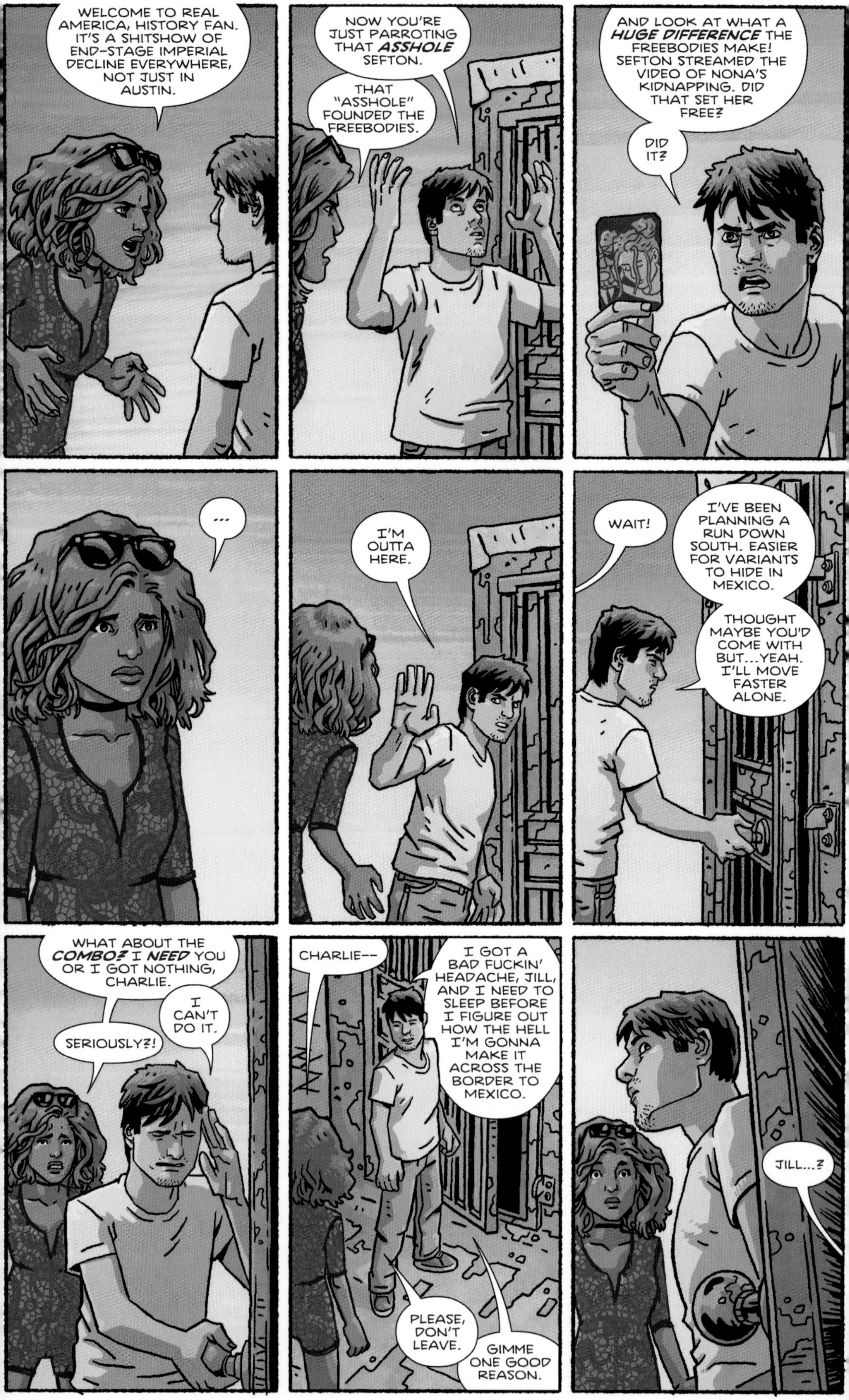
WELCOME TO REAL AMERICA, HISTORY FAN. IT'S A SHITSHOW OF END-STAGE IMPERIAL DECLINE EVERYWHERE, NOT JUST IN AUSTIN.
NOW YOU'RE JUST PARROTING THAT *ASSHOLE* SEFTON.
THAT "ASSHOLE" FOUNDED THE FREEBODIES.
AND LOOK AT WHAT A ***HUGE DIFFERENCE*** THE FREEBODIES MAKE! SEFTON STREAMED THE VIDEO OF NONA'S KIDNAPPING. DID THAT SET HER FREE?
DID IT?
...
I'M OUTTA HERE.
WAIT!
I'VE BEEN PLANNING A RUN DOWN SOUTH. EASIER FOR VARIANTS TO HIDE IN MEXICO.
THOUGHT MAYBE YOU'D COME WITH BUT... YEAH. I'LL MOVE FASTER ALONE.
WHAT ABOUT THE ***COMBO?*** I ***NEED*** YOU OR I GOT NOTHING, CHARLIE.
I CAN'T DO IT.
SERIOUSLY?!
CHARLIE--
I GOT A BAD FUCKIN' HEADACHE, JILL, AND I NEED TO SLEEP BEFORE I FIGURE OUT HOW THE HELL I'M GONNA MAKE IT ACROSS THE BORDER TO MEXICO.
PLEASE, DON'T LEAVE.
GIMME ONE GOOD REASON.
JILL...?

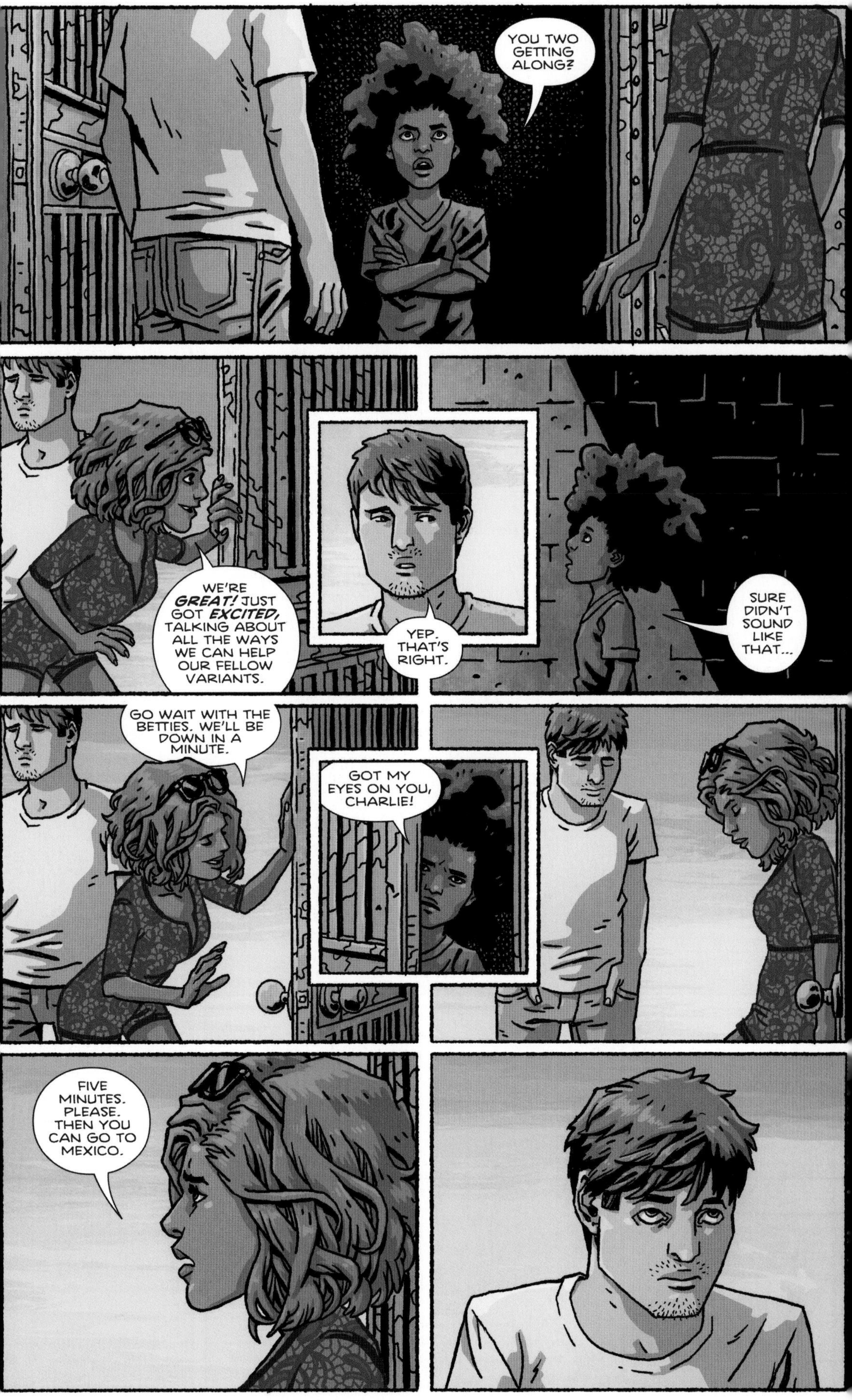
YOU TWO GETTING ALONG?
WE'RE *GREAT!* JUST GOT *EXCITED,* TALKING ABOUT ALL THE WAYS WE CAN HELP OUR FELLOW VARIANTS.
YEP. THAT'S RIGHT.
SURE DIDN'T SOUND LIKE THAT...
GO WAIT WITH THE BETTIES. WE'LL BE DOWN IN A MINUTE.
GOT MY EYES ON YOU, CHARLIE!
FIVE MINUTES. PLEASE. THEN YOU CAN GO TO MEXICO.

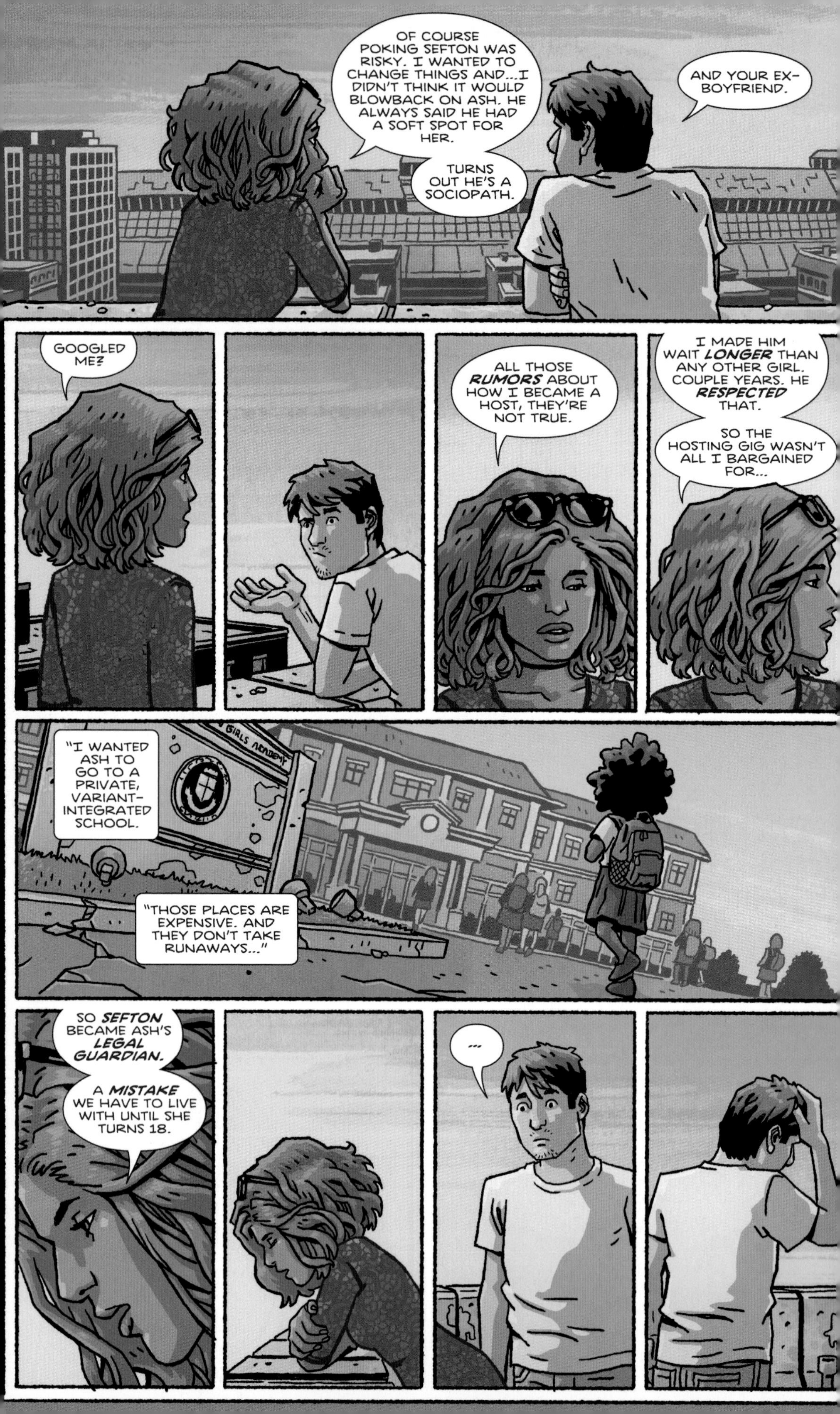

OF COURSE POKING SEFTON WAS RISKY. I WANTED TO CHANGE THINGS AND...I DIDN'T THINK IT WOULD BLOWBACK ON ASH. HE ALWAYS SAID HE HAD A SOFT SPOT FOR HER.
TURNS OUT HE'S A SOCIOPATH.
AND YOUR EX-BOYFRIEND.
GOOGLED ME?
ALL THOSE RUMORS ABOUT HOW I BECAME A HOST, THEY'RE NOT TRUE.
I MADE HIM WAIT LONGER THAN ANY OTHER GIRL. COUPLE YEARS. HE RESPECTED THAT.
SO THE HOSTING GIG WASN'T ALL I BARGAINED FOR...
"I WANTED ASH TO GO TO A PRIVATE, VARIANT-INTEGRATED SCHOOL.
GIRLS ACADEMY
"THOSE PLACES ARE EXPENSIVE. AND THEY DON'T TAKE RUNAWAYS..."
SO SEFTON BECAME ASH'S LEGAL GUARDIAN.
A MISTAKE WE HAVE TO LIVE WITH UNTIL SHE TURNS 18.
...

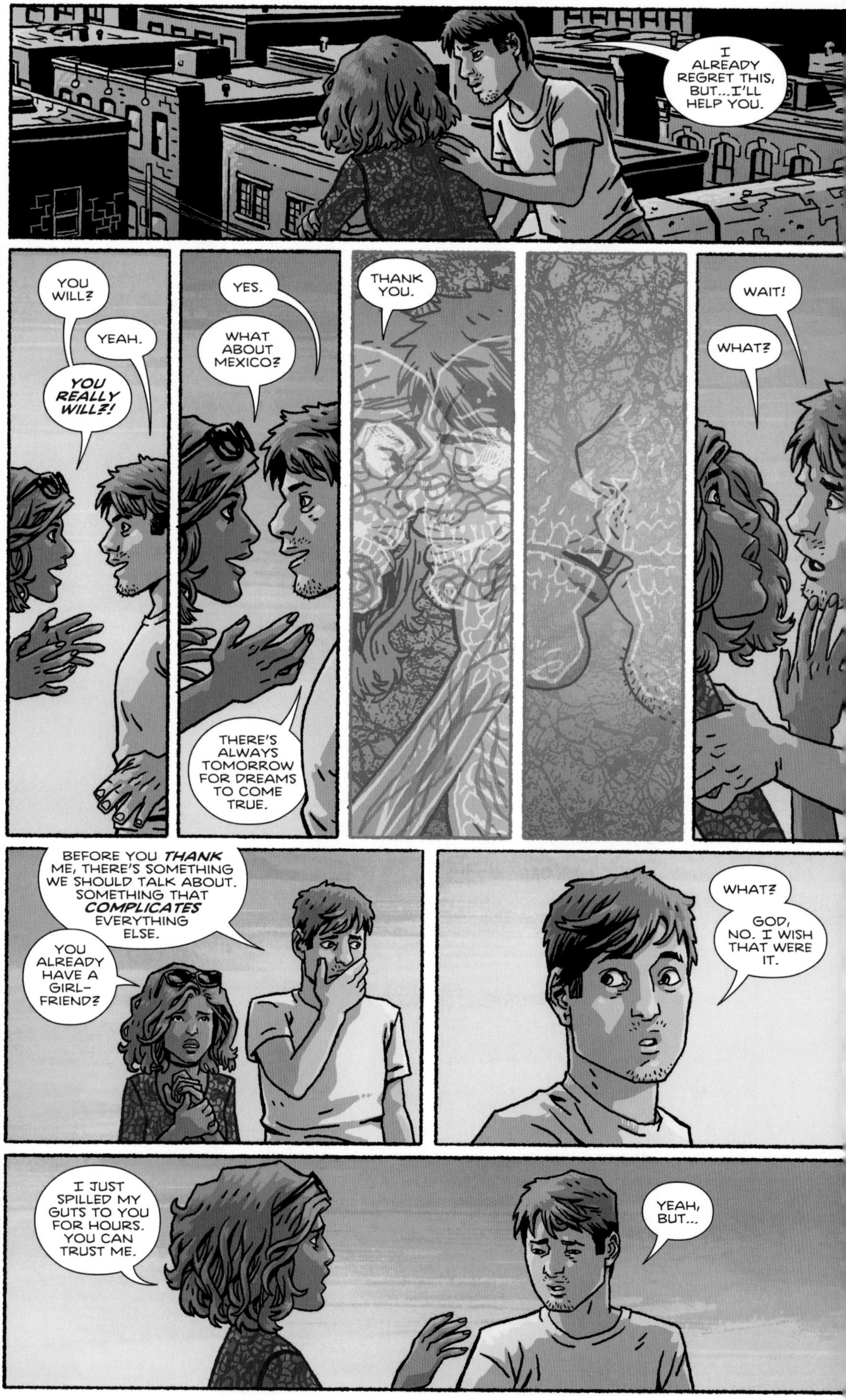

I ALREADY REGRET THIS, BUT...I'LL HELP YOU.
YOU WILL?
YEAH.
YOU REALLY WILL?!
YES.
WHAT ABOUT MEXICO?
THERE'S ALWAYS TOMORROW FOR DREAMS TO COME TRUE.
THANK YOU.
WAIT!
WHAT?
BEFORE YOU THANK ME, THERE'S SOMETHING WE SHOULD TALK ABOUT. SOMETHING THAT COMPLICATES EVERYTHING ELSE.
YOU ALREADY HAVE A GIRL-FRIEND?
WHAT?
GOD, NO. I WISH THAT WERE IT.
I JUST SPILLED MY GUTS TO YOU FOR HOURS. YOU CAN TRUST ME.
YEAH, BUT...

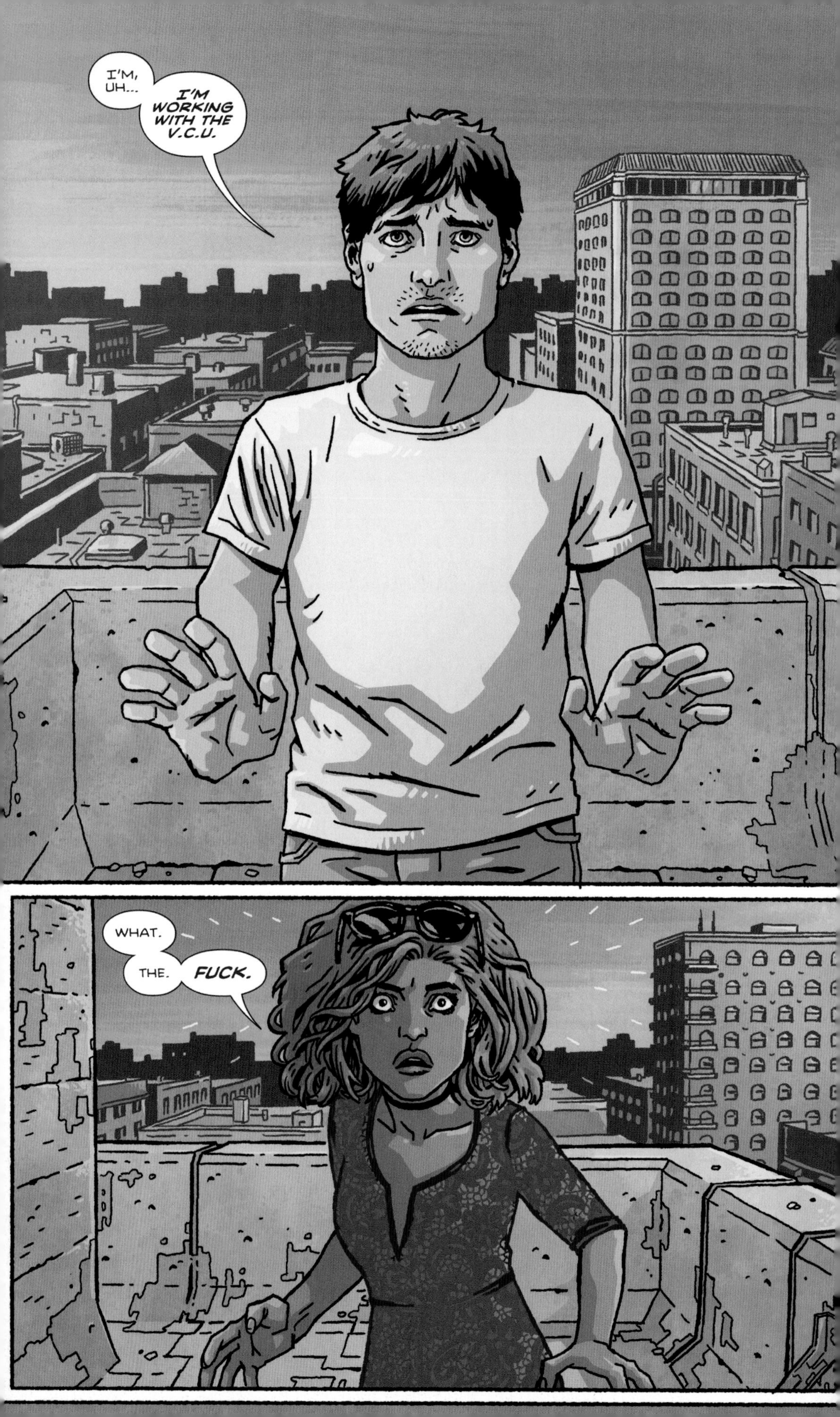
I'M, UH...
I'M WORKING WITH THE V.C.U.
WHAT.
THE.
FUCK.

CARNAGE REPORT

9:34 AM

U.S.A. Local Freedom Watch Pods Vids Options

VIOLENCE AGAINST THE VCU RISING

FREEBODIES AREN'T SO PEACEFUL AFTER ALL

By Sara-Beth Tompkinson

The Austin Variant Crimes Unit released new data today indicating a 74 percent rise in reports of violent attacks committed by civilians against uniformed VCU members in the city of Austin. The total number of attacks this year was 33, up from last year's count of 19. Every suspect in all 33 reports was a member of the Freebodies Variant supremacists movement.

"We've become soft on this community," said Austin VCU Captain Ramon Ruiz. "The Non-Lethal Act has emboldened left -wing extremists, and that's why we have Freebodies lobbing bricks at men and women in blue. For what? Proudly serving this community, folks. Keeping the peace and defending our national values against dangerous revolutionaries."

These statistics match trends in cities across Texas since the passage of TX SJR 2905, more commonly known as the "Non-Lethal Act" or "SJW 2905" for notoriously banning the use of lethal ammunition by police officers. The passage of SJR 2905 was universally denounced by GOP members of the State House and Senate, conservative icons, police unions, and the NRA. The unpopularity of this act led to the Red Wave that overturned a brief but seismic era of Democratic Party leadership across the Texas state legislature in the last election cycle.

Mainstream media has dogged the Austin VCU despite their use of non-lethal ammunition. Most recently, the non-lethal shock ammunition now utilized by the Austin VCU was accused of being "frequently deadly and deeply problematic" by Freebodies founder Sefton Smith.

Carnage Report did some testing of our own (available at this link). No subjects were killed across all our tests, which were personally executed by famed firearms expert, Marco Rambin, host of the popular stream, Rambin's Rules. Rambin himself even gamely requested a mouth guard and asked to be shot with a shock round. The celebrity host went bare-chested and drew a target over his heart. His assistant shot him directly on target and Rambin fell to the ground. Only moments later, he was back on his feet, concluding: "The shock ammo is completely safe."

Sefton Smith and the Freebodies continue to exaggerate the lethality of the Austin VCU's non-lethal ammo. But between our testing and the Austin VCU's statistics, it's not the VCU that people need to worry about. It's angry Freebodies turning violent, first against our men and women in blue, and next against our God-given rights as ordinary Americans.

_____ Published 11:19 AM ET, Wed Dec 09

ANM US News Trending Features Opinions Live TV Options

Cops Or Kidnappers?

Alarming reports of VCU-related disappearances prompt independent investigation by the Variant Minority Law center

By Jared Nissenbaum, ANM
Updated 7:01 PM ET, Mon December 7

(ANM) - A string of high-profile cases of missing Freebodies activists has Variants across America on edge. Nowhere is that tension felt more deeply than Austin, where a record 394 Freebodies have been reported missing this year.

Of those 394 cases, more than 60% of the Freebodies are reported to have disappeared after being arrested by the Austin VCU. In some cases, such as the arrest of political artist Nona Shaker, we have video evidence to corroborate claims that she was last seen being arrested by the VCU. Yet, Nona Shaker has not contacted her lawyer, her family, her friends, or her millions of social media followers. She has vanished.

When asked about Nona Shaker's status, Captain Ramon Ruiz of the Austin VCU replied, "I can confirm that Nona Shaker was arrested for graffiti, vandalism, and destruction of public property, as seen on your little video. She pleaded guilty on all counts, and now she's obliged to serve her time in the state correctional system."

There is no account of Nona Shaker's charges, trial, or guilty plea, nor is there any account of occupancy within the state correctional system. Information requests relayed to the state legislature and Governor Pritchard's office have all been denied.

Now, a legal team from the Variant Minority Law Center has begun an independent investigation to find out where Nona and her fellow missing Freebodies have gone. The VMLC is a non-profit initiative co-funded by Sefton Smith, founder and CEO of the Freebodies, who has frequently alleged that the Austin VCU is systematically campaigning to suppress protected speech in East Austin.

Candisse Williamson, a senior representative for the VMLC, offered the following statement regarding the investigation: "We know the Austin VCU uses shock rounds that were banned in 17 states for being too lethal to qualify as non-lethal ammunition. We know that Freebodies are being shocked and arrested, and then they're disappearing. We know that Governor Pritchard and her party accept millions in donations from private prison corporations, arms manufacturers, and the NRA."

She continues, "What we don't know is what Governor Pritchard and the Austin VCU have done with 394 Freebodies who went missing this year. Are they alive? Are they in jail? We don't know… but we will find our missing brothers and sisters. We will not give up on a single one. We will not forget them. This is America, and we demand to know where the government is hiding these people."

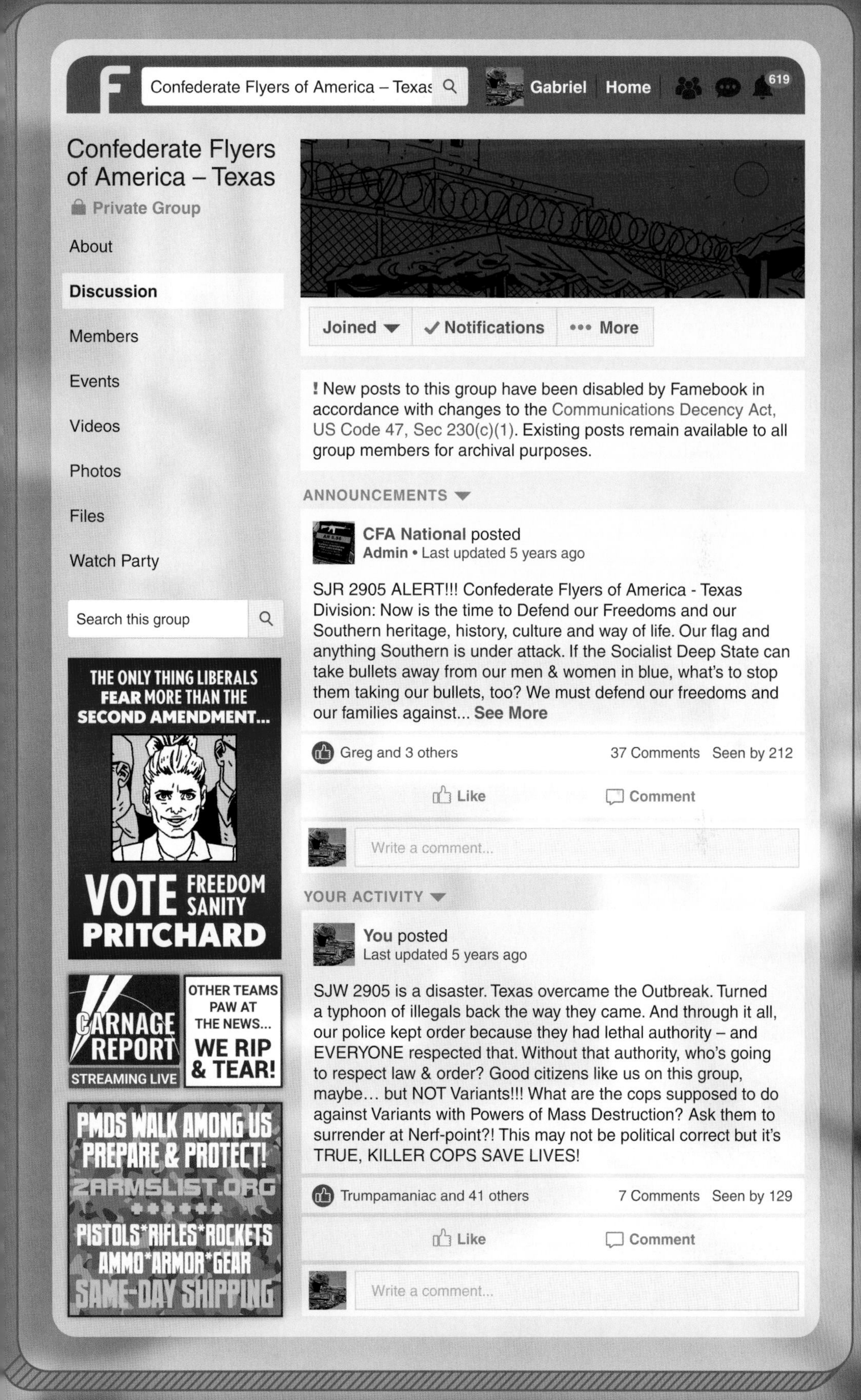
Confederate Flyers of America – Texas
Gabriel
Home
619
Confederate Flyers of America – Texas
Private Group
About
Discussion
Members
Events
Videos
Photos
Files
Watch Party
Search this group
THE ONLY THING LIBERALS FEAR MORE THAN THE SECOND AMENDMENT...
VOTE FREEDOM SANITY PRITCHARD
CARNAGE REPORT
STREAMING LIVE
OTHER TEAMS PAW AT THE NEWS...
WE RIP & TEAR!
PMDS WALK AMONG US
PREPARE & PROTECT!
2ARMSLIST.ORG
PISTOLS*RIFLES*ROCKETS
AMMO*ARMOR*GEAR
SAME-DAY SHIPPING
Joined
Notifications
More
! New posts to this group have been disabled by Famebook in accordance with changes to the Communications Decency Act, US Code 47, Sec 230(c)(1). Existing posts remain available to all group members for archival purposes.
ANNOUNCEMENTS
CFA National posted
Admin • Last updated 5 years ago
SJR 2905 ALERT!!! Confederate Flyers of America - Texas Division: Now is the time to Defend our Freedoms and our Southern heritage, history, culture and way of life. Our flag and anything Southern is under attack. If the Socialist Deep State can take bullets away from our men & women in blue, what's to stop them taking our bullets, too? We must defend our freedoms and our families against... See More
Greg and 3 others
37 Comments
Seen by 212
Like
Comment
Write a comment...
YOUR ACTIVITY
You posted
Last updated 5 years ago
SJW 2905 is a disaster. Texas overcame the Outbreak. Turned a typhoon of illegals back the way they came. And through it all, our police kept order because they had lethal authority – and EVERYONE respected that. Without that authority, who's going to respect law & order? Good citizens like us on this group, maybe… but NOT Variants!!! What are the cops supposed to do against Variants with Powers of Mass Destruction? Ask them to surrender at Nerf-point?! This may not be political correct but it's TRUE, KILLER COPS SAVE LIVES!
Trumpamaniac and 41 others
7 Comments
Seen by 129
Like
Comment
Write a comment...

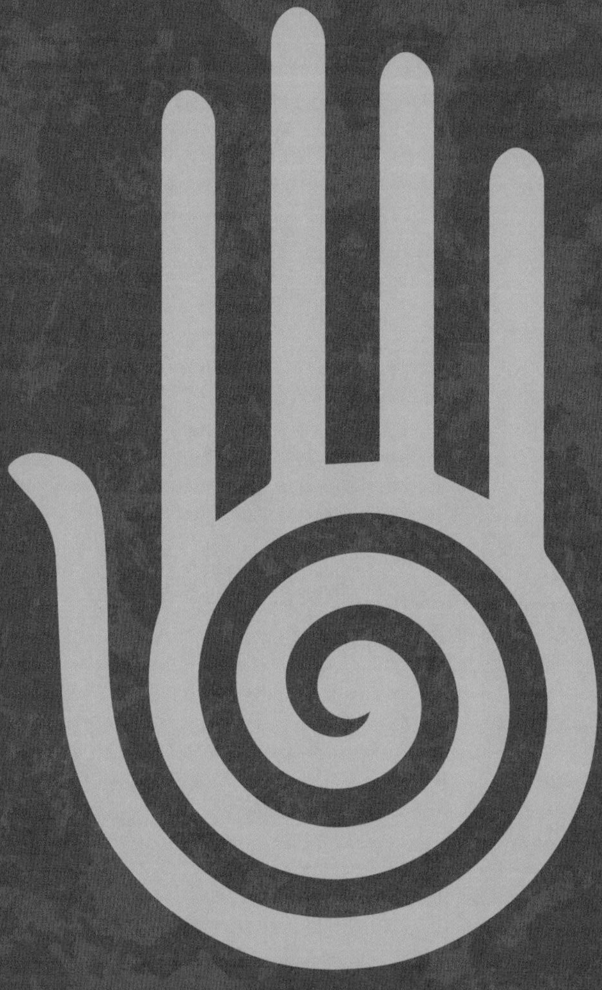

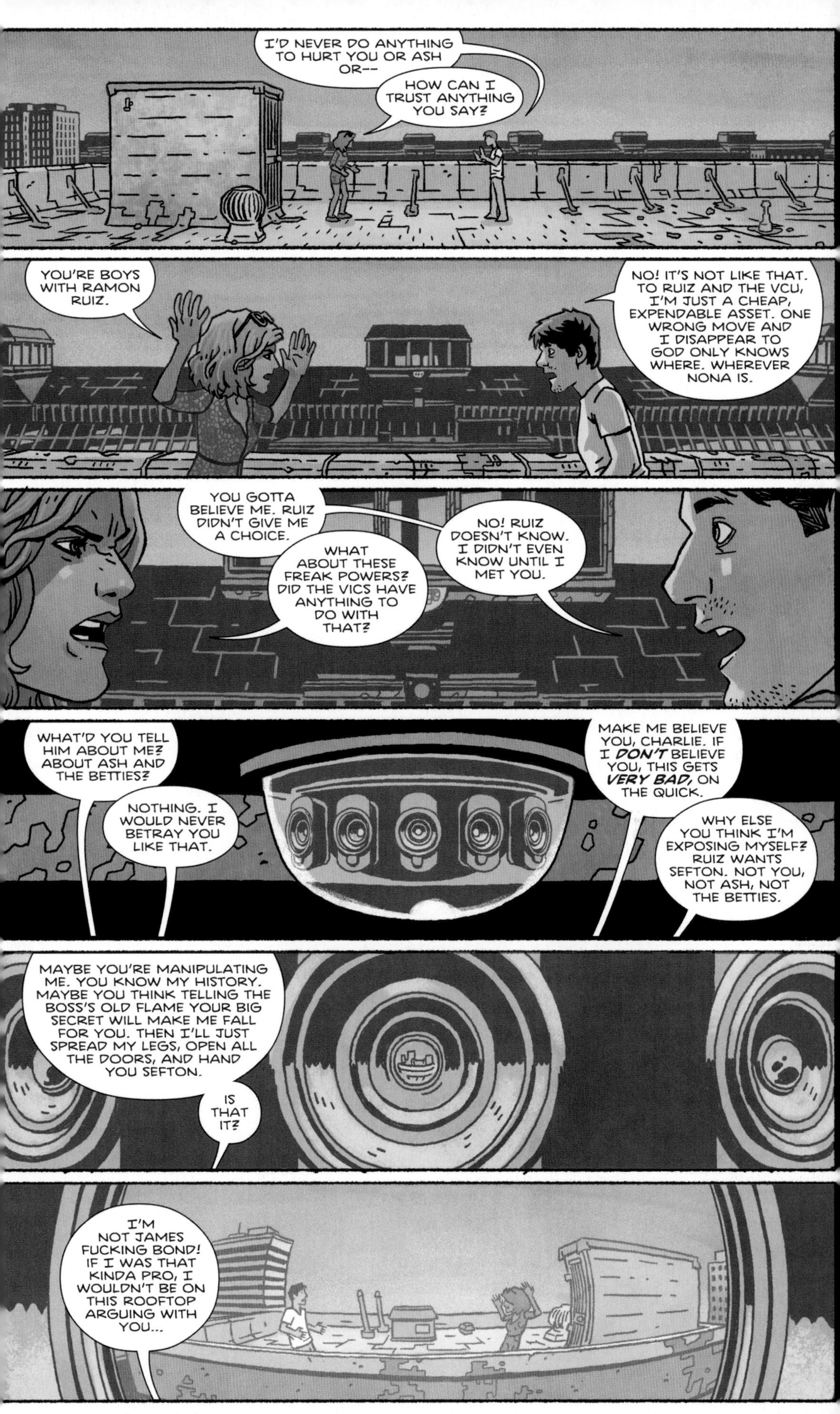
I'D NEVER DO ANYTHING TO HURT YOU OR ASH OR--
HOW CAN I TRUST ANYTHING YOU SAY?
YOU'RE BOYS WITH RAMON RUIZ.
NO! IT'S NOT LIKE THAT. TO RUIZ AND THE VCU, I'M JUST A CHEAP, EXPENDABLE ASSET. ONE WRONG MOVE AND I DISAPPEAR TO GOD ONLY KNOWS WHERE. WHEREVER NONA IS.
YOU GOTTA BELIEVE ME. RUIZ DIDN'T GIVE ME A CHOICE.
WHAT ABOUT THESE FREAK POWERS? DID THE VICS HAVE ANYTHING TO DO WITH THAT?
NO! RUIZ DOESN'T KNOW. I DIDN'T EVEN KNOW UNTIL I MET YOU.
WHAT'D YOU TELL HIM ABOUT ME? ABOUT ASH AND THE BETTIES?
NOTHING. I WOULD NEVER BETRAY YOU LIKE THAT.
MAKE ME BELIEVE YOU, CHARLIE. IF I DON'T BELIEVE YOU, THIS GETS VERY BAD, ON THE QUICK.
WHY ELSE YOU THINK I'M EXPOSING MYSELF? RUIZ WANTS SEFTON. NOT YOU, NOT ASH, NOT THE BETTIES.
MAYBE YOU'RE MANIPULATING ME. YOU KNOW MY HISTORY. MAYBE YOU THINK TELLING THE BOSS'S OLD FLAME YOUR BIG SECRET WILL MAKE ME FALL FOR YOU. THEN I'LL JUST SPREAD MY LEGS, OPEN ALL THE DOORS, AND HAND YOU SEFTON.
IS THAT IT?
I'M NOT JAMES FUCKING BOND! IF I WAS THAT KINDA PRO, I WOULDN'T BE ON THIS ROOFTOP ARGUING WITH YOU...

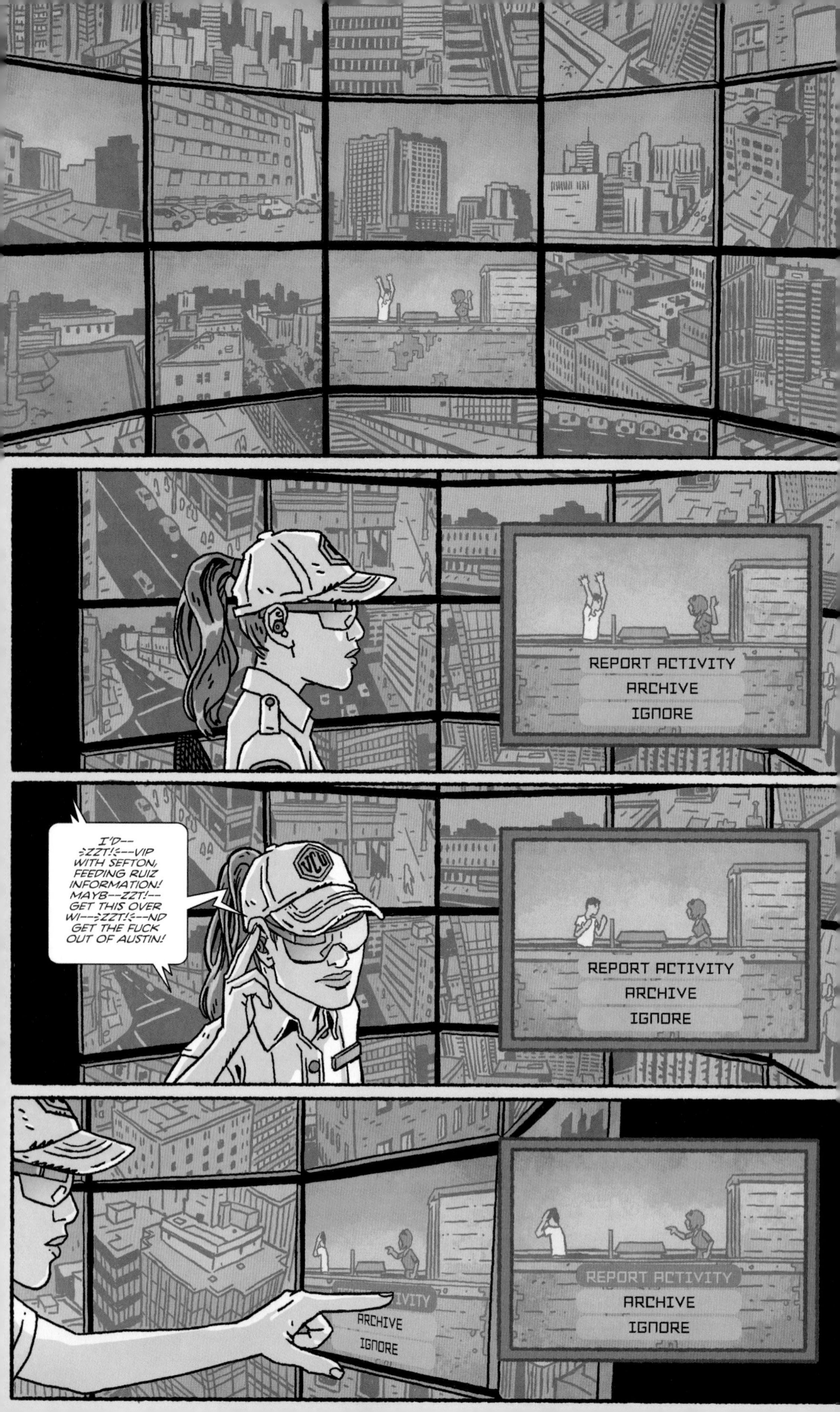
REPORT ACTIVITY
ARCHIVE
IGNORE
I'D-- ›ZZT!‹--VIP WITH SEFTON, FEEDING RUIZ INFORMATION! MAYB--ZZT!-- GET THIS OVER WI--›ZZT!‹--ND GET THE FUCK OUT OF AUSTIN!
REPORT ACTIVITY
ARCHIVE
IGNORE
ARCHIVE
IGNORE
REPORT ACTIVITY
ARCHIVE
IGNORE

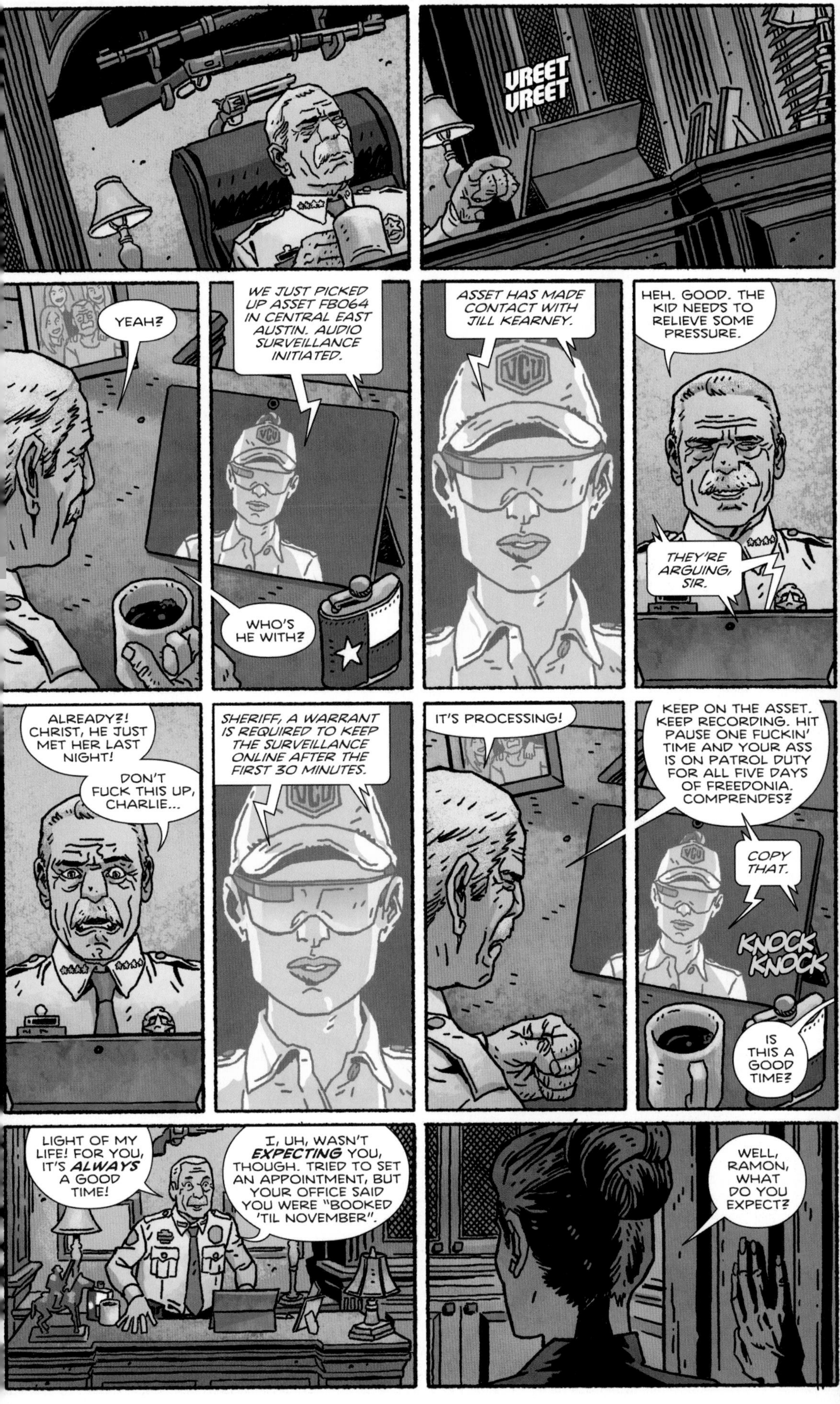
VREET VREET
YEAH?
WE JUST PICKED UP ASSET FB064 IN CENTRAL EAST AUSTIN. AUDIO SURVEILLANCE INITIATED.
WHO'S HE WITH?
ASSET HAS MADE CONTACT WITH JILL KEARNEY.
HEH. GOOD. THE KID NEEDS TO RELIEVE SOME PRESSURE.
THEY'RE ARGUING, SIR.
ALREADY?! CHRIST, HE JUST MET HER LAST NIGHT!
DON'T FUCK THIS UP, CHARLIE...
SHERIFF, A WARRANT IS REQUIRED TO KEEP THE SURVEILLANCE ONLINE AFTER THE FIRST 30 MINUTES.
IT'S PROCESSING!
KEEP ON THE ASSET. KEEP RECORDING. HIT PAUSE ONE FUCKIN' TIME AND YOUR ASS IS ON PATROL DUTY FOR ALL FIVE DAYS OF FREEDONIA. COMPRENDES?
COPY THAT.
KNOCK KNOCK
IS THIS A GOOD TIME?
LIGHT OF MY LIFE! FOR YOU, IT'S ALWAYS A GOOD TIME!
I, UH, WASN'T EXPECTING YOU, THOUGH. TRIED TO SET AN APPOINTMENT, BUT YOUR OFFICE SAID YOU WERE "BOOKED 'TIL NOVEMBER".
WELL, RAMON, WHAT DO YOU EXPECT?

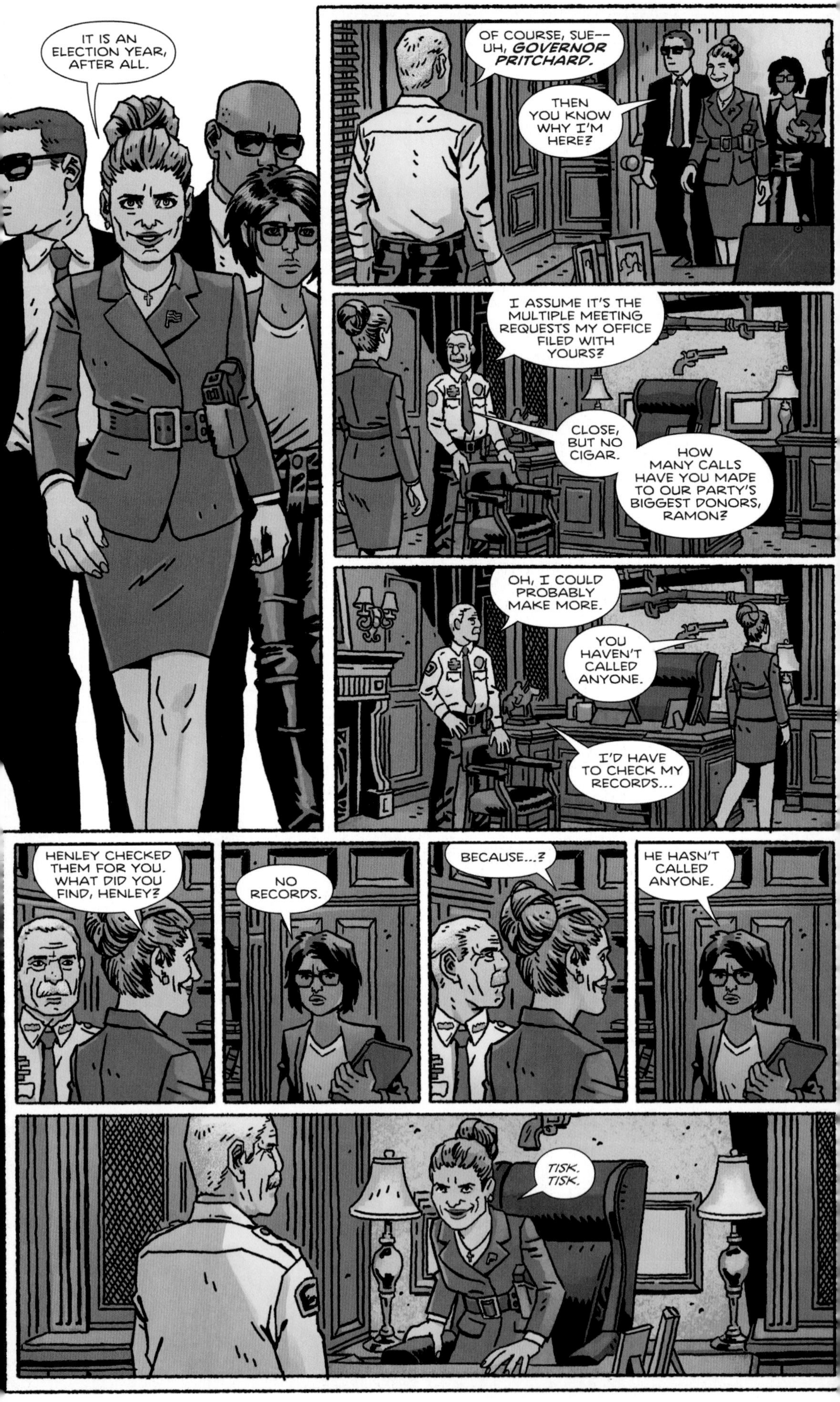
IT IS AN ELECTION YEAR, AFTER ALL.
OF COURSE, SUE-- UH, *GOVERNOR PRITCHARD.*
THEN YOU KNOW WHY I'M HERE?
I ASSUME IT'S THE MULTIPLE MEETING REQUESTS MY OFFICE FILED WITH YOURS?
CLOSE, BUT NO CIGAR.
HOW MANY CALLS HAVE YOU MADE TO OUR PARTY'S BIGGEST DONORS, RAMON?
OH, I COULD PROBABLY MAKE MORE.
YOU HAVEN'T CALLED ANYONE.
I'D HAVE TO CHECK MY RECORDS...
HENLEY CHECKED THEM FOR YOU. WHAT DID YOU FIND, HENLEY?
NO RECORDS.
BECAUSE...?
HE HASN'T CALLED ANYONE.
TISK. TISK.

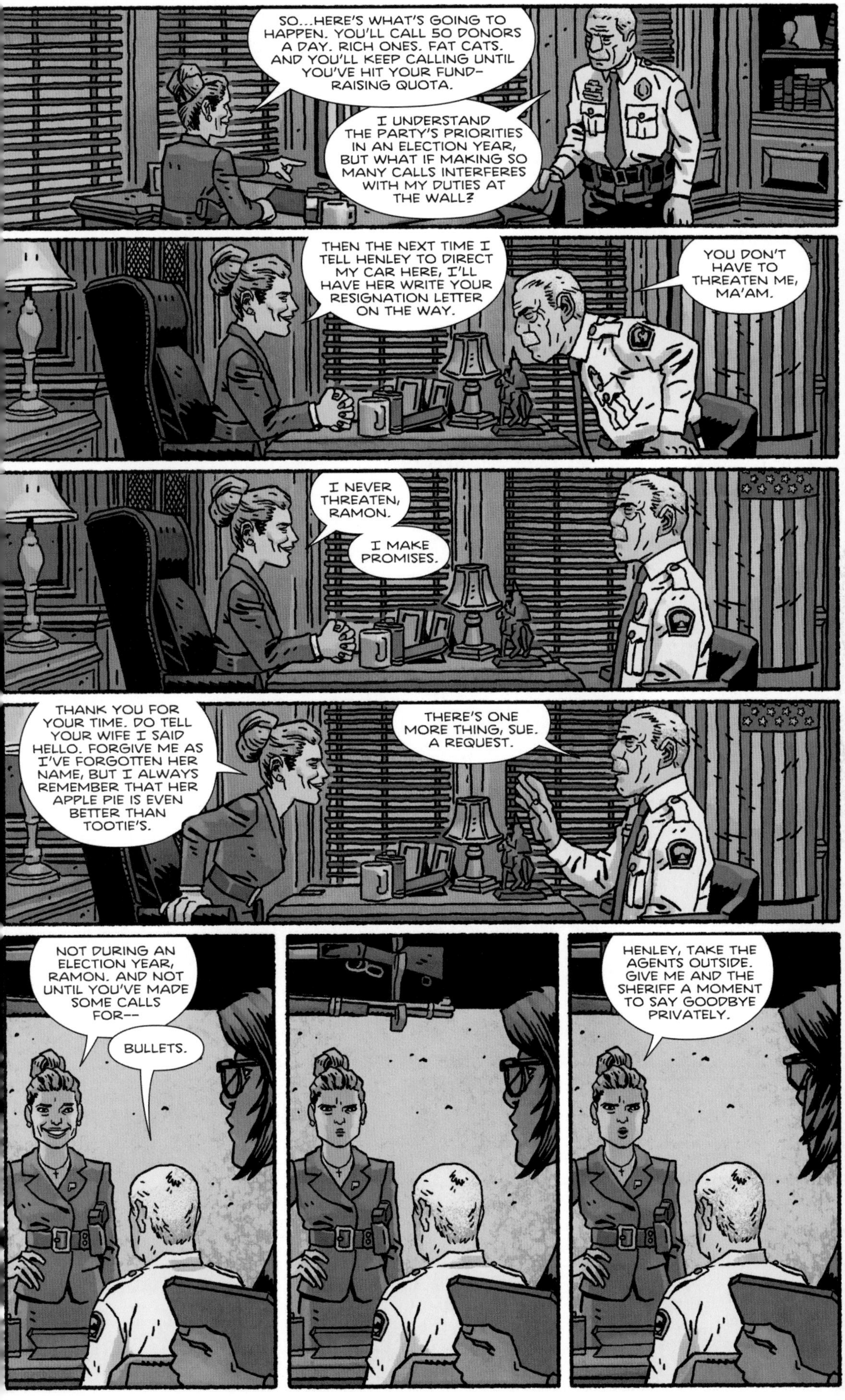
SO...HERE'S WHAT'S GOING TO HAPPEN. YOU'LL CALL 50 DONORS A DAY. RICH ONES. FAT CATS. AND YOU'LL KEEP CALLING UNTIL YOU'VE HIT YOUR FUND-RAISING QUOTA.
I UNDERSTAND THE PARTY'S PRIORITIES IN AN ELECTION YEAR, BUT WHAT IF MAKING SO MANY CALLS INTERFERES WITH MY DUTIES AT THE WALL?
THEN THE NEXT TIME I TELL HENLEY TO DIRECT MY CAR HERE, I'LL HAVE HER WRITE YOUR RESIGNATION LETTER ON THE WAY.
YOU DON'T HAVE TO THREATEN ME, MA'AM.
I NEVER THREATEN, RAMON.
I MAKE PROMISES.
THANK YOU FOR YOUR TIME. DO TELL YOUR WIFE I SAID HELLO. FORGIVE ME AS I'VE FORGOTTEN HER NAME, BUT I ALWAYS REMEMBER THAT HER APPLE PIE IS EVEN BETTER THAN TOOTIE'S.
THERE'S ONE MORE THING, SUE. A REQUEST.
NOT DURING AN ELECTION YEAR, RAMON. AND NOT UNTIL YOU'VE MADE SOME CALLS FOR--
BULLETS.
HENLEY, TAKE THE AGENTS OUTSIDE. GIVE ME AND THE SHERIFF A MOMENT TO SAY GOODBYE PRIVATELY.

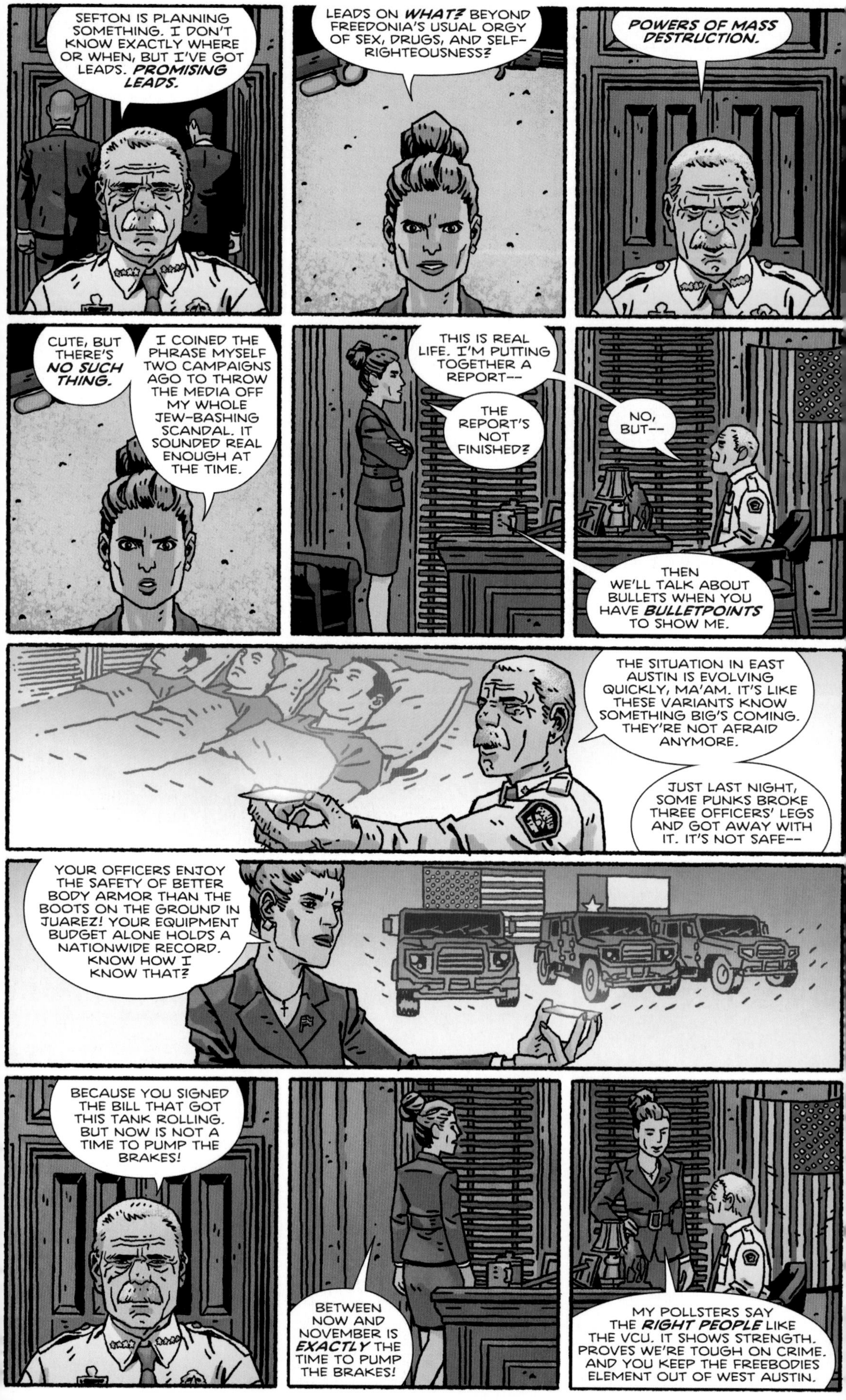
SEFTON IS PLANNING SOMETHING. I DON'T KNOW EXACTLY WHERE OR WHEN, BUT I'VE GOT LEADS. PROMISING LEADS.
LEADS ON WHAT? BEYOND FREEDONIA'S USUAL ORGY OF SEX, DRUGS, AND SELF-RIGHTEOUSNESS?
POWERS OF MASS DESTRUCTION.
CUTE, BUT THERE'S NO SUCH THING.
I COINED THE PHRASE MYSELF TWO CAMPAIGNS AGO TO THROW THE MEDIA OFF MY WHOLE JEW-BASHING SCANDAL. IT SOUNDED REAL ENOUGH AT THE TIME.
THIS IS REAL LIFE. I'M PUTTING TOGETHER A REPORT--
THE REPORT'S NOT FINISHED?
NO, BUT--
THEN WE'LL TALK ABOUT BULLETS WHEN YOU HAVE BULLETPOINTS TO SHOW ME.
THE SITUATION IN EAST AUSTIN IS EVOLVING QUICKLY, MA'AM. IT'S LIKE THESE VARIANTS KNOW SOMETHING BIG'S COMING. THEY'RE NOT AFRAID ANYMORE.
JUST LAST NIGHT, SOME PUNKS BROKE THREE OFFICERS' LEGS AND GOT AWAY WITH IT. IT'S NOT SAFE--
YOUR OFFICERS ENJOY THE SAFETY OF BETTER BODY ARMOR THAN THE BOOTS ON THE GROUND IN JUAREZ! YOUR EQUIPMENT BUDGET ALONE HOLDS A NATIONWIDE RECORD. KNOW HOW I KNOW THAT?
BECAUSE YOU SIGNED THE BILL THAT GOT THIS TANK ROLLING. BUT NOW IS NOT A TIME TO PUMP THE BRAKES!
BETWEEN NOW AND NOVEMBER IS EXACTLY THE TIME TO PUMP THE BRAKES!
MY POLLSTERS SAY THE RIGHT PEOPLE LIKE THE VCU. IT SHOWS STRENGTH. PROVES WE'RE TOUGH ON CRIME. AND YOU KEEP THE FREEBODIES ELEMENT OUT OF WEST AUSTIN.

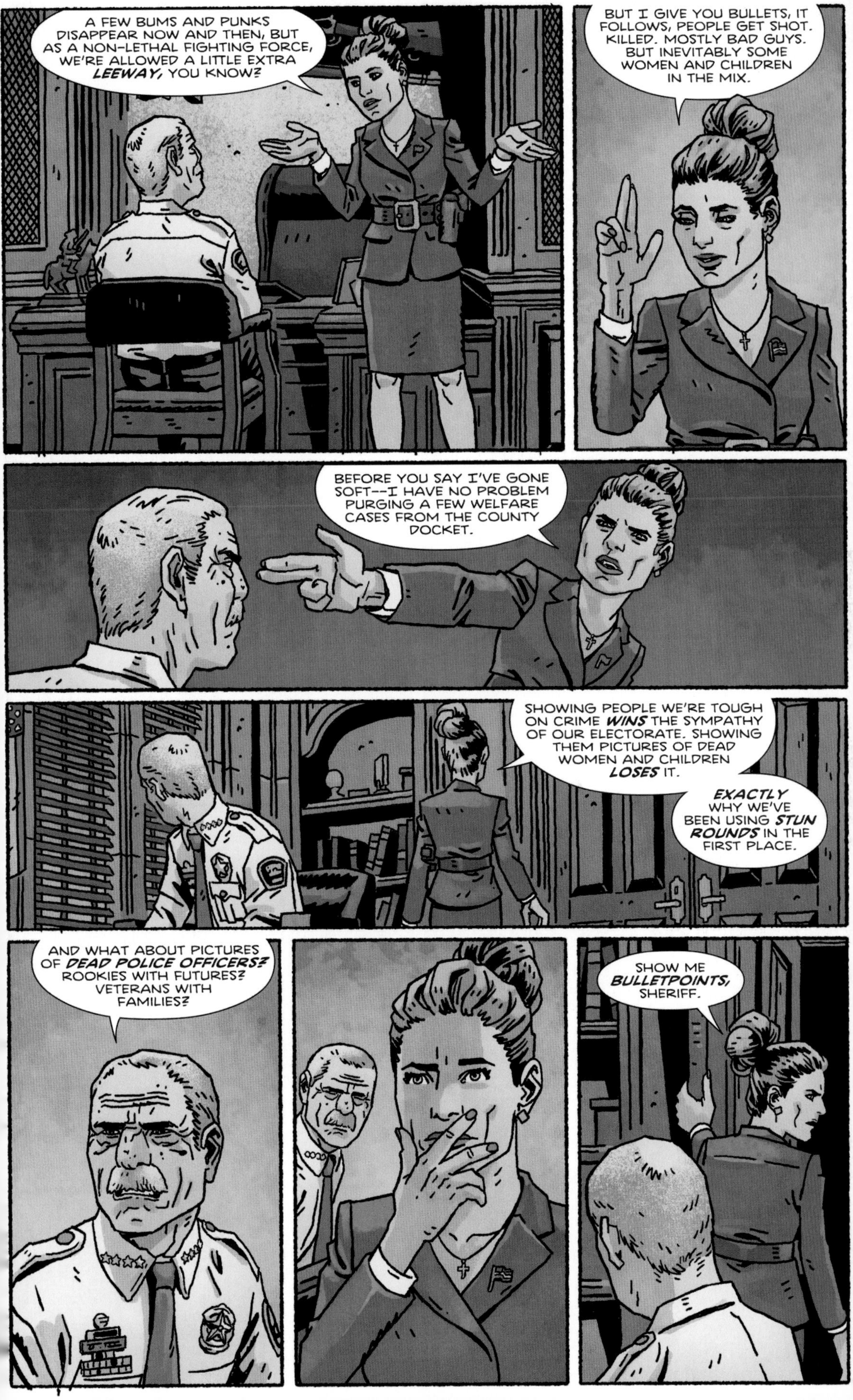
A FEW BUMS AND PUNKS DISAPPEAR NOW AND THEN, BUT AS A NON-LETHAL FIGHTING FORCE, WE'RE ALLOWED A LITTLE EXTRA *LEEWAY,* YOU KNOW?
BUT I GIVE YOU BULLETS, IT FOLLOWS, PEOPLE GET SHOT. KILLED. MOSTLY BAD GUYS. BUT INEVITABLY SOME WOMEN AND CHILDREN IN THE MIX.
BEFORE YOU SAY I'VE GONE SOFT--I HAVE NO PROBLEM PURGING A FEW WELFARE CASES FROM THE COUNTY DOCKET.
SHOWING PEOPLE WE'RE TOUGH ON CRIME *WINS* THE SYMPATHY OF OUR ELECTORATE. SHOWING THEM PICTURES OF DEAD WOMEN AND CHILDREN *LOSES* IT.
EXACTLY WHY WE'VE BEEN USING *STUN ROUNDS* IN THE FIRST PLACE.
AND WHAT ABOUT PICTURES OF *DEAD POLICE OFFICERS?* ROOKIES WITH FUTURES? VETERANS WITH FAMILIES?
SHOW ME *BULLETPOINTS,* SHERIFF.

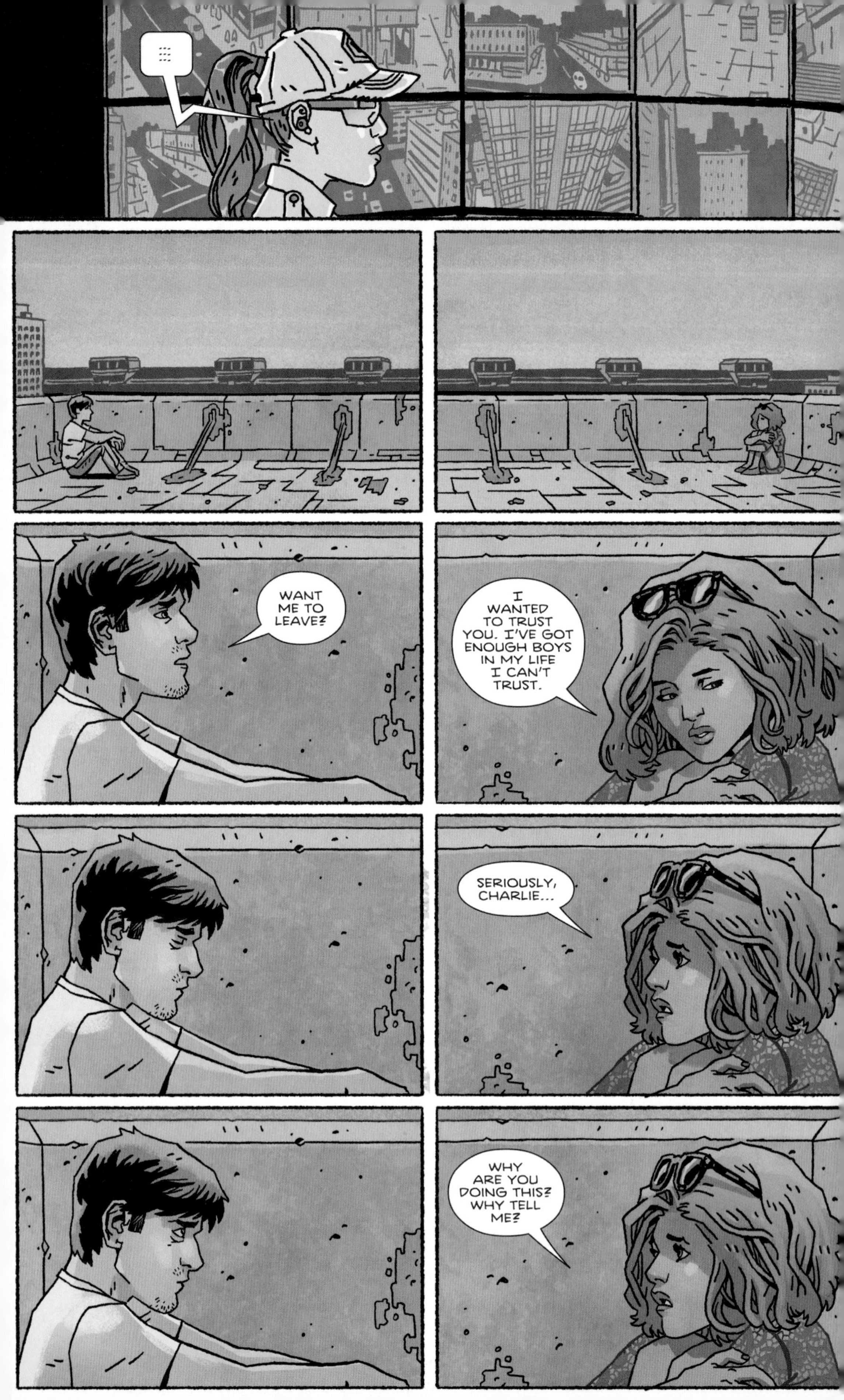
WANT ME TO LEAVE?
I WANTED TO TRUST YOU. I'VE GOT ENOUGH BOYS IN MY LIFE I CAN'T TRUST.
SERIOUSLY, CHARLIE...
WHY ARE YOU DOING THIS? WHY TELL ME?

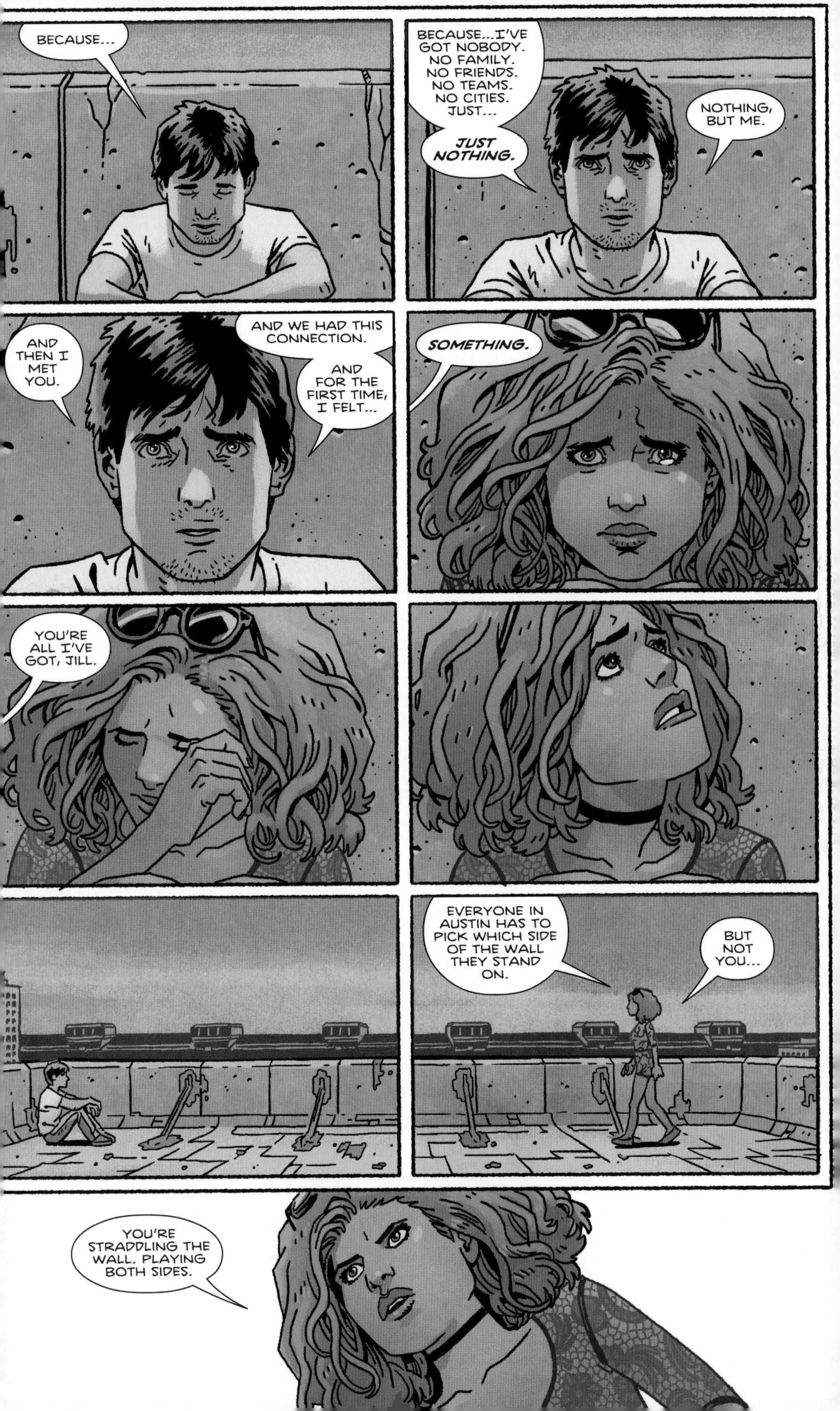
BECAUSE...
BECAUSE...I'VE GOT NOBODY. NO FAMILY. NO FRIENDS. NO TEAMS. NO CITIES. JUST...
JUST NOTHING.
NOTHING, BUT ME.
AND THEN I MET YOU.
AND WE HAD THIS CONNECTION.
AND FOR THE FIRST TIME, I FELT...
SOMETHING.
YOU'RE ALL I'VE GOT, JILL.
EVERYONE IN AUSTIN HAS TO PICK WHICH SIDE OF THE WALL THEY STAND ON.
BUT NOT YOU...
YOU'RE STRADDLING THE WALL. PLAYING BOTH SIDES.

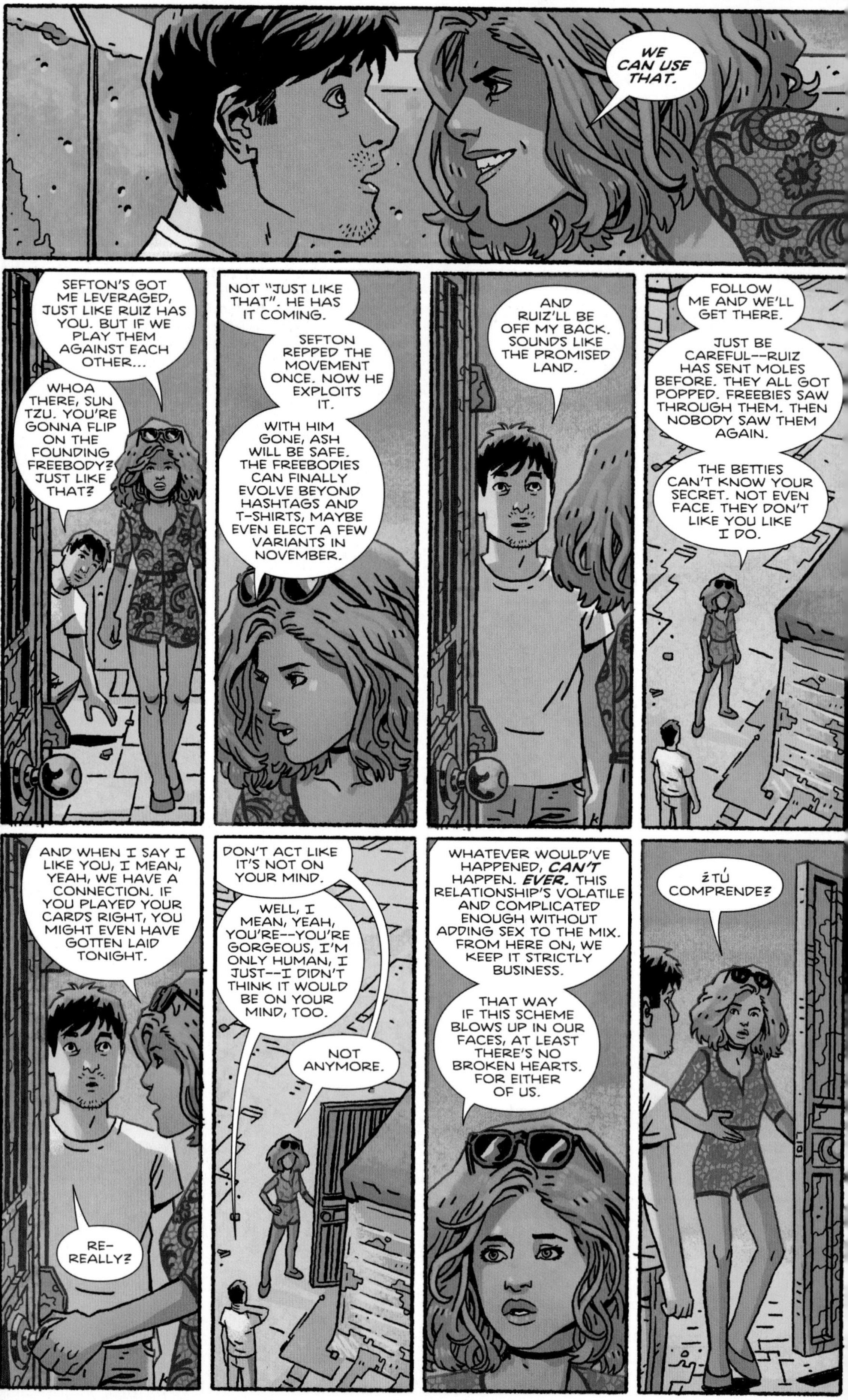
WE CAN USE THAT.
SEFTON'S GOT ME LEVERAGED, JUST LIKE RUIZ HAS YOU. BUT IF WE PLAY THEM AGAINST EACH OTHER...
WHOA THERE, SUN TZU. YOU'RE GONNA FLIP ON THE FOUNDING FREEBODY? JUST LIKE THAT?
NOT "JUST LIKE THAT". HE HAS IT COMING.
SEFTON REPPED THE MOVEMENT ONCE. NOW HE EXPLOITS IT.
WITH HIM GONE, ASH WILL BE SAFE. THE FREEBODIES CAN FINALLY EVOLVE BEYOND HASHTAGS AND T-SHIRTS, MAYBE EVEN ELECT A FEW VARIANTS IN NOVEMBER.
AND RUIZ'LL BE OFF MY BACK. SOUNDS LIKE THE PROMISED LAND.
FOLLOW ME AND WE'LL GET THERE.
JUST BE CAREFUL--RUIZ HAS SENT MOLES BEFORE. THEY ALL GOT POPPED. FREEBIES SAW THROUGH THEM. THEN NOBODY SAW THEM AGAIN.
THE BETTIES CAN'T KNOW YOUR SECRET. NOT EVEN FACE. THEY DON'T LIKE YOU LIKE I DO.
AND WHEN I SAY I LIKE YOU, I MEAN, YEAH, WE HAVE A CONNECTION. IF YOU PLAYED YOUR CARDS RIGHT, YOU MIGHT EVEN HAVE GOTTEN LAID TONIGHT.
RE-REALLY?
DON'T ACT LIKE IT'S NOT ON YOUR MIND.
WELL, I MEAN, YEAH, YOU'RE--YOU'RE GORGEOUS, I'M ONLY HUMAN, I JUST--I DIDN'T THINK IT WOULD BE ON YOUR MIND, TOO.
NOT ANYMORE.
WHATEVER WOULD'VE HAPPENED, CAN'T HAPPEN. EVER. THIS RELATIONSHIP'S VOLATILE AND COMPLICATED ENOUGH WITHOUT ADDING SEX TO THE MIX. FROM HERE ON, WE KEEP IT STRICTLY BUSINESS.
THAT WAY IF THIS SCHEME BLOWS UP IN OUR FACES, AT LEAST THERE'S NO BROKEN HEARTS. FOR EITHER OF US.
¿TÚ COMPRENDE?

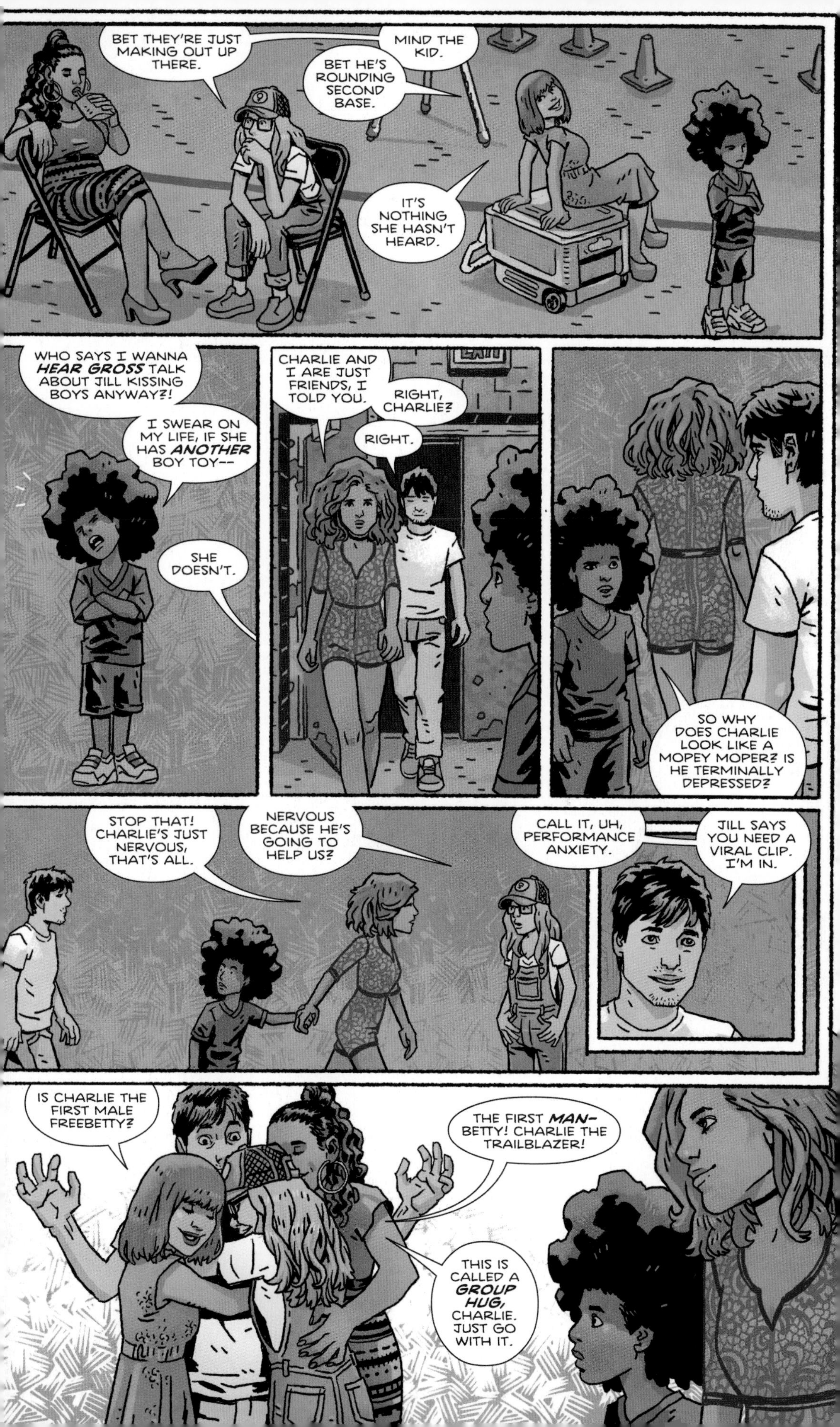
BET THEY'RE JUST MAKING OUT UP THERE.
MIND THE KID.
BET HE'S ROUNDING SECOND BASE.
IT'S NOTHING SHE HASN'T HEARD.
WHO SAYS I WANNA HEAR GROSS TALK ABOUT JILL KISSING BOYS ANYWAY?!
I SWEAR ON MY LIFE, IF SHE HAS ANOTHER BOY TOY--
SHE DOESN'T.
CHARLIE AND I ARE JUST FRIENDS, I TOLD YOU.
RIGHT, CHARLIE?
RIGHT.
SO WHY DOES CHARLIE LOOK LIKE A MOPEY MOPER? IS HE TERMINALLY DEPRESSED?
STOP THAT! CHARLIE'S JUST NERVOUS, THAT'S ALL.
NERVOUS BECAUSE HE'S GOING TO HELP US?
CALL IT, UH, PERFORMANCE ANXIETY.
JILL SAYS YOU NEED A VIRAL CLIP. I'M IN.
IS CHARLIE THE FIRST MALE FREEBETTY?
THE FIRST MAN-BETTY! CHARLIE THE TRAILBLAZER!
THIS IS CALLED A GROUP HUG, CHARLIE. JUST GO WITH IT.

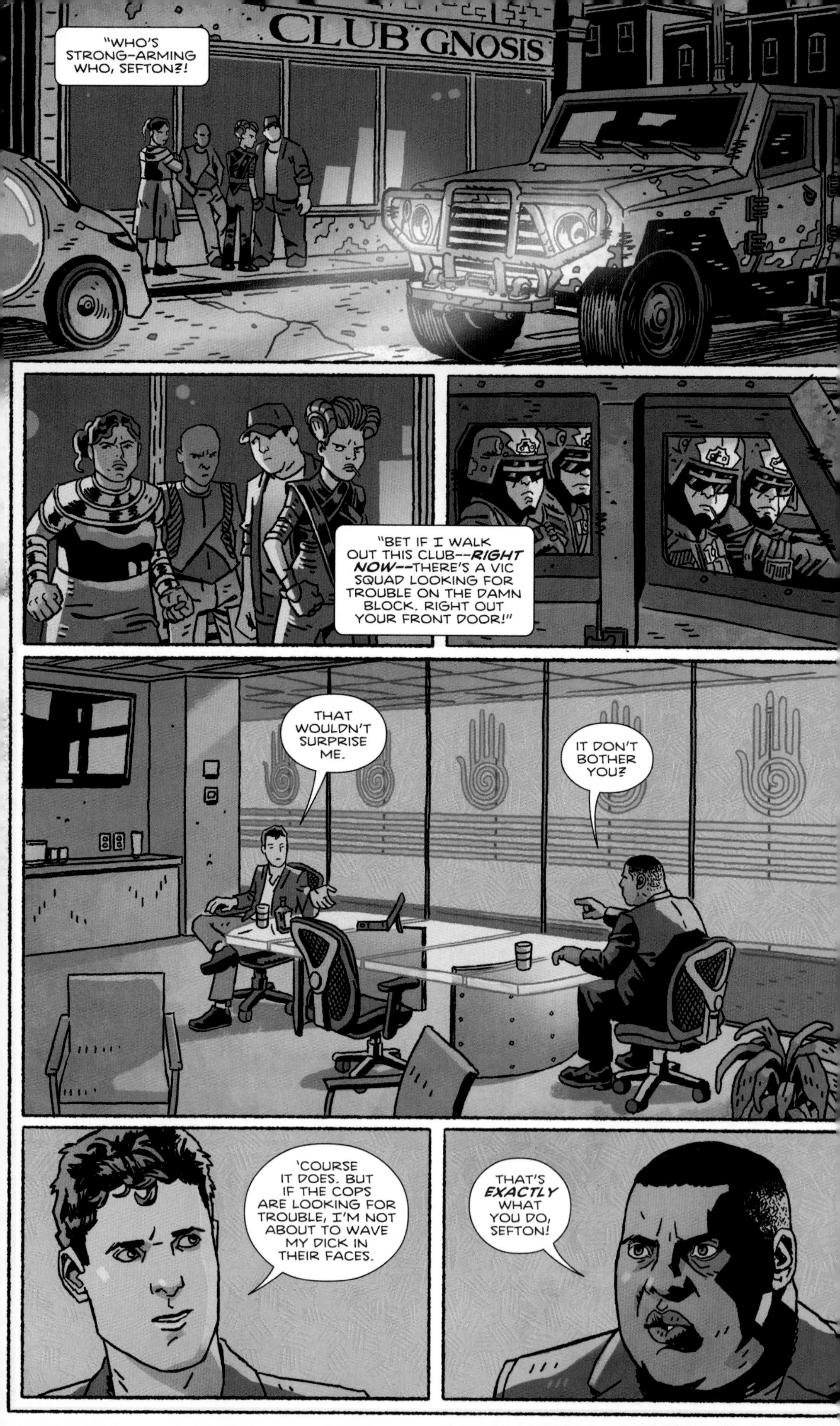
CLUB GNOSIS
"WHO'S STRONG-ARMING WHO, SEFTON?!
"BET IF I WALK OUT THIS CLUB--RIGHT NOW--THERE'S A VIC SQUAD LOOKING FOR TROUBLE ON THE DAMN BLOCK. RIGHT OUT YOUR FRONT DOOR!"
THAT WOULDN'T SURPRISE ME.
IT DON'T BOTHER YOU?
'COURSE IT DOES. BUT IF THE COPS ARE LOOKING FOR TROUBLE, I'M NOT ABOUT TO WAVE MY DICK IN THEIR FACES.
THAT'S EXACTLY WHAT YOU DO, SEFTON!

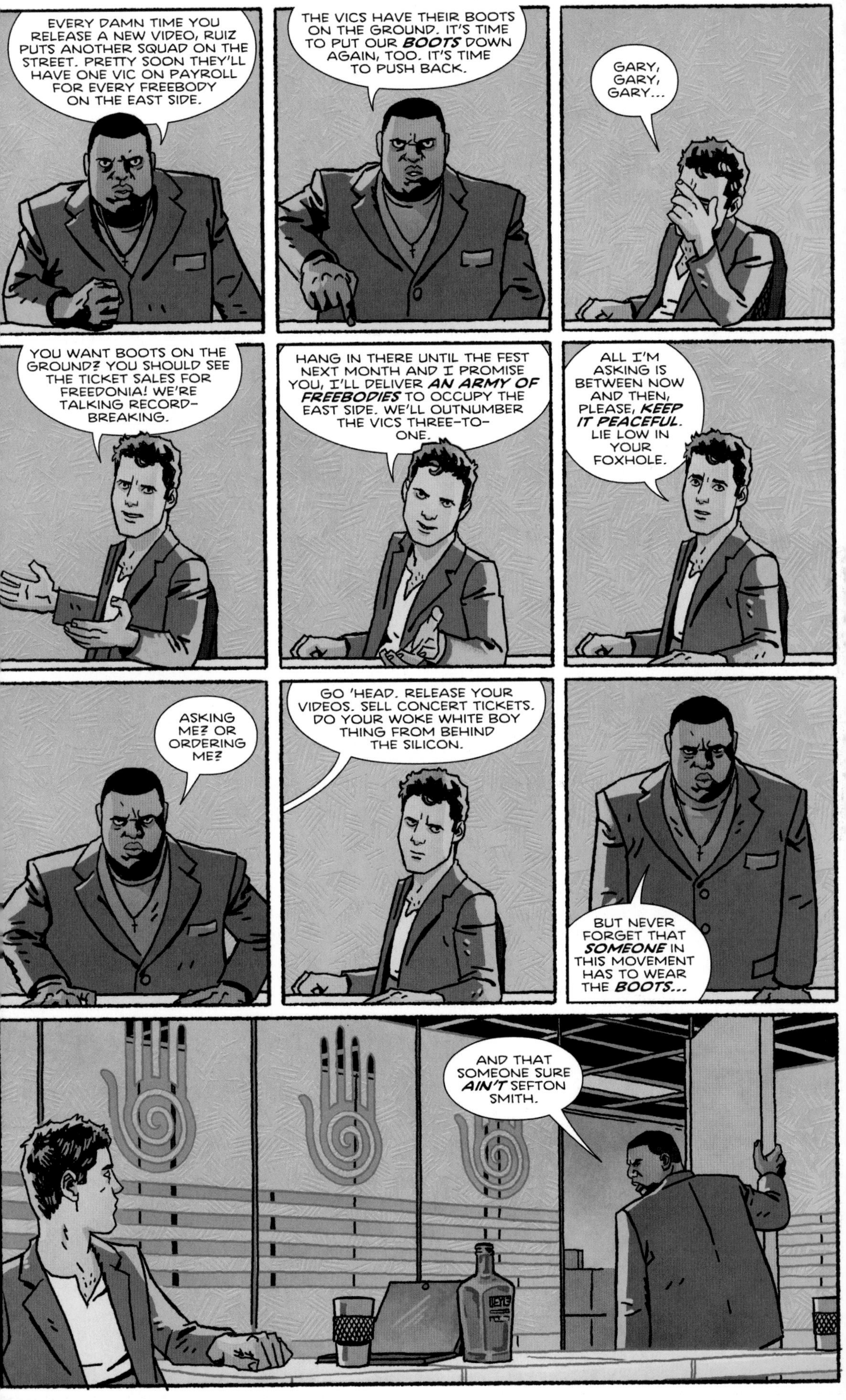
EVERY DAMN TIME YOU RELEASE A NEW VIDEO, RUIZ PUTS ANOTHER SQUAD ON THE STREET. PRETTY SOON THEY'LL HAVE ONE VIC ON PAYROLL FOR EVERY FREEBODY ON THE EAST SIDE.
THE VICS HAVE THEIR BOOTS ON THE GROUND. IT'S TIME TO PUT OUR BOOTS DOWN AGAIN, TOO. IT'S TIME TO PUSH BACK.
GARY, GARY, GARY...
YOU WANT BOOTS ON THE GROUND? YOU SHOULD SEE THE TICKET SALES FOR FREEDONIA! WE'RE TALKING RECORD-BREAKING.
HANG IN THERE UNTIL THE FEST NEXT MONTH AND I PROMISE YOU, I'LL DELIVER AN ARMY OF FREEBODIES TO OCCUPY THE EAST SIDE. WE'LL OUTNUMBER THE VICS THREE-TO-ONE.
ALL I'M ASKING IS BETWEEN NOW AND THEN, PLEASE, KEEP IT PEACEFUL. LIE LOW IN YOUR FOXHOLE.
ASKING ME? OR ORDERING ME?
GO 'HEAD. RELEASE YOUR VIDEOS. SELL CONCERT TICKETS. DO YOUR WOKE WHITE BOY THING FROM BEHIND THE SILICON.
BUT NEVER FORGET THAT SOMEONE IN THIS MOVEMENT HAS TO WEAR THE BOOTS...
AND THAT SOMEONE SURE AIN'T SEFTON SMITH.

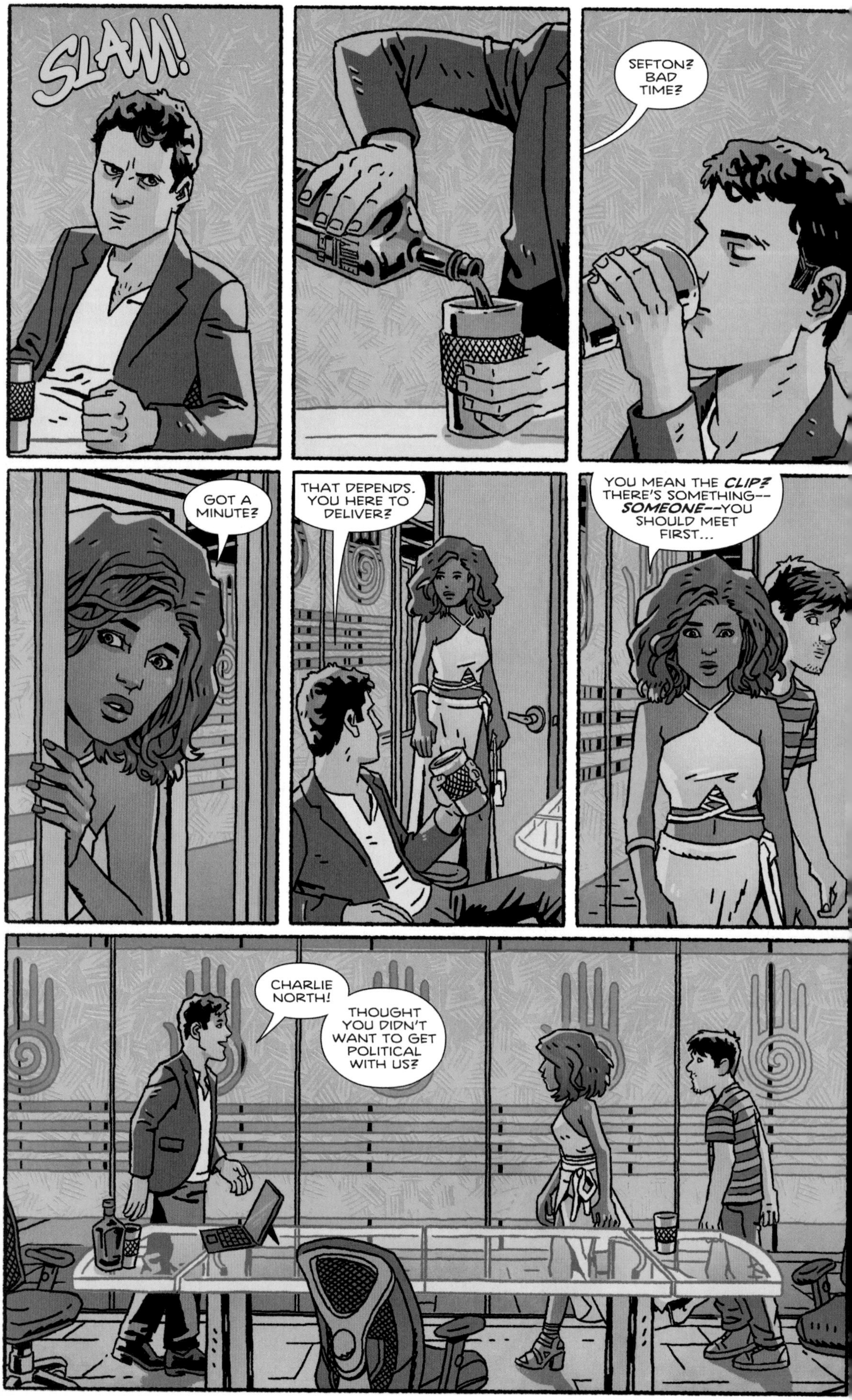
SLAM!
SEFTON? BAD TIME?
GOT A MINUTE?
THAT DEPENDS. YOU HERE TO DELIVER?
YOU MEAN THE *CLIP?* THERE'S SOMETHING-- ***SOMEONE***--YOU SHOULD MEET FIRST...
CHARLIE NORTH!
THOUGHT YOU DIDN'T WANT TO GET POLITICAL WITH US?

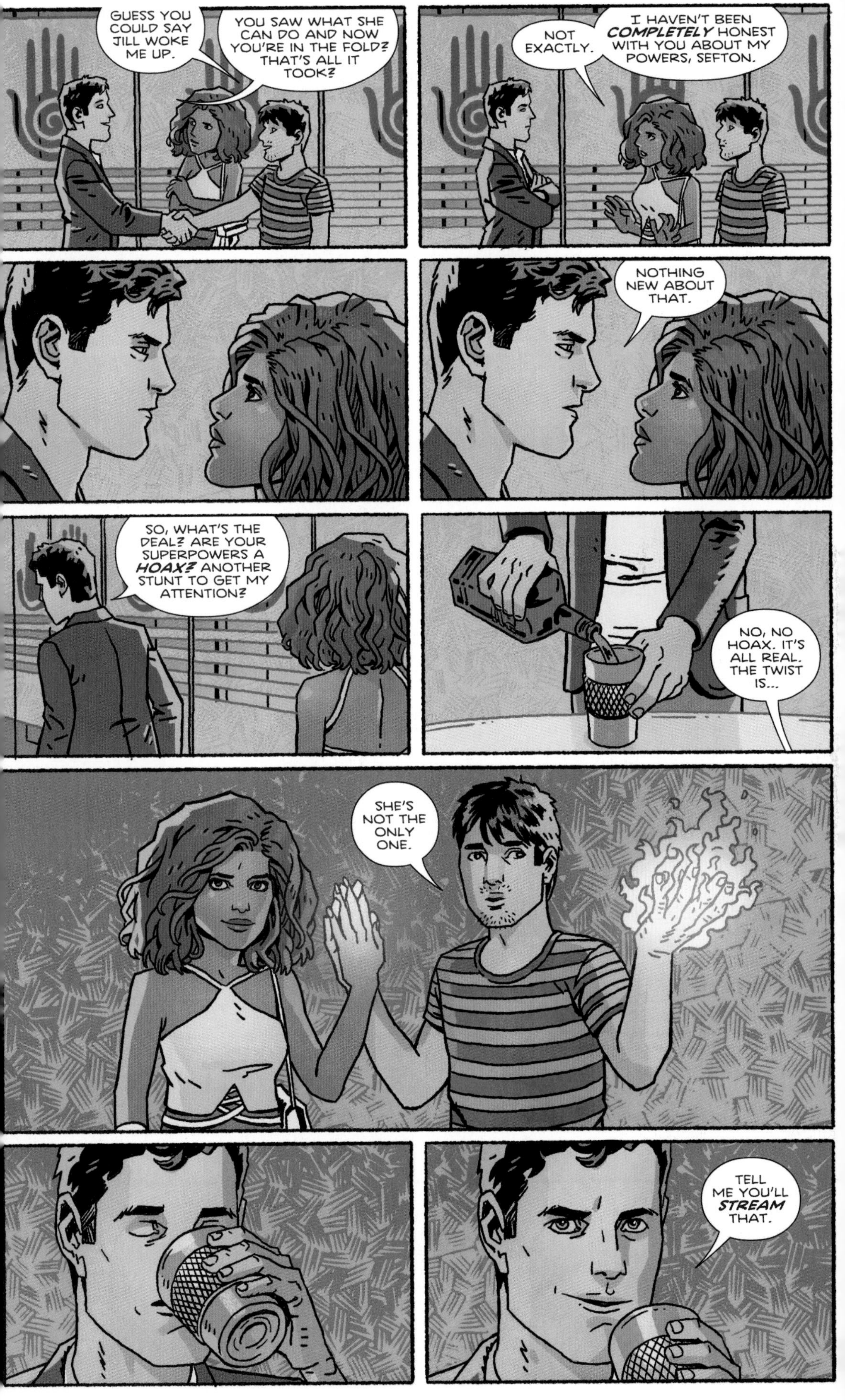
GUESS YOU COULD SAY JILL WOKE ME UP.
YOU SAW WHAT SHE CAN DO AND NOW YOU'RE IN THE FOLD? THAT'S ALL IT TOOK?
NOT EXACTLY.
I HAVEN'T BEEN COMPLETELY HONEST WITH YOU ABOUT MY POWERS, SEFTON.
NOTHING NEW ABOUT THAT.
SO, WHAT'S THE DEAL? ARE YOUR SUPERPOWERS A HOAX? ANOTHER STUNT TO GET MY ATTENTION?
NO, NO HOAX. IT'S ALL REAL. THE TWIST IS...
SHE'S NOT THE ONLY ONE.
TELL ME YOU'LL STREAM THAT.

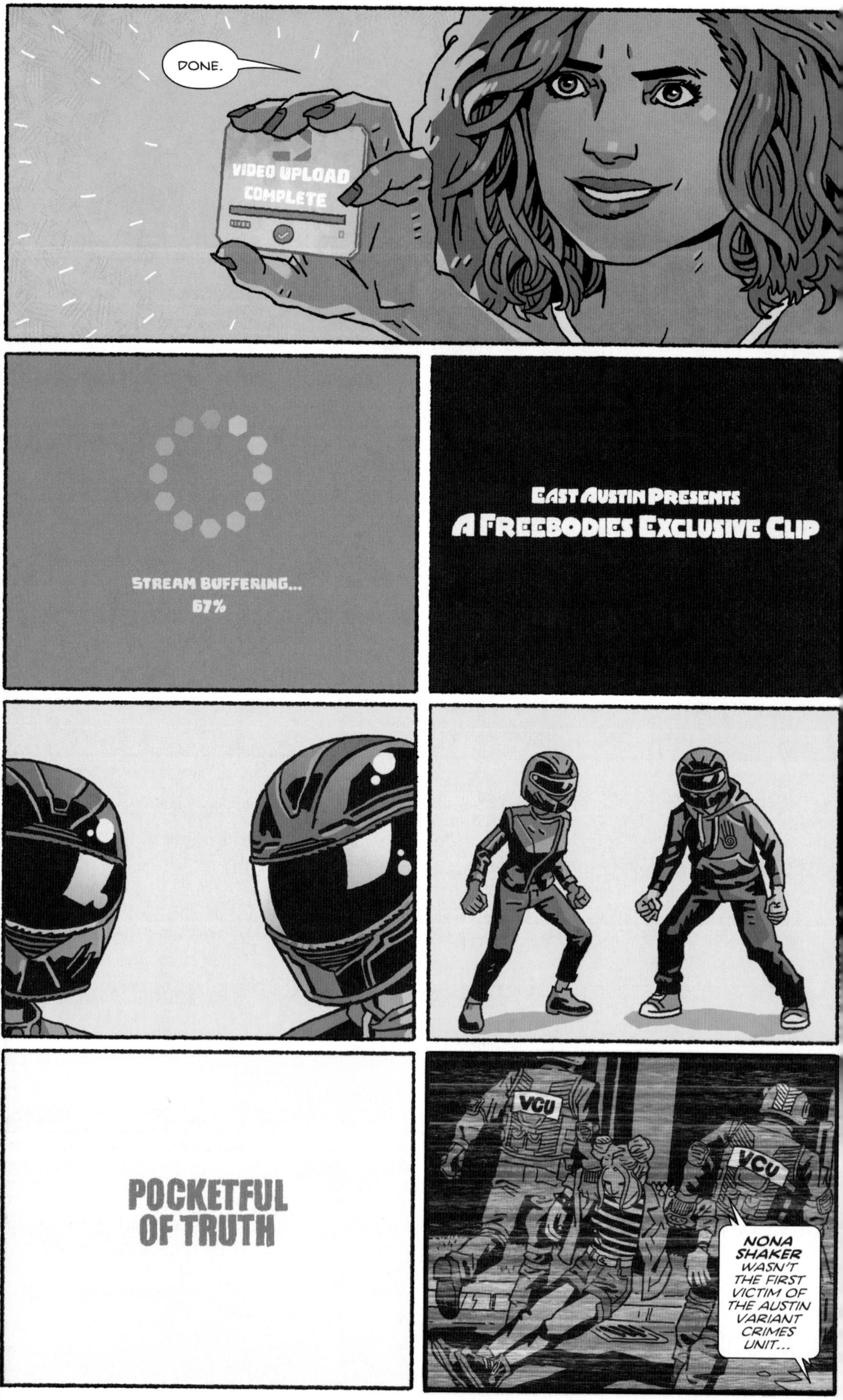
DONE.
VIDEO UPLOAD COMPLETE
STREAM BUFFERING...
67%
EAST AUSTIN PRESENTS
A FREEBODIES EXCLUSIVE CLIP
POCKETFUL OF TRUTH
VCU
VCU
NONA SHAKER WASN'T THE FIRST VICTIM OF THE AUSTIN VARIANT CRIMES UNIT...

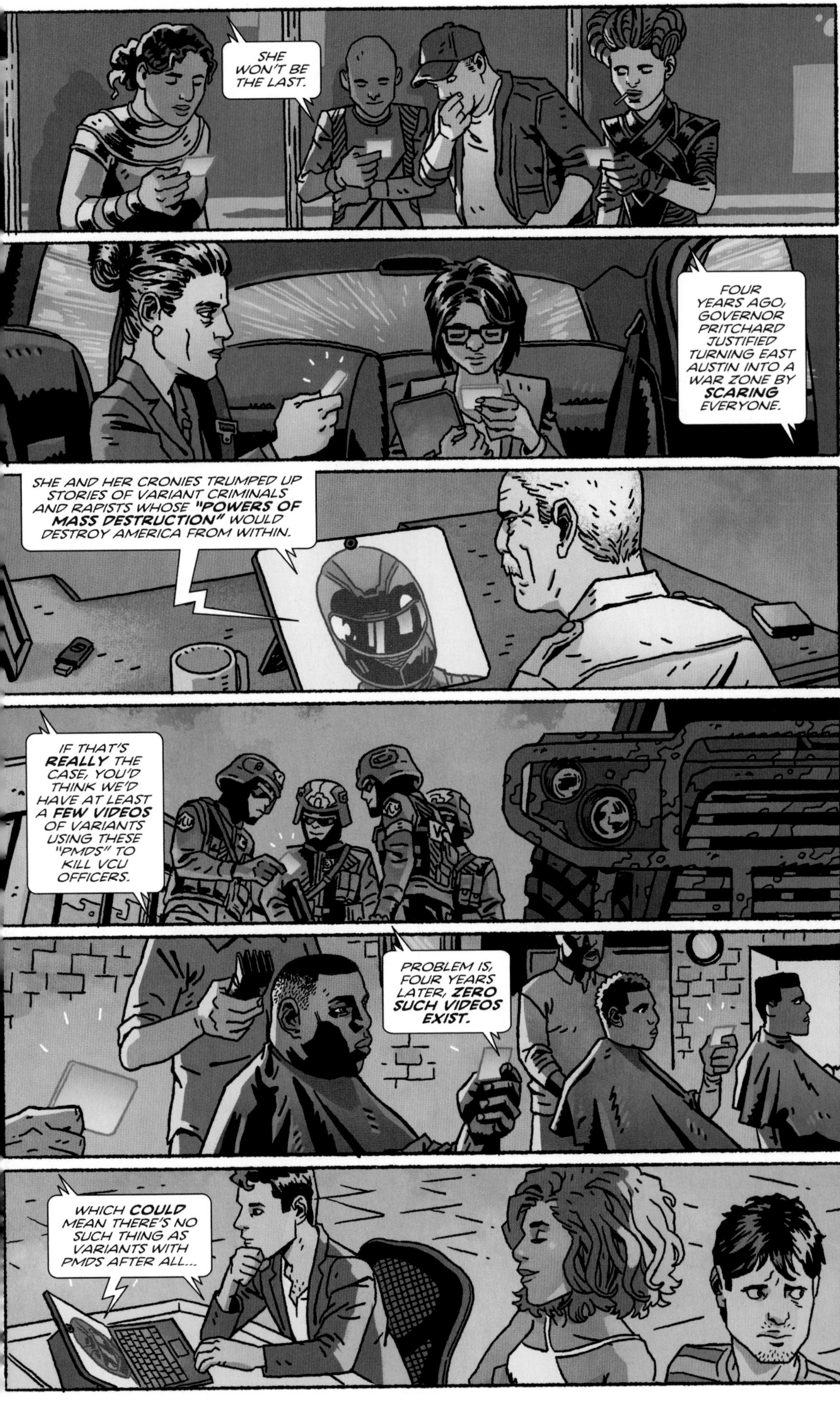
SHE WON'T BE THE LAST.
FOUR YEARS AGO, GOVERNOR PRITCHARD JUSTIFIED TURNING EAST AUSTIN INTO A WAR ZONE BY **SCARING** EVERYONE.
SHE AND HER CRONIES TRUMPED UP STORIES OF VARIANT CRIMINALS AND RAPISTS WHOSE **"POWERS OF MASS DESTRUCTION"** WOULD DESTROY AMERICA FROM WITHIN.
IF THAT'S **REALLY** THE CASE, YOU'D THINK WE'D HAVE AT LEAST A **FEW VIDEOS** OF VARIANTS USING THESE "PMDS" TO KILL VCU OFFICERS.
PROBLEM IS, FOUR YEARS LATER, **ZERO SUCH VIDEOS EXIST.**
WHICH **COULD** MEAN THERE'S NO SUCH THING AS VARIANTS WITH PMDS AFTER ALL...

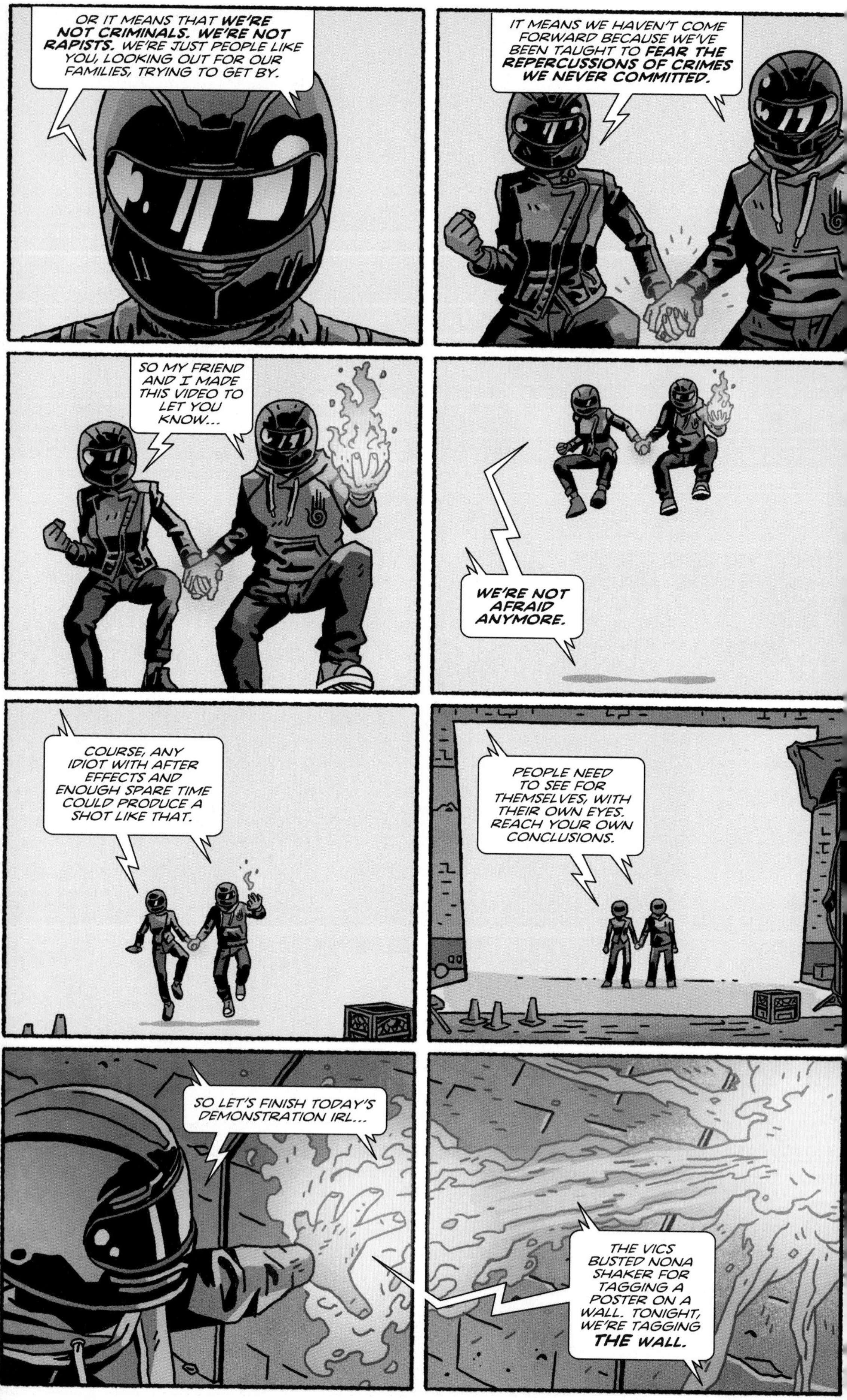

OR IT MEANS THAT WE'RE NOT CRIMINALS. WE'RE NOT RAPISTS. WE'RE JUST PEOPLE LIKE YOU, LOOKING OUT FOR OUR FAMILIES, TRYING TO GET BY.
IT MEANS WE HAVEN'T COME FORWARD BECAUSE WE'VE BEEN TAUGHT TO FEAR THE REPERCUSSIONS OF CRIMES WE NEVER COMMITTED.
SO MY FRIEND AND I MADE THIS VIDEO TO LET YOU KNOW...
WE'RE NOT AFRAID ANYMORE.
COURSE, ANY IDIOT WITH AFTER EFFECTS AND ENOUGH SPARE TIME COULD PRODUCE A SHOT LIKE THAT.
PEOPLE NEED TO SEE FOR THEMSELVES, WITH THEIR OWN EYES. REACH YOUR OWN CONCLUSIONS.
SO LET'S FINISH TODAY'S DEMONSTRATION IRL...
THE VICS BUSTED NONA SHAKER FOR TAGGING A POSTER ON A WALL. TONIGHT, WE'RE TAGGING THE WALL.

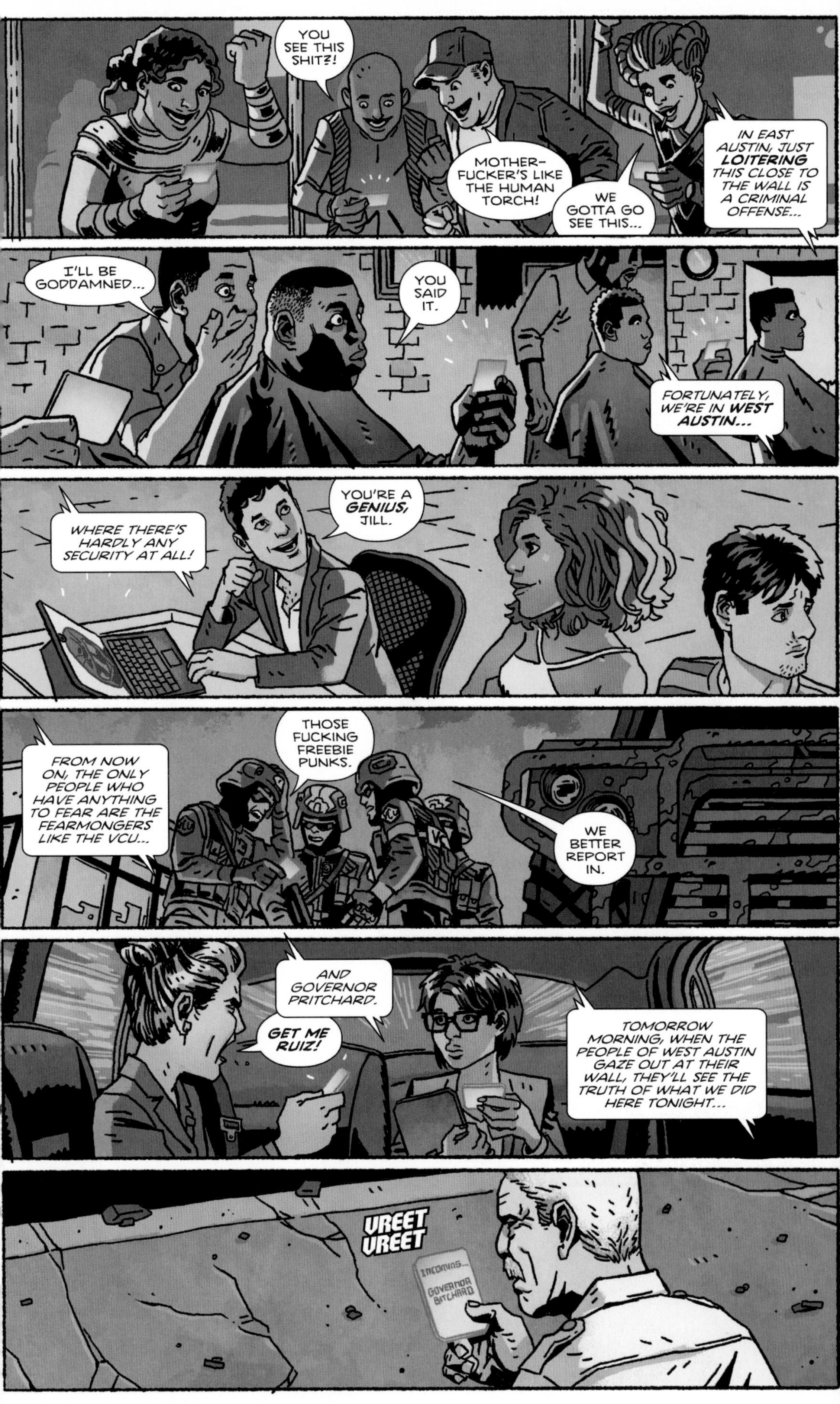

YOU SEE THIS SHIT?!
MOTHER-FUCKER'S LIKE THE HUMAN TORCH!
WE GOTTA GO SEE THIS...
IN EAST AUSTIN, JUST ***LOITERING*** *THIS CLOSE TO THE WALL IS A CRIMINAL OFFENSE...*
I'LL BE GODDAMNED...
YOU SAID IT.
FORTUNATELY, WE'RE IN ***WEST AUSTIN...***
WHERE THERE'S HARDLY ANY SECURITY AT ALL!
YOU'RE A ***GENIUS,*** JILL.
FROM NOW ON, THE ONLY PEOPLE WHO HAVE ANYTHING TO FEAR ARE THE FEARMONGERS LIKE THE VCU...
THOSE FUCKING FREEBIE PUNKS.
WE BETTER REPORT IN.
GET ME RUIZ!
AND GOVERNOR PRITCHARD.
TOMORROW MORNING, WHEN THE PEOPLE OF WEST AUSTIN GAZE OUT AT THEIR WALL, THEY'LL SEE THE TRUTH OF WHAT WE DID HERE TONIGHT...
VREET VREET

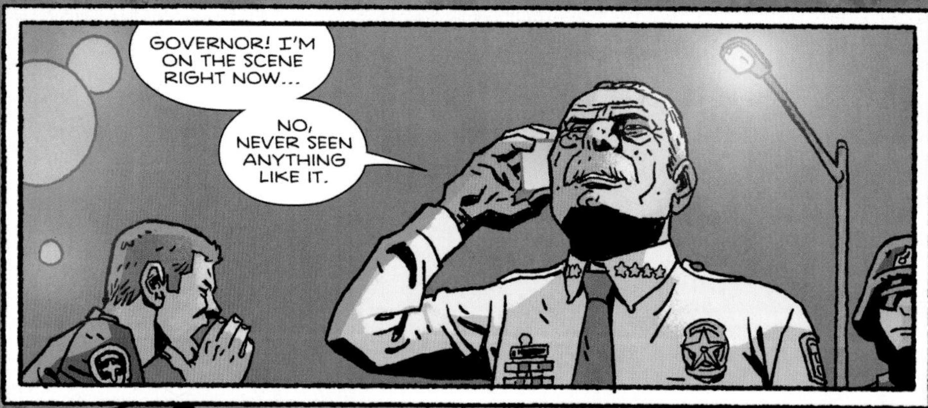
GOVERNOR! I'M ON THE SCENE RIGHT NOW...
NO, NEVER SEEN ANYTHING LIKE IT.

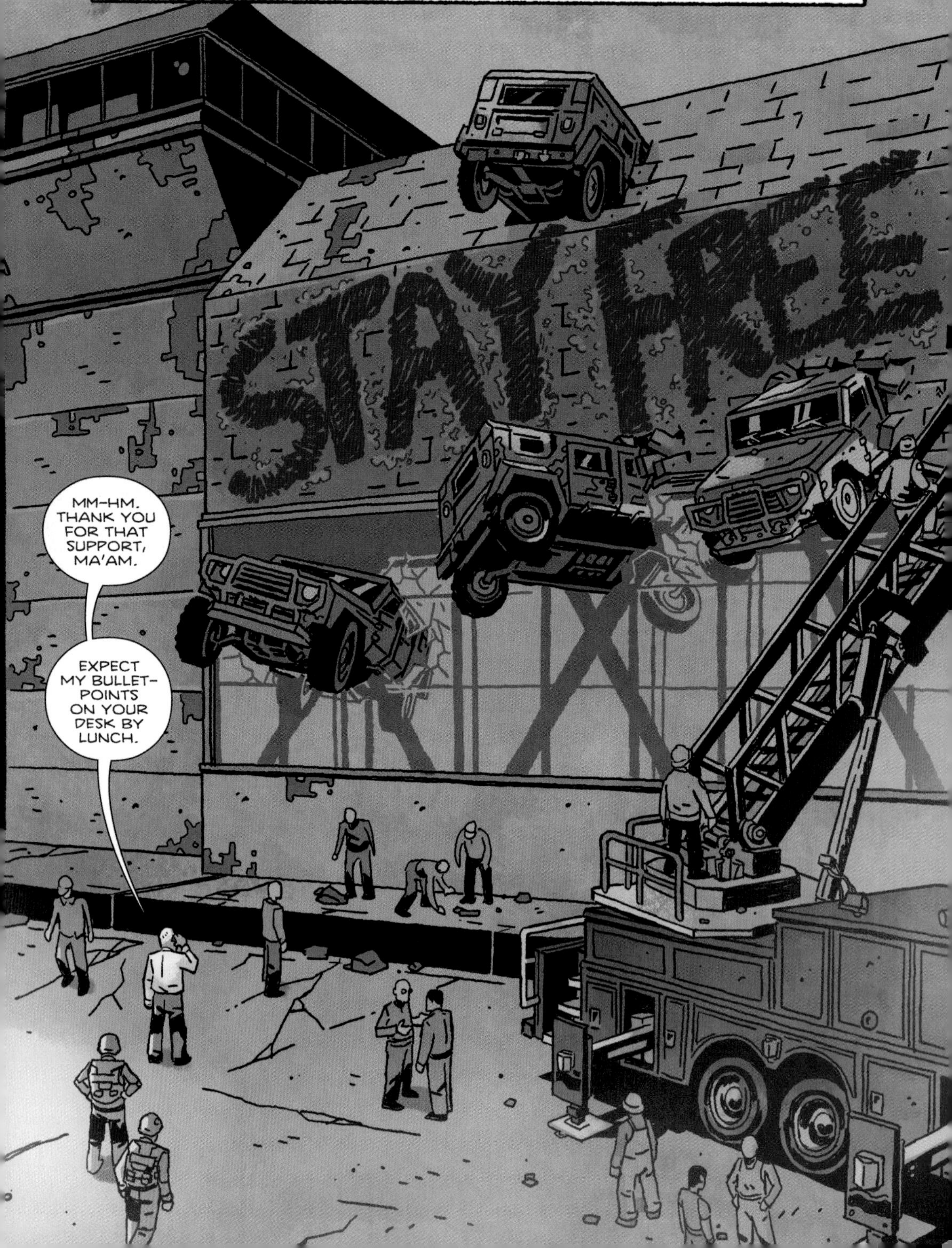
STAY FREE
MM-HM. THANK YOU FOR THAT SUPPORT, MA'AM.
EXPECT MY BULLET-POINTS ON YOUR DESK BY LUNCH.

ANM **US News** Trending Features Opinions Live TV Options

What Does It Mean To "Stay Free"?

Sefton Smith breaks down the resistance rallying cry

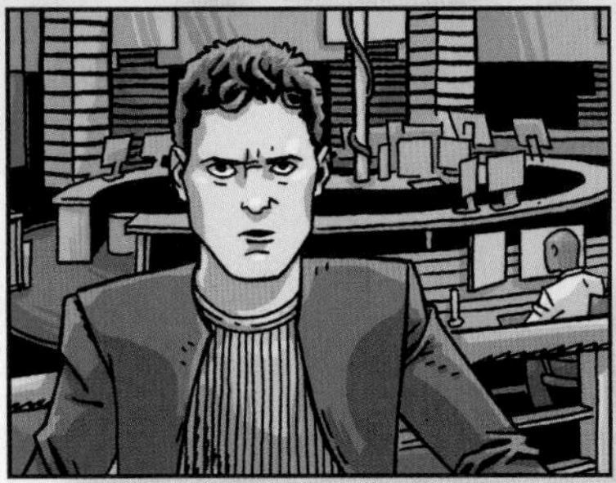

By Gabe Reiss & Maya Zach, ANM
Updated 10:32 AM ET, Wed January 19

(ANM) - Nobody expects to walk far in East Austin without hearing or seeing the words "Stay Free", but these days, that phenomenon is far from local. In Variant-friendly communities around the country, "Stay Free" is printed on T-shirts, painted on walls, and sung in popular songs like last fall's popcore banger, "STAY FREE (RESISTANCE IN F MAJOR)" by Teenie Stella ft. Winga-Ding Redd.

"Stay Free" was popularized by Sefton Smith, founder and CEO of the Freebodies, as the theme of his first Freedonia Festival. In the years since, that festival and the organization behind it have gathered momentum to become the fastest growing youth movement in America. Melding political activism with arts, culture, and fashion, the Freebodies have become a national brand, and "Stay Free" is their tagline.

As his movement grows, Sefton Smith has attracted controversy from all sides. To his critics on the right, Sefton is a cult leader wielding his influence to encourage hedonistic atavism and terrorist violence. To critics on the left, Sefton is a false prophet, his message of freedom and inclusion is corrupted by capitalist greed, and the Freebodies are merely a front for his own wealth and vanity.

In our attempts to learn more about "Stay Free", the substance behind it, and the future of the Freebodies, ANM sat down with Sefton Smith at his office in East Austin.

ANM: What does it mean to "Stay Free"?

Sefton: If your readers don't know that answer already, I don't think they're capable.

ANM: Humor us.

Sefton: It means exactly what it says. Stay. Free. All people, quote-unquote homo sapiens and Variants alike, are born free and should remain free. Confinement is against our nature. We were born to inhabit and master the wide-open spaces of this planet. Confining someone to a cage is almost worse than condemning them to death. Cages condemn people to madness and misery. We should be doing everything in our power to reduce the number of people in cages, to practice minimum viable incarceration… And yet, for some reason, 42% of Americans support parties, politicians, and policies that maximize incarceration rates, and these a******s are holding the rest of us hostage. F*** that!

ANM US News Trending Features Opinions Live TV Options

ANM: While "Stay Free" and the Freedonia Festival began as platforms to raise awareness about criminal justice—

Sefton: Criminal injustice. There's no justice in a system defined by racism and classicide.

ANM: The point we're trying to address is that these platforms were about raising awareness for social issues, but now they're about more than that. What else does "Stay Free" mean to you, besides advocating against mass incarceration?

Sefton: I've said this before, it's a state of mind. Don't put bodies in cages, don't put minds in boxes. Don't let your consciousness become a series of automatic, pre-selected responses to the narrow band of stimuli fed to you through big media—no offense.

ANM: None taken. How does "Stay Free" apply to capitalism?

Sefton: You know, a lot of people think I'm a Socialist, but I'm not. I straddle the political fence, so to speak. I'm a liberaltarian—a libertarian with liberal sympathies.

ANM: Is that a trademarked term?

Sefton: It should be! But I can't take credit for "liberaltarian," I owe that to the work of Will Wilkinson, one of the best policy minds of his time. He imagined the possibility of a popular political identity that values human liberty, in all its aspects, most seriously. This was decades ago, but he imagined it, and now I'm making it happen.

ANM: If being a Freebody is a political identity, and "Stay Free" is a political message, why aren't the Freebodies a non-profit organization?

Sefton: Because money matters in politics. We're starting a revolution, not a charity.

ANM: Ballpark, what portion of profits from Freedonia and the Freebodies are invested in activism, versus paid out to executives and investors like yourself?

Sefton: I'm the CEO, not the CPA. But I catch your drift. You want to know if I'm getting rich off the blood, sweat, and toil of eager young volunteers. Or, perhaps I'm stealing educational funds intended for at-risk youth in East Austin? Neither of which is true. Yes, I pay myself a world-class salary, but by any objective measure, I generate world-class value. And the Freebodies have been so successful, in financial reports we've publicly disclosed, that I can promise you there's enough money to go around between myself, my staff, and the many important causes that we champion.

I know where this is coming from, by the way. You've been listening to Gospel Gary.

ANM: [Popular Variant preacher and podcaster, Gospel Gary] is the second-most influential member of the Variant rights movement…

ANM US News Trending Features Opinions Live TV Options

Sefton: And he'd just love to be Number One, but I'm in his way. Ergo, he tries to paint me as the stereotype of a rich white a*****e. I'm not denying that I'm rich, or white, or even an a*****e, but I'm not the type who steals donor money from broke kids. F***, I'm the one donating most of the money when we do those drives, not to mention the dozen or so scholarships in my name in Austin alone. I do my part.

But, look, I get it. Gospel Gary is a founding father of Variant rights. I respect him. I admire him. There are certain things that he and I do not agree on. I believe in lasting, long-term social progress through policy and politics. Gary's more interested in lightning strikes. Protests, battles, shocks to the system of an indolent citizenry. That worked in the past but this isn't the 1960s. We can't march our way to change anymore. It's too dangerous, even without lethal ammunition. They won't kill you but they'll sure as s*** lock you the f*** up. And you know how I feel about that.

ANM: Looking to the other side, Governor Pritchard has her own criticisms of your work...

Sefton: Did you hear she's trying to cancel Freedonia? The State is suing Travis County to revoke all my licenses on the grounds of security risks. I mean, come on! We've never documented a violent incident at Freedonia. Not one. And then there are the millions—literally, hundreds of millions—of dollars that local Austin businesses will lose without a Freedonia. It's absurd. Pritchard is the epitome of the lying, corrupt gorgons that the party of Lincoln have become in the 21st century. I really shouldn't say more than that. I'll have my date with Princess Pritchard at City Hall in a few months.

ANM: What's next for the Freebodies?

Sefton: Godwilling, Freedonia. After that, I have plans. You'll find out more soon enough...

ANM: Would those plans involve an act of terrorism? Some people worry.

Sefton: *[laughs]* I'm not a violent person. I started the Freebodies to spread love. I use my fortune to spread love. Did you know that I was a sponsor and participant in the world's largest orgy? A record-breaking 699 people—the number was chosen with the greatest of care—all f*****g and sucking and licking and loving each other. Some people think that's shameful and disgusting. Which scenario would you rather live through: People f*****g and loving each other? Or fearing each other, and locking kids in cages?

ANM: Neither situation sounds particularly agreeable to our team... But given no other options, hypothetically, we prefer the orgy.

Sefton: I rest my case. Stay Free.

This interview has been edited for length, clarity, and mature content.

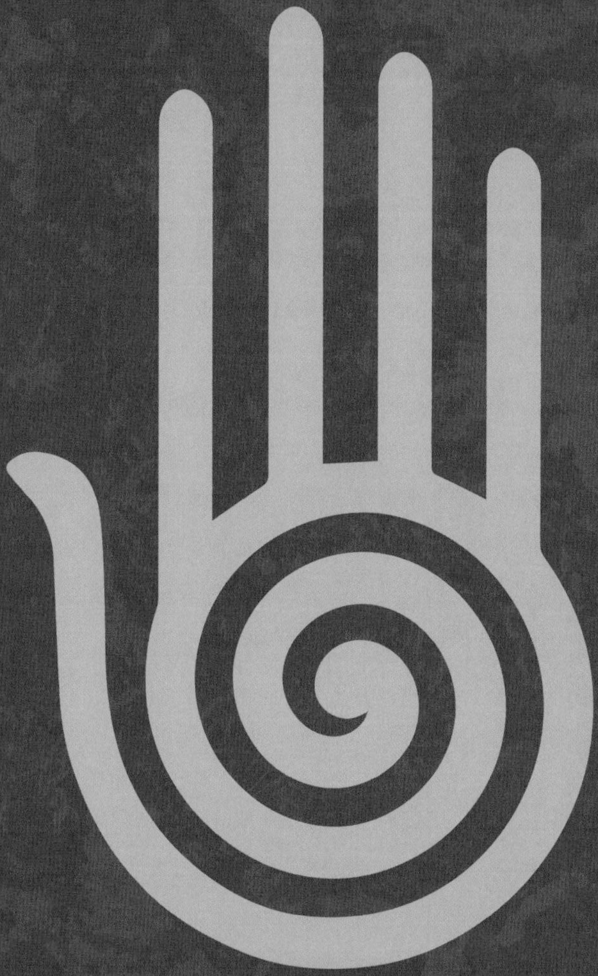

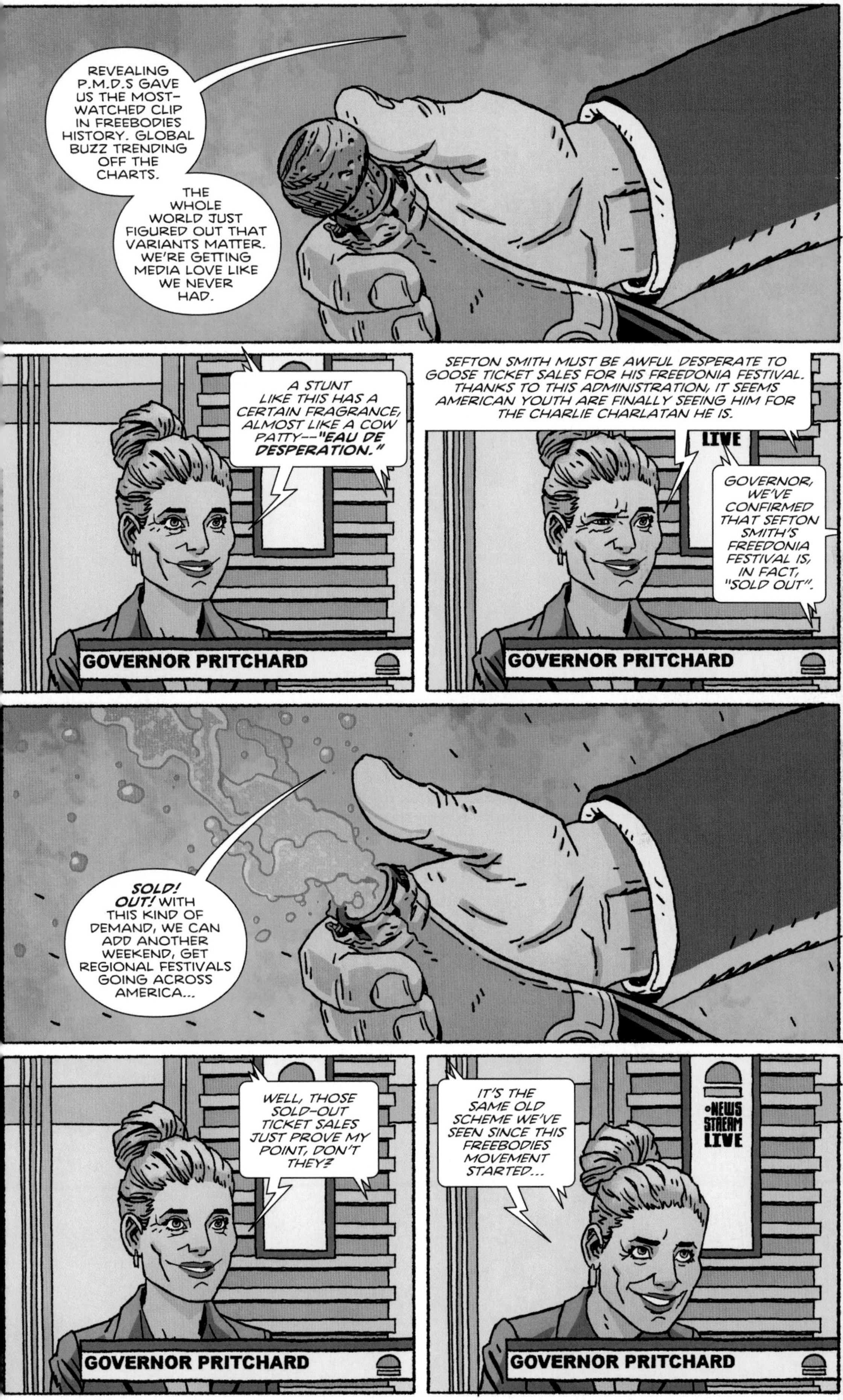
REVEALING P.M.D.S GAVE US THE MOST-WATCHED CLIP IN FREEBODIES HISTORY. GLOBAL BUZZ TRENDING OFF THE CHARTS.
THE WHOLE WORLD JUST FIGURED OUT THAT VARIANTS MATTER. WE'RE GETTING MEDIA LOVE LIKE WE NEVER HAD.
A STUNT LIKE THIS HAS A CERTAIN FRAGRANCE, ALMOST LIKE A COW PATTY--"EAU DE DESPERATION."
GOVERNOR PRITCHARD
SEFTON SMITH MUST BE AWFUL DESPERATE TO GOOSE TICKET SALES FOR HIS FREEDONIA FESTIVAL. THANKS TO THIS ADMINISTRATION, IT SEEMS AMERICAN YOUTH ARE FINALLY SEEING HIM FOR THE CHARLIE CHARLATAN HE IS.
LIVE
GOVERNOR, WE'VE CONFIRMED THAT SEFTON SMITH'S FREEDONIA FESTIVAL IS, IN FACT, "SOLD OUT".
GOVERNOR PRITCHARD
SOLD! OUT! WITH THIS KIND OF DEMAND, WE CAN ADD ANOTHER WEEKEND, GET REGIONAL FESTIVALS GOING ACROSS AMERICA...
WELL, THOSE SOLD-OUT TICKET SALES JUST PROVE MY POINT, DON'T THEY?
GOVERNOR PRITCHARD
NEWS STREAM LIVE
IT'S THE SAME OLD SCHEME WE'VE SEEN SINCE THIS FREEBODIES MOVEMENT STARTED...
GOVERNOR PRITCHARD

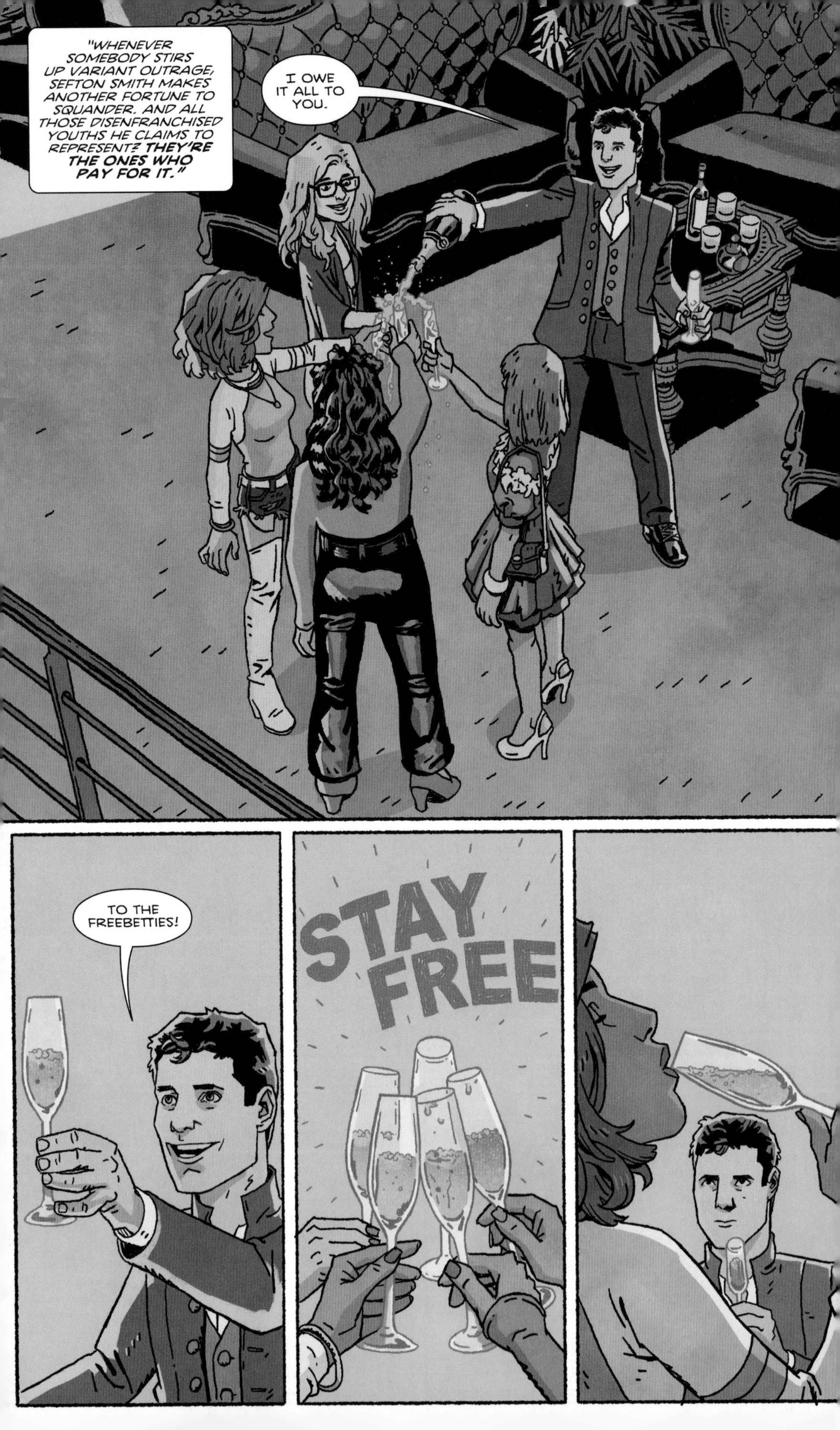
"WHENEVER SOMEBODY STIRS UP VARIANT OUTRAGE, SEFTON SMITH MAKES ANOTHER FORTUNE TO SQUANDER. AND ALL THOSE DISENFRANCHISED YOUTHS HE CLAIMS TO REPRESENT? THEY'RE THE ONES WHO PAY FOR IT."
I OWE IT ALL TO YOU.
TO THE FREEBETTIES!
STAY FREE

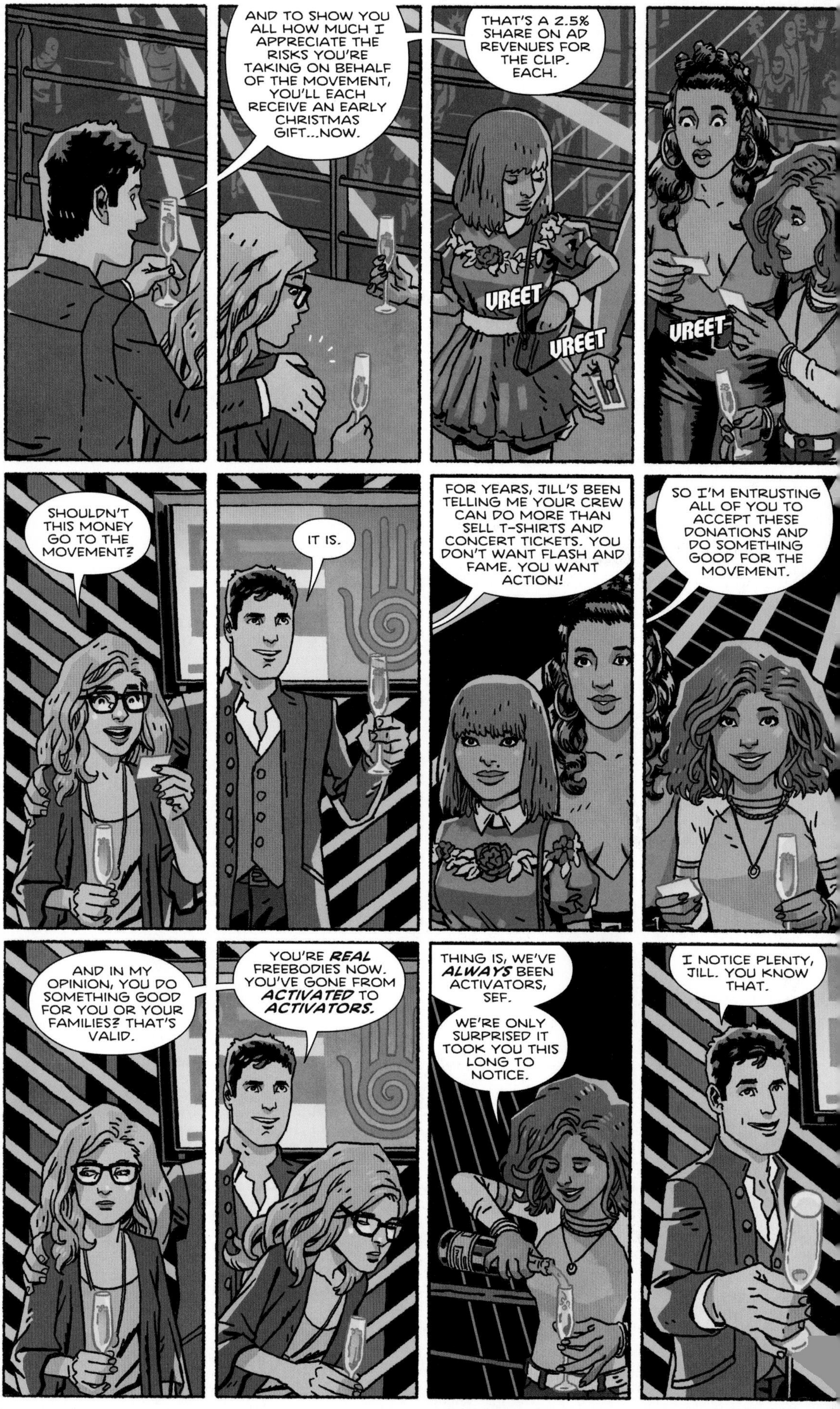
AND TO SHOW YOU ALL HOW MUCH I APPRECIATE THE RISKS YOU'RE TAKING ON BEHALF OF THE MOVEMENT, YOU'LL EACH RECEIVE AN EARLY CHRISTMAS GIFT...NOW.
THAT'S A 2.5% SHARE ON AD REVENUES FOR THE CLIP. EACH.
VREET
VREET
VREET
SHOULDN'T THIS MONEY GO TO THE MOVEMENT?
IT IS.
FOR YEARS, JILL'S BEEN TELLING ME YOUR CREW CAN DO MORE THAN SELL T-SHIRTS AND CONCERT TICKETS. YOU DON'T WANT FLASH AND FAME. YOU WANT ACTION!
SO I'M ENTRUSTING ALL OF YOU TO ACCEPT THESE DONATIONS AND DO SOMETHING GOOD FOR THE MOVEMENT.
AND IN MY OPINION, YOU DO SOMETHING GOOD FOR YOU OR YOUR FAMILIES? THAT'S VALID.
YOU'RE ***REAL*** FREEBODIES NOW. YOU'VE GONE FROM ***ACTIVATED*** TO ***ACTIVATORS.***
THING IS, WE'VE ***ALWAYS*** BEEN ACTIVATORS, SEF.
WE'RE ONLY SURPRISED IT TOOK YOU THIS LONG TO NOTICE.
I NOTICE PLENTY, JILL. YOU KNOW THAT.

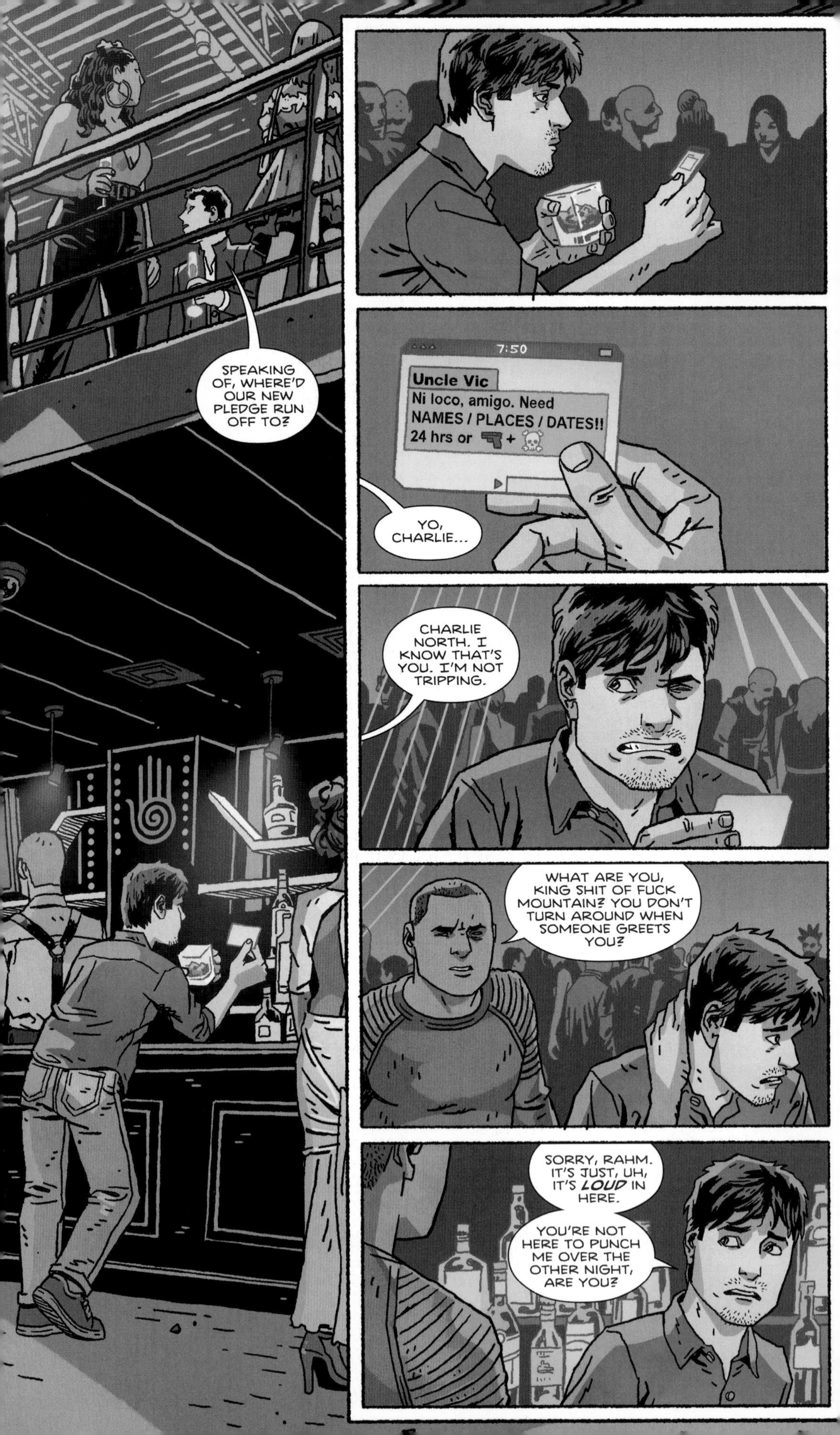
SPEAKING OF, WHERE'D OUR NEW PLEDGE RUN OFF TO?
7:50
Uncle Vic
Ni loco, amigo. Need
NAMES / PLACES / DATES!!
24 hrs or +
YO, CHARLIE...
CHARLIE NORTH. I KNOW THAT'S YOU. I'M NOT TRIPPING.
WHAT ARE YOU, KING SHIT OF FUCK MOUNTAIN? YOU DON'T TURN AROUND WHEN SOMEONE GREETS YOU?
SORRY, RAHM. IT'S JUST, UH, IT'S *LOUD* IN HERE.
YOU'RE NOT HERE TO PUNCH ME OVER THE OTHER NIGHT, ARE YOU?

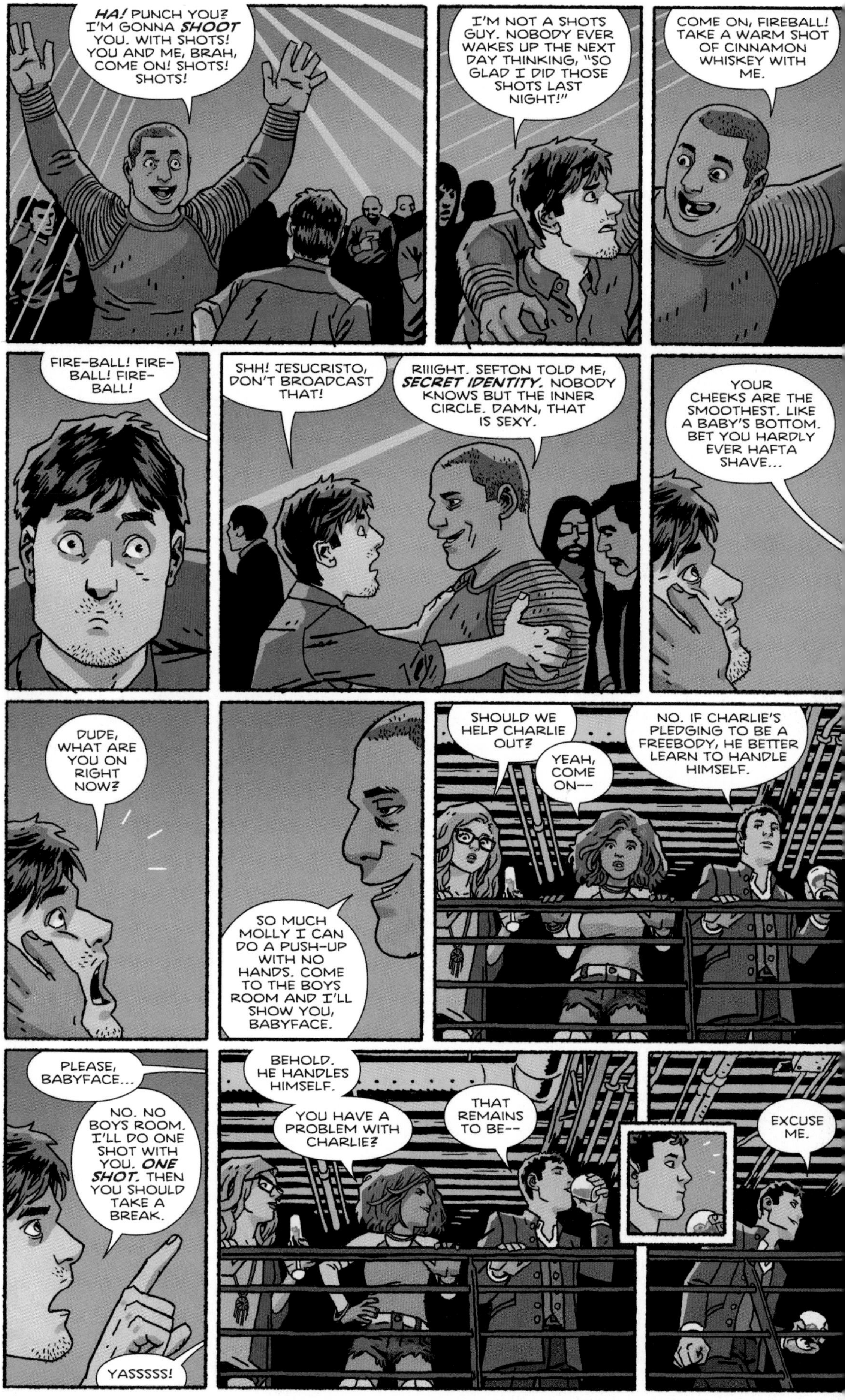
HA! PUNCH YOU? I'M GONNA SHOOT YOU. WITH SHOTS! YOU AND ME, BRAH, COME ON! SHOTS! SHOTS!
I'M NOT A SHOTS GUY. NOBODY EVER WAKES UP THE NEXT DAY THINKING, "SO GLAD I DID THOSE SHOTS LAST NIGHT!"
COME ON, FIREBALL! TAKE A WARM SHOT OF CINNAMON WHISKEY WITH ME.
FIRE-BALL! FIRE-BALL! FIRE-BALL!
SHH! JESUCRISTO, DON'T BROADCAST THAT!
RIIIGHT. SEFTON TOLD ME, SECRET IDENTITY. NOBODY KNOWS BUT THE INNER CIRCLE. DAMN, THAT IS SEXY.
YOUR CHEEKS ARE THE SMOOTHEST. LIKE A BABY'S BOTTOM. BET YOU HARDLY EVER HAFTA SHAVE...
DUDE, WHAT ARE YOU ON RIGHT NOW?
SO MUCH MOLLY I CAN DO A PUSH-UP WITH NO HANDS. COME TO THE BOYS ROOM AND I'LL SHOW YOU, BABYFACE.
SHOULD WE HELP CHARLIE OUT?
YEAH, COME ON--
NO. IF CHARLIE'S PLEDGING TO BE A FREEBODY, HE BETTER LEARN TO HANDLE HIMSELF.
PLEASE, BABYFACE...
NO. NO BOYS ROOM. I'LL DO ONE SHOT WITH YOU. ONE SHOT. THEN YOU SHOULD TAKE A BREAK.
YASSSSS!
BEHOLD. HE HANDLES HIMSELF.
YOU HAVE A PROBLEM WITH CHARLIE?
THAT REMAINS TO BE--
EXCUSE ME.

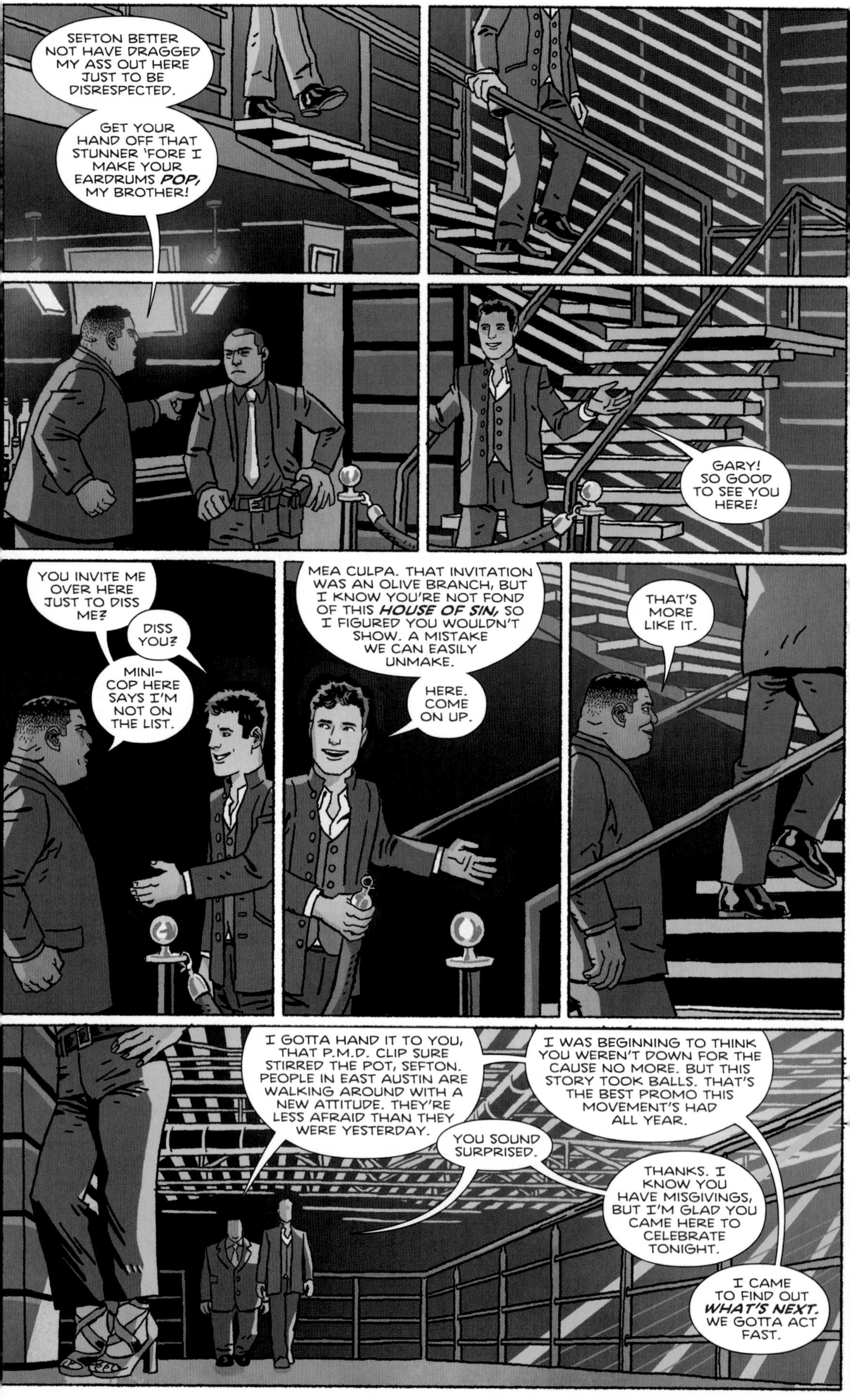
SEFTON BETTER NOT HAVE DRAGGED MY ASS OUT HERE JUST TO BE DISRESPECTED.
GET YOUR HAND OFF THAT STUNNER 'FORE I MAKE YOUR EARDRUMS *POP,* MY BROTHER!
GARY! SO GOOD TO SEE YOU HERE!
YOU INVITE ME OVER HERE JUST TO DISS ME?
DISS YOU?
MINI-COP HERE SAYS I'M NOT ON THE LIST.
MEA CULPA. THAT INVITATION WAS AN OLIVE BRANCH, BUT I KNOW YOU'RE NOT FOND OF THIS *HOUSE OF SIN,* SO I FIGURED YOU WOULDN'T SHOW. A MISTAKE WE CAN EASILY UNMAKE.
HERE. COME ON UP.
THAT'S MORE LIKE IT.
I GOTTA HAND IT TO YOU, THAT P.M.D. CLIP SURE STIRRED THE POT, SEFTON. PEOPLE IN EAST AUSTIN ARE WALKING AROUND WITH A NEW ATTITUDE. THEY'RE LESS AFRAID THAN THEY WERE YESTERDAY.
YOU SOUND SURPRISED.
I WAS BEGINNING TO THINK YOU WEREN'T DOWN FOR THE CAUSE NO MORE. BUT THIS STORY TOOK BALLS. THAT'S THE BEST PROMO THIS MOVEMENT'S HAD ALL YEAR.
THANKS. I KNOW YOU HAVE MISGIVINGS, BUT I'M GLAD YOU CAME HERE TO CELEBRATE TONIGHT.
I CAME TO FIND OUT *WHAT'S NEXT.* WE GOTTA ACT FAST.

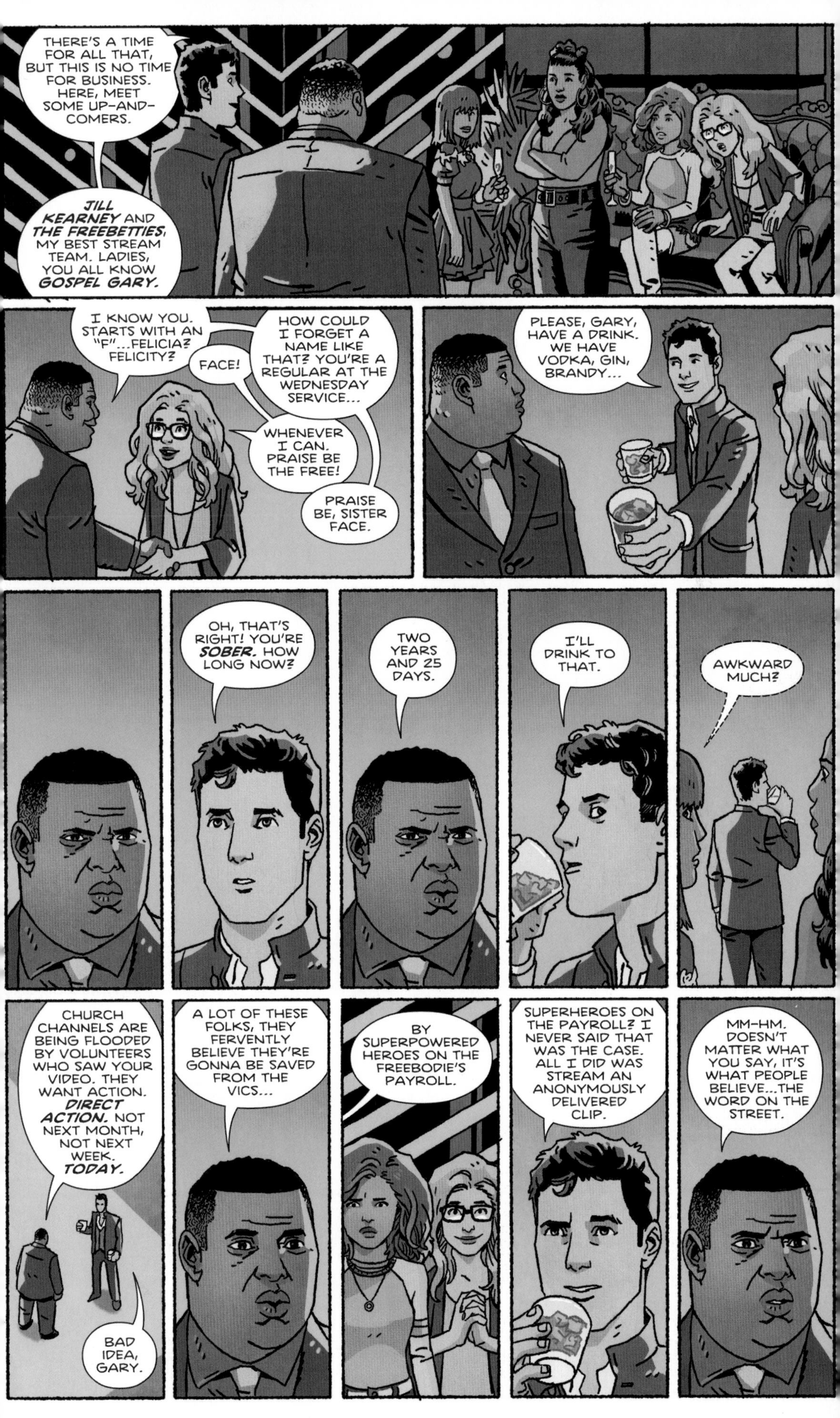
THERE'S A TIME FOR ALL THAT, BUT THIS IS NO TIME FOR BUSINESS. HERE, MEET SOME UP-AND-COMERS.
JILL KEARNEY AND THE FREEBETTIES, MY BEST STREAM TEAM. LADIES, YOU ALL KNOW GOSPEL GARY.
I KNOW YOU. STARTS WITH AN "F"...FELICIA? FELICITY?
FACE!
HOW COULD I FORGET A NAME LIKE THAT? YOU'RE A REGULAR AT THE WEDNESDAY SERVICE...
WHENEVER I CAN. PRAISE BE THE FREE!
PRAISE BE, SISTER FACE.
PLEASE, GARY, HAVE A DRINK. WE HAVE VODKA, GIN, BRANDY...
OH, THAT'S RIGHT! YOU'RE SOBER. HOW LONG NOW?
TWO YEARS AND 25 DAYS.
I'LL DRINK TO THAT.
AWKWARD MUCH?
CHURCH CHANNELS ARE BEING FLOODED BY VOLUNTEERS WHO SAW YOUR VIDEO. THEY WANT ACTION. DIRECT ACTION. NOT NEXT MONTH, NOT NEXT WEEK. TODAY.
BAD IDEA, GARY.
A LOT OF THESE FOLKS, THEY FERVENTLY BELIEVE THEY'RE GONNA BE SAVED FROM THE VICS...
BY SUPERPOWERED HEROES ON THE FREEBODIE'S PAYROLL.
SUPERHEROES ON THE PAYROLL? I NEVER SAID THAT WAS THE CASE. ALL I DID WAS STREAM AN ANONYMOUSLY DELIVERED CLIP.
MM-HM. DOESN'T MATTER WHAT YOU SAY, IT'S WHAT PEOPLE BELIEVE...THE WORD ON THE STREET.

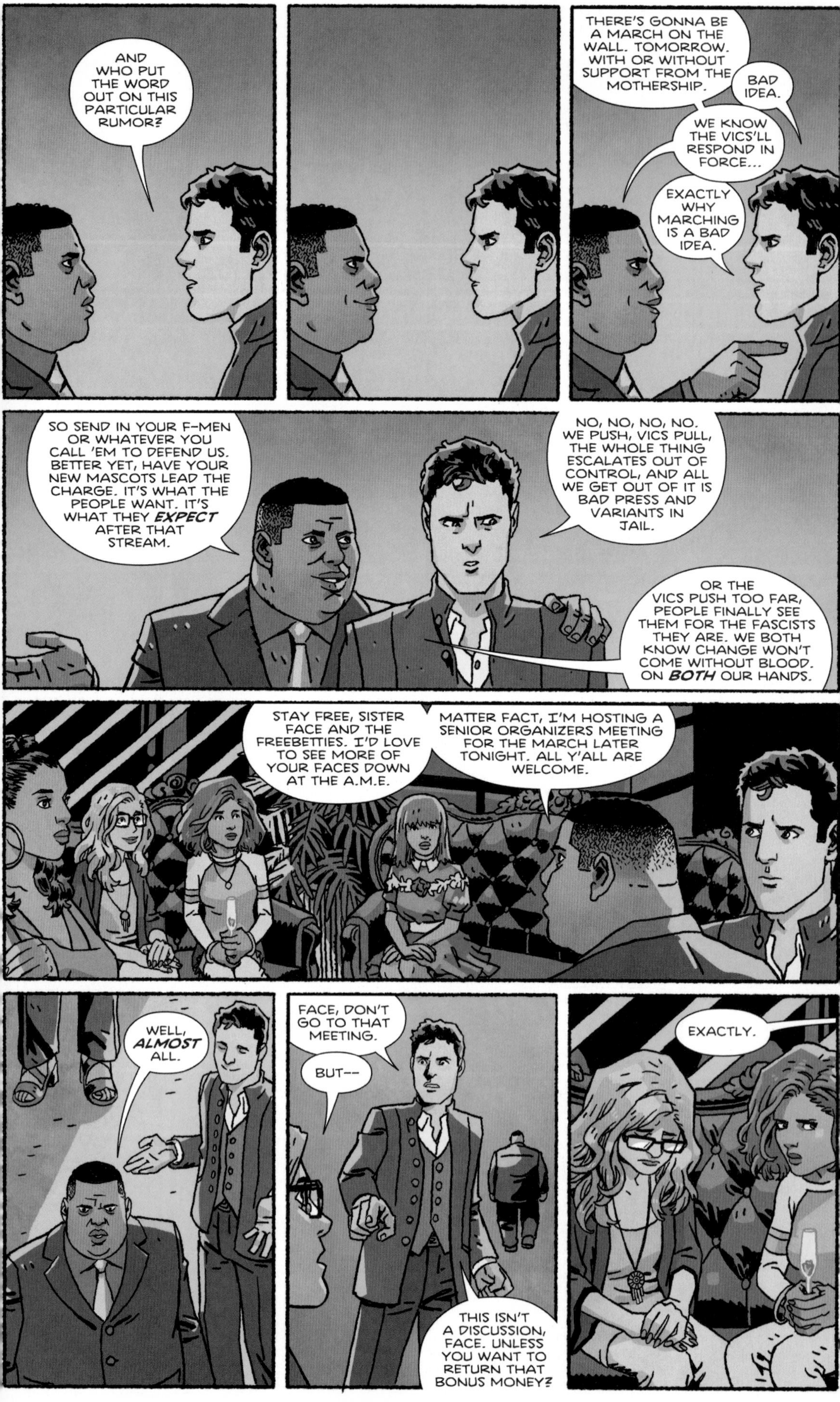
AND WHO PUT THE WORD OUT ON THIS PARTICULAR RUMOR?
THERE'S GONNA BE A MARCH ON THE WALL. TOMORROW. WITH OR WITHOUT SUPPORT FROM THE MOTHERSHIP.
BAD IDEA.
WE KNOW THE VICS'LL RESPOND IN FORCE...
EXACTLY WHY MARCHING IS A BAD IDEA.
SO SEND IN YOUR F-MEN OR WHATEVER YOU CALL 'EM TO DEFEND US. BETTER YET, HAVE YOUR NEW MASCOTS LEAD THE CHARGE. IT'S WHAT THE PEOPLE WANT. IT'S WHAT THEY *EXPECT* AFTER THAT STREAM.
NO, NO, NO, NO. WE PUSH, VICS PULL, THE WHOLE THING ESCALATES OUT OF CONTROL, AND ALL WE GET OUT OF IT IS BAD PRESS AND VARIANTS IN JAIL.
OR THE VICS PUSH TOO FAR, PEOPLE FINALLY SEE THEM FOR THE FASCISTS THEY ARE. WE BOTH KNOW CHANGE WON'T COME WITHOUT BLOOD. ON ***BOTH*** OUR HANDS.
STAY FREE, SISTER FACE AND THE FREEBETTIES. I'D LOVE TO SEE MORE OF YOUR FACES DOWN AT THE A.M.E.
MATTER FACT, I'M HOSTING A SENIOR ORGANIZERS MEETING FOR THE MARCH LATER TONIGHT. ALL Y'ALL ARE WELCOME.
WELL, ***ALMOST*** ALL.
FACE, DON'T GO TO THAT MEETING.
BUT--
THIS ISN'T A DISCUSSION, FACE. UNLESS YOU WANT TO RETURN THAT BONUS MONEY?
EXACTLY.

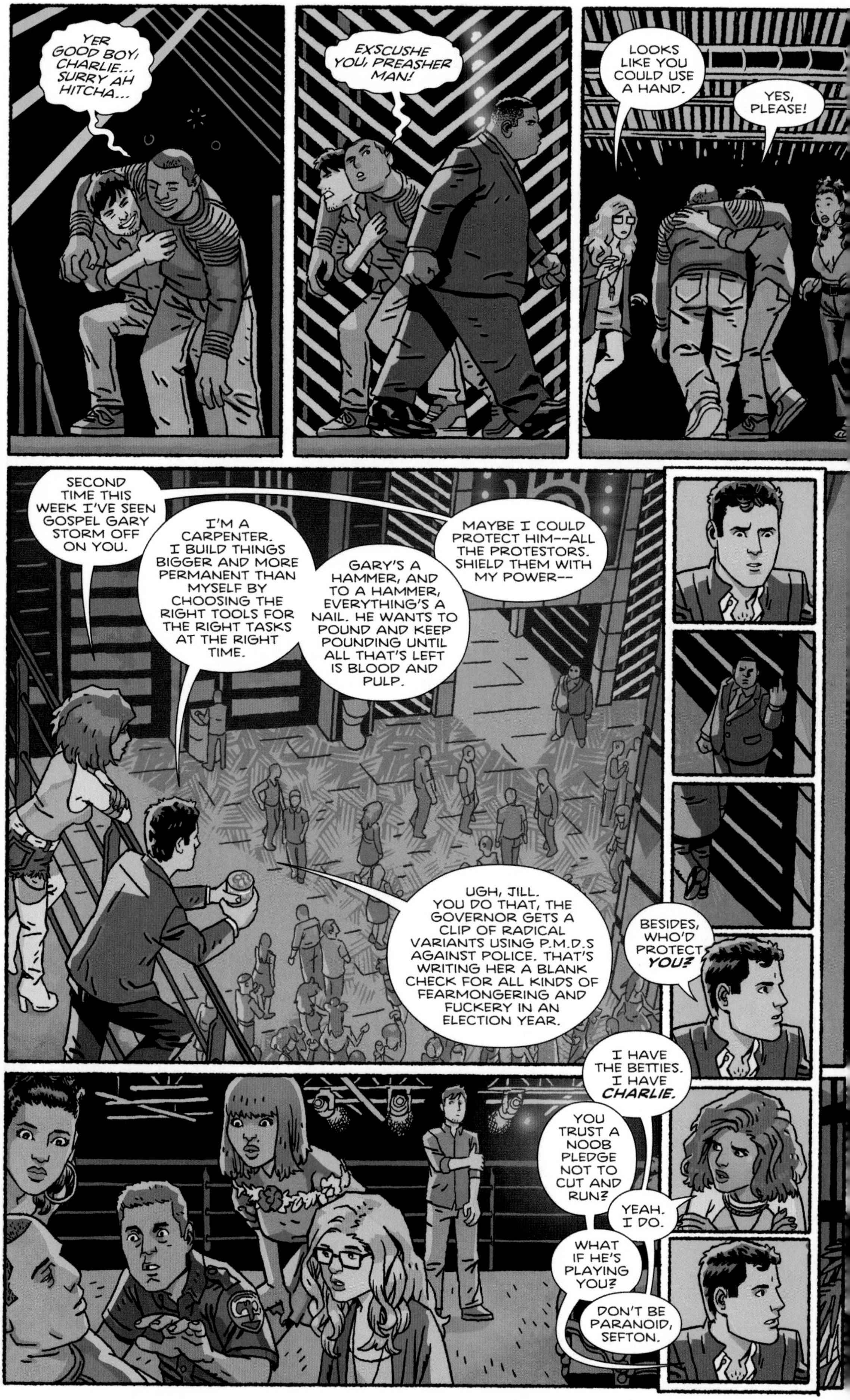
YER GOOD BOY, CHARLIE... SURRY AH HITCHA...
EXSCUSHE YOU, PREASHER MAN!
LOOKS LIKE YOU COULD USE A HAND.
YES, PLEASE!
SECOND TIME THIS WEEK I'VE SEEN GOSPEL GARY STORM OFF ON YOU.
I'M A CARPENTER. I BUILD THINGS BIGGER AND MORE PERMANENT THAN MYSELF BY CHOOSING THE RIGHT TOOLS FOR THE RIGHT TASKS AT THE RIGHT TIME.
GARY'S A HAMMER, AND TO A HAMMER, EVERYTHING'S A NAIL. HE WANTS TO POUND AND KEEP POUNDING UNTIL ALL THAT'S LEFT IS BLOOD AND PULP.
MAYBE I COULD PROTECT HIM--ALL THE PROTESTORS. SHIELD THEM WITH MY POWER--
UGH, JILL. YOU DO THAT, THE GOVERNOR GETS A CLIP OF RADICAL VARIANTS USING P.M.D.S AGAINST POLICE. THAT'S WRITING HER A BLANK CHECK FOR ALL KINDS OF FEARMONGERING AND FUCKERY IN AN ELECTION YEAR.
BESIDES, WHO'D PROTECT *YOU?*
I HAVE THE BETTIES. I HAVE *CHARLIE.*
YOU TRUST A NOOB PLEDGE NOT TO CUT AND RUN?
YEAH. I DO.
WHAT IF HE'S PLAYING YOU?
DON'T BE PARANOID, SEFTON.

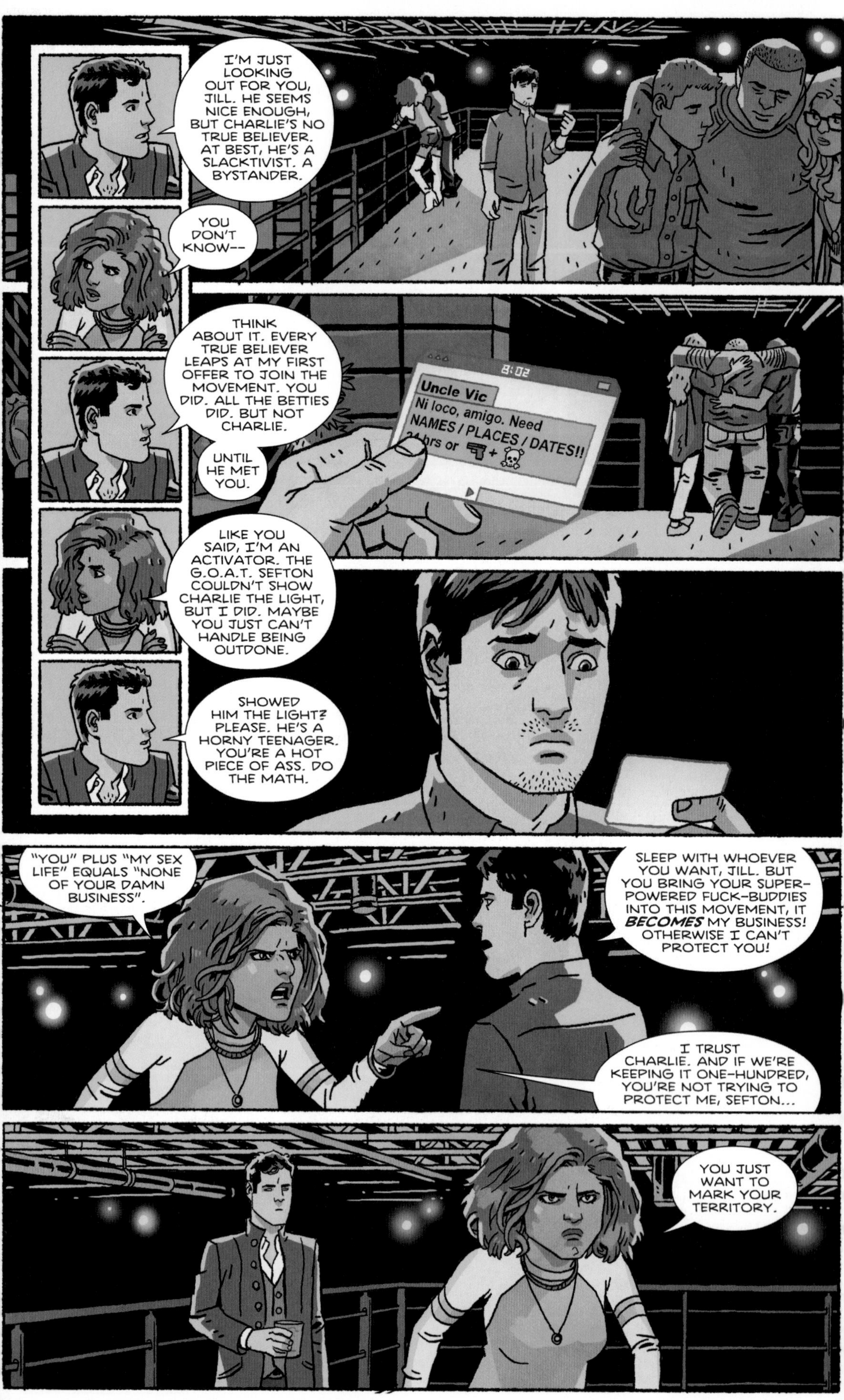

I'M JUST LOOKING OUT FOR YOU, JILL. HE SEEMS NICE ENOUGH, BUT CHARLIE'S NO TRUE BELIEVER. AT BEST, HE'S A SLACKTIVIST. A BYSTANDER.
YOU DON'T KNOW--
THINK ABOUT IT. EVERY TRUE BELIEVER LEAPS AT MY FIRST OFFER TO JOIN THE MOVEMENT. YOU DID. ALL THE BETTIES DID. BUT NOT CHARLIE.
UNTIL HE MET YOU.
8:02
Uncle Vic
Ni loco, amigo. Need NAMES / PLACES / DATES!!
24 hrs or
LIKE YOU SAID, I'M AN ACTIVATOR. THE G.O.A.T. SEFTON COULDN'T SHOW CHARLIE THE LIGHT, BUT I DID. MAYBE YOU JUST CAN'T HANDLE BEING OUTDONE.
SHOWED HIM THE LIGHT? PLEASE. HE'S A HORNY TEENAGER. YOU'RE A HOT PIECE OF ASS. DO THE MATH.
"YOU" PLUS "MY SEX LIFE" EQUALS "NONE OF YOUR DAMN BUSINESS".
SLEEP WITH WHOEVER YOU WANT, JILL. BUT YOU BRING YOUR SUPER-POWERED FUCK-BUDDIES INTO THIS MOVEMENT, IT *BECOMES* MY BUSINESS! OTHERWISE I CAN'T PROTECT YOU!
I TRUST CHARLIE. AND IF WE'RE KEEPING IT ONE-HUNDRED, YOU'RE NOT TRYING TO PROTECT ME, SEFTON...
YOU JUST WANT TO MARK YOUR TERRITORY.

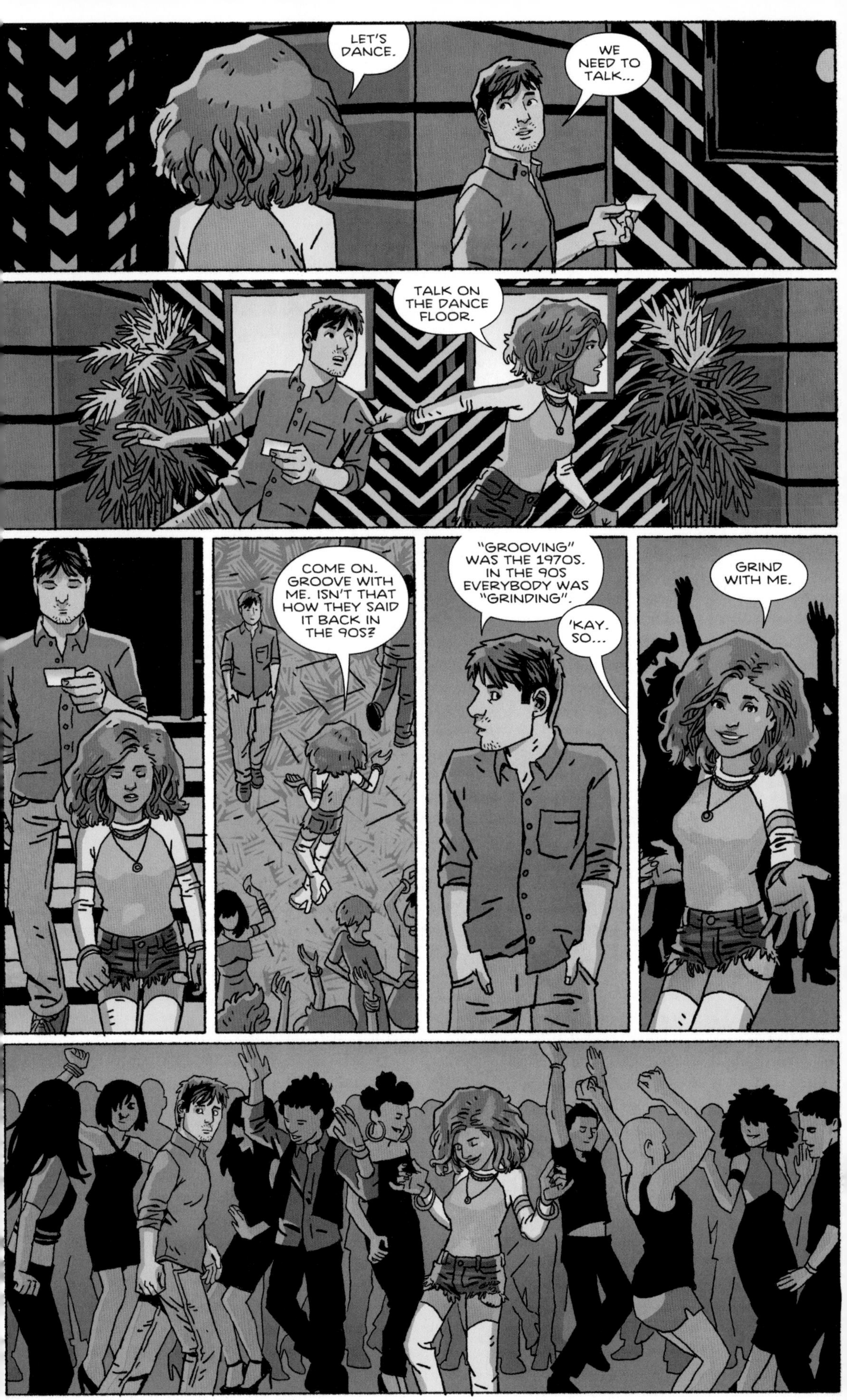
LET'S DANCE.
WE NEED TO TALK...
TALK ON THE DANCE FLOOR.
COME ON. GROOVE WITH ME. ISN'T THAT HOW THEY SAID IT BACK IN THE 90S?
"GROOVING" WAS THE 1970S. IN THE 90S EVERYBODY WAS "GRINDING".
'KAY. SO...
GRIND WITH ME.

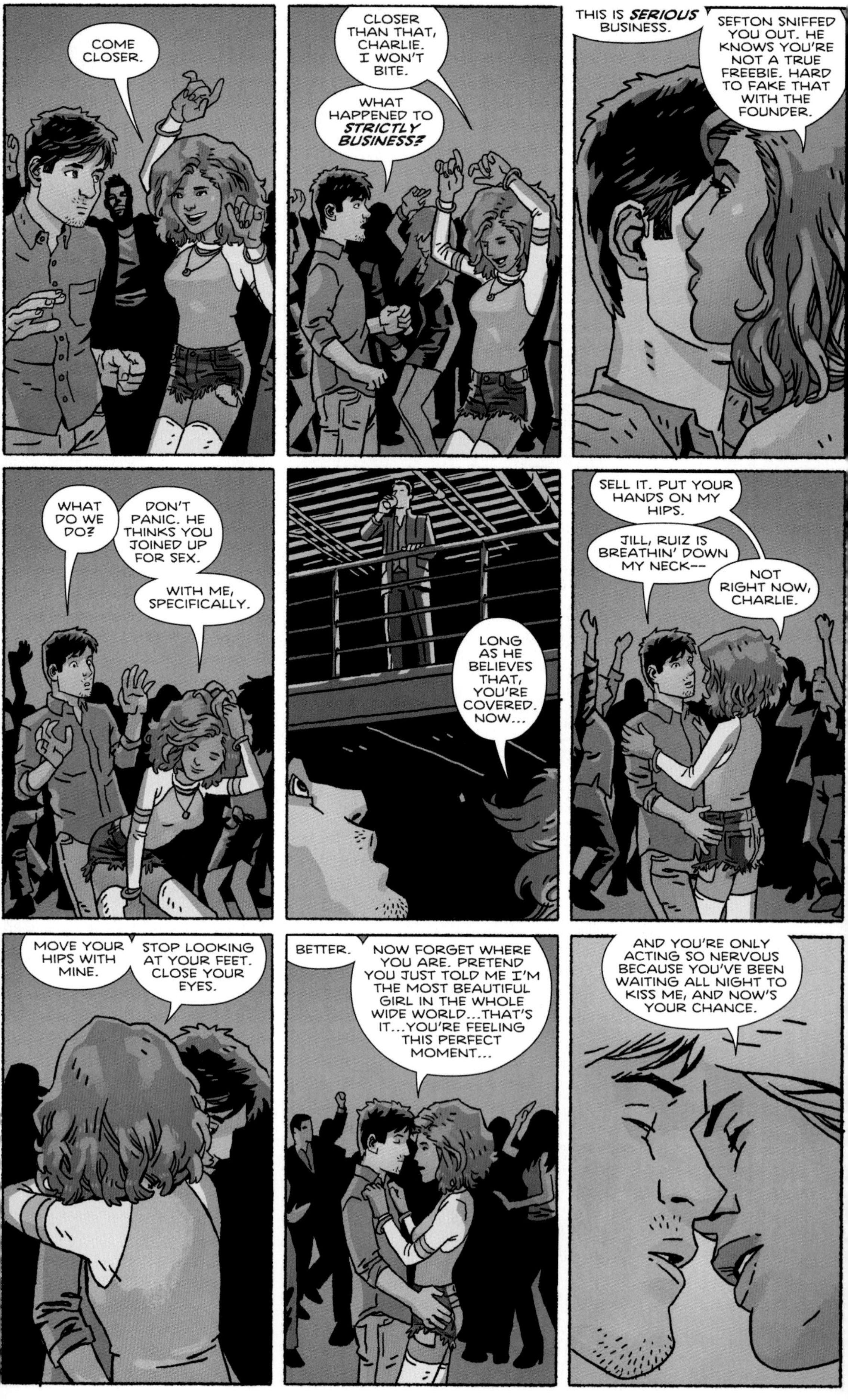
COME CLOSER.
CLOSER THAN THAT, CHARLIE. I WON'T BITE.
WHAT HAPPENED TO STRICTLY BUSINESS?
THIS IS SERIOUS BUSINESS.
SEFTON SNIFFED YOU OUT. HE KNOWS YOU'RE NOT A TRUE FREEBIE. HARD TO FAKE THAT WITH THE FOUNDER.
WHAT DO WE DO?
DON'T PANIC. HE THINKS YOU JOINED UP FOR SEX.
WITH ME, SPECIFICALLY.
LONG AS HE BELIEVES THAT, YOU'RE COVERED. NOW...
SELL IT. PUT YOUR HANDS ON MY HIPS.
JILL, RUIZ IS BREATHIN' DOWN MY NECK--
NOT RIGHT NOW, CHARLIE.
MOVE YOUR HIPS WITH MINE.
STOP LOOKING AT YOUR FEET. CLOSE YOUR EYES.
BETTER.
NOW FORGET WHERE YOU ARE. PRETEND YOU JUST TOLD ME I'M THE MOST BEAUTIFUL GIRL IN THE WHOLE WIDE WORLD...THAT'S IT...YOU'RE FEELING THIS PERFECT MOMENT...
AND YOU'RE ONLY ACTING SO NERVOUS BECAUSE YOU'VE BEEN WAITING ALL NIGHT TO KISS ME, AND NOW'S YOUR CHANCE.

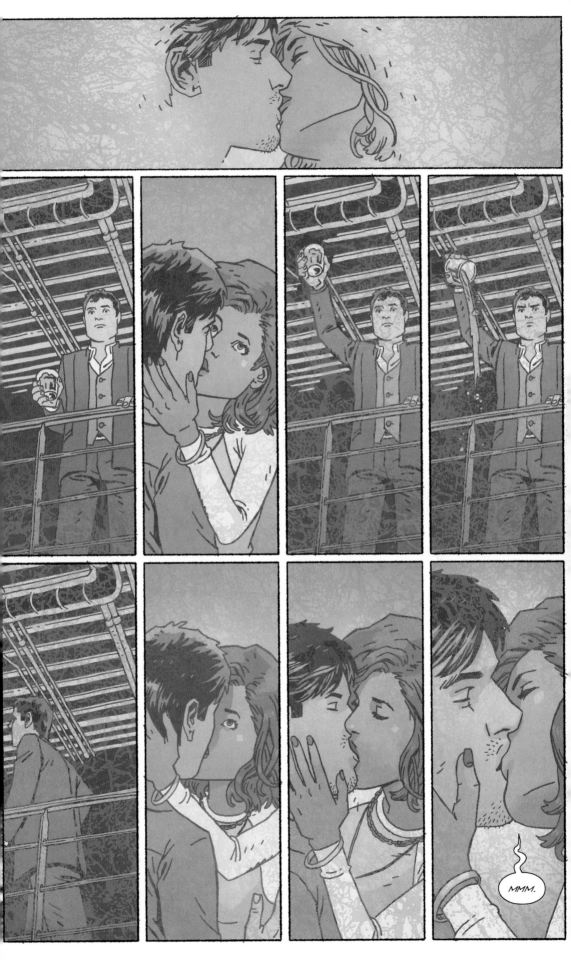

MMM.

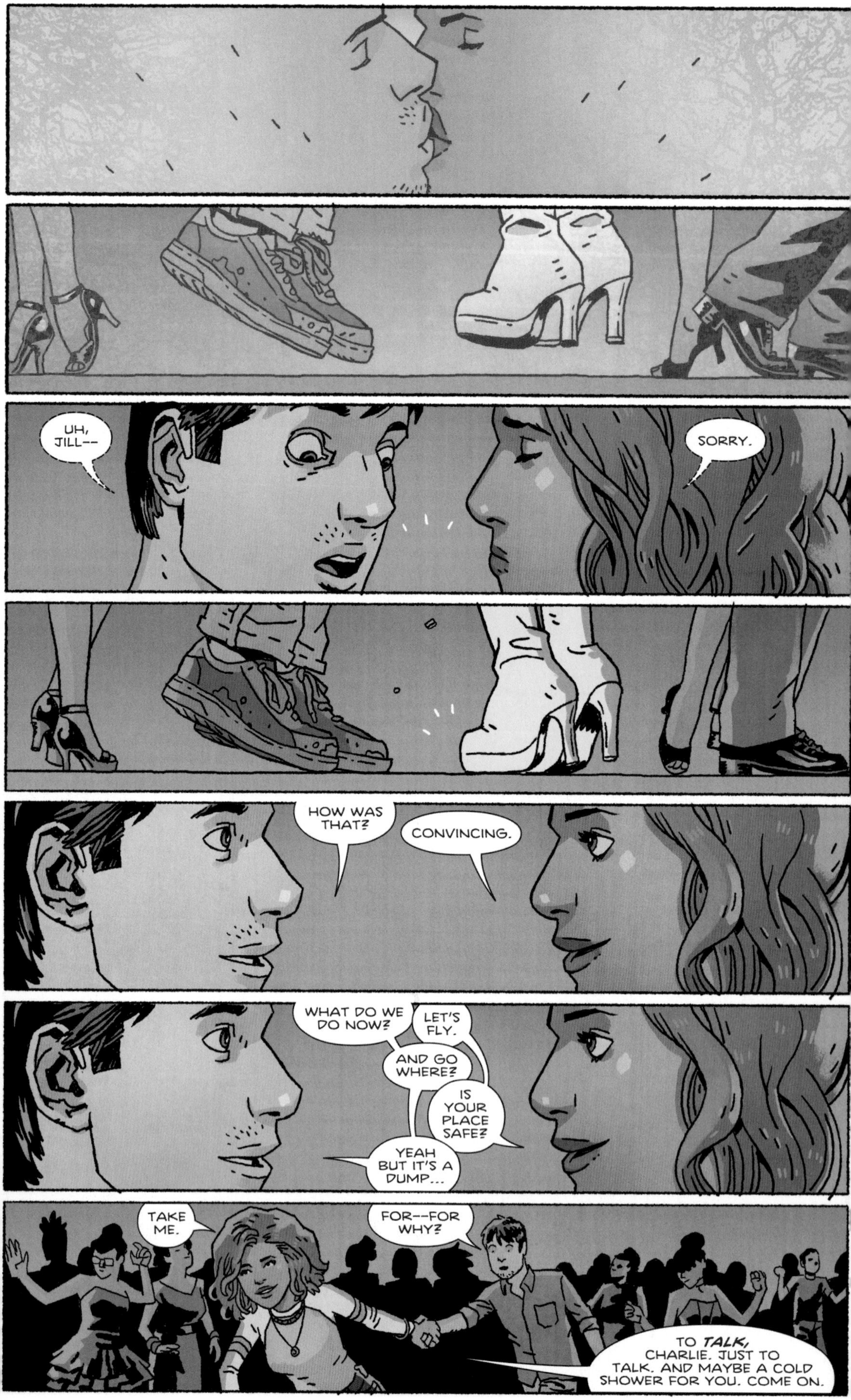
UH, JILL--
SORRY.
HOW WAS THAT?
CONVINCING.
WHAT DO WE DO NOW?
LET'S FLY.
AND GO WHERE?
IS YOUR PLACE SAFE?
YEAH BUT IT'S A DUMP...
TAKE ME.
FOR--FOR WHY?
TO *TALK,* CHARLIE. JUST TO TALK. AND MAYBE A COLD SHOWER FOR YOU. COME ON.

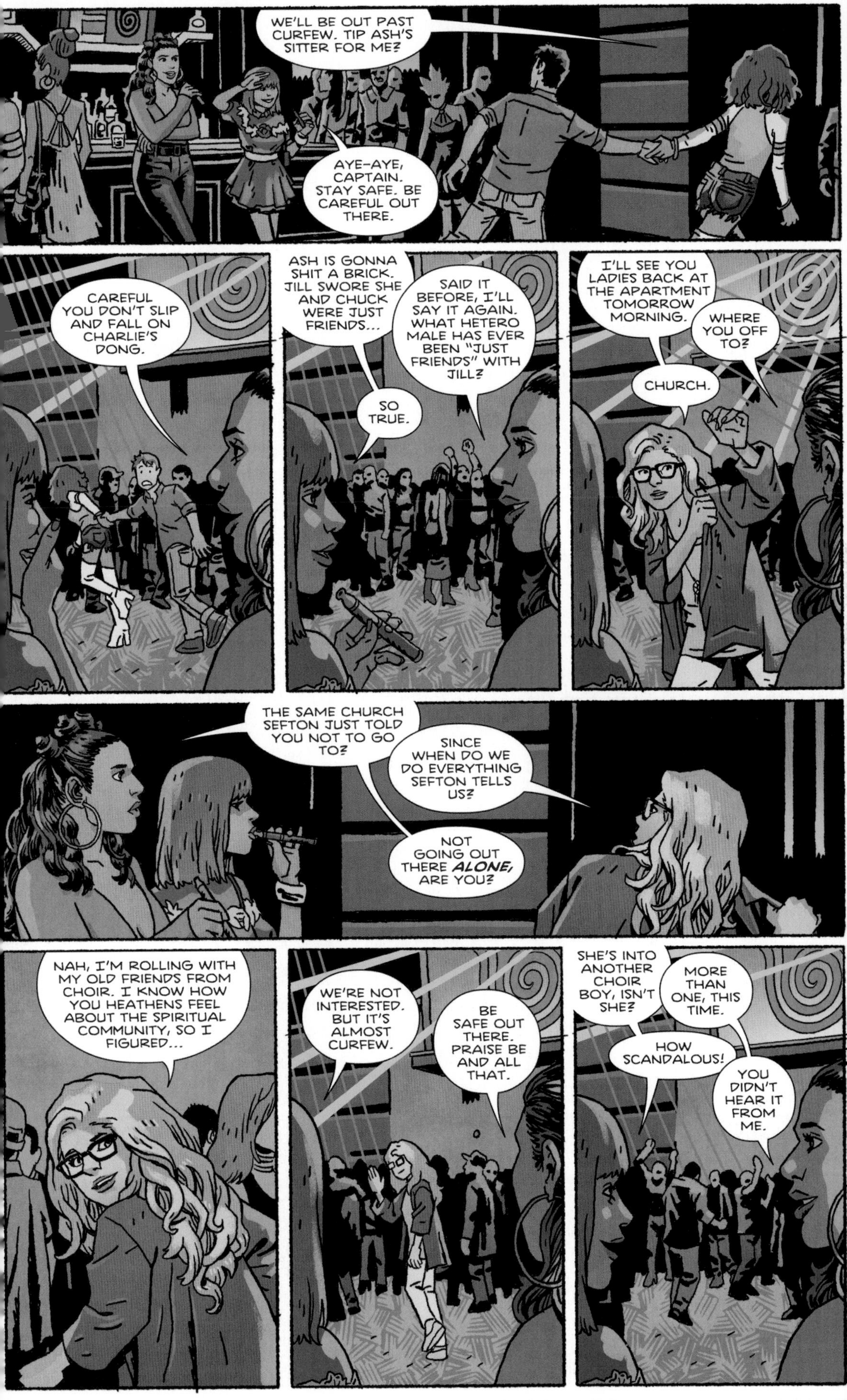
WE'LL BE OUT PAST CURFEW. TIP ASH'S SITTER FOR ME?
AYE-AYE, CAPTAIN. STAY SAFE. BE CAREFUL OUT THERE.
CAREFUL YOU DON'T SLIP AND FALL ON CHARLIE'S DONG.
ASH IS GONNA SHIT A BRICK. JILL SWORE SHE AND CHUCK WERE JUST FRIENDS...
SAID IT BEFORE, I'LL SAY IT AGAIN. WHAT HETERO MALE HAS EVER BEEN "JUST FRIENDS" WITH JILL?
SO TRUE.
I'LL SEE YOU LADIES BACK AT THE APARTMENT TOMORROW MORNING.
WHERE YOU OFF TO?
CHURCH.
THE SAME CHURCH SEFTON JUST TOLD YOU NOT TO GO TO?
SINCE WHEN DO WE DO EVERYTHING SEFTON TELLS US?
NOT GOING OUT THERE ALONE, ARE YOU?
NAH, I'M ROLLING WITH MY OLD FRIENDS FROM CHOIR. I KNOW HOW YOU HEATHENS FEEL ABOUT THE SPIRITUAL COMMUNITY, SO I FIGURED...
WE'RE NOT INTERESTED. BUT IT'S ALMOST CURFEW.
BE SAFE OUT THERE. PRAISE BE AND ALL THAT.
SHE'S INTO ANOTHER CHOIR BOY, ISN'T SHE?
MORE THAN ONE, THIS TIME.
HOW SCANDALOUS!
YOU DIDN'T HEAR IT FROM ME.

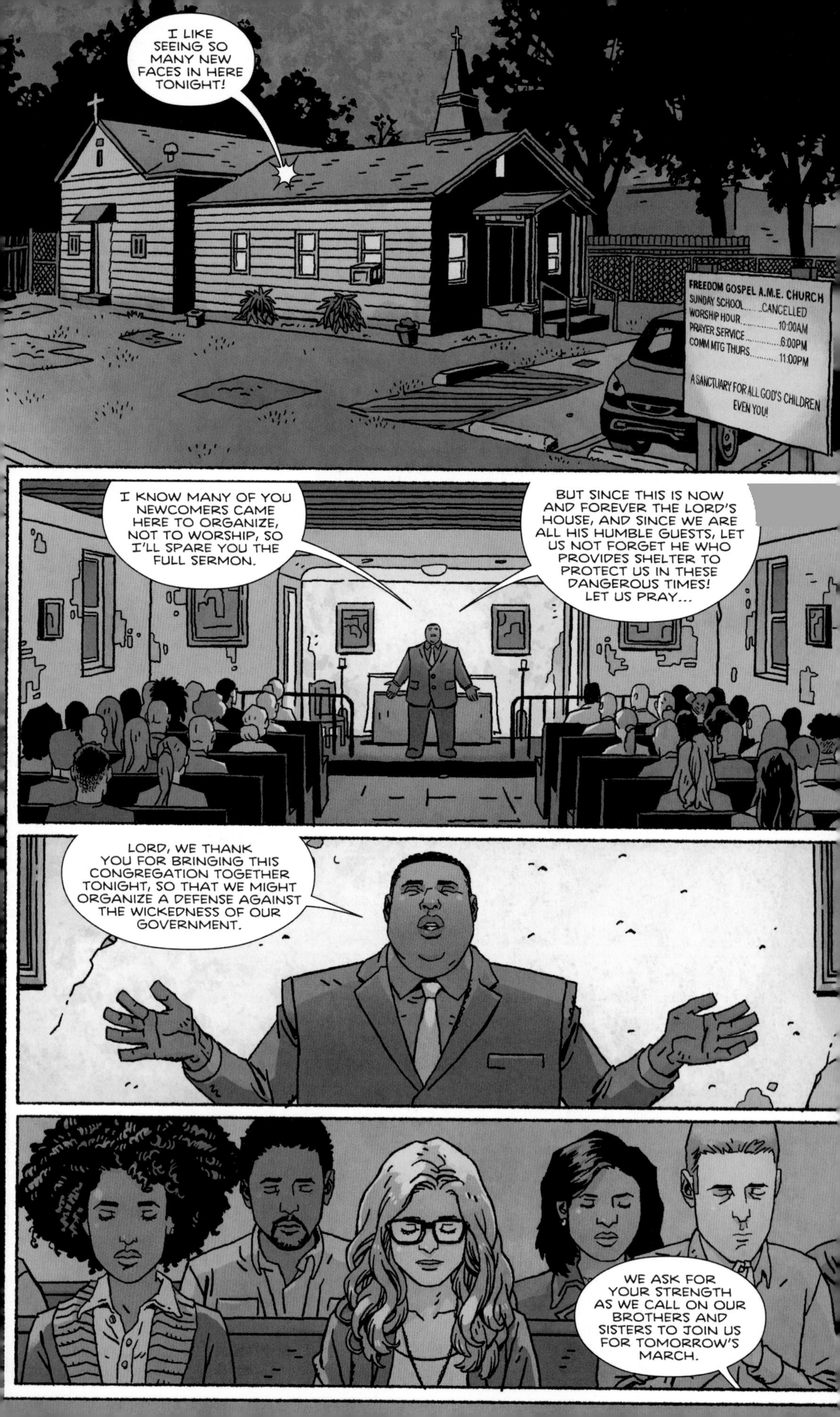
I LIKE SEEING SO MANY NEW FACES IN HERE TONIGHT!
FREEDOM GOSPEL A.M.E. CHURCH
SUNDAY SCHOOL......CANCELLED
WORSHIP HOUR..........10:00AM
PRAYER SERVICE..........6:00PM
COMM MTG THURS..........11:00PM
A SANCTUARY FOR ALL GOD'S CHILDREN
EVEN YOU!
I KNOW MANY OF YOU NEWCOMERS CAME HERE TO ORGANIZE, NOT TO WORSHIP, SO I'LL SPARE YOU THE FULL SERMON.
BUT SINCE THIS IS NOW AND FOREVER THE LORD'S HOUSE, AND SINCE WE ARE ALL HIS HUMBLE GUESTS, LET US NOT FORGET HE WHO PROVIDES SHELTER TO PROTECT US IN THESE DANGEROUS TIMES! LET US PRAY...
LORD, WE THANK YOU FOR BRINGING THIS CONGREGATION TOGETHER TONIGHT, SO THAT WE MIGHT ORGANIZE A DEFENSE AGAINST THE WICKEDNESS OF OUR GOVERNMENT.
WE ASK FOR YOUR STRENGTH AS WE CALL ON OUR BROTHERS AND SISTERS TO JOIN US FOR TOMORROW'S MARCH.

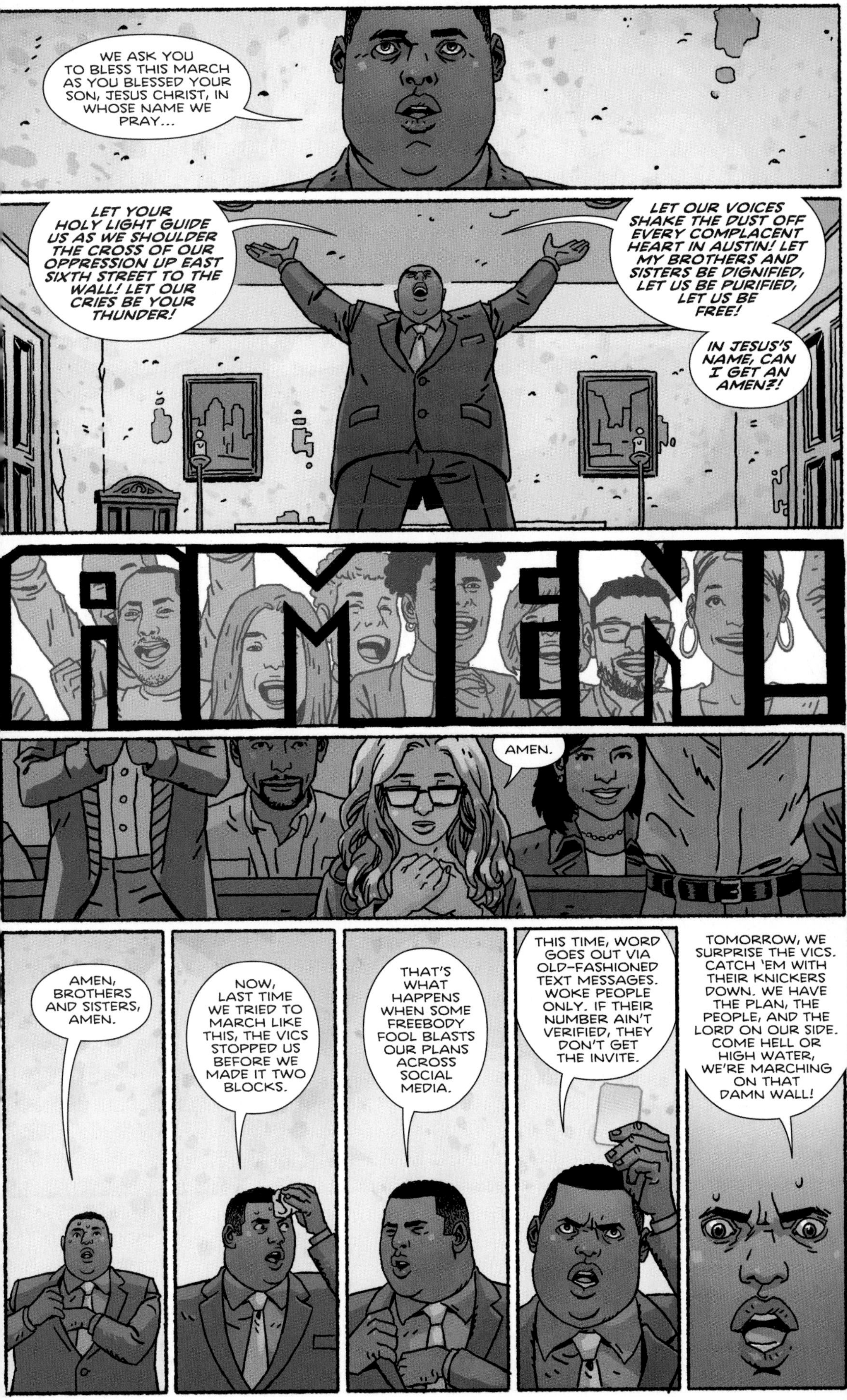
WE ASK YOU TO BLESS THIS MARCH AS YOU BLESSED YOUR SON, JESUS CHRIST, IN WHOSE NAME WE PRAY...
LET YOUR HOLY LIGHT GUIDE US AS WE SHOULDER THE CROSS OF OUR OPPRESSION UP EAST SIXTH STREET TO THE WALL! LET OUR CRIES BE YOUR THUNDER!
LET OUR VOICES SHAKE THE DUST OFF EVERY COMPLACENT HEART IN AUSTIN! LET MY BROTHERS AND SISTERS BE DIGNIFIED, LET US BE PURIFIED, LET US BE FREE!
IN JESUS'S NAME, CAN I GET AN AMEN?!
¡AMEN!
AMEN.
AMEN, BROTHERS AND SISTERS, AMEN.
NOW, LAST TIME WE TRIED TO MARCH LIKE THIS, THE VICS STOPPED US BEFORE WE MADE IT TWO BLOCKS.
THAT'S WHAT HAPPENS WHEN SOME FREEBODY FOOL BLASTS OUR PLANS ACROSS SOCIAL MEDIA.
THIS TIME, WORD GOES OUT VIA OLD-FASHIONED TEXT MESSAGES. WOKE PEOPLE ONLY. IF THEIR NUMBER AIN'T VERIFIED, THEY DON'T GET THE INVITE.
TOMORROW, WE SURPRISE THE VICS. CATCH 'EM WITH THEIR KNICKERS DOWN. WE HAVE THE PLAN, THE PEOPLE, AND THE LORD ON OUR SIDE. COME HELL OR HIGH WATER, WE'RE MARCHING ON THAT DAMN WALL!

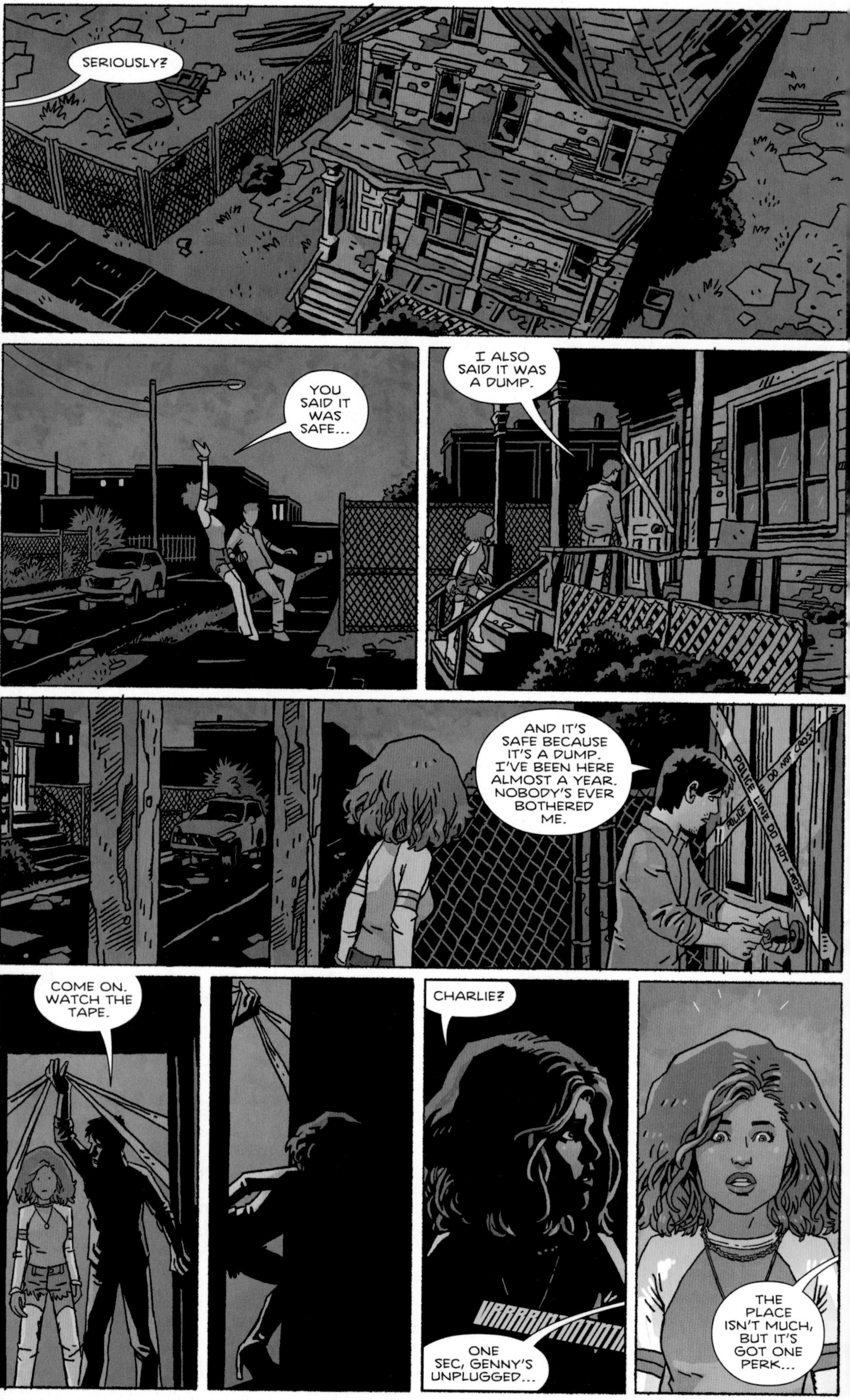
SERIOUSLY?
YOU SAID IT WAS SAFE...
I ALSO SAID IT WAS A DUMP.
AND IT'S SAFE BECAUSE IT'S A DUMP. I'VE BEEN HERE ALMOST A YEAR. NOBODY'S EVER BOTHERED ME.
POLICE LINE DO NOT CROSS
COME ON. WATCH THE TAPE.
CHARLIE?
VRRRRMMMMM
ONE SEC, GENNY'S UNPLUGGED...
THE PLACE ISN'T MUCH, BUT IT'S GOT ONE PERK...

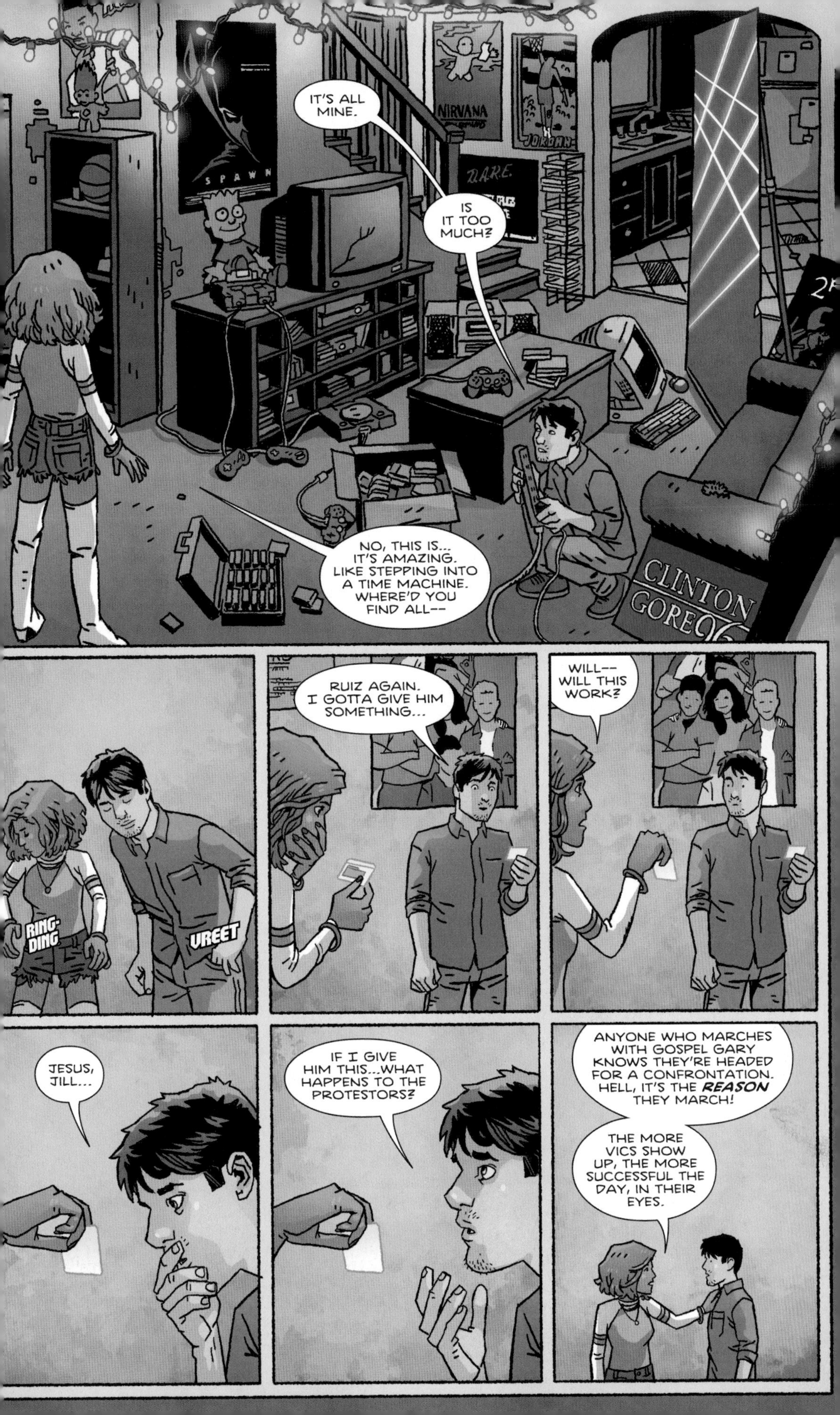
IT'S ALL MINE.
IS IT TOO MUCH?
NO, THIS IS... IT'S AMAZING. LIKE STEPPING INTO A TIME MACHINE. WHERE'D YOU FIND ALL--
CLINTON GORE 96
RING-DING
VREET
RUIZ AGAIN. I GOTTA GIVE HIM SOMETHING...
WILL-- WILL THIS WORK?
JESUS, JILL...
IF I GIVE HIM THIS...WHAT HAPPENS TO THE PROTESTORS?
ANYONE WHO MARCHES WITH GOSPEL GARY KNOWS THEY'RE HEADED FOR A CONFRONTATION. HELL, IT'S THE *REASON* THEY MARCH!
THE MORE VICS SHOW UP, THE MORE SUCCESSFUL THE DAY, IN THEIR EYES.

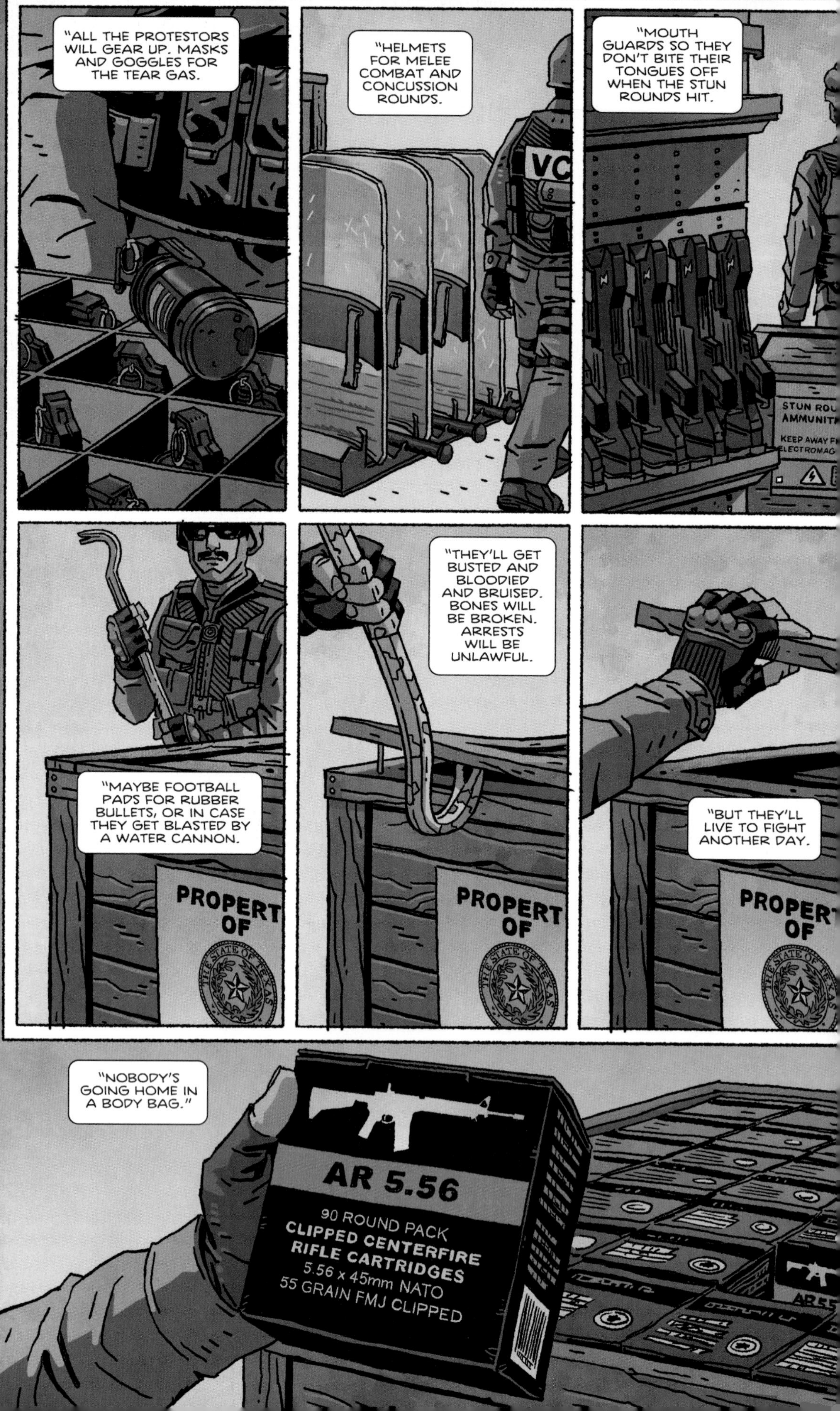
"ALL THE PROTESTORS WILL GEAR UP. MASKS AND GOGGLES FOR THE TEAR GAS.
"HELMETS FOR MELEE COMBAT AND CONCUSSION ROUNDS.
VC
"MOUTH GUARDS SO THEY DON'T BITE THEIR TONGUES OFF WHEN THE STUN ROUNDS HIT.
"MAYBE FOOTBALL PADS FOR RUBBER BULLETS, OR IN CASE THEY GET BLASTED BY A WATER CANNON.
PROPERT OF
"THEY'LL GET BUSTED AND BLOODIED AND BRUISED. BONES WILL BE BROKEN. ARRESTS WILL BE UNLAWFUL.
PROPERT OF
"BUT THEY'LL LIVE TO FIGHT ANOTHER DAY.
PROPERT OF
"NOBODY'S GOING HOME IN A BODY BAG."
AR 5.56
90 ROUND PACK
CLIPPED CENTERFIRE RIFLE CARTRIDGES
5.56 x 45mm NATO
55 GRAIN FMJ CLIPPED

+1 512-555-0316

🔒 Encrypted Conversation + 1 512-555-0316

Thurs 09:38 Sister Face! This is Justice Harrison from Freedom Gospel A.M.E. I'm sure you've seen the PMD video that's got the VCU shook. Now is the time to show them our strength. We need to march! You've supported Gospel Gary before. Can he count on your support now?

Thurs 09:46 FUCKIN HELL YEAH!

I mean... HEAVEN YEAH!!

Thurs 09:47 Awesome! The following info is confidential and invite-only. DO NOT SHARE ON SOCIAL CHANNELS. We congregrate for morning prayers @ dawn @ the corner of East 5th & Pedernales. The day will be long, so we suggest you bring a water bottle and snacks. ALL weapons are banned. Body armor is discouraged; it sends the wrong message. Gospel Gary wants to avoid violence at all costs. Will we see you tomorrow morning?

Thurs 09:49

I am so down!

Thurs 09:50 God bless you, Sister Face. See you tomorrow. Meanwhile, if you have the means, Gospel Gary humbly asks that you donate to keep Freedom Gospel alive for our impoverished brethren. You can donate here: https://freedomgospel. church/blessings

Thurs 10:03 God is great! Stay free!

Thurs 19:48 Sister Face! Justice here again. Gospel Gary personally requests your presence at tonight's senior organizers meeting. Kicks off 8:30 @ Freedom Gospel. We know it's short notice, but can you make it?

Thurs 19:53 Gospel Gary can count on me!

Thurs 19:55 God bless, Sister. Do you need escort? Gospel Gary can provide.

Thurs 19:57 I'm cool thx!

Thurs 19:59 Be safe out there. See you soon!

RATIONAL REVIEW DONATE CHANNELS LOGIN SUBSCRIBE

LAW & THE COURTS

The Farcical Innocence of Gospel 'Guilty' Gary

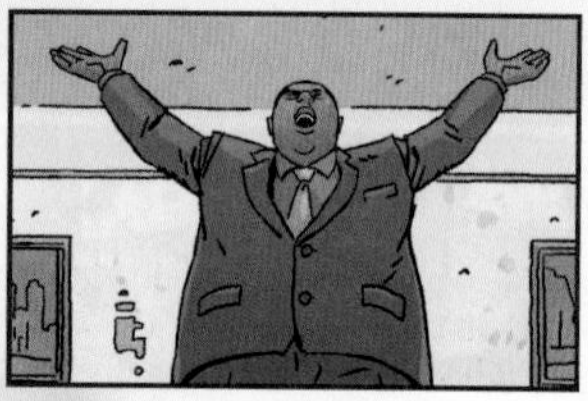

By HALEY HICKS | February 9, 6:30 AM

Activist stokes racial fears to delegitimize law enforcement.

This week, "Gospel" Gary Mendo, who hails himself as a "preacher, activist, and humanitarian," will give a keynote speech at the annual Clean Hands Network conference in Austin, TX. The theme of the event, whose attendees work to prevent and undo wrongful convictions, is "The Presumption of Innocence."

I've covered many confounding things in my five years as a columnist, author, influencer, and pageant host, but this one takes my breath away.

Gospel Gary is a serial firestarter. He has been arrested a dozen times for crimes ranging from "battery against a police officer" to "willful incitement of a riot". Seven of those arrests resulted in guilty convictions and prison sentences. The remaining five were dismissed or withdrawn following sustained campaigns of public pressure and harassment perpetrated by Gary's loyal followers after he tweeted the names of his accusers. The average Gospel Gary tweet generates over two million impressions.

This man is to innocence as Antifa is to civility. Rather than speak on the "Presumption of Innocence," Gary's keynote will reliably consist of baseless attacks on police officers. Time after time, he presumes malice and racism if an officer even sneezes in the direction of a minority, let alone if that officer legitimately arrests a guilty suspect. At the end of his keynote, he will lead a march on the Capitol, hoping to incite police violence to prove his own point.

Former Cleveland police detective Sergeant Jon Margolis serves on the board of Blue Justice, which advocates for wrongfully convicted police officers. Margolis told me: "Gospel Gary's agenda is to instill in people a fear of the police. He creates an environment conducive to deadly confrontations... The whole truth is never reported in these investigations. Evidence that favors the police is diminished or omitted entirely when it hits the news."

What exactly is "humanitarian" or exemplary about such an attitude? This is race-hustling cynicism at its worst. That's par for the twisted course for Gospel Gary, a seven-times-convicted offender who nonetheless treats people as guilty until proven innocent and threatens those who call him out (including critics within the Freebodies who allege he has ripped off the movement).

EXECUTIVE ORDER BY THE GOVERNOR OF THE STATE OF TEXAS

THE STATE OF TEXAS EXECUTIVE DEPARTMENT
OFFICE OF THE GOVERNOR   AUSTIN, TEXAS

EXECUTIVE ORDER SAP 83

Relating to the Use of Lethal Ammunition by Law Enforcement in the State of Texas

WHEREAS, I, SUZANNA A. PRITCHARD, Governor of Texas, issued an emergency proclamation certifying the threat of Powers of Mass Destruction against the Travis County Sheriff's Department – Variant Crimes Unit and other law enforcement agencies in the State of Texas; and

WHEREAS, it was first enshrined in the 2nd Amendment of the Constitution of the United States of America that "a well regulated Militia, being necessary to the security of a free State, the right of the people to keep and bear Arms, shall not be infringed;" and

WHEREAS, law enforcement officers of the State have been denied their 2nd Amendment rights in the wake of a Socialist coup that resulted in the unconstitutional passage of S.J.R.-2905, which forbade the use of lethal arms in the pursuit of justice; and

WHEREAS, the imminent threat posed by Powers of Mass Destruction endangers the lives of all law enforcement officers;

NOW, THEREFORE, by the authority vested in me by the Constitution and the laws of this State, I do hereby invoke executive privilege to revoke SJR-2905 as it applies to State law enforcement agencies that include, but are not limited to, the following:

Texas Department of Public Safety

-      Texas Highway Patrol

-      Texas Ranger Division

Texas and Southwestern Cattle Raisers Association Special Rangers

Travis County Sheriff's Department – Variant Crimes Unit

University of Texas System Police

AND HEREBY charge the Texas Secretary of State to supervise the immediate distribution of lethal ammunition to State law enforcement agencies.

This executive order supersedes all previous orders on this matter that are in conflict or inconsistent with its terms, and this order shall remain in effect and in full force until modified, amended, rescinded, or superseded by me or by a succeeding governor.

Given under my hand,
Suzanna A. Pritchard, Governor

IN TESTIMONY WHEREOF, I have hereunto set my
hand and caused the Great Seal of the State of Texas
to be affixed. Done at the Capitol in the City of Austin.

By the Governor

Blair C. Scott
Secretary of the State

Suzanna A. Pritchard
Governor of Texas

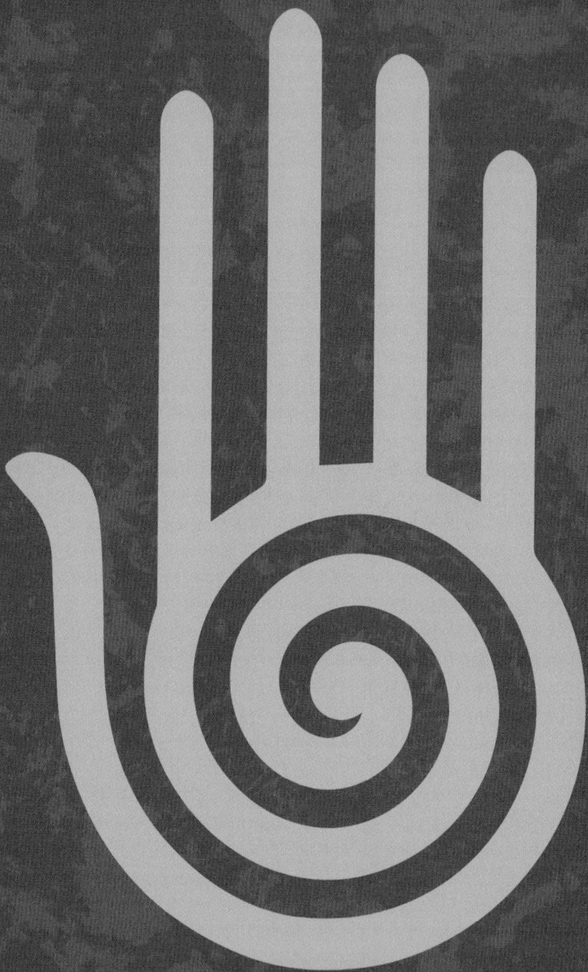

NOW

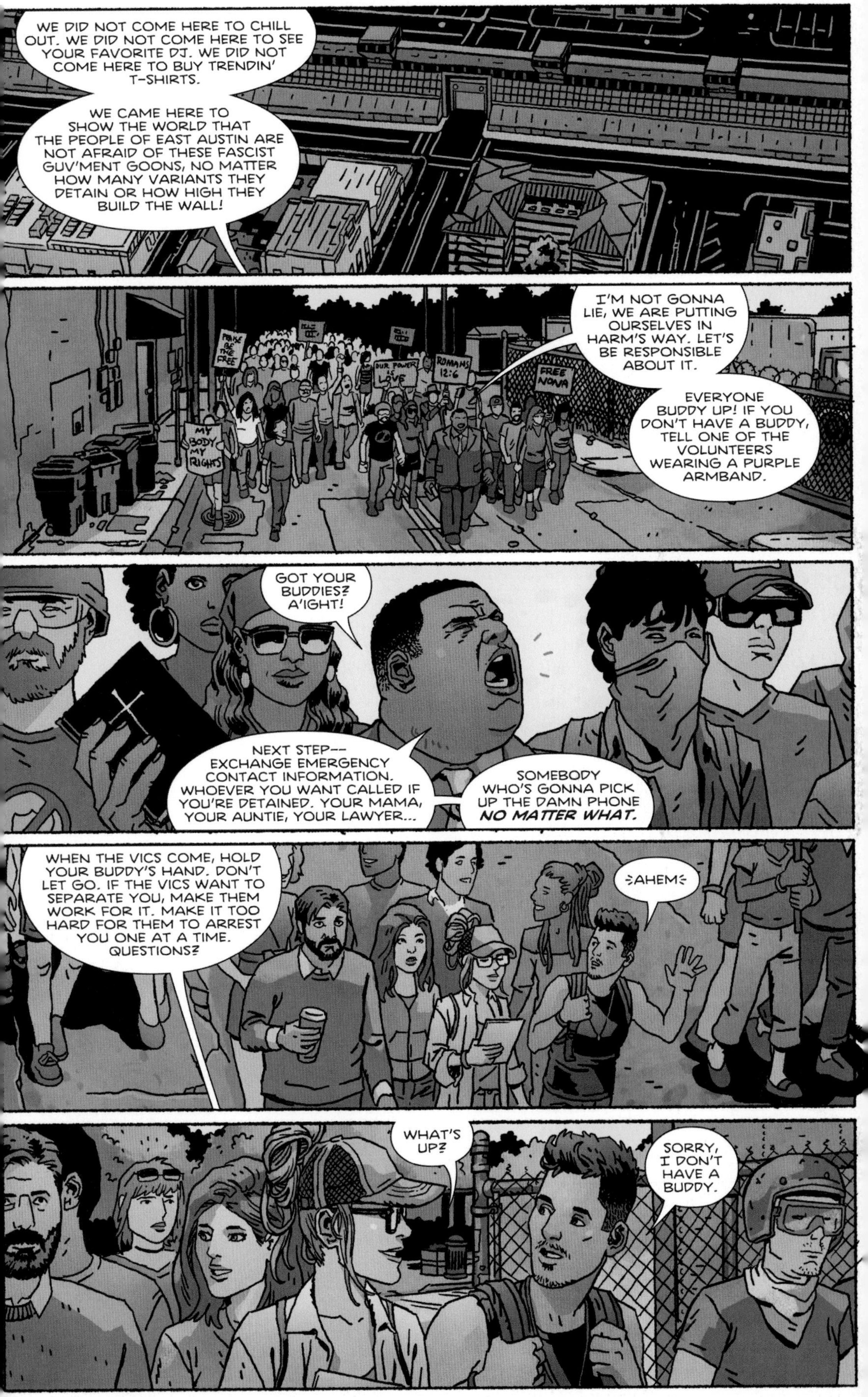
WE DID NOT COME HERE TO CHILL OUT. WE DID NOT COME HERE TO SEE YOUR FAVORITE DJ. WE DID NOT COME HERE TO BUY TRENDIN' T-SHIRTS.
WE CAME HERE TO SHOW THE WORLD THAT THE PEOPLE OF EAST AUSTIN ARE NOT AFRAID OF THESE FASCIST GUV'MENT GOONS, NO MATTER HOW MANY VARIANTS THEY DETAIN OR HOW HIGH THEY BUILD THE WALL!
PRAISE BE THE FREE
OUR POWER IS LOVE
ROMANS 12:6
FREE NOVA
MY BODY MY RIGHTS
I'M NOT GONNA LIE, WE ARE PUTTING OURSELVES IN HARM'S WAY. LET'S BE RESPONSIBLE ABOUT IT.
EVERYONE BUDDY UP! IF YOU DON'T HAVE A BUDDY, TELL ONE OF THE VOLUNTEERS WEARING A PURPLE ARMBAND.
GOT YOUR BUDDIES? A'IGHT!
NEXT STEP-- EXCHANGE EMERGENCY CONTACT INFORMATION. WHOEVER YOU WANT CALLED IF YOU'RE DETAINED. YOUR MAMA, YOUR AUNTIE, YOUR LAWYER...
SOMEBODY WHO'S GONNA PICK UP THE DAMN PHONE *NO MATTER WHAT.*
WHEN THE VICS COME, HOLD YOUR BUDDY'S HAND. DON'T LET GO. IF THE VICS WANT TO SEPARATE YOU, MAKE THEM WORK FOR IT. MAKE IT TOO HARD FOR THEM TO ARREST YOU ONE AT A TIME. QUESTIONS?
AHEM
WHAT'S UP?
SORRY, I DON'T HAVE A BUDDY.

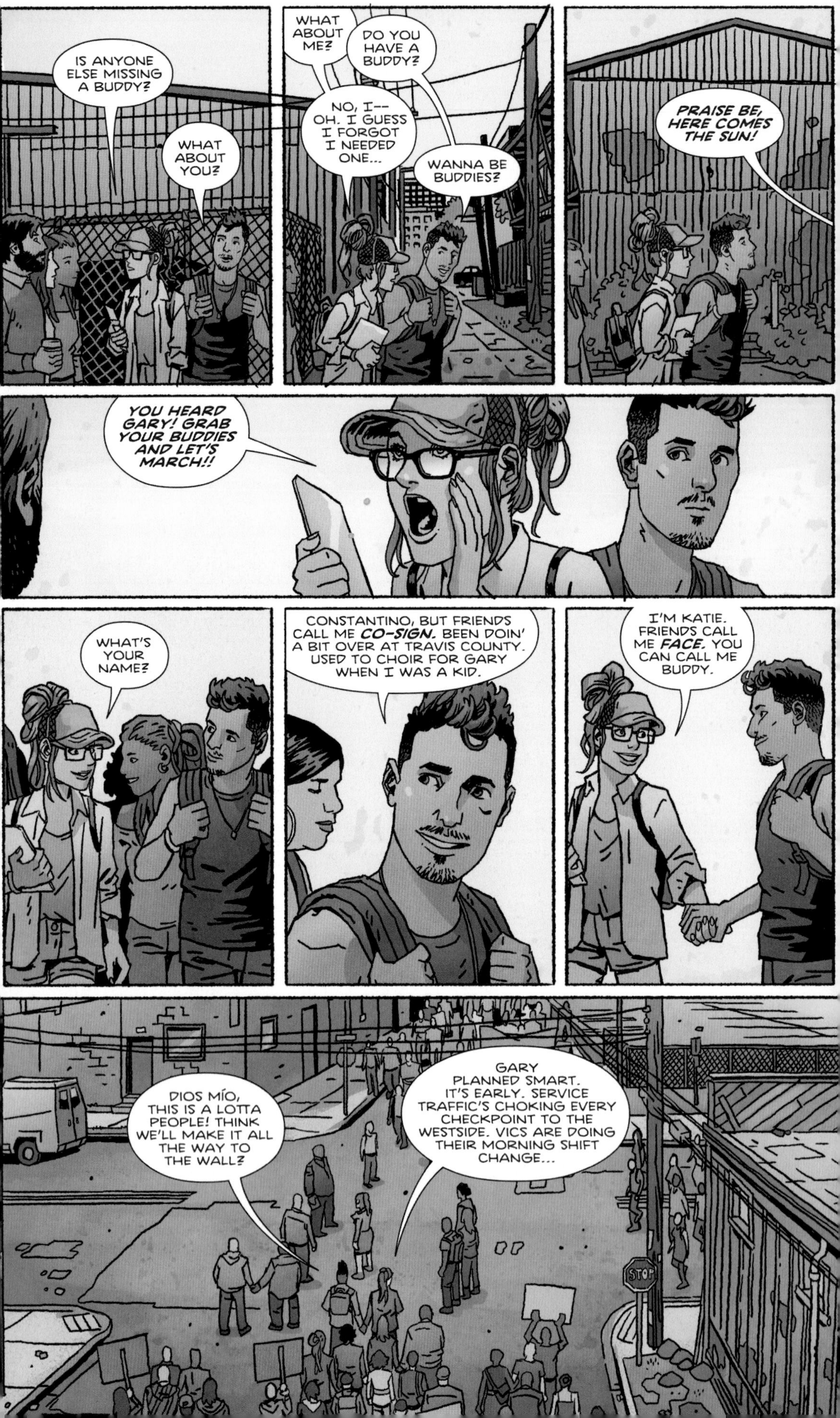

IS ANYONE ELSE MISSING A BUDDY?
WHAT ABOUT YOU?
WHAT ABOUT ME?
DO YOU HAVE A BUDDY?
NO, I-- OH. I GUESS I FORGOT I NEEDED ONE...
WANNA BE BUDDIES?
PRAISE BE, HERE COMES THE SUN!
YOU HEARD GARY! GRAB YOUR BUDDIES AND LET'S MARCH!!
WHAT'S YOUR NAME?
CONSTANTINO, BUT FRIENDS CALL ME CO-SIGN. BEEN DOIN' A BIT OVER AT TRAVIS COUNTY. USED TO CHOIR FOR GARY WHEN I WAS A KID.
I'M KATIE. FRIENDS CALL ME FACE. YOU CAN CALL ME BUDDY.
DIOS MÍO, THIS IS A LOTTA PEOPLE! THINK WE'LL MAKE IT ALL THE WAY TO THE WALL?
GARY PLANNED SMART. IT'S EARLY. SERVICE TRAFFIC'S CHOKING EVERY CHECKPOINT TO THE WESTSIDE. VICS ARE DOING THEIR MORNING SHIFT CHANGE...
STOP

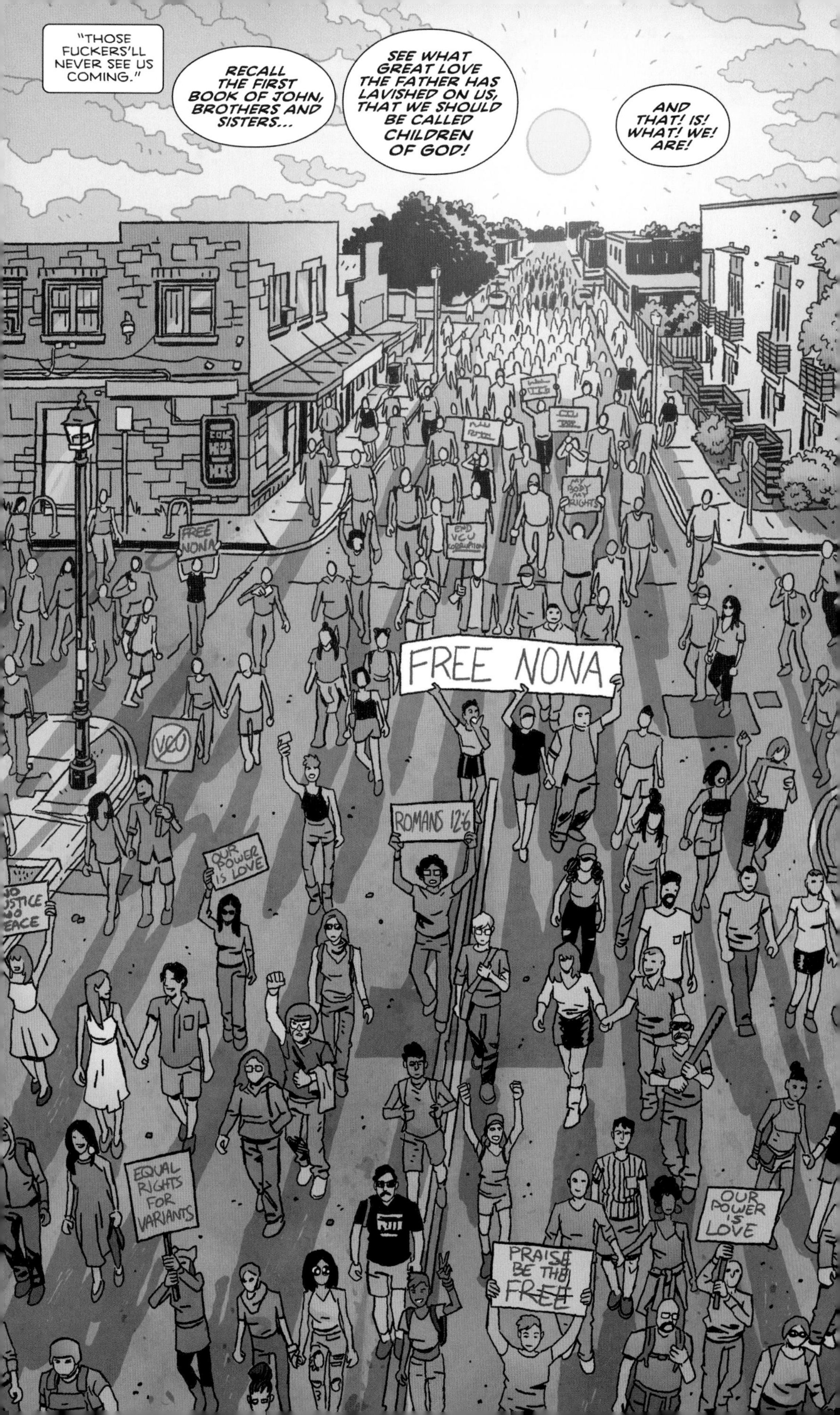
"THOSE FUCKERS'LL NEVER SEE US COMING."
RECALL THE FIRST BOOK OF JOHN, BROTHERS AND SISTERS...
SEE WHAT GREAT LOVE THE FATHER HAS LAVISHED ON US, THAT WE SHOULD BE CALLED CHILDREN OF GOD!
AND THAT! IS! WHAT! WE! ARE!
FREE NONA
END VCU CORRUPTION
MY BODY MY RIGHTS
FREE NONA
VCU
ROMANS 12:6
OUR POWER IS LOVE
EQUAL RIGHTS FOR VARIANTS
PRAISE BE THE FREE
OUR POWER IS LOVE

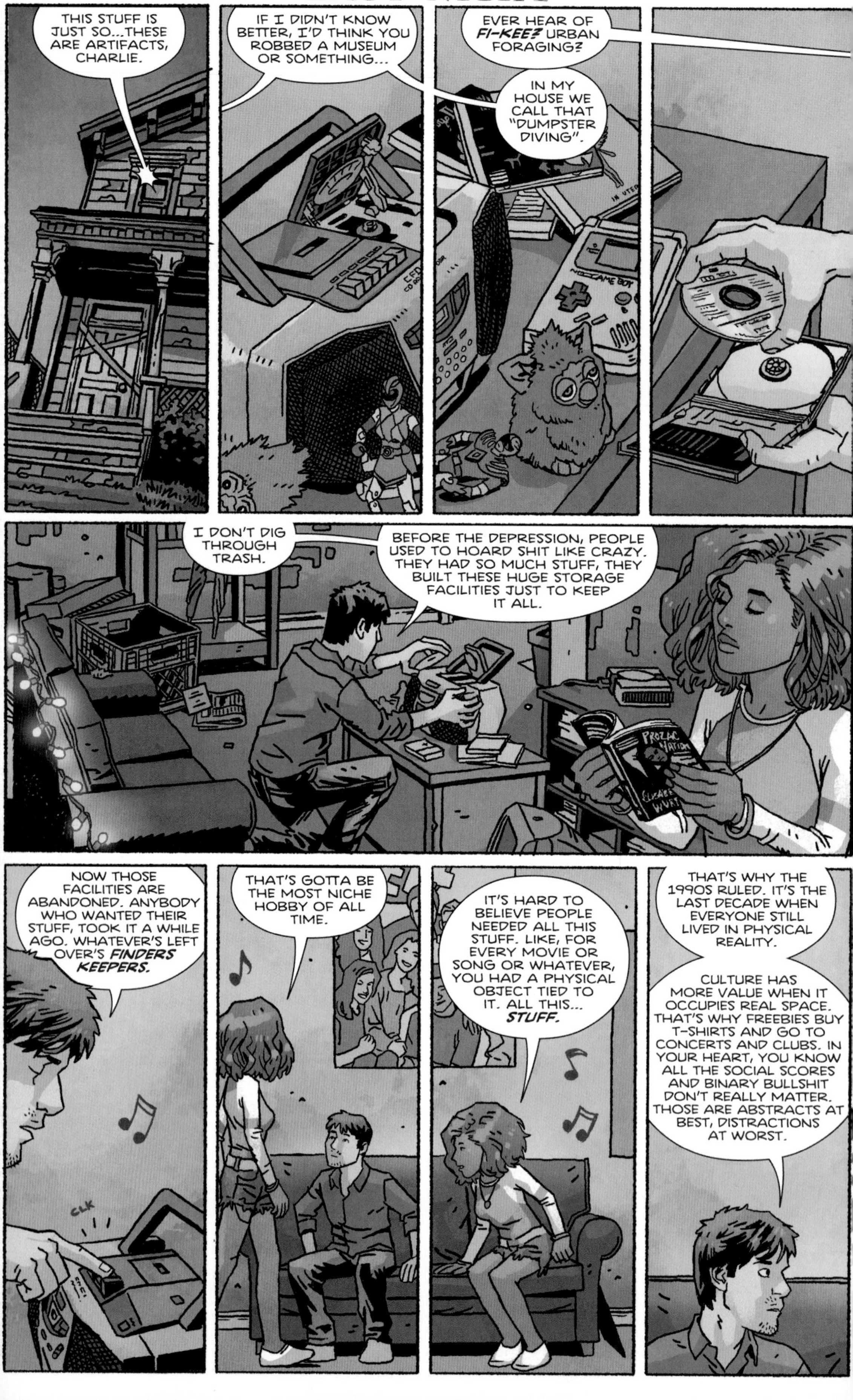
THIS STUFF IS JUST SO...THESE ARE ARTIFACTS, CHARLIE.
IF I DIDN'T KNOW BETTER, I'D THINK YOU ROBBED A MUSEUM OR SOMETHING...
EVER HEAR OF *FI-KEE?* URBAN FORAGING?
IN MY HOUSE WE CALL THAT "DUMPSTER DIVING".
I DON'T DIG THROUGH TRASH.
BEFORE THE DEPRESSION, PEOPLE USED TO HOARD SHIT LIKE CRAZY. THEY HAD SO MUCH STUFF, THEY BUILT THESE HUGE STORAGE FACILITIES JUST TO KEEP IT ALL.
PROZAC NATION
NOW THOSE FACILITIES ARE ABANDONED. ANYBODY WHO WANTED THEIR STUFF, TOOK IT A WHILE AGO. WHATEVER'S LEFT OVER'S *FINDERS KEEPERS.*
CLK
THAT'S GOTTA BE THE MOST NICHE HOBBY OF ALL TIME.
IT'S HARD TO BELIEVE PEOPLE NEEDED ALL THIS STUFF. LIKE, FOR EVERY MOVIE OR SONG OR WHATEVER, YOU HAD A PHYSICAL OBJECT TIED TO IT. ALL THIS... *STUFF.*
THAT'S WHY THE 1990S RULED. IT'S THE LAST DECADE WHEN EVERYONE STILL LIVED IN PHYSICAL REALITY.
CULTURE HAS MORE VALUE WHEN IT OCCUPIES REAL SPACE. THAT'S WHY FREEBIES BUY T-SHIRTS AND GO TO CONCERTS AND CLUBS. IN YOUR HEART, YOU KNOW ALL THE SOCIAL SCORES AND BINARY BULLSHIT DON'T REALLY MATTER. THOSE ARE ABSTRACTS AT BEST, DISTRACTIONS AT WORST.

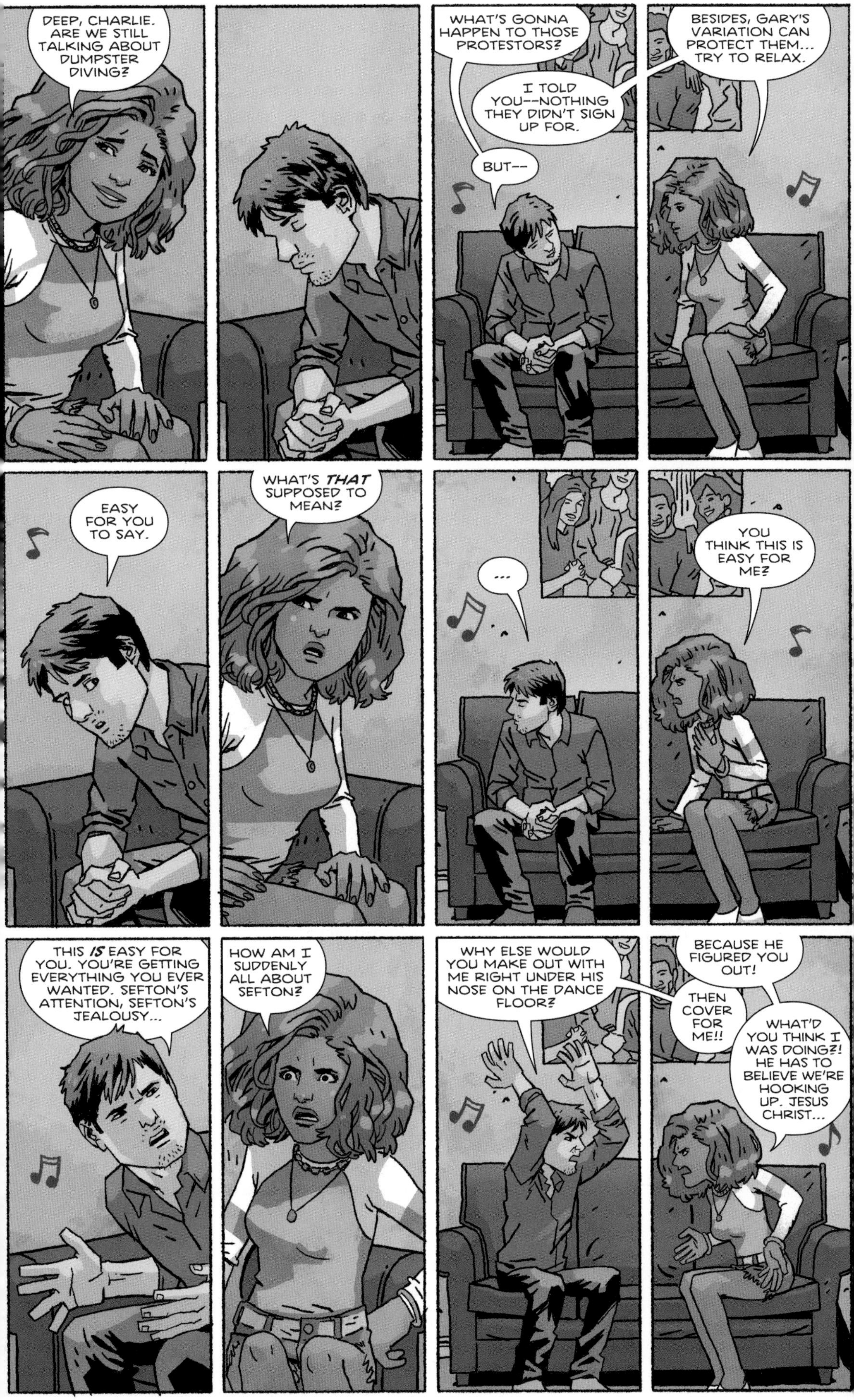
DEEP, CHARLIE. ARE WE STILL TALKING ABOUT DUMPSTER DIVING?
WHAT'S GONNA HAPPEN TO THOSE PROTESTORS?
I TOLD YOU--NOTHING THEY DIDN'T SIGN UP FOR.
BUT--
BESIDES, GARY'S VARIATION CAN PROTECT THEM... TRY TO RELAX.
EASY FOR YOU TO SAY.
WHAT'S *THAT* SUPPOSED TO MEAN?
...
YOU THINK THIS IS EASY FOR ME?
THIS *IS* EASY FOR YOU. YOU'RE GETTING EVERYTHING YOU EVER WANTED. SEFTON'S ATTENTION, SEFTON'S JEALOUSY...
HOW AM I SUDDENLY ALL ABOUT SEFTON?
WHY ELSE WOULD YOU MAKE OUT WITH ME RIGHT UNDER HIS NOSE ON THE DANCE FLOOR?
BECAUSE HE FIGURED YOU OUT!
THEN COVER FOR ME!!
WHAT'D YOU THINK I WAS DOING?! HE HAS TO BELIEVE WE'RE HOOKING UP. JESUS CHRIST...

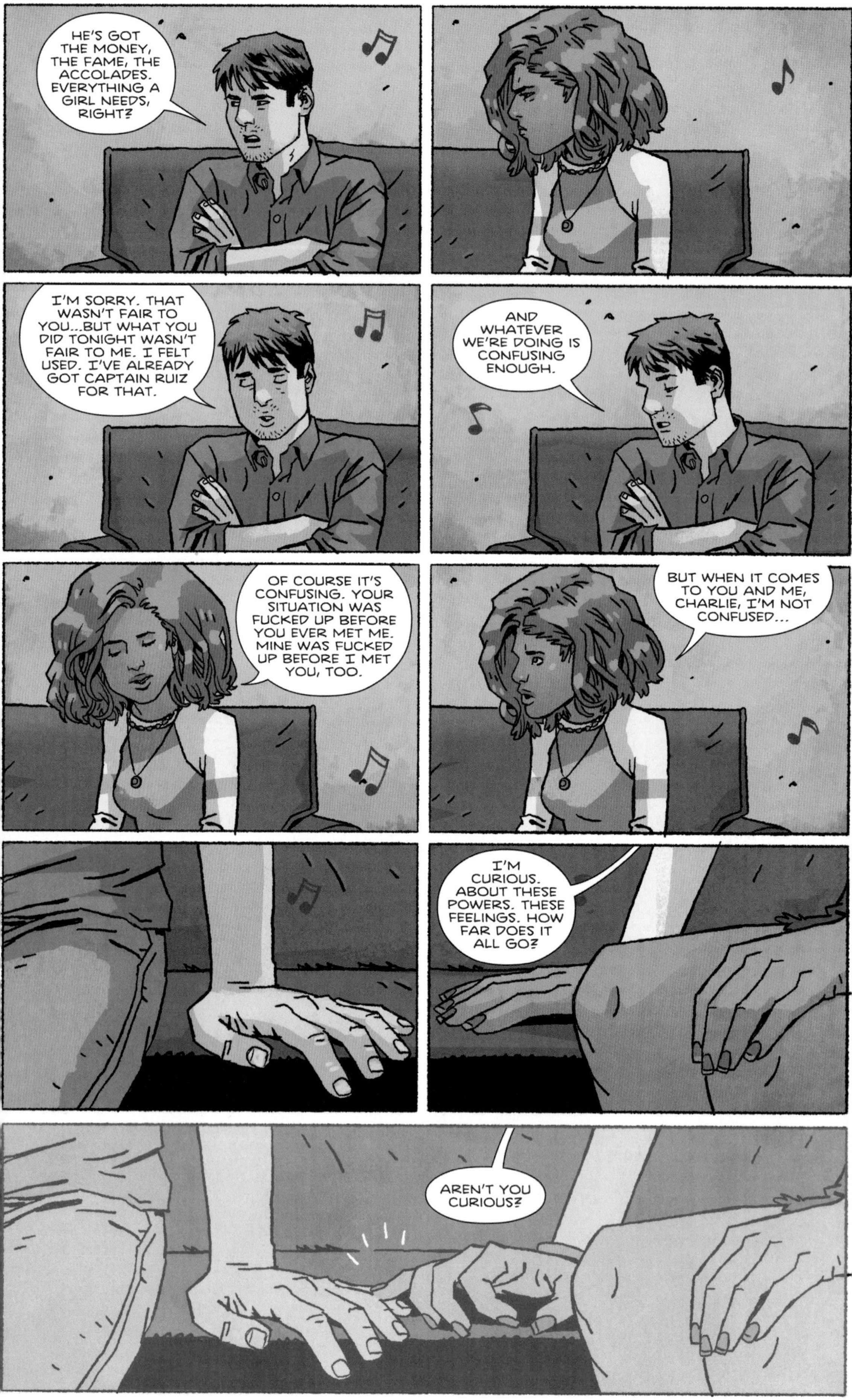
HE'S GOT THE MONEY, THE FAME, THE ACCOLADES. EVERYTHING A GIRL NEEDS, RIGHT?
I'M SORRY. THAT WASN'T FAIR TO YOU...BUT WHAT YOU DID TONIGHT WASN'T FAIR TO ME. I FELT USED. I'VE ALREADY GOT CAPTAIN RUIZ FOR THAT.
AND WHATEVER WE'RE DOING IS CONFUSING ENOUGH.
OF COURSE IT'S CONFUSING. YOUR SITUATION WAS FUCKED UP BEFORE YOU EVER MET ME. MINE WAS FUCKED UP BEFORE I MET YOU, TOO.
BUT WHEN IT COMES TO YOU AND ME, CHARLIE, I'M NOT CONFUSED...
I'M CURIOUS. ABOUT THESE POWERS. THESE FEELINGS. HOW FAR DOES IT ALL GO?
AREN'T YOU CURIOUS?

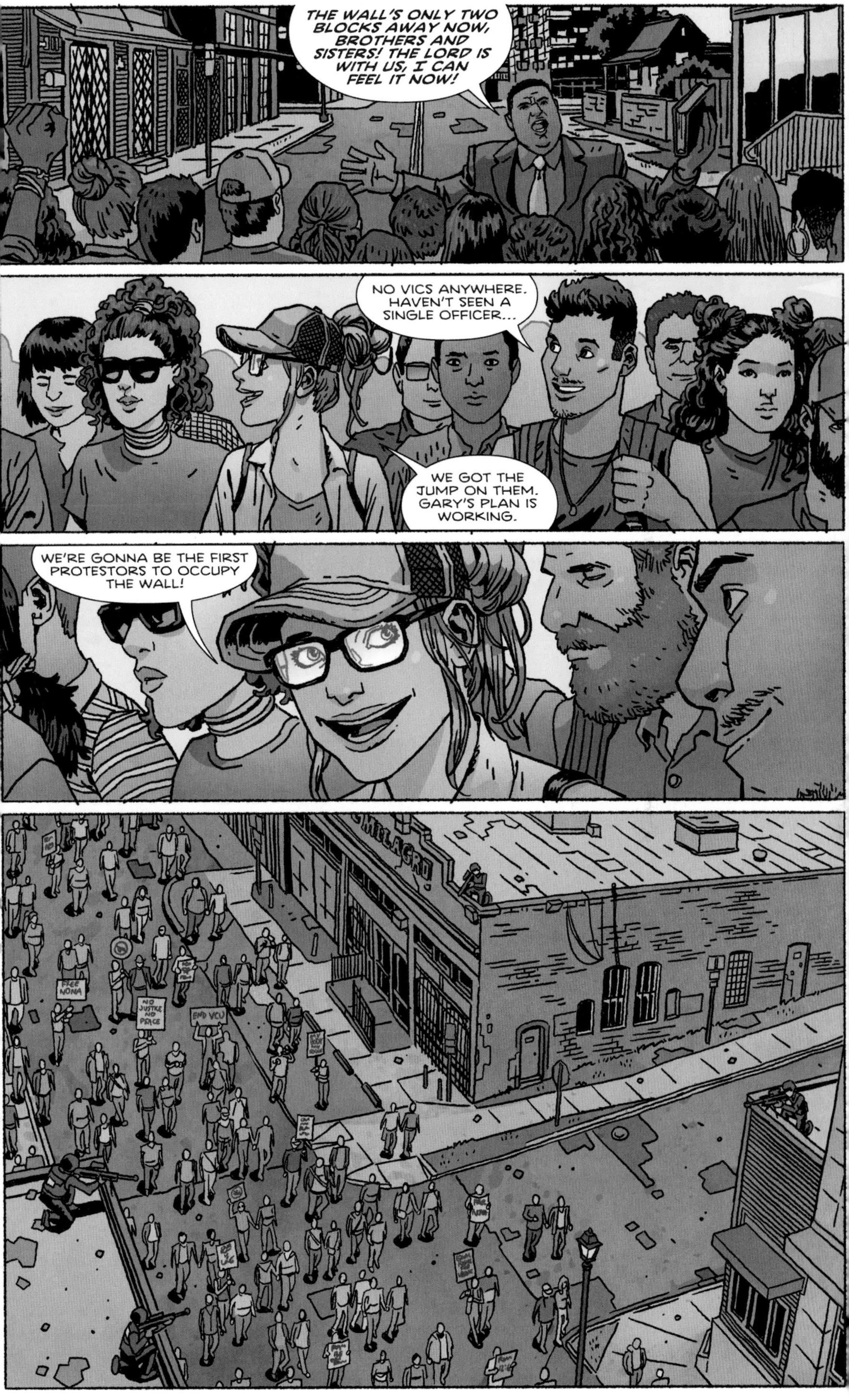
THE WALL'S ONLY TWO BLOCKS AWAY NOW, BROTHERS AND SISTERS! THE LORD IS WITH US, I CAN FEEL IT NOW!
NO VICS ANYWHERE. HAVEN'T SEEN A SINGLE OFFICER...
WE GOT THE JUMP ON THEM. GARY'S PLAN IS WORKING.
WE'RE GONNA BE THE FIRST PROTESTORS TO OCCUPY THE WALL!
FREE NONA
NO JUSTICE NO PEACE
END VCU

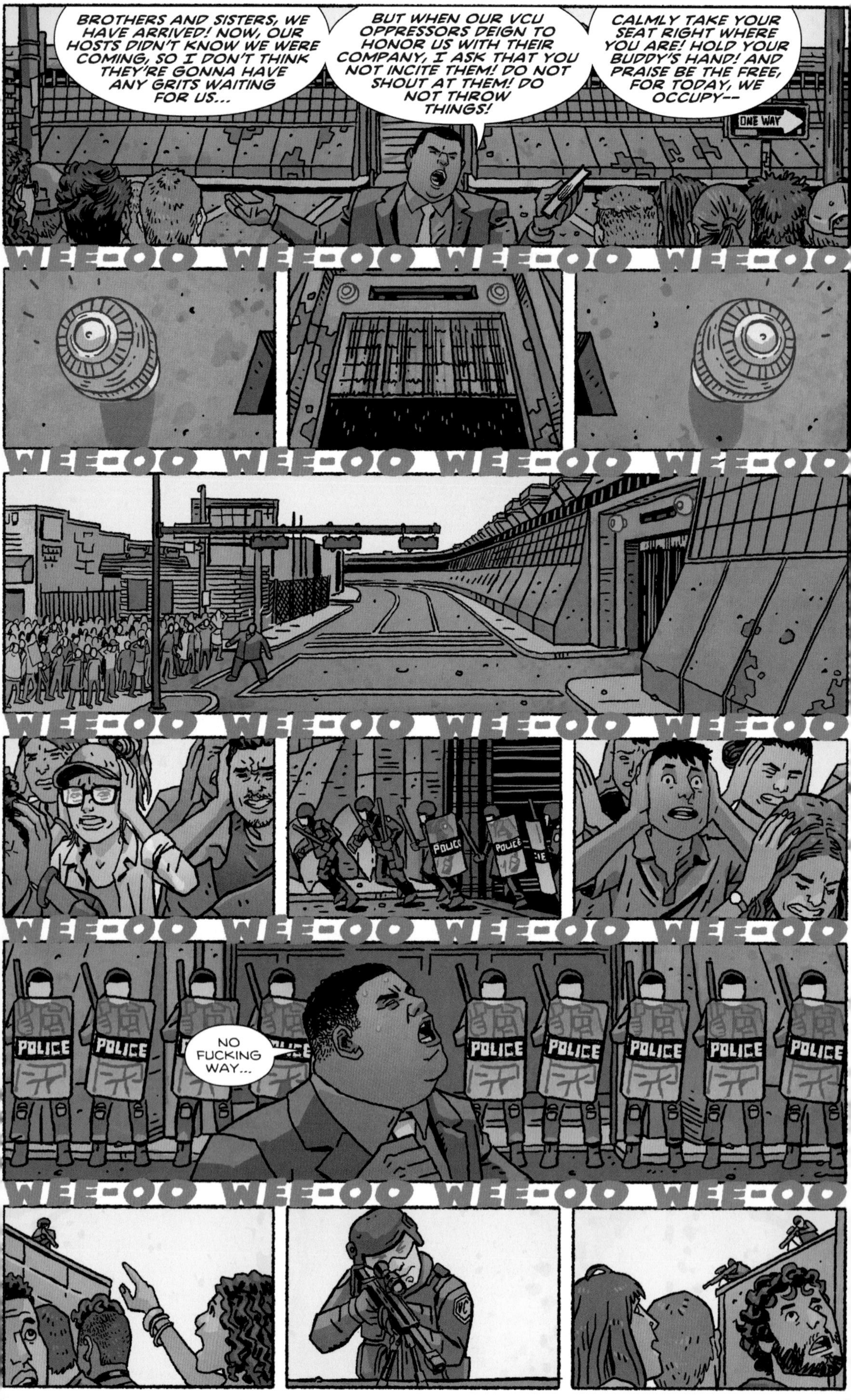
BROTHERS AND SISTERS, WE HAVE ARRIVED! NOW, OUR HOSTS DIDN'T KNOW WE WERE COMING, SO I DON'T THINK THEY'RE GONNA HAVE ANY GRITS WAITING FOR US...
BUT WHEN OUR VCU OPPRESSORS DEIGN TO HONOR US WITH THEIR COMPANY, I ASK THAT YOU NOT INCITE THEM! DO NOT SHOUT AT THEM! DO NOT THROW THINGS!
CALMLY TAKE YOUR SEAT RIGHT WHERE YOU ARE! HOLD YOUR BUDDY'S HAND! AND PRAISE BE THE FREE, FOR TODAY, WE OCCUPY--
ONE WAY
WEE-OO WEE-OO WEE-OO WEE-OO
WEE-OO WEE-OO WEE-OO WEE-OO
WEE-OO WEE-OO WEE-OO WEE-OO
POLICE
POLICE
WEE-OO WEE-OO WEE-OO WEE-OO
POLICE
POLICE
POLICE
POLICE
POLICE
POLICE
POLICE
POLICE
NO FUCKING WAY...
WEE-OO WEE-OO WEE-OO WEE-OO

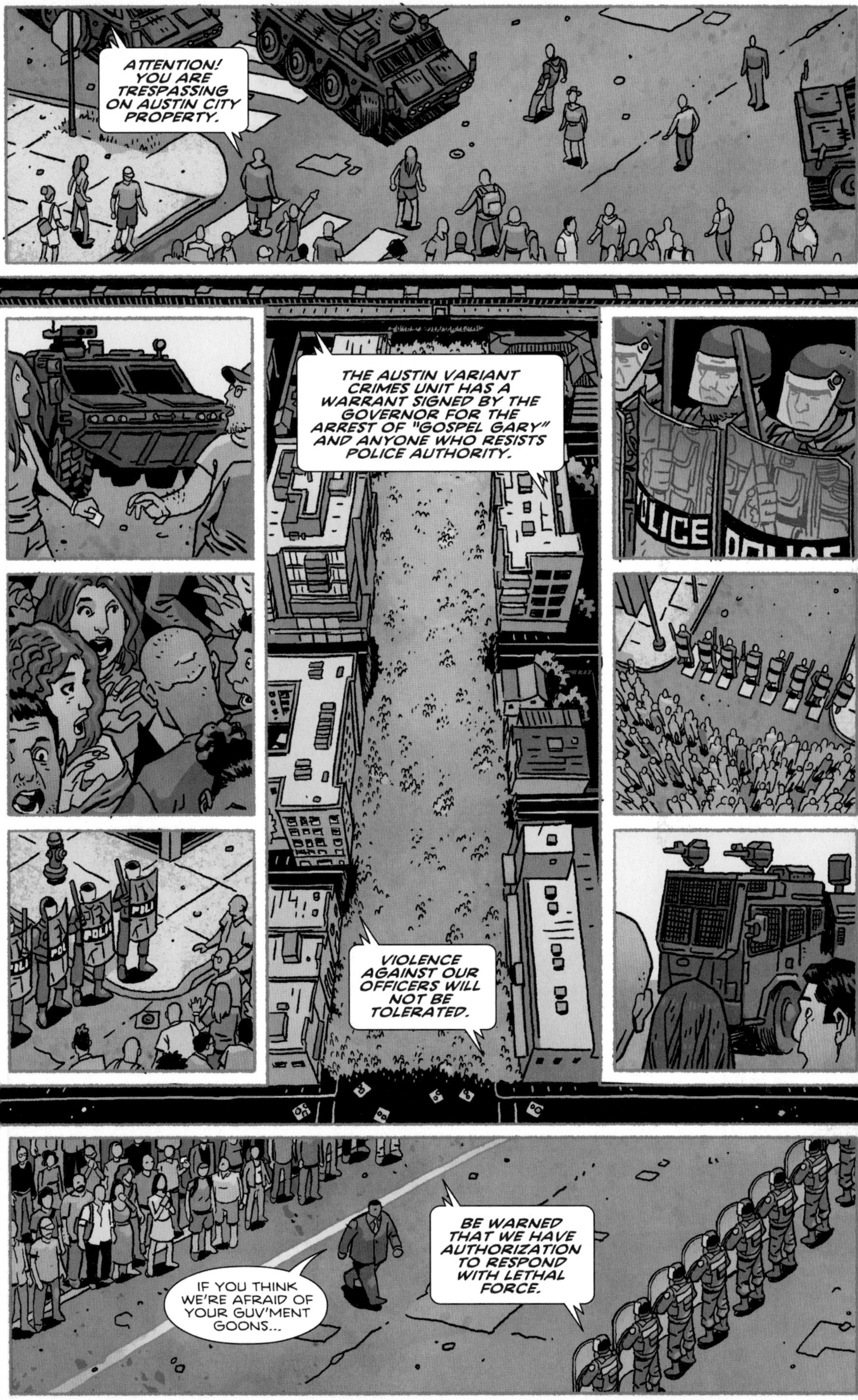

ATTENTION! YOU ARE TRESPASSING ON AUSTIN CITY PROPERTY.
THE AUSTIN VARIANT CRIMES UNIT HAS A WARRANT SIGNED BY THE GOVERNOR FOR THE ARREST OF "GOSPEL GARY" AND ANYONE WHO RESISTS POLICE AUTHORITY.
POLICE
POLICE
POLI
POLI
POLI
VIOLENCE AGAINST OUR OFFICERS WILL NOT BE TOLERATED.
BE WARNED THAT WE HAVE AUTHORIZATION TO RESPOND WITH LETHAL FORCE.
IF YOU THINK WE'RE AFRAID OF YOUR GUV'MENT GOONS...

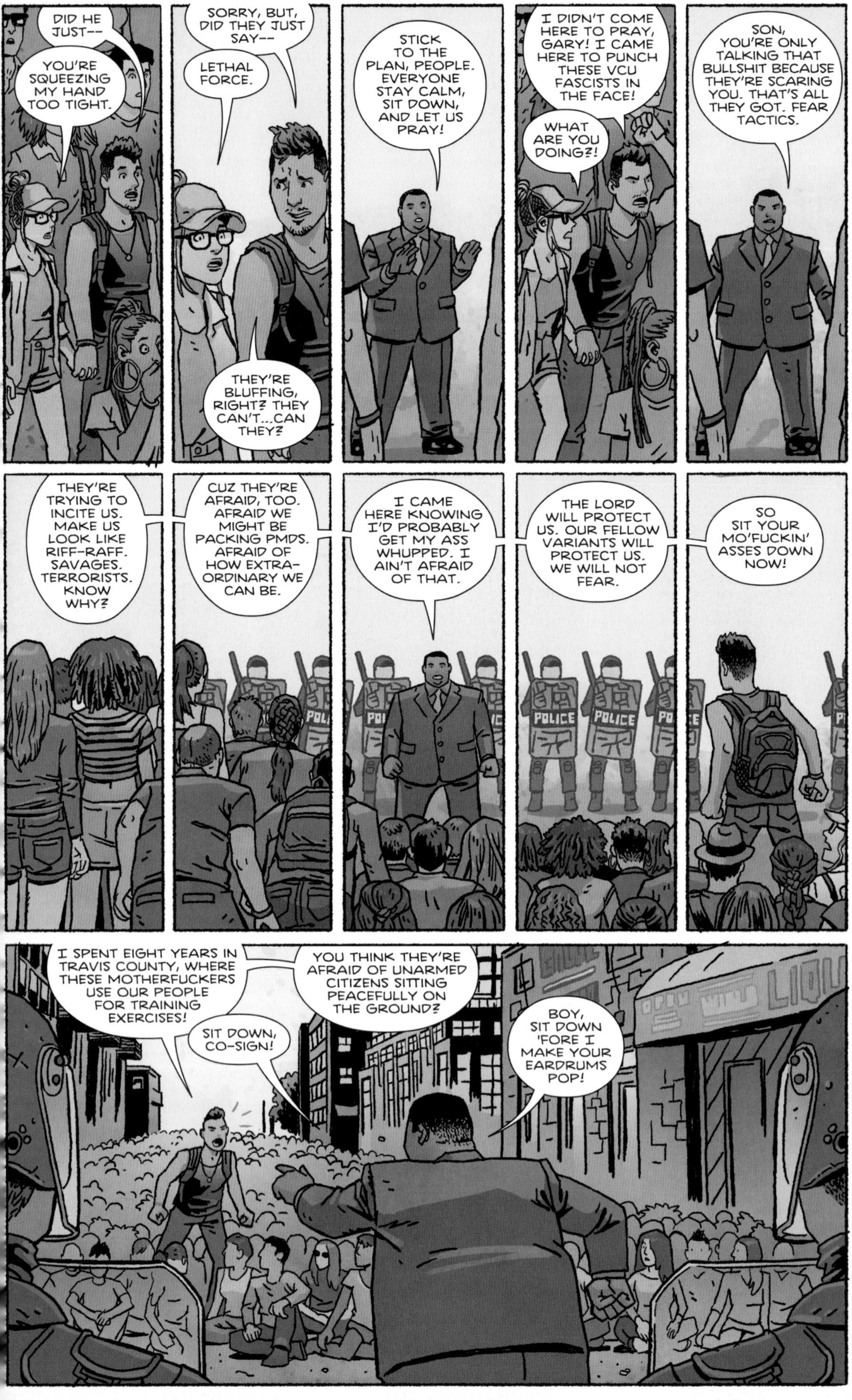
DID HE JUST--
YOU'RE SQUEEZING MY HAND TOO TIGHT.
SORRY, BUT, DID THEY JUST SAY--
LETHAL FORCE.
THEY'RE BLUFFING, RIGHT? THEY CAN'T...CAN THEY?
STICK TO THE PLAN, PEOPLE. EVERYONE STAY CALM, SIT DOWN, AND LET US PRAY!
I DIDN'T COME HERE TO PRAY, GARY! I CAME HERE TO PUNCH THESE VCU FASCISTS IN THE FACE!
WHAT ARE YOU DOING?!
SON, YOU'RE ONLY TALKING THAT BULLSHIT BECAUSE THEY'RE SCARING YOU. THAT'S ALL THEY GOT. FEAR TACTICS.
THEY'RE TRYING TO INCITE US. MAKE US LOOK LIKE RIFF-RAFF. SAVAGES. TERRORISTS. KNOW WHY?
CUZ THEY'RE AFRAID, TOO. AFRAID WE MIGHT BE PACKING PMDS. AFRAID OF HOW EXTRA-ORDINARY WE CAN BE.
I CAME HERE KNOWING I'D PROBABLY GET MY ASS WHUPPED. I AIN'T AFRAID OF THAT.
THE LORD WILL PROTECT US. OUR FELLOW VARIANTS WILL PROTECT US. WE WILL NOT FEAR.
SO SIT YOUR MO'FUCKIN' ASSES DOWN NOW!
POLICE
I SPENT EIGHT YEARS IN TRAVIS COUNTY, WHERE THESE MOTHERFUCKERS USE OUR PEOPLE FOR TRAINING EXERCISES!
YOU THINK THEY'RE AFRAID OF UNARMED CITIZENS SITTING PEACEFULLY ON THE GROUND?
SIT DOWN, CO-SIGN!
BOY, SIT DOWN 'FORE I MAKE YOUR EARDRUMS POP!

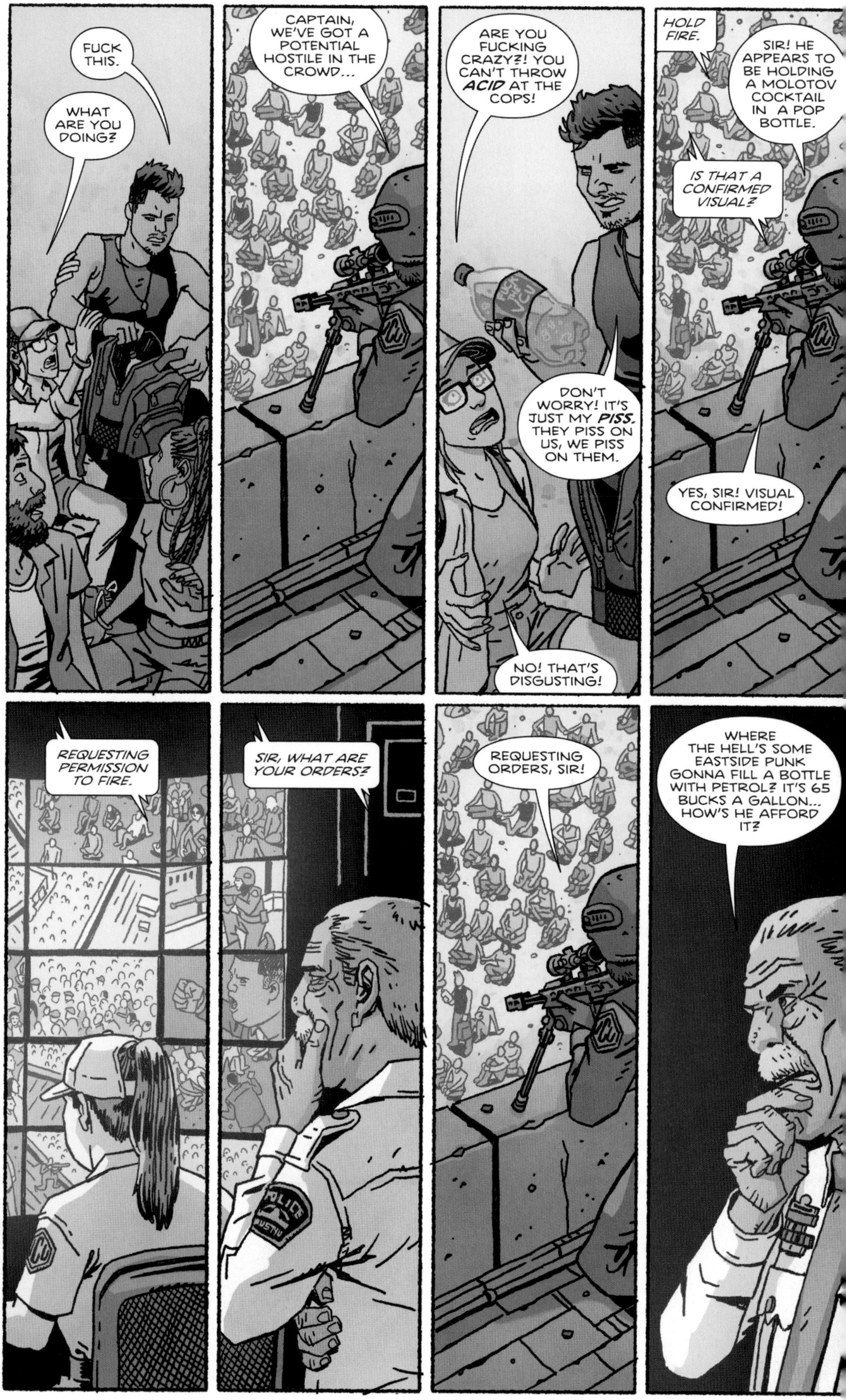
FUCK THIS.
WHAT ARE YOU DOING?
CAPTAIN, WE'VE GOT A POTENTIAL HOSTILE IN THE CROWD...
ARE YOU FUCKING CRAZY?! YOU CAN'T THROW ACID AT THE COPS!
DON'T WORRY! IT'S JUST MY PISS. THEY PISS ON US, WE PISS ON THEM.
NO! THAT'S DISGUSTING!
HOLD FIRE.
SIR! HE APPEARS TO BE HOLDING A MOLOTOV COCKTAIL IN A POP BOTTLE.
IS THAT A CONFIRMED VISUAL?
YES, SIR! VISUAL CONFIRMED!
REQUESTING PERMISSION TO FIRE.
SIR, WHAT ARE YOUR ORDERS?
REQUESTING ORDERS, SIR!
WHERE THE HELL'S SOME EASTSIDE PUNK GONNA FILL A BOTTLE WITH PETROL? IT'S 65 BUCKS A GALLON... HOW'S HE AFFORD IT?

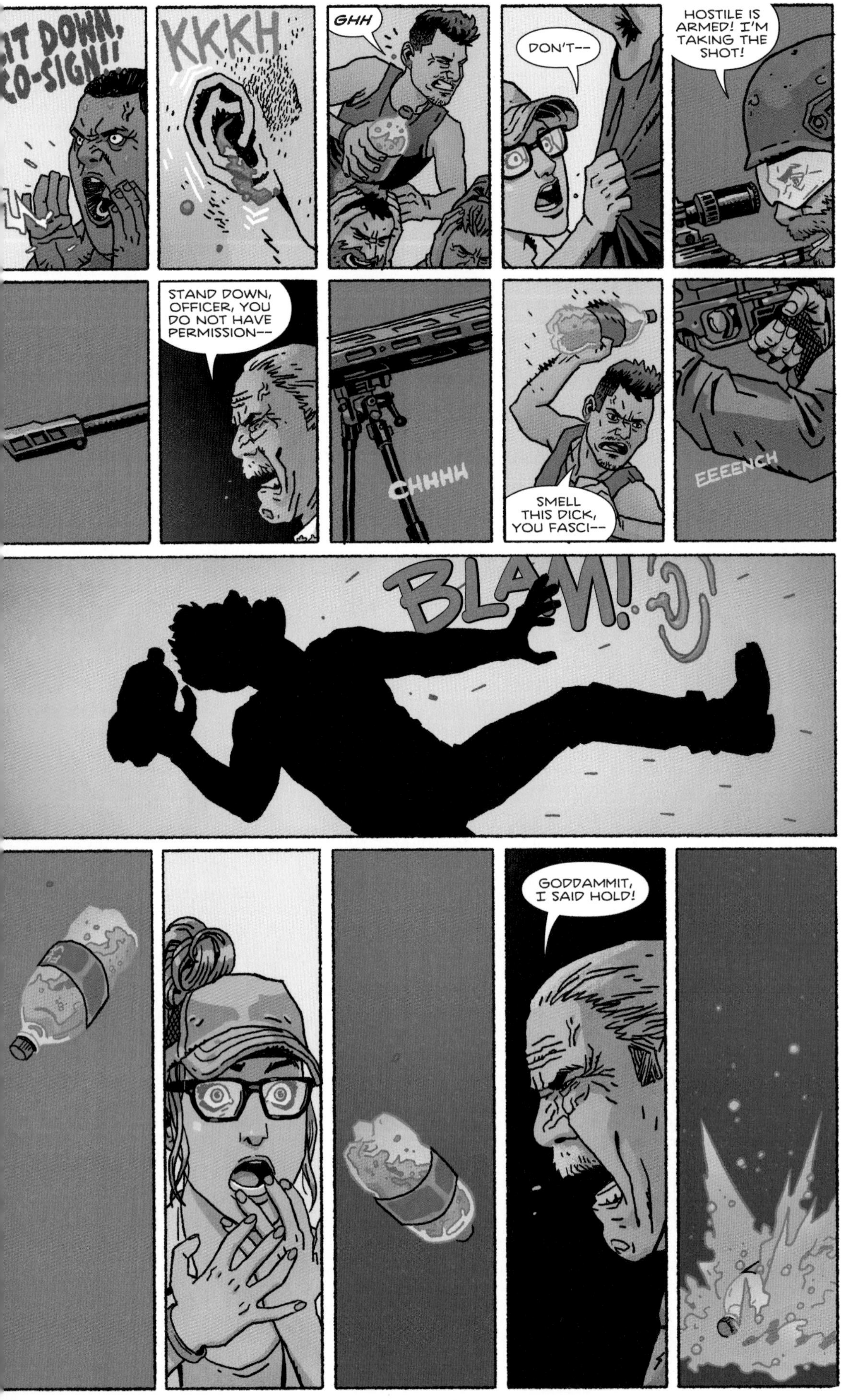
IT DOWN, CO-SIGN!!
KKKH
GHH
DON'T--
HOSTILE IS ARMED! I'M TAKING THE SHOT!
STAND DOWN, OFFICER, YOU DO NOT HAVE PERMISSION--
CHHHH
SMELL THIS DICK, YOU FASCI--
EEEENCH
BLAM!
GODDAMMIT, I SAID HOLD!

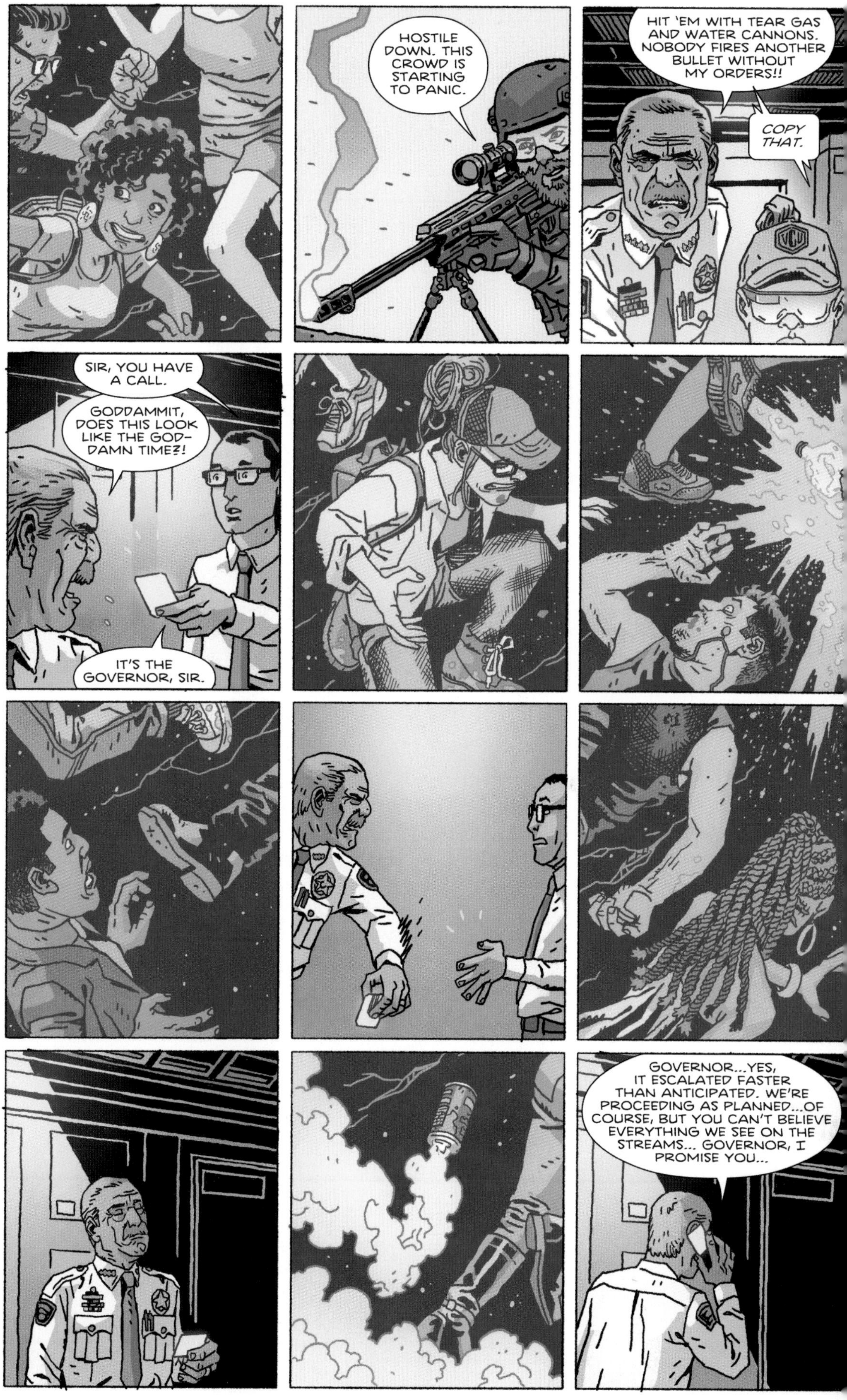
HOSTILE DOWN. THIS CROWD IS STARTING TO PANIC.
HIT 'EM WITH TEAR GAS AND WATER CANNONS. NOBODY FIRES ANOTHER BULLET WITHOUT MY ORDERS!!
COPY THAT.
SIR, YOU HAVE A CALL.
GODDAMMIT, DOES THIS LOOK LIKE THE GOD-DAMN TIME?!
IT'S THE GOVERNOR, SIR.
GOVERNOR...YES, IT ESCALATED FASTER THAN ANTICIPATED. WE'RE PROCEEDING AS PLANNED...OF COURSE, BUT YOU CAN'T BELIEVE EVERYTHING WE SEE ON THE STREAMS... GOVERNOR, I PROMISE YOU...

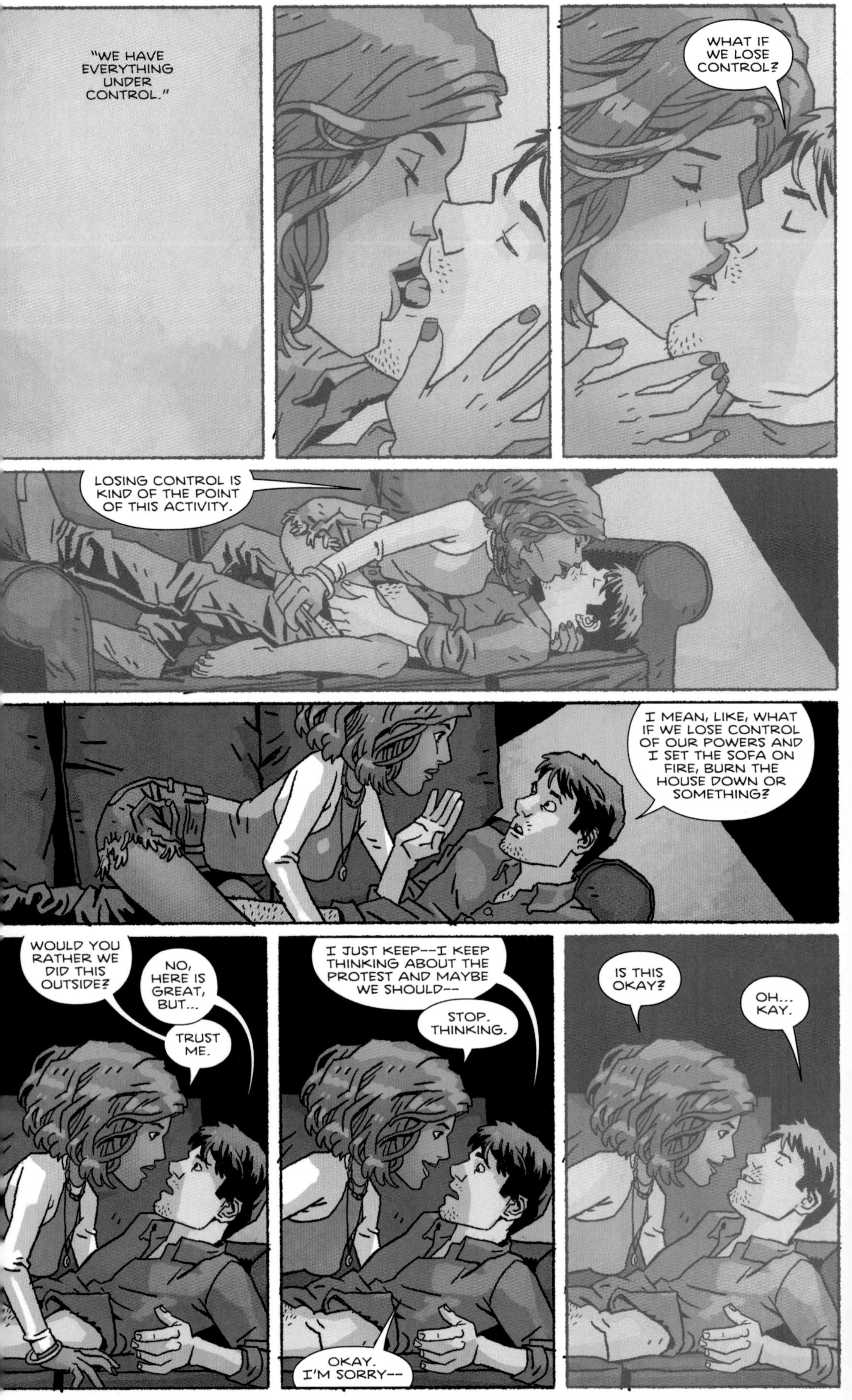
"WE HAVE EVERYTHING UNDER CONTROL."
WHAT IF WE LOSE CONTROL?
LOSING CONTROL IS KIND OF THE POINT OF THIS ACTIVITY.
I MEAN, LIKE, WHAT IF WE LOSE CONTROL OF OUR POWERS AND I SET THE SOFA ON FIRE, BURN THE HOUSE DOWN OR SOMETHING?
WOULD YOU RATHER WE DID THIS OUTSIDE?
NO, HERE IS GREAT, BUT...
TRUST ME.
I JUST KEEP--I KEEP THINKING ABOUT THE PROTEST AND MAYBE WE SHOULD--
STOP. THINKING.
OKAY. I'M SORRY--
IS THIS OKAY?
OH... KAY.

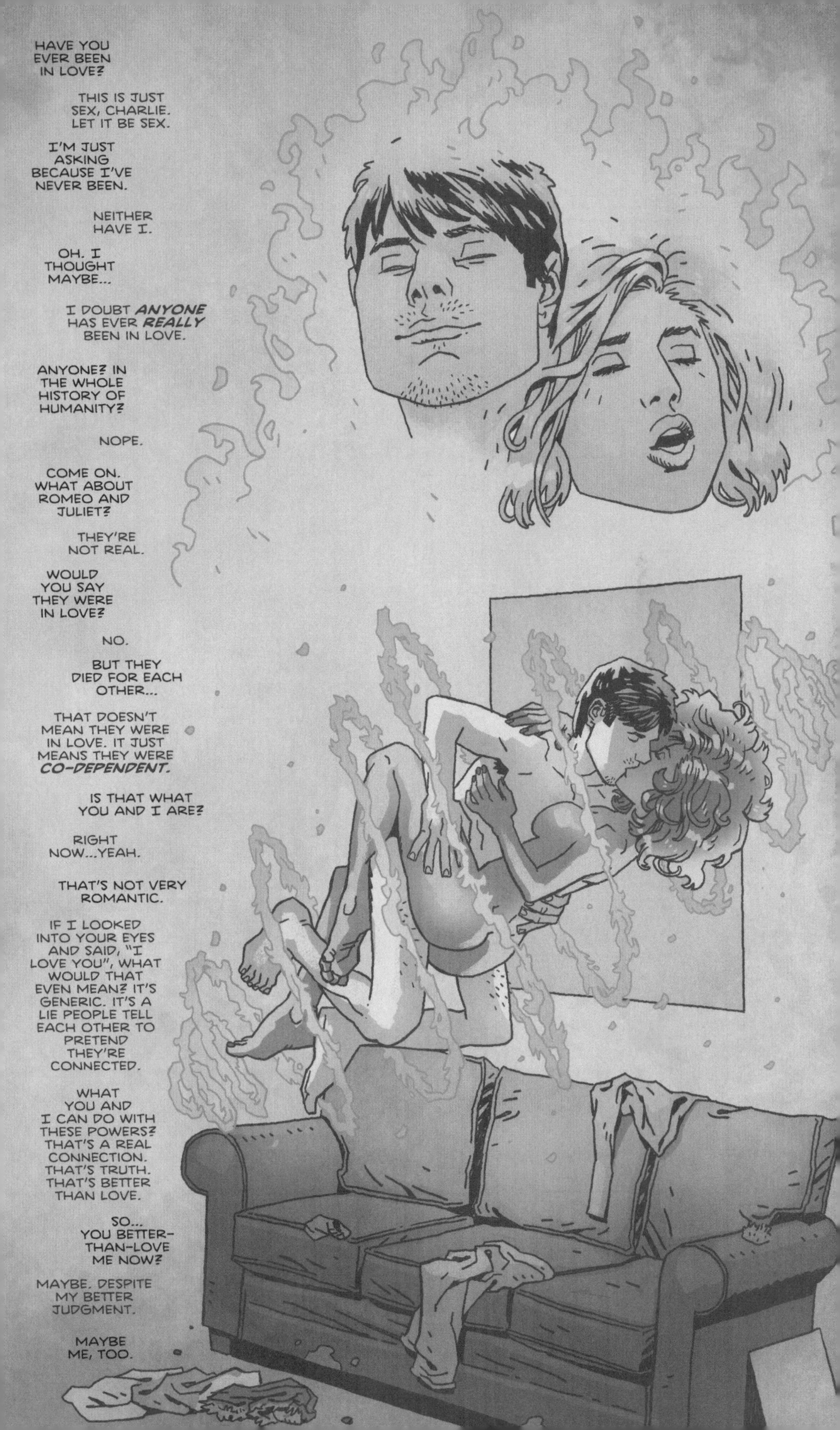
HAVE YOU EVER BEEN IN LOVE?
THIS IS JUST SEX, CHARLIE. LET IT BE SEX.
I'M JUST ASKING BECAUSE I'VE NEVER BEEN.
NEITHER HAVE I.
OH. I THOUGHT MAYBE...
I DOUBT ANYONE HAS EVER REALLY BEEN IN LOVE.
ANYONE? IN THE WHOLE HISTORY OF HUMANITY?
NOPE.
COME ON. WHAT ABOUT ROMEO AND JULIET?
THEY'RE NOT REAL.
WOULD YOU SAY THEY WERE IN LOVE?
NO.
BUT THEY DIED FOR EACH OTHER...
THAT DOESN'T MEAN THEY WERE IN LOVE. IT JUST MEANS THEY WERE CO-DEPENDENT.
IS THAT WHAT YOU AND I ARE?
RIGHT NOW...YEAH.
THAT'S NOT VERY ROMANTIC.
IF I LOOKED INTO YOUR EYES AND SAID, "I LOVE YOU", WHAT WOULD THAT EVEN MEAN? IT'S GENERIC. IT'S A LIE PEOPLE TELL EACH OTHER TO PRETEND THEY'RE CONNECTED.
WHAT YOU AND I CAN DO WITH THESE POWERS? THAT'S A REAL CONNECTION. THAT'S TRUTH. THAT'S BETTER THAN LOVE.
SO... YOU BETTER-THAN-LOVE ME NOW?
MAYBE. DESPITE MY BETTER JUDGMENT.
MAYBE ME, TOO.

NOW

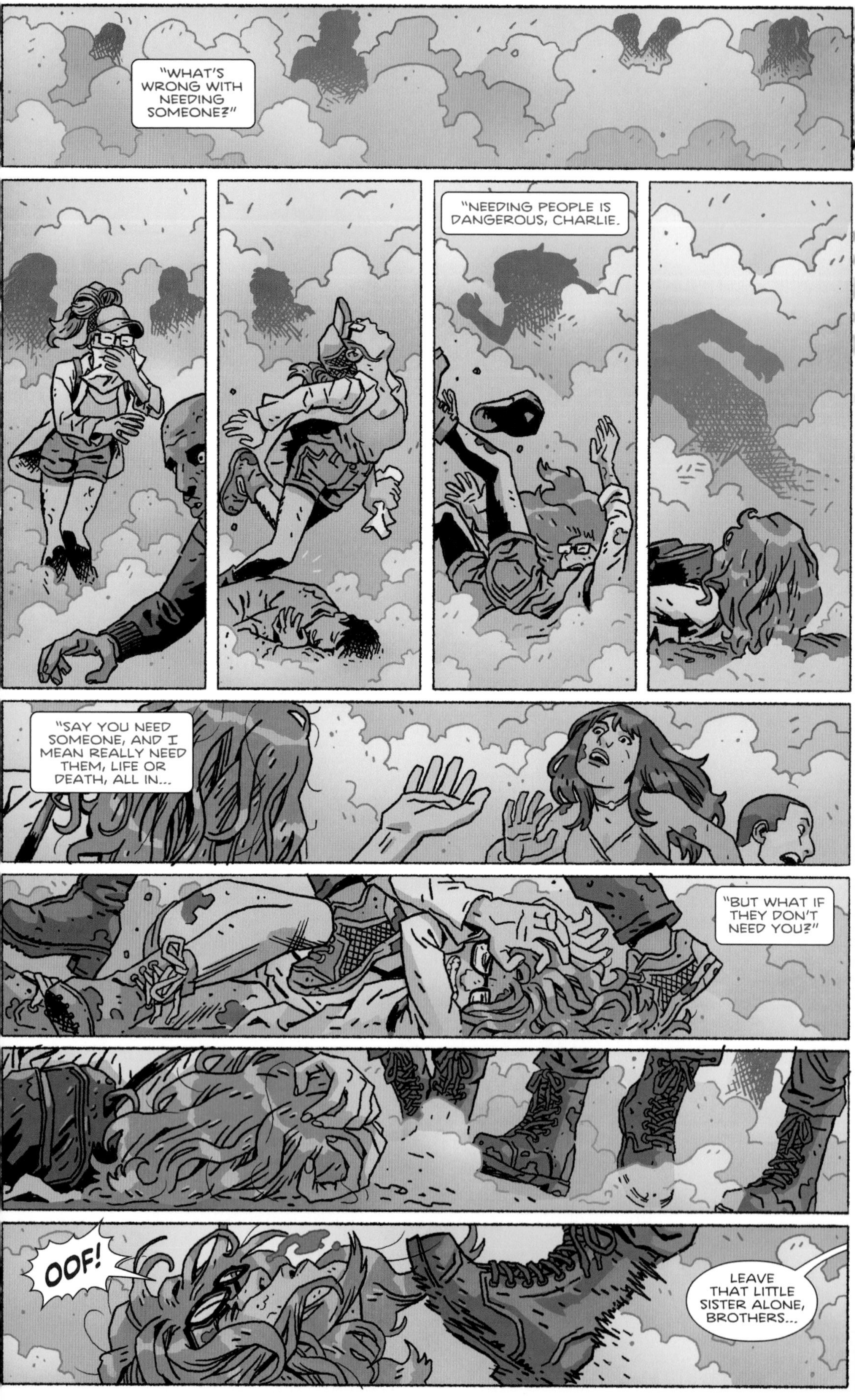
"WHAT'S WRONG WITH NEEDING SOMEONE?"
"NEEDING PEOPLE IS DANGEROUS, CHARLIE.
"SAY YOU NEED SOMEONE, AND I MEAN REALLY NEED THEM, LIFE OR DEATH, ALL IN...
"BUT WHAT IF THEY DON'T NEED YOU?"
OOF!
LEAVE THAT LITTLE SISTER ALONE, BROTHERS...

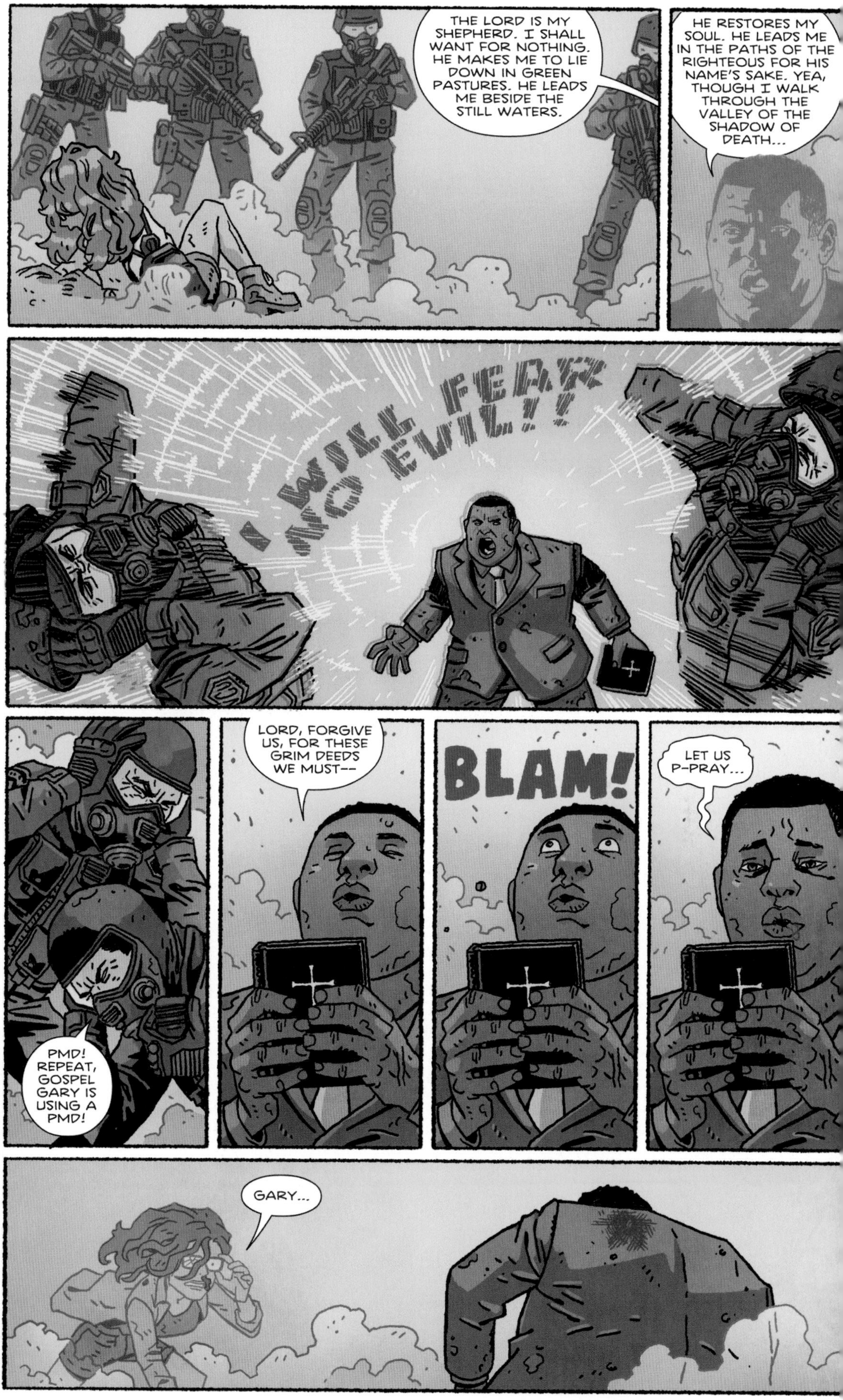
THE LORD IS MY SHEPHERD. I SHALL WANT FOR NOTHING. HE MAKES ME TO LIE DOWN IN GREEN PASTURES. HE LEADS ME BESIDE THE STILL WATERS.
HE RESTORES MY SOUL. HE LEADS ME IN THE PATHS OF THE RIGHTEOUS FOR HIS NAME'S SAKE. YEA, THOUGH I WALK THROUGH THE VALLEY OF THE SHADOW OF DEATH...
I WILL FEAR NO EVIL!!
PMD! REPEAT, GOSPEL GARY IS USING A PMD!
LORD, FORGIVE US, FOR THESE GRIM DEEDS WE MUST--
BLAM!
LET US P-PRAY...
GARY...

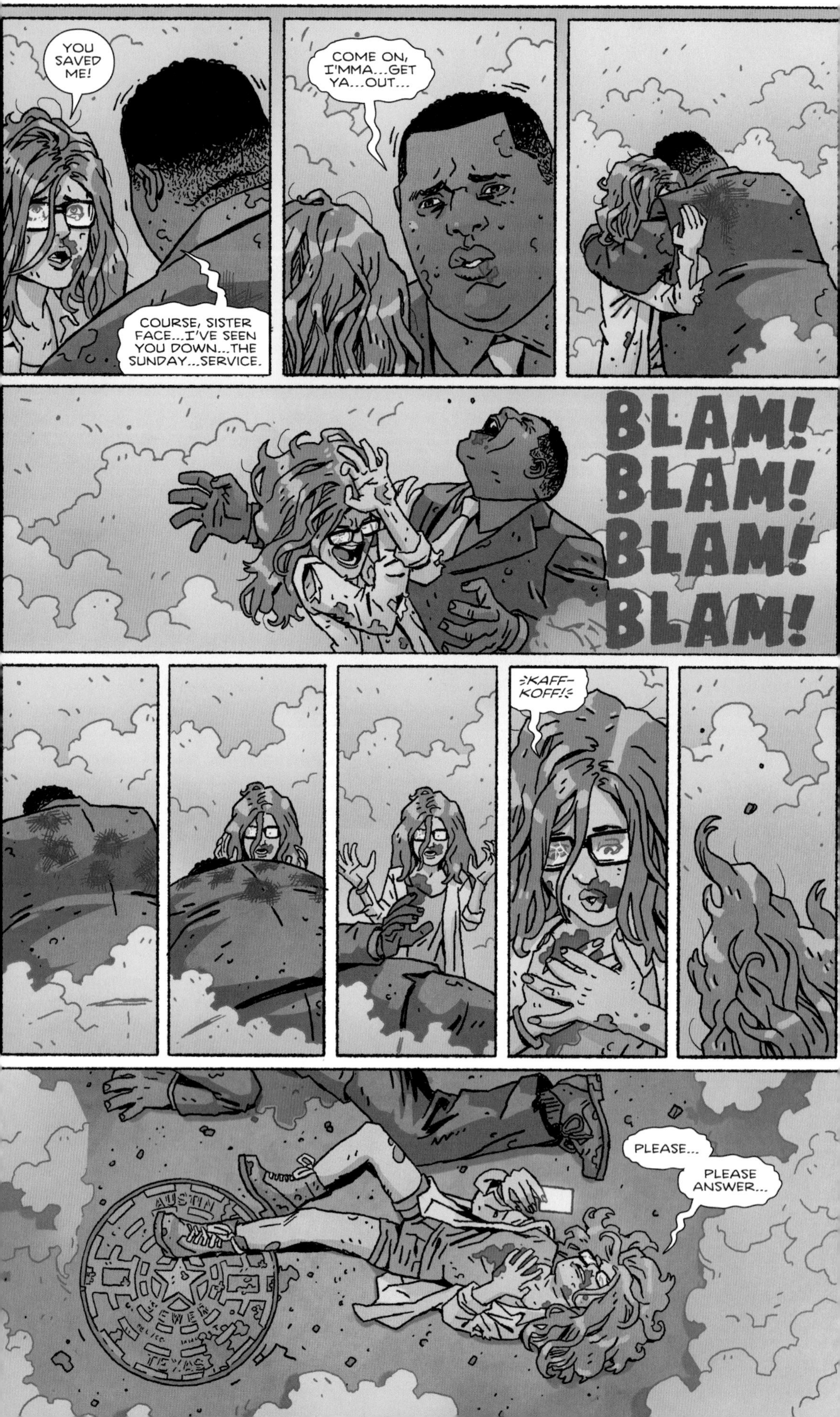
YOU SAVED ME!
COURSE, SISTER FACE...I'VE SEEN YOU DOWN...THE SUNDAY...SERVICE.
COME ON, I'MMA...GET YA...OUT...
BLAM! BLAM! BLAM! BLAM!
KAFF-KOFF!
AUSTIN
SEWER
TEXAS
PLEASE...
PLEASE ANSWER...

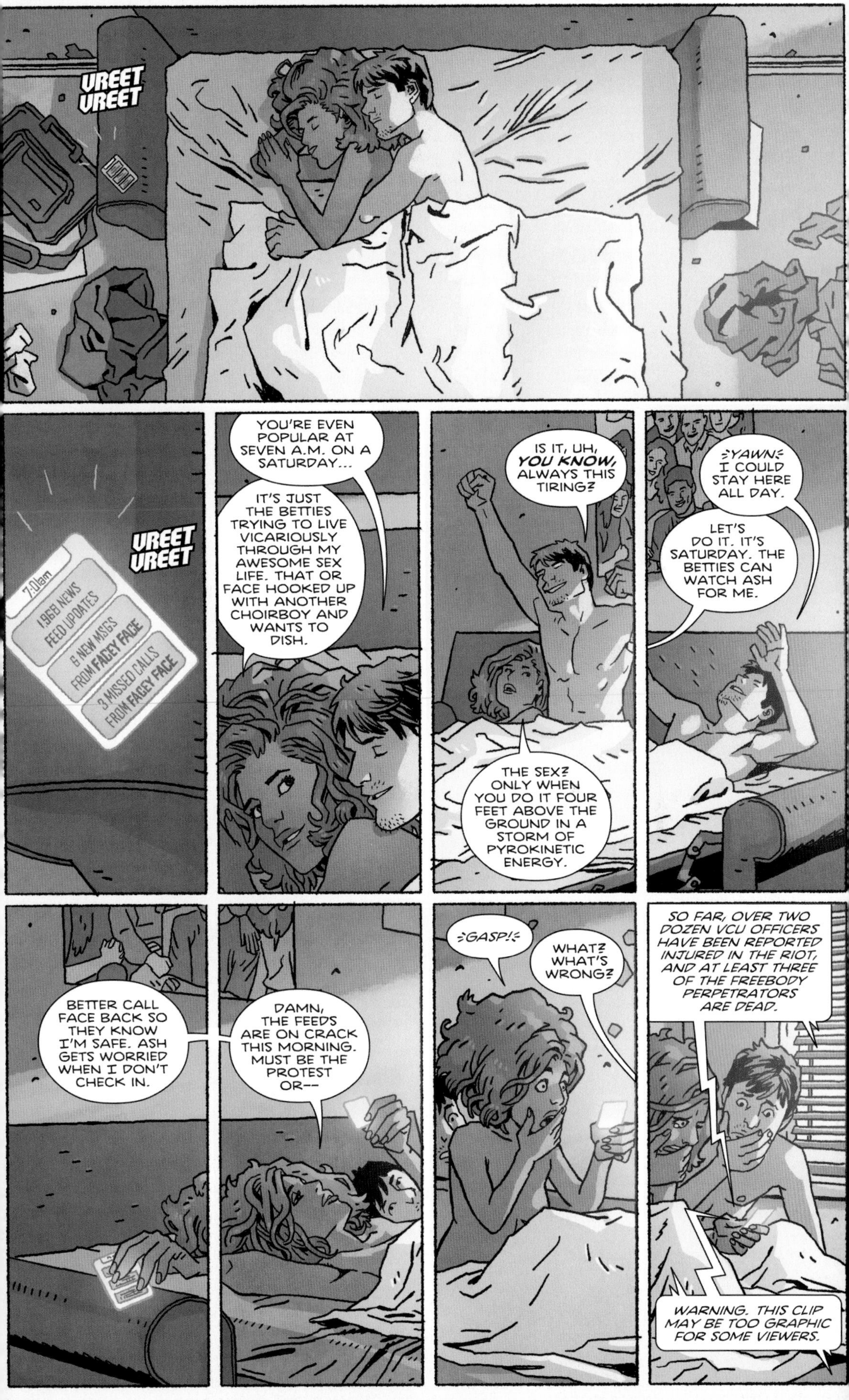

UREET UREET
UREET UREET
7:01am
1968 NEWS FEED UPDATES
6 NEW MSGS FROM FACEY FACE
3 MISSED CALLS FROM FACEY FACE
YOU'RE EVEN POPULAR AT SEVEN A.M. ON A SATURDAY...
IT'S JUST THE BETTIES TRYING TO LIVE VICARIOUSLY THROUGH MY AWESOME SEX LIFE. THAT OR FACE HOOKED UP WITH ANOTHER CHOIRBOY AND WANTS TO DISH.
IS IT, UH, YOU KNOW, ALWAYS THIS TIRING?
THE SEX? ONLY WHEN YOU DO IT FOUR FEET ABOVE THE GROUND IN A STORM OF PYROKINETIC ENERGY.
YAWN I COULD STAY HERE ALL DAY.
LET'S DO IT. IT'S SATURDAY. THE BETTIES CAN WATCH ASH FOR ME.
BETTER CALL FACE BACK SO THEY KNOW I'M SAFE. ASH GETS WORRIED WHEN I DON'T CHECK IN.
DAMN, THE FEEDS ARE ON CRACK THIS MORNING. MUST BE THE PROTEST OR--
GASP!
WHAT? WHAT'S WRONG?
SO FAR, OVER TWO DOZEN VCU OFFICERS HAVE BEEN REPORTED INJURED IN THE RIOT, AND AT LEAST THREE OF THE FREEBODY PERPETRATORS ARE DEAD.
WARNING. THIS CLIP MAY BE TOO GRAPHIC FOR SOME VIEWERS.

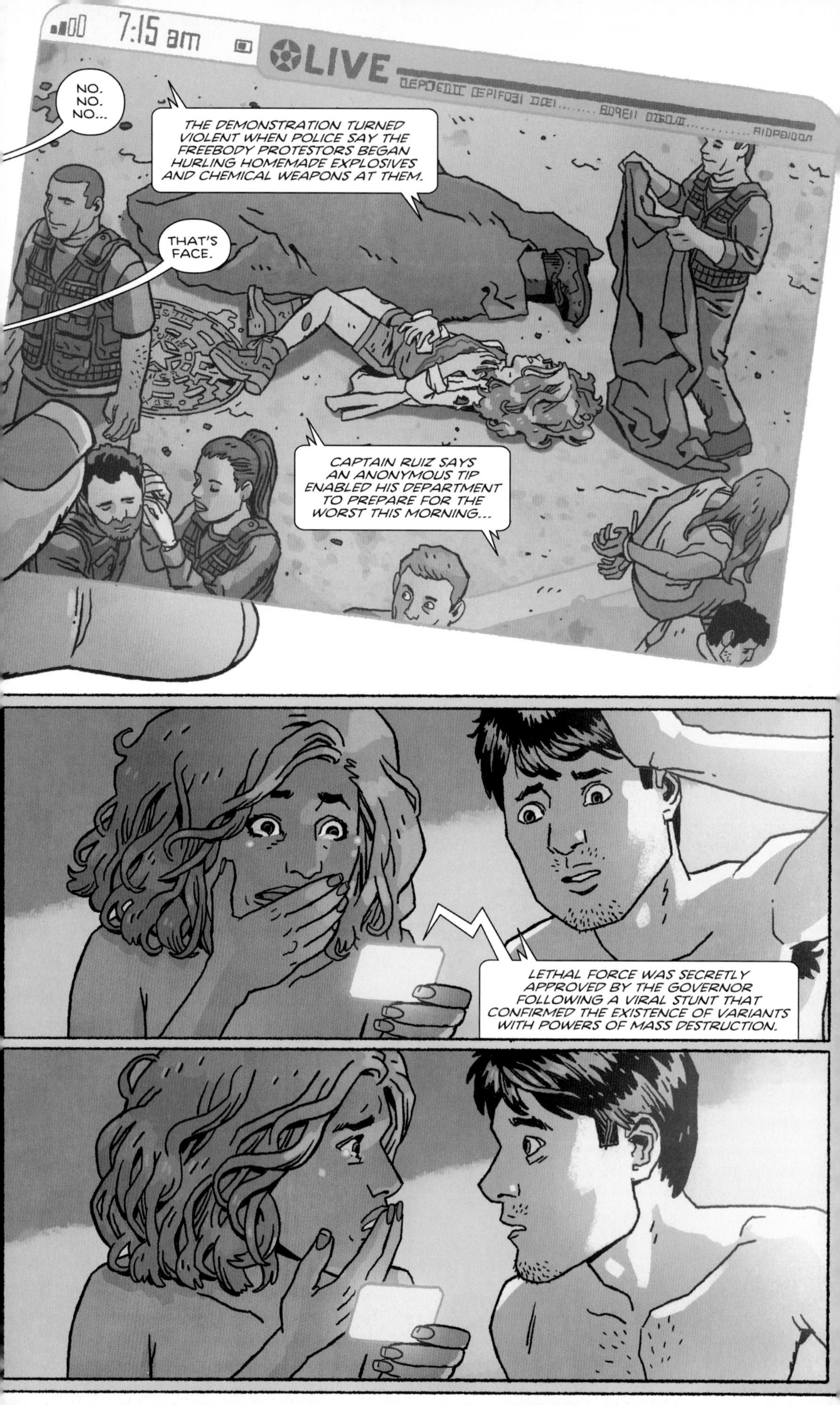
7:15 am
LIVE
NO. NO. NO...
THE DEMONSTRATION TURNED VIOLENT WHEN POLICE SAY THE FREEBODY PROTESTORS BEGAN HURLING HOMEMADE EXPLOSIVES AND CHEMICAL WEAPONS AT THEM.
THAT'S FACE.
CAPTAIN RUIZ SAYS AN ANONYMOUS TIP ENABLED HIS DEPARTMENT TO PREPARE FOR THE WORST THIS MORNING...
LETHAL FORCE WAS SECRETLY APPROVED BY THE GOVERNOR FOLLOWING A VIRAL STUNT THAT CONFIRMED THE EXISTENCE OF VARIANTS WITH POWERS OF MASS DESTRUCTION.

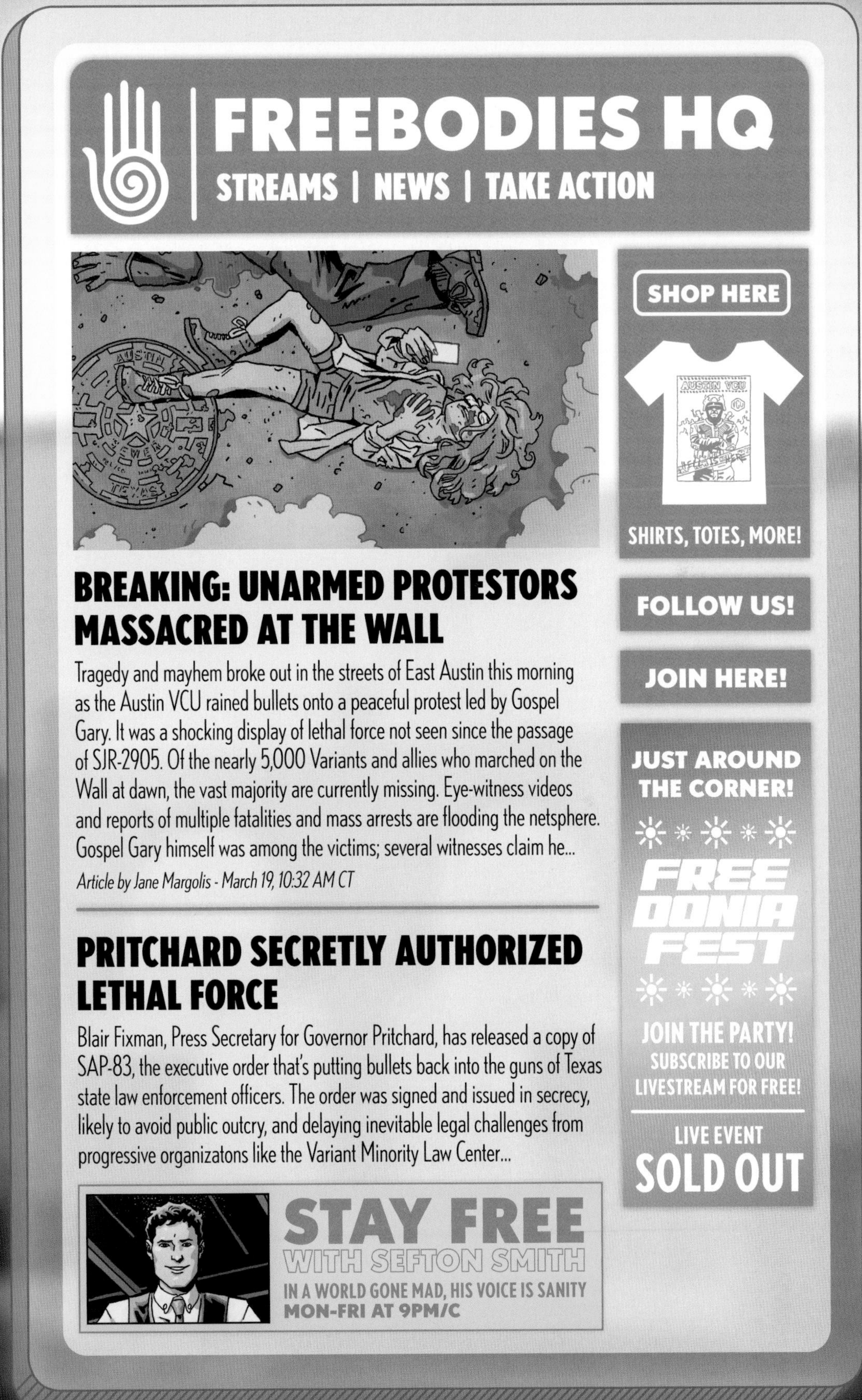
FREEBODIES HQ
STREAMS | NEWS | TAKE ACTION
AUSTIN
SEWER
TEXAS
BREAKING: UNARMED PROTESTORS MASSACRED AT THE WALL
Tragedy and mayhem broke out in the streets of East Austin this morning as the Austin VCU rained bullets onto a peaceful protest led by Gospel Gary. It was a shocking display of lethal force not seen since the passage of SJR-2905. Of the nearly 5,000 Variants and allies who marched on the Wall at dawn, the vast majority are currently missing. Eye-witness videos and reports of multiple fatalities and mass arrests are flooding the netsphere. Gospel Gary himself was among the victims; several witnesses claim he...
Article by Jane Margolis - March 19, 10:32 AM CT
PRITCHARD SECRETLY AUTHORIZED LETHAL FORCE
Blair Fixman, Press Secretary for Governor Pritchard, has released a copy of SAP-83, the executive order that's putting bullets back into the guns of Texas state law enforcement officers. The order was signed and issued in secrecy, likely to avoid public outcry, and delaying inevitable legal challenges from progressive organizatons like the Variant Minority Law Center...
STAY FREE
WITH SEFTON SMITH
IN A WORLD GONE MAD, HIS VOICE IS SANITY
MON-FRI AT 9PM/C
SHOP HERE
AUSTIN VCU
SHIRTS, TOTES, MORE!
FOLLOW US!
JOIN HERE!
JUST AROUND THE CORNER!
FREE DONIA FEST
JOIN THE PARTY!
SUBSCRIBE TO OUR LIVESTREAM FOR FREE!
LIVE EVENT
SOLD OUT

ANM **US News** Trending Features Opinions Live TV Options

Bullets fly, PMDs unleashed as Austin VCU clash with protesters

Gov. Pritchard declares state of emergency after authorizing use of lethal force against variants

By Arune Singh, ANM
Updated 12:27 PM ET, Mon March 19

This story will be updated as new information is confirmed. For the latest news live from Austin, watch our ANM Stream-on-the-Scene.

(ANM) - Just before dawn, an estimated 4,000 Variant rights activists assembled under the leadership of Gospel Gary to march across East Austin and protest the Wall. They were prepared to confront stun rounds, tear gas, water cannons, and batons. They could not know they would be met with full-metal jackets, open-tips, and hollow points, among the many forms of lethal ammunition that Texas law officers are prohibited from using under SJR-2905.

But as of this morning, SJR-2905 no longer applies in Texas. The publicly divisive law was once a moonshot in the eyes of progressive activists. Its surprising passage by the state legislature was enabled by a confluence of events: the aftermath of GOP-Russia scandals, a Blue Wave electoral cycle in which Texans elected their first Democratic governor since the 20th century, and global outrage over a supercut of Texas officers killing a record-breaking 76 protestors during the World Climate Day riots.

In the wake of SJR-2905, Texas law enforcement adopted the use of stun ammunition and other non-lethal methods. Fatal police shootings in Texas dropped from 732 to 0, year over year. The law proved so undeniably effective and surprisingly popular that Governor Suzanna Pritchard (R) refused to challenge SJR-2905 while campaigning on a nationalist platform of "law, order, and securing the existence of our people and a future for our children." Despite Pritchard's landslide victory in that election, SJR-2905 seemed bulletproof for three years of her administration.

No longer. Recent events have emboldened Governor Pritchard. ANM has now confirmed with her Press Secretary, Blair Fixman, that in the hours after anonymous Freebodies activists provided recorded evidence of the existence of powers of mass destructions (PMDs), Governor Pritchard secretly signed an executive order, SAP-83, revoking the majority of SJR-2905 provisions, effectively restoring the use of lethal force for Texas law enforcement.

Sure enough, within days of receiving SAP-83, sidewalks in East Austin have been stained with the blood of civilians. A written statement from Governor Pritchard cites the revelation that at least three Variants possess PMDs as just cause for the bloodshed. Documented PMDs include the two anonymous Freebodies who demonstrated telekinesis (the ability to move objects without touching them) and pyrokinesis (the ability to command fire and heat) by defacing a section of the Wall in West Austin.

The third PMD has been identified as Gospel Gary Mendo, a popular East Austin preacher and community organizer. The Austin VCU claims that today's protest at the Wall escalated

CARNAGE REPORT
9:34 AM

U.S.A. Local Freedom Watch Pods Vids Options

AUSTIN VCU SUPPRESSES VIOLENT RIOT

PROOF OF PMDS JUSTIFIES USE OF LETHAL FORCE

By Michael Maverick

PMDs were unleashed on the streets of East Austin in a dramatic showdown between activists and police today. A crowd of aggressive anti-police Variants stormed the Wall at dawn. Mainstream outlets estimate this crowd at 4,000-5,000 activists strong; Carnage Report sources who were there tell us the crowd was actually much smaller at 1,500 or less.

This crowd's declared intention was a "peaceful occupation" of the Wall, yet for some reason, they came ready to fight, armed with homemade weapons, projectiles, and the aforementioned PMDs. They belligerently taunted the VCU, chanting insults and shouting threats as they approached the Wall. When confronted by VCU officers ordering them to disperse, the Variants' "peaceful" protest quickly escalated into a riot. The ensuing violence sent several officers to St. David's Medical Center with serious injuries.

Those officers would be dead, had it not been for the courage and heroic foresight of Governor Pritchard, whose executive order revoking SJR-2905 enabled our brave men and women in blue to defend themselves against violent radicals, the most notorious of these being preacher and agitator Gary Mendo, who took the occasion to reveal his own PMDs – deafening vocal blasts that left several officers with bleeding eardrums. Gary Mendo's inhumane assault on our protectors of law and order was mercifully pacified by skilled VCU sharpshooters.

We cannot underestimate the scale of wanton destruction that would surely have befallen East Austin without the brave efforts of these heroic officers. The VCU should honor them with a parade, but we know they can't, because for years Freebodies have hijacked and disrupted every public display of support for law enforcement.

I bet these Freetards will think twice now that they know the VCU is re-licensed to kill. If the decisive action of SAP-83 results in anything less than a landslide re-election for Governor Pritchard in November, I'll eat my sneakers.

There is bound to be handwringing and outrage from socialists and Variant apologists on the Left over the reported deaths of Gary Mendo and a number of his cohorts. They will say the police used excessive force (they did not). They will say the protestors carried no firearms (they did). They will say SAP-83 is illegal (it's legal). They will say anything to portray Gary Mendo and his radical contingents of miscreants and hooligans as victims of state authority.

They should consider this: Not a single one of the officers who served at the Wall today woke up intending to kill or hurt someone. Our men and women in blue woke up, put their pants on one leg at a time just like you and me, then went to work to guard their community and uphold our laws. Contrast that with Gary Mendo and his radical adherents. They woke up with an intention to offend, incite, and do harm to the Austin VCU. As they marched across East Austin, as they slandered our heroes and disrespected the laws and norms of democracy, they made their intentions clear.

— Published 12:18 PM ET, Mon March 19

A PLEA FOR RATIONAL RECOVERY
BY TOPHER CARLSBERG

SOCIALISM IS FOR SERFS
REAL AMERICANS KNOW BETTER
CORPORATISM WILL SAVE US
A CARNAGE REPORT SPECIAL FEATURE

90's Mix for JILL

CD #1 Freebetties Banger Mix
1) Bikini Kill - Double Dare Ya
2) Bomfunk Mc's - Freestyler
3) Ricky Martin - La Copa de la Vida
4) Corona - Rhythm of the Night
5) Boyz II Men - Motownphilly
6) La Mafia - Un Millon de Rosas
7) Freak Nasty - Da Dip
8) Montell Jordan - This is How We Do It
9) Madonna - Vogue
10) Mc Hammer - U Can't Touch This
11) Fatboy Slim - The Rockafeller Skank
12) No Doubt - Just A Girl

CD #2 Resistance Rock + Rap Mix
1) Alice in Chains - Man in the Box
2) Rage Against the Machine - Killing in the Name Of
3) The Smashing Pumpkins - Disarm
4) The Cranberries - Zombie
5) Manic Street Preachers - If You Tolerate This Your Children Will Be Next
6) Michael Jackson - They Don't Care About Us
7) 2Pac - Trapped
8) Snow - Informer
9) KRS-One - Sound of Da Police
10) Public Enemy - Fight the Power

CD #3 C♡J Mix
1) Juan Gabriel - Estoy Enamorado de Ti
2) NSYNC - Tearin' Up My Heart
3) Spin Doctors - Two Princes
4) Extreme - More Than Words
5) Fugees - Killing Me Softly
6) Jon Secada - Otro Pía Más sin verte
7) Bryan Adams - Everything I Do
8) Westlife - Swear It Again
9) Mariah Carey - Always Be My Baby
10) Janet Jackson - Together Again
11) Aerosmith - I Don't Want To Miss A Thing
12) Selena - I Could Fall

TO BE CONTINUED...

…OM ROBERT KIRKMAN AND SKYBOUND

ROBERT KIRKMAN
LORENZO DE FELICI
ANNALISA LEONI
OBLIVION SONG
CHAPTER FOUR

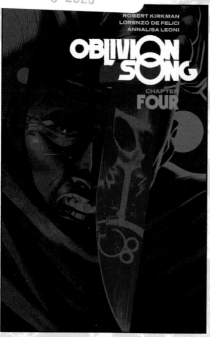

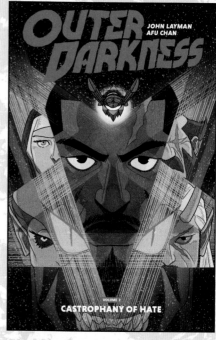

CHAPTER ONE TP
ISBN: 978-1-5343-0642-4
$ 9.99

CHAPTER TWO
ISBN: 978-1-5343-1057-5
$16.99

CHAPTER THREE
ISBN: 978-1-5343-1326-2
$16.99

CHAPTER FOUR
ISBN: 978-1-5343-1517-4
$16.99

OUTER DARKNESS
JOHN LAYMAN
AFU CHAN
VOLUME 2
CASTROPHANY OF HATE

VOL. 1: EACH OTHER'S THROATS
ISBN: 978-1-5343-1210-4
$16.99

VOL. 2: CASTROPHANY OF HATE
ISBN: 978-1-5343-1370-5
$16.99

VOLUME EIGHT
LIVE BY THE SWORD

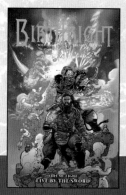

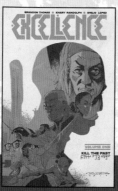

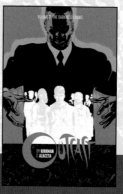

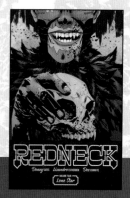

VOL. 1: HOMECOMING
ISBN: 978-1-63215-231-2
$9.99

VOL. 2: CALL TO ADVENTURE
ISBN: 978-1-63215-446-0
$12.99

VOL. 3: ALLIES AND ENEMIES
ISBN: 978-1-63215-683-9
$12.99

VOL. 4: FAMILY HISTORY
ISBN: 978-1-63215-871-0
$12.99

VOL. 5: BELLY OF THE BEAST
ISBN: 978-1-5343-0218-1
$12.99

VOL. 6: FATHERHOOD
ISBN: 978-1-53430-498-7
$14.99

VOL. 7: BLOOD BROTHERS
ISBN: 978-1-5343-1053-7
$14.99

VOL. 8: LIVE BY THE SWORD
ISBN: 978-1-5343-1368-2
$14.99

BRANDON THOMAS
KHARY RANDOLPH
EMILIO LOPEZ
EXCELLENCE
VOLUME ONE
KILL THE PAST

VOL. 1: KILL THE PAST
ISBN: 978-1-5343-1362-0
$16.99

VOLUME 7: THE DARKNESS GROWS
BY KIRKMAN & AZACETA
OUTCAST

VOL. 1: A DARKNESS SURROUNDS HIM
ISBN: 978-1-63215-053-0
$9.99

VOL. 2: A VAST AND UNENDING RUIN
ISBN: 978-1-63215-448-4
$14.99

VOL. 3: THIS LITTLE LIGHT
ISBN: 978-1-63215-693-8
$14.99

VOL. 4: UNDER DEVIL'S WING
ISBN: 978-1-5343-0050-7
$14.99

VOL. 5: THE NEW PATH
ISBN: 978-1-5343-0249-5
$16.99

VOL. 6: INVASION
ISBN: 978-1-5343-0751-3
$16.99

VOL. 7: THE DARKNESS GROWS
ISBN: 978-1-5343-1239-5
$16.99

REDNECK
Donny Cates
Lisandro Estherren
Dee Cunniffe
VOLUME FOUR
Lone Star

VOL. 1: DEEP IN THE HEART
ISBN: 978-1-5343-0331-7
$16.99

VOL. 2: THE EYES UPON YOU
ISBN: 978-1-5343-0665-3
$16.99

VOL. 3: LONGHORNS
ISBN: 978-1-5343-1050-6
$16.99

VOL. 4: LONE STAR
ISBN: 978-1-5343-1367-5
$16.99